MW00474341

# WICKED INTENTIONS

WICKED GAMES BOOK 3

J.T. GEISSINGER

Published by J.T. Geissinger, Inc.

ISBN 978-0-9969358-9-0

Cover design by Letitia Hasser RBA Designs

Editing by Linda Ingmanson

To Jay, for everything

# 1

## MARIANA

When sizing up a potential mark, a thief of any intelligence must answer one crucial question before committing to the job.

Is the risk worth the reward?

I know it sounds simple enough. Believe me, it's anything but.

Take my current situation, as an example. After weeks of painstaking planning and an airplane flight halfway around the world, I'm tucked into a comfortable chair at a table in an outdoor bar at a luxury resort in St. Croix, sipping a strawberry daiquiri and pretending to flip through a travel magazine while actually performing covert reconnaissance through the mirrored lenses of my sunglasses. My target—or mark, in criminal parlance—is sitting on the edge of the infinity pool several meters away, laughing loudly, blond head thrown back, straight white teeth glinting in the tropical sun.

Americans. Always the boisterous laughs and good dental work. I envy everything about them.

This particular one has the muscular, golden good looks of a Hemsworth. At first glance, he could be mistaken for an actor or model, maybe one of those self-obsessed Instagram pseudo-celebrities shilling soft drinks and designer clothing to a legion of teenage fans. But on closer inspection, interesting details emerge.

The Marine Corps tattoo on his right shoulder. The hawklike awareness in his blue eyes. The trio of shiny round divots marring the taut skin of his stomach.

I've seen enough bullet scars to recognize them. That he survived three shots to the gut makes him intriguing. In my experience, most people die after one.

Golden Boy sits on the edge of the pool, legs dangling in the crystalline water, chatting and laughing with the most unlikely of companions. A redhead with a constellation of tattoos on her slender limbs has her arms linked around the waist of a beast of a man with linebacker shoulders, close-cropped black hair, and a megawatt smile. An attractive Black woman in a yellow bikini canoodles with a pale man half her size in a blue speedo who has a wild thatch of hair.

With them is a teenage girl with a rat on her head.

She treads water in the pool a short distance away from her companions. With her mop of curly brown hair and distinct facial features, she doesn't look related to any of the adults. The fat black-and-white rat, contentedly perched atop her hair as if it's a permanent fixture, seems to be enjoying the conversation as much as the warm afternoon sun.

After a few moments, the girl swims to the edge of the pool and pulls herself up with her skinny arms to sit beside Golden Boy, her back turned to me.

I wince when I see the scar.

Ragged and lurid pink, it traces a vicious path from between her narrow shoulder blades to the small of her back. It's too irregular to be a surgical scar. An accident, perhaps? Whatever its origin, it's recent. No more than a few months by my best guess.

*Dios mio, poor baby.*

I suspect that out of all of her companions, the two of us have the most in common.

"Another daiquiri, ma'am?" A smiling waiter in white shorts and flip-flops bends over me.

"No, thank you."

The waiter nods and walks away.

On paper, this job is straightforward. Gain access to the room of honeymooning Saudi Prince Khalid, relieve his new bride of her wedding present—a one-hundred-carat ruby necklace with a flawless twenty-carat stone as its centerpiece—and escape with my head intact.

In reality, there are a few substantial kinks.

One, Prince Khalid travels with a cadre of heavily armed bodyguards.

Two, the necklace won't be sitting out on the coffee table, waiting to be swiped. Cracking a safe is inevitable. And safe-cracking takes time, especially if done quietly.

Three, there's only one road to and from this exclusive resort, which will quickly be shut down if the necklace is discovered missing, thereby blocking my exit unless I can arrange to escape via scuba gear into the Caribbean Sea. Which I won't, because I can't swim.

And last but not least, there's Golden Boy.

Who is staying in the room directly beneath Prince Khalid's suite.

Who, if properly handled, could invite me up for a nightcap, thereby providing access to Prince Khalid's suite via the balcony. It involves a climb up a drainpipe and a series of low walls, but I can't hack the front door keycard reader as I normally would because Khalid's door is guarded by men with semiautomatic weapons, so the only other way in is through the balcony. And the only way to get *there* is from the balcony of the room below.

Unfortunately, Golden Boy must have had his hotel room

broken into in the past, because in addition to the keycard reader, he's installed a portable door lock with an alarm that will sound if the door's opened. And if he's gone to the trouble to do that, the probability that there are other security devices inside is high. Which means my best bet to safely access his room is by "befriending" the man himself.

Luckily, he just glanced at me for the third time in five minutes.

God bless my mother. My long legs and high cheekbones are all hers. If I'd taken after my father, I'd look like a hobbit. Not a bad thing in and of itself, but certainly not helpful in seducing handsome American men who carry themselves as if their whole life has been one extended homecoming king coronation party.

But Golden Boy isn't your average skirt-chasing playboy with more money than brains. Though he works hard to appear casual and normal, I see past his façade. He's a wolf in sheep's clothing. This one has a taste for blood. Which brings me back to my original question.

Is the risk worth the reward?

Of course it is. Wolves are no match for me.

Smiling, I rise from my chair and head to the bar, walking slowly so Golden Boy can take his time eyeing my bare legs. He slides off the edge of the pool and stands waist-deep in the water so he can get a better look at me.

I make a bet with myself on how long it'll take him to make his move. Judging by the way he's staring, another five minutes, tops.

"Do you have a lunch menu?" I ask the bartender as I slither onto a barstool and cross my legs. I'm wearing a plunging white maillot that sets off my tanned skin and showcases my cleavage, white kitten heels, and a sheer cover-up that skims the tops of my bare thighs. Even from this distance, I can feel Golden Boy's gaze on my skin, hotter than the Caribbean sun.

"Of course," says the bartender, a serious young man with a

gap between his crooked front teeth. He hands me a leather folio. "The conch croquettes are amazing."

I pretend to study the menu while eavesdropping on Golden Boy and his companions. The first thing I note is that my mark has a sleepy Southern drawl to go along with his muscles and baby blues. Texas? No, Georgia.

"I'll try them, thank you," I tell the bartender, letting the lilt of a fake Parisian accent infiltrate my words. Then I close my eyes, tip my head back, and fan myself with the menu as I stretch my neck. My hair slides off my shoulders and down my back. A waft of humid air drifts between my breasts. Golden Boy falters in the middle of his sentence, and then abruptly continues.

"...got Tabby on a plane."

"Connor gives incredible pep talks," says a female voice, warm with laughter. "I think this man could convince me to do anything."

"Oh yeah?" says a male voice, not Golden Boy's. Judging by the deep, commanding tone, my money's on the big beast, not the pale one with the woman in the yellow bikini. Tabby must be the redhead, then.

I listen, lazily fanning air over my cleavage, swinging my leg back and forth, a black widow patiently waiting for her prey to enter the web.

"There's a few things I'd *definitely* like to convince you to do, woman," says the beast, chuckling. Then there are some exaggerated kissing noises, which prompt a chorus of groans.

"Get a room, you two!" scolds another female. Must be Yellow Bikini. The voice is too adult to be the scarred girl.

"They spend any more time in their room, Darcy, we won't see 'em at all," drawls Golden Boy.

"They're newlyweds! Give them a break!" says a different male voice. He has a German accent. Blue speedo.

"Speakin' of breaks, I need another beer. Anybody else ready?"

Golden Boy takes drink orders from his companions. I hear the splash as he jumps out of the pool. Trying not to smirk, I start a silent countdown in my head. *Five, four, three, two—*

"'Scuse, me, bartender? Can we get another round?"

I open my eyes to find Golden Boy standing next to me. He's looking at the bartender at the end of the bar, who nods in acknowledgment. Then Golden Boy turns his head and looks at me.

Electricity jolts through me when our eyes meet. It's disturbing how strong it is. It's been years since I felt serious attraction to anyone, and muscular blonds aren't my type in the first place. Dark and dangerous is more my thing.

Although, admittedly, Golden Boy has the dangerous part down. The look in his eyes is anything but tame.

"Hi," he says, staring at me with blazing intensity.

Here's the part where I need to figure out his type. Dumb and bubbly? Smoldering seductress? Girl next door? There's a key that unlocks the door to every man's libido. And once his libido is engaged, his brain takes a nap for the duration.

I'm so grateful I'm a woman. We can get turned on without completely losing our intellect to our genitals.

"Hello," I say neutrally. I remove my sunglasses. Neither of us smiles.

He asks, "What part of Paris you from?"

I have to physically force myself not to blink. There's a slight difference between a Parisian accent and other French accents, and the fact that he picked it out is alarming.

And impressive. I'm inclined to like him, but of course I don't allow myself to.

"You know Paris?" I ask coyly, avoiding his question.

He cocks his head. "A little."

Hmm. That could mean he's only seen the city in movies, or he lived there for years. He's giving away about as much as I am.

"The eighth arrondissement," I parry, testing him. "Gare Saint-Lazare."

His face remains impassive. "Swanky neighborhood. You from there originally?"

I get the sense he's testing me, too. Why do I like it? I decide to change the subject to see how he handles it. "What's your name?"

One corner of his mouth turns up. A roguish little dimple appears in his cheek. "You avoided my question."

"And you just avoided mine."

"Yeah, but only because you started it."

"Funny, you don't strike me as a man who lets anyone else take the lead."

He chuckles. "With a rear view as fine as yours, darlin', you can take the lead anytime you like."

Now we're smiling at each other. For the first time in a long time, I'm having what could almost be described as fun.

The bartender arrives with the drinks. "Shall I charge it to your room, Mr. McLean?"

"Yep," Golden Boy answers without looking away from me.

The bartender leaves with a promise that my conch croquettes are almost ready.

I say, "So, Mr. McLean, where in Georgia are you from?"

If he's surprised I pegged his accent, he doesn't show it. He lifts a shoulder, self-confident, nonchalant. "Little town nobody's ever heard of."

"Oh come on. Now you have to tell me."

The dent in his cheek grows deeper. "Perry."

My smile widens. Unfortunately for him and his ego, I've spent a lot of time in the American South. I say, "Home to the annual Georgia National Fair. Cute little historic town center. There's, what, ten thousand residents in Perry?"

Golden Boy watches me with blistering focus. "Fifteen. What did you say your name was?"

I let the silence stretch out between us before saying softly, "I didn't."

When his eyes flash with desire, I know how I'm going to play him. He likes a challenge. Which means Girl Next Door and Dumb and Bubbly are out the window, and Smoldering Seductress is in the house. I moisten my lips with the tip of my tongue, lower my chin, and look up at him from beneath my lashes.

He sets his empty beer bottle on the counter and slides onto the barstool next to me, all without taking his gaze from my face. His big thighs are spread open on either side of mine, effectively trapping me.

"So," he says, "beautiful, nameless mademoiselle. Are we going to be friends or not?"

I can't help myself. I laugh at his directness. "I don't know, handsome American Marine. Perhaps we should take a moment to discuss your definition of 'friends.'"

He leans closer. He's bare chested, barefoot, and soaking wet from the waist down. The bulge in his black swim shorts is clearly visible, and impressively large. Five-o'clock shadow glints copper along his square jaw. If I were any other woman, this man would be devastating.

Into my ear, he says softly, "Anything you want it to be."

*Does he think I'm a prostitute?* I'm not offended, but this is awfully forward, even for an American. Most men take a lot longer than five minutes to get to the propositioning.

Obviously he's not like most men. I need to be careful with this one.

When he leans back, I tilt my head and consider him.

Up close, he's even more handsome than he looked in the pool. Masculine and a little gritty, in spite of his sleepy Southern drawl and baby-blue eyes. He's got big, rough hands, a superhero's square jaw, an appealing cleft in his chin, and a lot of tattoos on his chest and arms that I'd like to trace with my fingers. Or tongue.

But I don't ever sleep with a mark. It's a policy I've never broken. If he takes me up to his room, I've got two potent pills to slip into his drink that will conveniently allow me to side step the minefield of sex with a stranger.

I might take a quick peek into his shorts while he's passed out to check out that bulge he's packing, but that's as far as it will go.

"I already have a lot of friends." I say it with just enough warmth that he knows it's not a brush-off.

"I bet you do." His voice is husky now. He lets his gaze drift to my lips, then to my cleavage, then down my legs, boldly and unapologetically eating me up with his eyes.

Under his admiring gaze, I feel like a cat that's been stroked down its back. I wouldn't be surprised if I started to purr. "And so do you." I nod in the direction of his companions in the pool, who watch us with open interest.

"They can wait. I wanna get to know you better first."

I stifle the urge to laugh again. He's making this too easy. "Such an eager beaver!"

His eyes grow hotter. "A word of advice, darlin'," he drawls, grinning. "Don't say any words that are euphemisms for your lady parts unless you want me to think you're flirtin' with me."

"I see. No mentions of muffins, cookies, secret gardens, or cockpits. Got it."

His grin is so wide, it's practically blinding. "You *are* flirtin' with me."

Bat, bat, bat go my eyelashes. "Would you mind if I were?"

His grin fades. He reaches out and gently strokes a lock of hair off my shoulder. He skims his fingertips slowly down my arm until he reaches my wrist. His touch leaves a trail of sparks in its wake.

He cuffs my wrist in his big hand, settles his index finger over my pulse point, and, after a moment of silence where I think he's counting my heartbeat, says gruffly, "You know I wouldn't.

But I've got another warnin' for you, beautiful mademoiselle. I don't do small talk. When I want a woman, I go after her."

He raises my wrist to his lips and brushes a sweet, soft kiss across the pulse pounding there. Electricity crackles through my body. All my nerve endings sit up and suck in a startled breath.

Looking into my eyes, my new friend Mr. McLean says, "So unless you tell me right now you don't wanna play this game, I'm comin' after *you*."

Mierde santa. *This man must get laid a dozen times a week.*

Suddenly I'm filled with longing so strong and bittersweet, it steals my breath. I wish I were a normal woman, a tourist on vacation with her friends who could indulge herself in a summer fling with a sexy stranger. I wish I could say yes to this beautiful man, let him make love to me, let myself go.

I wish I could forget all the sins that led me to this moment.

But I can't. They follow me like a shadow, dogging my every step. My only path to freedom is repayment of my debts, and Prince Khalid's new bride's ruby necklace is next on my debtor's list.

So I smile and toss my hair and pretend to be someone I'm not, stuffing my longing for a different life into a dark, abandoned corner of my heart where all my other useless yearnings go.

"I like to play games, Mr. McLean," I say lightly. "But since you've warned me, I should warn you, too. I always win."

When he smiles, he does it with his whole body. It's like he lights up from the inside out. "It's Ryan," he says. "And *damn*, this is gonna be fun. Tell me your name."

I use the fake name on my fake passport and say, "Angeline Lemaire."

Ryan nods. "It's a pleasure to meet you, Angeline."

Before I can say another word, he tugs me closer and crushes his mouth to mine.

# 2

## RYAN

She tastes like strawberries and sunshine and secrets that go deep, and kisses like it's her last day alive. Whoever this siren calling herself Angeline really is, she's sexy as fuck.

She's also clearly dangerous.

If my cock were any harder, it would be titanium.

Her hands are balled to fists on my chest, the one sign of resistance to the otherwise total surrender her body melts into as we kiss. Along with everything else about her, it's an intriguing contradiction. Like the sadness in her eyes that's paired with cold calculation. The self-confidence paired with the vulnerability. The pounding pulse paired with the disinterested smile.

She makes a sound deep in her throat, a soft, feminine moan. It makes my cock twitch. I tighten my arms around her and pull her closer.

"Wait!" She gasps, breaking away. Her eyes are startled. She lets out a surprised little laugh. "Wait a minute!"

Breathing hard, we stare at each other, our noses inches apart. I give her five seconds to get her bearings. Then I growl,

"That's as long as I can stand," and take her mouth again, fisting my hands in her hair to hold her head in place.

From somewhere far off, I hear catcalls and clapping.

Her hands flatten over my pecs. After a moment, she winds her arms around my shoulders. Then she gives me her weight, leaning into me with a little sigh as she goes slack against my body. The kiss softens but also deepens, so now it's slower and less greedy, but somehow even more intense.

Judging by how hard her nipples are against my bare chest, how irregular her breathing is, and how she's digging her nails into my skin, I'd say she's just as turned on as I am.

When the kiss finally ends, a minute or a century later, I'm dizzy. I mutter, "Fuck." My voice sounds like I've swallowed a handful of gravel.

Her laugh is low and throaty. "Well said."

I open my eyes and look at her. She's flushed. Her eyes are half-lidded. She has that hazy, satisfied look a woman gets after she comes.

The amount of blood leaving the rest of my body to boil in my cock can't be healthy. Pretty soon I won't be able to remain upright.

I grin at her. "This is already turning out to be a fantastic friendship."

She stares at me for a second, then breaks into full-throated laughter, her head thrown back.

Goddamn. If I thought she was gorgeous before, watching her laugh is on a whole other level. She's fucking *stunning*.

The waiter arrives with her conch croquettes. When he glares at me as he sets the plate down on the bar, I know he was hoping to be in the exact position I am now. *You and every other guy in the place, buddy.*

I smile blandly at him. He stalks off like a wounded puppy.

Angeline gently pushes me away, smooths a hand over her hair, and looks like she's trying to rearrange her face into something a little more composed than the horny-sex-kitten expression she's wearing now.

I say, "Hey, Angel." When she glances at me sharply, I explain. "I'm calling you Angel now. Less formal, since we're such good friends and all. As I was saying—*Angel*—I have to go distribute these drinks before one of those animals in the pool throws something at me, so I want you to sit here and think about what you're gonna say to me when I get back."

I stand, pop one of her conch croquettes into my mouth, chew, and swallow. "And make it good. If I find out you're just a pretty face, I'll be sorely disappointed."

Her smile is the definition of smug. With that seductive accent, she says, "A pretty face who can make a soldier who survived three shots to the stomach swoon from just a kiss."

She takes one of the conch croquettes and bites into it with the unstudied elegance of a queen. I want to grab her, throw her over my shoulder, take her upstairs to my room, and fuck the living daylights out of her until we're both exhausted, but I smile at her instead.

Time enough for that later. Right now I've gotta distribute some drinks.

I grab the beers and Tabby's water and leave Angeline with a wink. She rolls her eyes and shakes her head, but she's smiling, so I know she thinks I'm cute. Pretending my dick isn't tenting the front of my shorts like the big top at a circus, I swagger back to the pool.

When I get there, Darcy takes one look at my crotch and says, "Uh, Ryan? Unless you're starring in a Viagra commercial we don't know about, you might wanna wrap a towel around your waist. That thing needs its own zip code."

Connor hoots. Tabby and Kai look politely in different directions. Juanita says with perfect teenage disdain, "Ew."

"Cut the poor guy some slack," says Connor, chuckling. "He's on vacation."

Darcy snorts. "So that means we all have to be subjected to a front-row viewing of his monster boner? I don't think so. I mean, it's a beautiful thing, Ry, but seriously, you might as well be naked."

She stares right at my dick the entire time she talks. Kai frowns and nudges her with his elbow. She says innocently, "What? I'm telling him to put it away!"

Juanita slides into the pool with a muttered "You guys are gross," and swims off.

I crouch down, set all the drinks on the edge of the pool, and say in a low voice, "So don't be surprised if I miss dinner tonight. Somethin' else came up."

Darcy laughs. "You don't say!"

Tabby says, "Why don't you bring your new friend to dinner with us?"

When I cast a doubtful glance at her, she sighs. "It's our last night on the island, Ryan. Who knows when we'll all be together like this again. C'mon. You can sacrifice *one* hour in between..." She waves a hand vaguely in the air. "Whatever it is you'll be doing."

If I'm being honest, I don't think I can. That one taste of Angeline knocked me flat on my ass. I feel like a junkie after a high. All I want is more, more, more.

But tomorrow Connor and Tabby are off to island-hop for the rest of their honeymoon, and the rest of us are back to our real lives in New York, so Tabby has a valid point. It would be impolite to bail on our last dinner together just for some mind-blowingly hot sex with an incredibly beautiful, sensual, and fascinating stranger.

I mean...right?

Watching my face, Tabby says drily, "Don't break your brain trying to decide, Boner Boy."

"Leave him alone, woman." Connor wraps his arm around Tabby's waist and drags her against him. He smiles down at her.

"If he makes it, he makes it. If he doesn't, I can't honestly say I blame him." He lowers his voice. "Seriously, princess. *Look* at her."

Tabby's brows lift. "Oh, you think she's hot, jarhead?"

Darcy mutters, "Uh-oh."

"Not my type," Connor says instantly. "But I can see the appeal." When Tabby just keeps staring at him, he clears his throat. "For someone else. Not me, obviously."

Tabby says, "Mm-hmm."

Darcy makes an "ooo" sound that's like *You are so dead right now*, while Kai watches the exchange with his typical batshit-crazy grin.

My friends are so weird.

"Okay, in the name of marital harmony, I'll commit to dinner," I say, itching to get back to Angeline and her strawberry-flavored mouth. I stand and salute Connor, who gives me a pleading look like he really wants me to stay and help defuse the situation.

I leave him with a smirk. He's my brother-in-arms and I love the guy, but I'd rather take another three shots to the gut than deal with a pissed-off Tabitha West.

Angeline watches me return with the focused concentration of a predator contemplating a meal. Why that should be such a fucking turn-on, I have no idea.

I stop beside her and lean an elbow on the bar. "So. What'd you come up with, Angel?" When she opens her mouth, I warn, "And remember, it better be good."

She waits a beat and then says tartly, "Is it my turn to talk now?"

*Mercy. A goddess* and *a smartass. I'm done for.* I say mildly, "Be my guest."

A secret smile hovers around her lips. She crooks a finger, inviting me closer. I'm in her face so fast, I've probably set a new land speed record. She puts her lips against my ear and whispers, "You don't really think I'm going to sleep with a man I met five minutes ago, do you?"

Something inside my chest does this flopping, dying fish thing that doesn't seem healthy. I have to stifle a groan. I want this woman so bad, I can taste it.

I turn my head a fraction and now we're nose to nose, staring into each other's eyes. Hers are a gorgeous caramel brown, twinkling with mischief.

I say, "Of course not. I'm a gentleman. I was gonna let you finish those conch croquettes first."

She slow blinks and smiles.

My titanium boner is in serious jeopardy of exploding in my shorts.

"You haven't even asked what I'm doing in St. Croix." Angeline leans back and lazily selects another of the croquettes from the plate. "I could be vacationing with my husband."

"No ring," I counter, watching her make eating a piece of fried seafood look like dirty fetish porn.

She swallows and licks her lips, obviously enjoying torturing me. "My boyfriend, then."

"You don't have a boyfriend."

My tone of total confidence makes her arch an eyebrow. "No? What makes you so certain of that?"

"Because you kiss like you're starving, you look at me like a little kid looks at all the presents under the tree on Christmas morning, and you're not the type of woman who cheats on her man. You're too serious for that, even though you try to seem carefree."

Something crosses her face, a look of surprise or irritation, instantly erased. She says, "I had no idea I was so transparent."

Though her tone is casual, I can tell she's disturbed. She doesn't want me to look too closely, to notice things about her. Naturally, that makes me want to notice even more. I'm a bloodhound with the fresh scent of fox in my nose.

*Let the hunt begin.*

"Ignore me," I say, watching her compose herself. "I've been out in the sun too long. So tell me, Angel, what brings you to St. Croix?"

She flips a lock of long brown hair over her shoulder and swivels on the stool so she's facing the bar counter, her eyes turned away. "Work."

I look at the infinity pool, the lush green mountains in the distance, the sparkling Caribbean Sea dotted with sailboats. Then I look back at her, in all her exotic glory. "Lemme guess. You're a model."

"I'm a travel writer, doing a piece on the fine resorts of the Caribbean."

"A writer." *Sure you are. And I'm Dolly Parton.* I slide onto the barstool next to her and take a slug of my warm beer. "Guess you're not just a pretty face after all."

I'm gifted with her full-throated laugh again. "You mean you couldn't tell from that line I used on you when you came back from the pool?"

"So it was a *line*," I drawl, gently bumping her shoulder with mine. When she looks at me, I grin. "You *are* gonna sleep with me."

She tries to look offended but completely fails. "You think you're extremely charming, don't you?" she says, all prim and proper. Now it's my turn to laugh.

"Hardly. My mama always said I've got the manners God gave a goat. I'm just a beer-drinkin' good ol' boy from Georgia with more balls than brains."

Angeline eyes me. She lets her gaze linger on my tattoos, the scars on my stomach, and my hands, which have spent near equal time on the keys of a piano as they have on an M16 rifle. She says softly, "Or maybe that's what you *want* people to think."

Our eyes lock. A strange sensation makes its way through my

stomach. It's fizzy. Fluttery. If I didn't know fucking better, I'd describe it as butterflies.

"I'm leavin' tomorrow," I say abruptly, holding her gaze.

"Me, too."

"So…ticktock, beautiful mademoiselle."

She knows exactly what I mean. Her lips curve upward. "I appreciate your candor, Mr. McLean—"

"Ryan," I correct her. "Good friends call each other by their first names, Angel."

Her eyes do this incredible thing when she smiles. They sparkle like sunshine glimmering off water. Or is that the stars in my own eyes I'm seeing?

*Sweet baby Jesus, I'm losing my shit. Pull it together, dickhead!*

"Okay," Angeline says. "As I was saying, I appreciate your candor, Ryan. And I'd be lying if I said I wasn't tempted. You're very sexy."

Her gaze travels hungrily up and down my body as she says "sexy." If she keeps looking at me like that, I might have an accident in my shorts.

Then she lets out this sad little sigh and lifts a shoulder. "But I don't do one-night stands. It's not my thing."

Like I'm gonna let that stop me. I immediately switch into problem-solving mode. "No one-nighters. No problem. You live in Paris, right?"

Her brows pull together. "Yes. Why?"

"I'm in New York."

She cocks her head, waiting.

I say, "It's only about an eight-hour flight between the two, and I've got a shit-ton of frequent flier miles. And since you're a travel writer, I figure you probably do, too."

She stares at me without blinking. Then she says, "We've known each other for ten minutes and you're suggesting we enter into a long-distance relationship?"

I shrug but don't break eye contact. "You want me. I want you. You don't do one-night stands. You got a better solution?"

I'm not sure if her expression is horror or amusement. "You're actually serious."

"As a heart attack, Angel."

Shaking her head, she lets out a small, astonished laugh and mutters something to herself in French.

I lean closer, wrap my hand around her arm, and give it a squeeze. When she looks at me, I say softly, "The way you move. The way you look at me. Your laugh. *That kiss*. I'm thirty-four years old, Angel, and I've had my share of women. Not a single one has ever challenged me, made me laugh, called me on my shit, looked at me like they understood me, *and* given me a boner that could cut glass while at the same time makin' me feel like a teenager with his first crush. I wouldn't care if you lived in fuckin' Antarctica. This is gonna happen."

*Even if you* are *lying to me about who you are.*

After a long time, she simply says, "Wow."

I grin at her. "You just fell in love with me, didn't you? You're totally in love with me now."

Her laugh is disbelieving. "*Or* I'm wondering where the nearest police station is so I can file a restraining order!"

"Nah. I'm tellin' you, it's love. A year from now, we'll be back here on our honeymoon."

She drops her face into her hands and groans. "*Mon Dieu*, please stop talking."

From the pool comes a shout. "Whatever he just said, he meant, sweetheart!"

It's Connor. Over my shoulder, I casually flip him the bird. His booming laugh echoes across the pool and through the bar.

I say, "Listen."

Angeline looks at me warily.

"We're havin' dinner tonight in the hotel restaurant, the six of us." I jerk my thumb in the direction of the pool and the gang of misfits I call friends. "Now seven, including you. After dinner, you and I will go up to my room, we'll talk, we'll have a drink, we'll pretend like you're not already madly in love with me and wild to have my babies."

She interrupts me before I've got the last word out of my mouth. "There is something seriously wrong with you, Ryan McLean. Are you aware of that?"

"Yeah, but you still think I'm cute. Which means there's somethin' seriously wrong with *you*. Which makes us a perfect match."

She starts to laugh and can't stop. I go right on talking.

"Then you'll decide if your one-night stand rule applies to the beginning of a long-distance relationship with the man of your dreams. And I'm just pointin' out here that it *wouldn't* be a one-night stand if it's at the start of a relationship. Anyway. Whatever you decide, we'll spend some time, get to know each other better, share a few stories, make out. Probably mostly make out."

She continues to laugh. I'm having a hard time keeping a straight face too.

"So whaddya say, Angel?"

When she finally catches her breath, her eyes are alight, her cheeks are pink, and her smile is as brilliant as the sun. She says, "Okay, cowboy. You're on. But don't even think about stepping out of line with me, because I'm a knife-fencing expert. Put a hand where it isn't wanted, and you'll lose it."

Now I'm the one laughing, but not because I don't believe her. I *do*. And this is major progress.

It's the first thing she's told me about herself that's the truth.

# 3

## MARIANA

There's a part of me that's thrilled about the way things are going. Ryan's making this all extremely easy on me, that's for sure. But there's another part of me—a bigger part—that's worried.

I like him.

For someone in my line of work, that can be deadly.

It's not just the way Ryan looks or kisses, or his straightforward, no-bullshit style. It's not only his wacky sense of humor or his obvious intelligence. It's all that, *plus* he's this big, macho Marine with a cocky swagger who's strong enough to survive gunshots but touches me with true gentleness, both with his hands and his eyes.

The man has a sensitive side.

There's nothing more irresistible to my cynical heart than rugged masculinity paired with tenderness. Every other man I know is ruthless to his core.

It's times like these I wish I weren't so observant.

"Dinner's at eight," says Ryan, smiling his signature cocksure smile. "What room you in, Angel? I'll pick you up."

No matter how much I like him, the odds of me letting this

man into my room are about as good as the odds that lightning will strike me dead where I sit. "Let's meet in the lobby."

Before he can ask why, I lean forward and kiss him.

It proves an effective distraction.

He takes my face in his hands—another thing I like more than I should—and softly groans into my mouth as our tongues sweep together. Dangerous adrenaline floods my veins. I try to maintain intellectual distance, like an outside observer, but the man is a champion kisser. His lips are filled with mind-altering chemicals. They must be, because within seconds, I'm lost, clinging to him like I'm drowning and he's the only thing that can save me from going under the next big wave.

"I dig the little noises you make," he whispers, gently biting my lower lip as he cradles my head.

"Noises?" I repeat, too blissed out to be horrified I might be making some kind of unattractive animal sounds into his mouth.

When was the last time I was kissed like this?

Never.

"Little growly kitten noises." He kisses one corner of my mouth, then the other. He says hotly into my ear, "I wonder what kind of noises you'll make when I have my face between your legs."

I summon a vivid picture of myself naked on my back in a bed, Ryan's golden head between my thighs, writhing and screaming my way through a thermonuclear orgasm. I try not to pant.

He allows me to pull away, but the expression on his face is dark and intense. I think he might grab me at any moment and haul me off into the bushes, caveman style.

Over the roar of my pulse, I say coolly, "Don't get ahead of yourself, cowboy. You're still in the friend zone. Any more assumptions about where this is headed and the friend zone is where you'll stay."

I amuse him, evidenced by his gruff chuckle and jaunty salute. "Yes, ma'am."

I toss my hair and rise from the barstool. Instantly, he's on his feet, too.

"See you at eight," I say.

He looks crestfallen, like a little boy left alone at the playground. "You're leavin' already? It's not even four!"

*Mierde. Why does he have to be so adorable?* The contrast between his sweet, boyish side and his macho, mouthy side is maddeningly disarming. "I have some work to finish up this afternoon. My article's due to my editor today, and I haven't wrapped it up yet."

He looks at me for a beat. His expression changes into something unreadable. Gone is the little boy. In his place is a man who is watchful and speculative, his eyes the chilly blue of an iceberg. It's the wolf I saw earlier, the one lurking behind the swagger and smiles.

"Of course," he says, without a shred of emotion in his voice. "I understand. Duty calls."

This time when he smiles, it sends a shiver down my spine.

I dig some cash from the clutch I brought with me to the pool and leave it on the bar for the conch croquettes. Ryan looks skyward and sighs. He picks up the money and waves it in my face. Confused, I take it.

Ryan says, "Don't insult me, Angel. And before you get any other dumb ideas, I'm buyin' dinner, too, *compris*?"

My heart skips a beat. "You speak French?"

His shrug is the picture of nonchalance. "A little," he says. "Used to date a French girl."

*Sure you did.* I narrow my eyes. His cool smile grows suspiciously wider. Suddenly, I feel like we're in the middle of a film noir standoff, two spies on opposite sides of a bridge waiting to see who'll draw their gun first.

"See you at eight, Angel." Ryan kisses me on the cheek, slaps me on the ass, and saunters off, whistling, toward the pool.

I watch him go, convinced I've made a miscalculation.

I'm dealing with something far more dangerous than a wolf.

~

Back in my room, I unlock the safe and remove the burner phone I bought at the airport. I dial a number I know by heart. There's a distant hiss, then a click as the line is answered.

"Reynard," says a cultured British voice.

"It's Dragonfly," I say, relieved. Reynard always answers the line, he's as reliable as Big Ben, but there are so few reliable things in this world, I still can't take him for granted.

"My darling!" he says, pleased. "Have you completed your article already?"

"I need to check a source."

A short pause follows. "I see. One moment." Fingers tap a keyboard thousands of miles away. "Proceed."

"Ryan McLean. Unsure if it's M-C or M-A-C. Male, thirty-four, American, from Perry, Georgia. Served in the Marines. Unsure of the service dates. Blond hair, blue eyes, approximately six foot two, two hundred twenty pounds. Multiple tattoos. Perfect teeth."

More typing. I know it won't be long, but I'm impatient anyway, tapping my foot on the plush carpet as I wait.

Finally, a low chuckle comes through the phone. "Oh my. That's quite a smile. I've seen sharks less deadly. Careful, my darling, this one's got a serious bite."

"Tell me."

"Ryan Tiberius McLean—"

"Tiberius?" I'm incredulous. "He was named after a Roman emperor? Who does that to their child?"

"May I continue, or would you like to amuse yourself by repeating everything I say and asking rhetorical questions?"

I smile but don't laugh. Under no circumstances does one laugh at Reynard. "My apologies. Please continue."

"As I was saying. Ryan Tiberius McLean, born August tenth, nineteen eighty-three, to Betty Anne Rasmussen, a homemaker, and Thomas Robert McLean, a peach farmer." Reynard's pause drips with condescension. "Humble beginnings, indeed."

I don't point out that my father was a farmer too. Avocadoes. To this day, I still can't bear to look at them. They'll forever be paired in my memory with gunfire, bodies, and blood.

"August tenth," I muse. "So he's a Leo. That fits."

Reynard sighs. I can almost hear the eye roll. "My darling. Astrology isn't an actual science."

"I know, but there could be *something* to it. If you met him, you'd agree he's very lionlike."

Though Reynard doesn't reply, I know exactly what he's doing at this moment. He's shaking his head in silent disappointment. I miss him with a sudden, violent ache.

He's the closest thing to family I've got.

Reynard continues, sounding bored. "Two older siblings, Missy and Cleo—you're right, these names are dreadful—graduated Perry High School top of his class, football scholarship to Georgia State..." Reynard pauses. "Both parents killed in a drive-by shooting on a vacation to Los Angeles to celebrate their twentieth wedding anniversary."

The breath leaves my chest in an audible rush. The room starts to spin. The words get stuck in my head, replaying over and over until I want to press my hands over my ears and scream.

*Parents killed. Shooting. Parents killed. Shooting. Killed.*

*Killed.*

*Killed.*

I sit heavily on the edge of the bed and swallow back the hot, acid sting of bile.

If Reynard guesses the effect those words have had on me, he doesn't mention it. He continues in the same monotone as before.

"Graduated Georgia State and entered the United States Marines. Seems your Mr. McLean excelled there. Commendations galore, rose rapidly through the ranks, selected for Special Ops, etcetera, etcetera… Oh, this is interesting. Areas of specialty include reconnaissance, close-quarter battle tactics, and edged weapons."

"He's a *knife-fighting* expert," I say dully. "Why does God hate me, Reynard?"

"Again with the rhetorical questions. I wasn't quite finished, my darling."

I groan. "Don't tell me there's more."

"You'll love this. After aging out of Special Ops and leaving the corps, he was recruited to a private security firm—"

"Security firm?" My eyes bulge in horror.

"Wait for it…where he provides armed security services for high-profile clients, federal and local governments, law enforcement and intelligence agencies, and multinational corporations. Looks like he's primarily doing extractions now. Retrieving the Russian oligarch's kidnapped daughter from the clutches of the Serbian Mafia, that kind of thing."

My silence must last a long time, because Reynard eventually asks, "Are you still there?"

"He's a merc," I say, miserable with disbelief. "Of all the men in all the world who could've been staying in that room, he's a mercenary. A knife-wielding, kidnapped-daughter-extracting, goddamn *mercenary*."

"Yes," Reynard drawls, amused. "He certainly is. Am I to take it your article won't be completed by deadline? That could be problematic, my darling."

I grit my teeth and straighten my spine. "I've never missed a deadline yet, have I?"

"That's my girl," says Reynard, his voice a purr. "See you on the other side."

As always, he hangs up with that cryptic goodbye.

I say aloud to the empty room, "Well, it could be worse. At least it's not raining. The climb up to Khalid's balcony would be really treacherous in the rain."

From somewhere off in the distant mountains comes a low roll of thunder. I flop onto my back on the bed and close my eyes.

*You've got to be kidding me.*

# 4

## RYAN

If my boner doesn't chill pretty soon, I'm gonna have to seek medical attention.

"For fuck's sake," I mutter, looking down at the big guy jutting out from the front of the towel wrapped around my waist. "Would you behave?"

He doesn't answer. He also doesn't budge. I've got an organ that's been sticking out at a ninety-degree angle from my body for the past three and a half hours. If I didn't love him so much, I'd grab a length of duct tape and tape him to my leg.

I wipe the steam from the bathroom mirror, slap my face with a dollop of foam, and start to shave. It's awkward because I have to tilt my hips back so I don't bash my dick on the edge of the sink. I finish the shave, brush my teeth, comb my wet hair, and throw on clean clothes, thinking the entire time about a brown-haired siren who seems about as likely to kiss me as she is to stab me in the back with an ice pick.

I haven't been this turned on in years.

Whistling, I set the motion detectors and alarms that will send an alert to my cell if they're tripped, and lock my hotel door. I'm ten minutes early, but I don't want to miss Angeline coming off the elevator. The woman moves like poetry. I've got the perfect spot in mind where I'm gonna stand and wait until she comes down.

*Angeline Lemaire, age twenty-six, born and raised in Paris, France. Freelance travel writer for Condé Nast and National Geographic Travel, among others. Graduated from the Sorbonne with a degree in journalism, never married, no children, no criminal record, pays her taxes on time.*

Biggest load of bullshit ever invented. Boring, too. If I were gonna invent a background for myself, you can bet it would include something awesome like astronaut or race car driver. A writer? Seriously? She looks like a Bond girl, all slinky strides and knife-blade eyes. She should've gone with "international lingerie model/boner inducer." It would've been way more believable.

Fuck, this is gonna be fun.

So. Much. *Fun.*

I have to remember to thank Tabby for updating Metrix's computer systems. The search program she installed is amazing. I have a suspicion it's somehow linked to the National Security Administration's database, but hell if I'm gonna ask. The less I know the better.

I take my time as I make my way through the hotel to the lobby. Anticipation buzzes inside my gut like I've swallowed a beehive. All my senses are heightened. Sharpened. I've got that jacked-up feeling I get right before a midnight raid.

The lobby of the hotel is swanky but understated, decorated in classic, laid-back island style. The scent of rain and orchids perfume the air. One entire wall is open to the view of the ocean, letting the balmy evening breezes drift in. The guests are swanky too, jet-set types from around the world, dripping diamonds and scorn.

I make a quick loop through the lobby to check the exits—old habits die hard—then take my position in front of a stand of potted palms between the main elevators and the entrance to the restaurant. By my calculation, Angeline will have to walk toward me for a good thirty seconds, giving me plenty of time to enjoy the view.

Unfortunately, Darcy and Kai get off the elevator first. They spot me instantly.

"Ryan!" Darcy shouts from halfway down the hall.

I lift a hand. "Yo, Darcy."

She hustles over, Kai in tow. When they stop beside me, Darcy huffs and gives me a side-eyed look. "What're you doing over here lurking by the plants?"

"I'm not lurking. I'm waiting."

Darcy looks at Kai and waggles her eyebrows. "For Miss Thang."

Kai grins at her. "Love is a cruel master, *mein kleines Häschen.*"

I don't allow myself to react to him calling her his little bunny rabbit in German.

But then the conversation comes to a screeching halt because the elevator doors open again. Angeline steps into the room, and all the air goes out.

Feeling like I've been stabbed in the gut, I say faintly, "Holy shit."

Darcy and Kai turn to look in the direction I'm looking. When Darcy sees Angeline, she turns back to me, chuckling.

"This bitch ain't playin'. Good luck, sucker. We'll be at the bar."

She pats me on the shoulder, then drags Kai off toward the restaurant, leaving me standing alone with my mouth open like I'm trying to catch flies.

Angeline is a supermodel, and the lobby is her runway. Scarlet lips, scarlet dress with a slit from ankle to hip, long legs flashing in slow motion. Glossy hair tumbling over her shoulders. Dangerous eyes. A radiant smile. Impressions hit me one after another as she moves toward me. The long skirt of her dress billows behind her like a sail.

Her waist is narrow, her hips are round, and my dick and my brain are in total agreement: she's a fucking knockout.

When she reaches me, she rests her hands on my shoulders and kisses me lightly on both cheeks. I'm wrapped in the scent of her skin, fresh and peppery, like watercress.

"You look wonderful," she says softly, holding my gaze. "Have you been waiting long?"

Against impossible odds, I regain the power of speech. "Only my whole life."

She laughs, thinking I'm joking.

I make a motion with my index finger, indicating she should turn around. I have to see this masterpiece from all angles. She takes a step back and twirls. It looks professional, like she's been performing spins in front of a camera for years. Two guys near the front desk who are watching look like they're having heart attacks.

"That's some dress, Angel."

"This old thing?" She bats her lashes at me. It's my turn to laugh.

I grab her, pull her against my chest, bury my face in her hair, and inhale deeply. "Have you been rolling around in a clover field?" I murmur against her neck. "You smell like spring. And spices."

"That's my perfume. It's Caron's *Poivre*. You like it?"

I lightly bite her neck. I whisper, "It's edible. Like you."

A little shudder runs through her body. She pulls away and tilts her head toward the restaurant. "Shall we?"

"Yes. But don't be surprised if I drag you off halfway through dinner. This dress is testing the limits of my self-control."

Her smile is pleased. Apparently, devastation of the male population was her goal when she dressed. *Nailed it.*

She takes my arm. We stroll toward the restaurant while I enjoy the unexpected pleasure of being the envy of every man in sight. Even some of the women look like they'd like to take my place. The rest look like they're hoping Angeline will trip.

"So, did you finish your article?"

There's not a quiver in her voice when she answers. "I did."

"How'd it go?"

From the corner of my eye, I see her mysterious smile. "There are always some unexpected difficulties near the end, but nothing insurmountable. I think my editor will be very pleased with how it turns out."

"Turns" out, not "turned" out. Which indicates the work is still in progress, but she just said she finished it.

*Interesting*. I make a vague "hmm" sound and settle my arm around her waist. Our steps fall in sync like we've been walking together for years.

When we reach the restaurant, I check in with the hostess. She says the rest of our party is in the bar, so we head over, holding hands.

"Hiya, kids," I say when we reach them. "This is Angeline."

I introduce her to Tabby, who's wearing ponytails and what looks like a turquoise tube sock for a dress, Connor, in his usual all-black ensemble of T-shirt, cargo pants, and boots, and Darcy and Kai. Juanita is nowhere to be seen.

After the introductions are made and everyone has said a friendly hello, I ask Tabby, "Where's Juanita?"

"She found an MMA match on cable. I left her in front of the TV with Elvis and enough Red Bull and Cheetos to last a lifetime."

Angeline says, "Elvis?"

Tabby nods. "The rat she never goes anywhere without."

When Angeline's brows lift, Tabby grins. "It's a long story. I love your dress, by the way."

"And I love your Tinker Bell tattoo," Angeline counters,

looking at Tabby's ankle. "She was always my favorite Disney character."

"Mine, too!" says Tabby, smiling. "She's badass."

"But also fragile. She can't exist unless Peter believes in her. Faith is the only thing that keeps her alive."

I see it the instant Tabby's curiosity kicks into gear. If she were a cat, her ears would've just pricked and her tail would've begun twitching. She says, "All you need is faith, trust, and a little bit of pixie dust."

Without hesitation, Angeline responds. "Never say goodbye, because goodbye means going away, and going away means forgetting."

Tabby claps her hands and hoots. "Oh my God! I think I love you, Angeline!"

I look at Connor. "Brother, you have any idea what's happening?"

"Let's eat," says Kai, stroking Darcy's arm and staring up at her in adoration. "My *Häschen* needs fuel for later."

They exchange a pair of truly lascivious smiles. Before the conversation can get any weirder, I motion for the hostess to seat us.

An hour later, dinner is over, Kai and Darcy are fondling each other under the table, and Tabby and Angeline have become fast friends.

"You do *not* like Hello Kitty!" pronounces Tabby. She's been peppering Angeline with questions for the past twenty minutes as Connor and I listened, stealing amused glances at each other.

Angeline nods, swallowing another spoonful of her dessert. She delicately pats her lips with her napkin. "I know you probably think it's silly, but I was obsessed with her for my entire teenage years. I had this backpack I carried everywhere. It was pink, with little butterflies and flowers—"

"And Kitty was wearing an embroidered kimono," interrupts Tabby in a low, thrilled voice. "I had *the exact same one*."

Angeline blinks. "You like Hello Kitty?"

Tabby pounds both fists on the table and shouts, "I fucking *love* her!"

They beam at each other.

I say, "Would you two like to get a room?"

Tabby says, "Don't hate, Ryan. Kitty's worth seven billion dollars a *year*. What're you bringing in annually?"

Connor says, "Not enough. He's due for a raise."

Now he's got my attention. "Oh yeah? This is news."

He smiles and slings his arm over the back of Tabby's chair. "Just got a bonus from Karpov. A big one. And that's thanks to you, brother. That job would never have gone so well if it weren't for you. I think the guy wants to put you in his will or something. He wouldn't shut up about how you saved his daughter's life."

I chuckle. "Well, you never know when you might need a favor from a Russian oligarch. His gratitude could come in handy someday."

Beside me, Angeline falls still. Her gaze cuts from Connor to me. "You two work together?"

"Yep. This big ape recruited me straight outta the corps into his security firm. I thought we talked about that."

"No, we didn't. You said you knew each other in the military, and then we all started talking about the wedding."

I think for a minute. "Oh yeah." I shrug. "Anyway, we work together. Tabby helps, too."

Angeline turns to Tabby with a new look on her face, one of wariness, as if she's seeing her for the first time. "Oh?"

Tabby leans back into Connor's arm and smiles at him.

"*Technically* I work for the government, but these bozos need a little assistance from time to time."

Angeline says tightly, "Assistance?"

Tabby looks back at Angeline and says what she always says when someone asks what she does, with the same flat, *no more questions* delivery. "I'm in computers."

It's like a wall comes down over Angeline's face. Her smile vanishes. The light goes out in her eyes. She says tonelessly, "You're a hacker."

That almost jolts me out of my seat. *How the fuck did she put that together?* Connor and I glance sharply at each other. Tabby merely smiles.

"I prefer the term social engineer."

Angeline carefully sets her spoon on the edge of her dessert plate. "How interesting. I've been thinking about writing a book about hackers, actually. Which branch of the government do you work for?"

Tabby's way too smart not to notice the sudden change of vibe from Angeline, but she's also too smart to let that show. She says brightly, "Well, I could tell you, but then I'd have to kill you!" Then she laughs.

Angeline stifles the small tremor in her right hand by sliding it into her lap and curling it into a fist. "And you, Darcy? Do you work for the government, too?"

Darcy snorts. "Girlfriend, I couldn't work for Uncle Sam even if I wanted to. I've got *waaay* too many skeletons in my closet. It's like a damn boneyard in there. Nope, I'm a food blogger. And me and my baby, here"—she tenderly kisses Kai's temple—"just published our first cookbook!"

Angeline's smile looks like someone is holding a gun to her head and ordering her to act normal on pain of death. "That's wonderful. So you're writers, too."

Kai politely belches behind his hand. "I'm a chef. Darcy does the writing. She's the one with all the talent."

Darcy pets his golf hat like he's her favorite Chihuahua she dressed up and brought to dinner. "Aww, baby, that's so sweet! But without your recipes, there would've been no cookbook. *You're* the talent. I just transcribe your genius onto paper."

Kai is incandescent with pride. Meanwhile, I'm too focused on every nuance of Angeline's reaction to this conversation to pay much attention to anything else.

She's pretty good at concealing her emotions, but I'm better at reading people. And right now, the thing she most wants to do is bolt.

I reach out and give her clenched fist a squeeze. Instantly, it loosens. She threads her fingers through mine and sends me a small smile.

I lean over and murmur, "You ready to go?"

"Yes." She gazes gratefully at me, like she's surrounded by highway bandits and I've just charged in on my white steed, brandishing a sword.

"Well, kids, this has been fun," I say, addressing the group. "Sayonara."

I stand, pull a wad of cash from my wallet, throw it on the table, grab Angeline's hand, and pull her to her feet.

"Guess we'll say our goodbyes in the morning!" Connor calls out after us as I stride away from the table without a backward glance. The sound of everyone's laughter fades quickly as I lead the way through the lobby, Angeline by my side.

When we get to the elevator bank, I stab my finger on the call button. Beside me, Angeline is silent and tense. The doors open, we get in, and the doors shut behind us. As soon as we're in motion, I turn and press the emergency stop button. The elevator jolts to a halt.

Angeline lets out a little yip of surprise and grabs the handrail for balance. Then she flattens herself against the wall as I advance. Her eyes widen. When we're chest to chest, toe to toe, I say, "Let's play a game, Angel. It's called Truth or Dare."

She swallows.

I say, "I'll go first. I choose Truth. Ask me anything you want, and I'll answer it truthfully."

Angeline silently searches my face for a moment. I wonder what she sees.

In a husky whisper, she asks, "Can I trust you?"

"Now *that's* an interesting question." I brush my fingertips across her jaw, slide my hand into her hair, and cup the back of her neck. "I could ask you the same thing. But since it's my turn, I'll honor the rules of the game and give you an answer." I lean in and softly press my lips to hers. Against her mouth, I say, "It depends."

An alarm buzzes. We ignore it.

"Depends on what?"

"How you define trust."

She drops her tiny handbag and grabs fistfuls of my shirt, her arms braced against my chest, pushing me away at the same time she's pulling me closer. "That's not an answer."

I dip my head and skim my nose down her neck to her collarbone. She shivers but tries to suppress it, which makes me smile. I wrap my arms around her body and nuzzle my face into her hair. My hands find the full, round perfection of her ass, and squeeze.

Into her neck I ask, "Can I trust *you*?"

She arches against me, moaning softly when she finds me hard for her. When I open my mouth over the pulse on her neck, her next moan is almost drowned by that damn buzzer.

I lift my head and stare into her eyes. "Can I trust you, Angeline?"

"Of course you can," she says, staring earnestly back at me.

I throw my head back and laugh. "Fuck, I love the way you lie!"

Then I kiss her until we're both panting and the buzzer gets too loud to ignore. I press the button for my floor and turn back to Angeline with a smile.

"Okay, sweetheart. Since we're obviously not gonna do too well with Truth, let's move on to Dare."

My gaze drops to the neckline of her dress.

# 5

## MARIANA

The look in Ryan's eyes is savage. I know exactly what's coming next.

Time to apply the brakes.

I place a hand flat on his chest, lock my elbow, and level him with a look. "Let's *not* move on to Dare. Let's just have a drink, cowboy, and slow this rodeo down."

Beneath my hand, his heart thuds like there's someone inside his rib cage whacking it with a sledgehammer. Mine is doing the same thing. Not only because he turns me on like nobody's business, but also because I'm unsettled.

This man can sniff out a lie like a dog sniffs out a rat.

And worse than that? Far worse?

He knows I'm lying, *and he doesn't care.*

I don't know what to make of that. I don't know what he has planned. All I know is that I'm far out in rough water, there's a dangerous riptide, and something with a mouthful of sharp, hungry teeth is closing in.

Ryan takes my hand from my chest and kisses it. He sends me a dazzling game-show-host smile. "Sure thing, darlin'. I can go slow. I can go as slow as you like."

His smile turns filthy. Unexpectedly, I laugh.

"You have a dirty mind."

Chuckling, he pushes the button to start the elevator's ascent. "Angel, you have no idea."

But I do, and it intrigues me. Just one more part of the problem.

When we arrive at his room, I watch in fascination as he takes several minutes to disarm and unlock a series of electronic and mechanical security devices hidden behind various pieces of furniture and on all the doors, including the one to the bathroom. His paranoia seems like overkill, even to the woman planning on drugging his drink.

Amused, I ask, "Were you expecting company? Other than me, I mean."

He turns to me with a twinkle in his eye. "Better safe than sorry, in my experience. You never know when someone with sticky fingers might take a stroll through your door."

My heart stops. It starts back up with a painful beat, then flutters erratically while I draw a breath.

I decide the best way to handle this is with a frontal attack. He'll know if I'm bullshitting anyway. Looking him dead in the eye, I say, "I'm not here to steal from you."

His smile comes on slow. He wanders over to me, moving casually, his arms loose at his sides. He stops in front of me and murmurs, "I know. I just haven't figured out what you *are* here for."

I can't tell if he's talking about here in his room, here in this hotel, or here on this island. Possibly all three. Everything he says to me now seems layered with meaning. It's all innuendoes and undertones. Insinuation is his middle name.

*Better than Tiberius.*

He touches my cheek. "Why're you smilin' like that, Angel?"

"I'm trying to decide if I like you or not."

"Oh, you do. You just don't want to. The question is why."

Suddenly, I'm tired, and more than a little depressed. He's worn me out with his eagle-eyed intuition. I've never met a man so perceptive. It's exhausting.

"Can I ask a favor, Ryan?" I ask quietly, holding his gaze.

He answers without hesitation. "Yes."

"Can we pretend, just for tonight, that nothing bad has ever happened to either one of us? That we still have faith that the world is a good place, filled with good people? That all our tomorrows can be as good as today?"

He searches my face in silence. He lifts his hand and cups my cheek. When he speaks, his voice is husky with emotion. "When you let me see you, the *real* you, it's the most beautiful thing I've ever seen. If you give me more of that, I'll pretend anything you want."

We stare at each other. My pulse gallops like a whipped horse. Finally, I decide *what the hell.* I'll never see him again. I've got two hours until Khalid passes out—as he does every night like clockwork after half a dozen cocktails. I might as well spend it being the real me with a stranger while we pretend everything is what it's not.

I nod. "Okay. That's sufficiently fucked up for my liking. But I'm warning you, I haven't been the real me in so long, it might take a minute for me to remember who that is. And I have one condition, but it's nonnegotiable."

Ryan might as well be a live wire for all his crackling energy. He says, "Which is?"

"We don't talk about work. Mine *or* yours."

He replies instantly. "Deal."

I'm so relieved, I want to collapse into hysterical laughter onto the floor. "Good. Pour me a drink while I take off these heels. They're killing me. Being a femme fatale is hell on the feet."

He blinks. Then he laughs. It's a sound I enjoy far too much for my own good.

Grinning, he says, "I've got a full minibar, Angel. Name your poison."

"Bourbon."

His eyebrows lift. He nods approvingly. "America's number one spirit. Interestin' choice for a girl from Paris." He winks and saunters across the room toward the wet bar, leaving me astonished once again.

He knows I'm not from Paris.

*How* does he know?

Who *is* this guy?

I pronounce, "I'm going to snoop around now."

"Knock yourself out, sweetheart. I got nothin' to hide from you." He doesn't even turn, just casually proceeds to pour us drinks.

Teetering between exasperation, exhilaration, and the urge to abandon the job altogether and run away quick as I can, I kick off my heels, set my handbag on the TV console, and look around.

His room is large, with one wall missing and open to the view of the sea, as all the rooms in the resort are. Built right into the side of a mountain, the resort is the playground for the rich and famous, those who require both luxury and privacy. Everything about the décor and architecture supports both needs, from the thousand-thread-count Egyptian cotton sheets to the huge wading pools on the balconies to the ban on camera use in all the public spaces.

I walk through the living room and stare at the view. In the distance, the ocean sparkles under patchy moonlight. Fat gray thunderclouds slink down the hills. A humid breeze stirs my hair.

Ryan appears silently beside me and hands me my drink. "Gonna be a storm tonight." He looks sideways at me. He's not smiling.

I gulp the bourbon. It sears a stinging path down my throat. *Steady, Mari. Steady.*

I begin my inspection of the room.

First stop is the dresser. I pull open a drawer and peer inside. Underwear. White cotton briefs, folded with military precision. I resist the urge to touch them and close the drawer. The next drawer holds T-shirts, all of them plain black, all of them exactly alike. He must look amazing in them, tattooed biceps bulging from beneath the sleeves, the color setting off his golden skin and hair…

*Who's running this show, Mari? You, or your ovaries?*

I close my eyes, take another swig of my drink, and close that drawer, too.

Ryan relaxes onto the sofa. He watches with cynical interest as I open and close the rest of the dresser drawers. He drawls, "If you're lookin' for my gun, Angel, I'm wearin' it."

I smile at him. "Hammerless slimline .38 strapped to your left ankle. I know."

The laser-beam look he gives me would slice a lesser woman in two, but I merely smile wider, enjoying myself, and stroll over to the teak armoire. I swing open the door.

A row of white dress shirts, spotless and crisp, like the one he's wearing. Dark-wash jeans, also like the ones he's wearing, hang next to the shirts. On the floor are three pairs of shoes, black leather Ferragamos, same as the ones he's wearing, and a lone pair of flip-flops. I turn and look at him.

"You have very specific taste in clothing."

"And women."

He takes a drink, watching me over the rim of the glass. One arm is stretched casually over the back of the sofa. His legs are spread wide. He takes up a lot of space just sitting there. He fills up the whole room. I've never met a man with so much presence.

*The necklace, Mari. Eyes on the prize.*

I turn away from Ryan and stroll into the bathroom, thoughtfully swirling what's left of the bourbon in my glass.

Razor, comb, shaving cream, toothbrush, and a tube of toothpaste are laid out on the marble bathroom counter in a straight row. Though I know he showered and shaved before dinner, there isn't a stray hair or drop of water in sight. All the towels hang, perfectly folded, from their racks.

"You're freakishly neat," I observe aloud.

"Or maybe the maid came in and straightened up during dinner."

I look at him over my shoulder. "Without tripping one of your alarms? I don't think so."

The corners of his mouth tip up. I can tell he's enjoying our strange little game as much as I am.

"Finished with your inspection yet?" he inquires, so casually he almost sounds bored.

I glance at the laptop on the coffee table.

"You said no work," he reminds me. "And that"—he tips his head at the laptop—"is all work."

I know exactly what I'll be firing up as soon as he passes out. The urge to know more about him feels like the nail-biting habit I had when I was a kid. Irresistible. Obsessive. Something you know isn't good for you, but you're helpless to stop it.

I say lightly, "You're right. No work. Take out your wallet."

He chuckles. "It's in my back pocket, Angel. You wanna snoop in it? Come and get it."

I hesitate. I don't believe he'll harm me, but this is dangerous anyway. Being physically close to him is dangerous. It makes me think of hot kisses and big, rough hands and the pulse between my legs like a little heartbeat when he touches my skin.

I take a moment to fortify myself with one last swig of bourbon, then cross to him and set the empty glass on the coffee table. I expect him to stand, but he just looks up at me, a glint of mischief shining in his blue eyes.

*Son of a bitch.*

I lift my skirt and straddle him.

Which of course is what he wanted, evidenced by the smug-as-shit smile he gives me.

"Well, *howdy*, sweetheart," he drawls. He leaves the one arm stretched out over the back of the sofa, but settles his other hand on my bare thigh. It's heavy and warm, and feels strangely possessive.

"Howdy yourself." I reach around, trying to stuff my hand under his butt so I can get to his back pocket. It's almost impossible. I can wriggle my fingers just past his hip, but he's too heavy to make much headway otherwise.

Naturally, he doesn't assist by adjusting his weight. He just smiles at me while I struggle.

"Never had a woman fondle my ass on the first date," he muses.

"I'm not *fondling*, cowboy, I'm investigating. And you're not helping, by the way."

"Why on earth would I help when it's so much fun watchin' you work?"

His gaze drops to my chest.

My dress has a low neckline and spaghetti straps, and I'm not wearing a bra, so my breasts aren't exactly hidden. In fact, they're popping out all over, mere inches from his face.

He moistens his lips.

It's such a simple thing, yet utterly seductive. I imagine those lips latching on to one of my nipples and drawing it into the wet heat of his mouth. Lust rips through me, razor sharp.

His gaze flashes up to mine. It's blistering hot. "Your heart-beat just went all catawampus, darlin'."

I say, "Your lips are so—"

My face goes molten hot.

"So what?" he prompts, holding perfectly still.

I swallow. The heat between us is like a current on a circuit, cycling back and forth on a loop, growing hotter and brighter with every breath. My answer comes on the barest of whispers. "Sensual."

His hand tightens on my thigh, but otherwise, he doesn't react. Even his voice remains unruffled. "And you say *I'm* the one with a dirty mind."

"I can't help it if you have an abnormally pretty mouth," I say, staring at the subject in question.

"Pretty?" he repeats, offended.

"Sulky and pretty, like a girl's." I manage to make my tone lighter, more in control, but he's looking at me like *his* control is quickly unraveling.

He says gruffly, "Now you're just bein' mean."

I touch a finger to the bow of his lips, then follow the curve down to the corner of his full and perfectly sculpted mouth. "No," I say, my voice faint. "I'm not."

Our eyes lock. Heat flashes over my body. Goose bumps erupt over my skin.

Ryan whispers, "Tell me you feel that too. Tell me I'm not crazy and you can feel that."

Seconds tick by in silence as we stare at each other. Ryan's expression is that of a man trying to solve a fascinating, frustrating puzzle.

He abandons his drink on the back of the sofa and slides both hands into my hair. Then he pulls me closer and buries his nose in it, inhaling deeply, combing his fingers through the strands. I allow it and concentrate on quelling the tremor in my body. I dig my fingers into his shoulders and breathe in and out with my eyes closed, every nerve in my body primed to his touch.

*This is unprofessional. And dangerous. You don't do this. You* never *do this!*

"I won't do anything you don't want me to do," Ryan murmurs against my neck. "You're in control of this. Tell me to stop, and I will."

His intuition is preternatural. How does he know what I need to hear right now? Somehow I've got to make my mind go blank. *Think of Reynard. Think of the necklace. Think of how close you are to being free.*

Then I can't think at all because Ryan slowly pulls my head back, exposing my neck. He skims his lips from my earlobe down to my collarbone, inhaling at the base of my throat.

"Fuck, I love the way you smell."

His voice is guttural with desire. I bite my lip to stop the groan from escaping.

Using my hair as a tether and the circle of his arms to keep me in place, he trails his nose down my chest and nuzzles it into my cleavage. His breath is hot against my skin. His erection is hard against the back of my thigh. I lose my fight with the tremors, and a shudder runs through me.

I'm strung so tightly that when the tip of his tongue touches my skin, I jerk.

He makes a masculine sound deep in his throat and flexes his hips. I barely resist the instinct to rock against the bulge in his jeans.

Barely.

I sense that he's smiling, but I can't look down to check.

Soft kisses press against the swell of my breasts. He's being so gentle. So slow. It's maddening.

"You're panting, Angel," he says, tightening his arms around me. "Do you want me to stop?"

"Yes. No. Yes. Fuck."

His laugh is soft and dark. "Hmm. I'd say you need more input before you can make an informed decision."

Right through the filmy material of my dress, he gently bites my hard nipple.

It feels incredible. I moan like a porn star.

Still in perfect control, he releases one hand from my hair so he can squeeze my breast. He suckles my nipple through the fabric. I whimper helplessly as fire roars through my veins.

He drags the neckline of my dress down. Warm air caresses my breast. Then I feel his hand, rough and strong, cupping my flesh, then his tongue and lips, hot and decadent, draw against my nipple.

Lost to the sensation, I arch into his mouth.

He makes that sound in his throat again and sucks harder.

My shaking fingers slip around the back of his neck. He releases my hair and cups both my breasts in his hands, nosing the fabric away so I'm bared to him. My chest rises and falls rapidly with my labored breathing. Then he goes back and forth between my breasts, licking, sucking, gently biting my nipples and the flesh around them until I'm certain I'll pass out.

I've never felt quite so lavished. So worshipped. The desire to squirm on his lap to find some relief for the ache between my legs is almost irresistible.

"Talk to me, Angel," he murmurs, circling his thumbs over the rigid nubs of my nipples. "If you want me to stop, now's the time to say so, because next I'm gonna get you on your back and get my face between your legs and eat your pussy until you scream my name."

*Mierda santa.* My body wants that so much, a riot breaks out inside me. My brain is battered with lust hormones wielding hammers until rational thought is all but impossible.

"I…I want…please…"

My voice is the husky tenor of a phone-sex operator. I don't recognize it at all.

"That's a yes if I've ever heard one," mutters Ryan. In one lightning-fast motion, he flips me onto my back on the sofa and kneels between my spread legs.

My dress slides languidly down my bare thighs and pools around my waist. Ryan stares down at me like he's been electrocuted.

"Sweet Jesus, woman," he whispers. "You're beautiful."

Out in the dark night sky, thunder booms. The breeze picks

up, fluttering the pages of a magazine on the coffee table. And my heart aches like it might be dying.

No one has ever looked at me like this. Like I'm a wild, endangered animal that needs to be treasured and protected if it's going to survive. He might as well be a penitent kneeling in front of a cross for all the reverence in his eyes. The fervor in his gaze is religious.

He slowly slides his hands down my spread thighs. When he reaches my waist, he circles it and squeezes, learning my shape. Then he pushes the dress up past my hips, exposing my stomach all the way to my ribs, the entire time staring down with intense concentration.

He traces his index finger lightly around the tattoo near my left hip. His questioning gaze flashes up to mine.

"Dragonflies live a short life," I whisper, mesmerized by the ardor in his eyes. "They know they have to make every moment matter."

His eyes are piercing. "I've heard that a dragonfly landing on you is a dead loved one coming to visit."

My heart twists so violently, I suck in a breath. I turn my head away and close my eyes to hide.

Ryan lowers himself onto me, resting his weight on his elbows. He murmurs into my ear, "Okay. Sore spot. We won't go there tonight."

The way he says "tonight" lets me know he has every intention of getting it out of me in the future, however.

But there's no future here. This is one of those unexpected things that pops up randomly in life. A fleeting spark between two strangers, a moment in time that's special exactly because it's so short.

Things like this aren't meant to last. A few hours of pleasure in a lifetime of pain is the best we can hope for.

It dawns on me that I'm being offered an incredible gift.

It doesn't really matter that I'm here on a job and my initial intention was only to use him as a pawn to make my play. It doesn't matter that I've never crossed this line before, or that I'll never see this man again after tonight.

What matters is that this connection—this strange and beautiful thing—is real. Ryan makes me feel alive. He makes me feel special. He makes me feel *seen*, something I never truly am.

I'm a fool if I let him slip through my fingers when I could have a memory that could sustain me through all the dark times to come.

The decision made, I relax on multiple levels. I exhale my final resistance, take his face in my hands, and look into his beautiful eyes, the blue of opals and clear summer skies.

"No, we won't go there tonight. But let's go everywhere else, Ryan. Let's go all the places we need to go. Let's do it all."

There's a long, tense moment where he doesn't respond. He just stares at me, searching my face. Then a smile curves his lips, dangerous in its intensity.

"*There* you are," he says softly.

I warn, "You only have a few hours until I turn into a pumpkin. Make them count."

He chuckles. "God*damn*, I love a bossy woman."

"Then you're in luck, cowboy." I pull his face toward mine. "Now shut up."

When I kiss him, he's still smiling.

# 6

## MARIANA

There are kisses, and there are *kisses*. Slow, deep, and incredibly hot, this one wins best in show. Only seconds in, I'm helplessly squirming.

I wonder briefly how many women it must've taken for him to perfect his technique, then decide I don't care. For tonight, his talented mouth is all mine.

It's so good, I bite his lower lip and sink my fingernails into his back, desperate for more.

He laughs softly against my greedy lips. "Easy, killer. What's your rush?"

"It's been too long. And you're delicious." I'm panting. Close to begging. Long-dormant nerve endings are waking up, ravenous with hunger, like vampires at dusk.

"Right back atcha, Angel. But we're not rushing anything." His eyes are dark, so dark they're almost black. His voice drops to a growl. "I'm gonna savor you, inch by inch."

I shiver, thrilled by the sound of that, and he laughs at me again. My eagerness pleases him. His smile is devilish. We both know he's got me exactly where he wants me.

For now.

I say, "Okay. But hurry up."

He puts a finger over my lips and proceeds to ignore my demand.

He starts at the sensitive spot just below my earlobe, investigating it with his lips, gently stroking the skin with the tip of his tongue. Then he moves his mouth slowly down my neck, pressing soft kisses every half inch, cradling my head in his hands as his lips go to work on me.

My eyes drift shut. This is heaven. I have to remember this. I have to sear this memory into my mind so I can take it out and admire it later on.

I make a small sound of desperation. He quietly shushes me. His hands glide to my shoulders. His fingers toy with the straps of my dress.

He rests his cheek on my chest for a moment, listening to the clamor of my heart. It's terribly intimate. I know my heartbeat sounds like gunfire. My cheeks burning, I turn my face to the cushion and clench my hands to fists.

"No hiding," he whispers, lifting his head. "There's no hiding from me now, Angel. It's too late for that."

I don't open my eyes or indicate I've heard him. When his hand slides around my throat and gently squeezes, my lids snap open. My entire body tenses.

Instantly, he releases his grip on my throat. His eyes search mine.

"Don't restrain me," I say, my voice shaking. "I can't stand that."

A furrow appears between his eyebrows. He considers me in silence, then says gently, "Thank you for tellin' me. Do you want to stop?"

A spike of pain pierces my heart.

Passion, I can handle. Though it's unexpected, it's welcome. This gentleness, though, this tender attention to my emotional state… What the hell is this? I'm not familiar with this from a man. I have no idea what to do with it. It's terrifying.

Finally, I say, "No. Just don't hold me down."

I'm rewarded with a string of the sweetest kisses all over my chest, just above where my heart is frantically beating. His voice both soft and rough, Ryan says, "Anything you don't like, just tell me, sweetheart. I only wanna make you feel good."

I'm dreaming. This can't be happening. Obviously, I took a bad fall somewhere and am lying in a hospital bed in a medically induced coma.

This man is a mercenary. He was trained by his government to hunt, maim, and kill. His paranoia is such that he carries a concealed weapon even on vacation and rigs his hotel room with spy gear like something out of a Bond movie. He obviously knows I'm not being truthful about a lot of things, yet he's handling me like a fragile piece of expensive china. Like a treasure.

Like a gift.

Desperate to get my pulse under control, I exhale raggedly. Against my skin, Ryan makes a husky coo of support. He knows I'm struggling. If he keeps this up, I'll crack wide open.

He presses kiss after kiss to my chest, shoulders, and neck. His hair tickles my cheek. He's heavy and hot on top of me, but I like the way he feels. I like the way he smells, clean male and soft musk. I like the way he tastes, and the way he tastes me.

I like everything about him.

*Mierde*! What the hell is *wrong* with me?

"Open your eyes," he commands.

I look at him. He stares back at me with piercing intensity, like nothing else exists in the world except us. Enunciating every syllable, he says, "You can trust me. You have my word."

The promise hangs there between us, dangerous as a lit stick of dynamite.

I want him to take it back. Promises are even more dangerous than explosives.

I say, "That's not going to happen."

But I've forgotten something crucial about him. Challenges—the more difficult, the better—are exactly what make him tick.

He says, "Maybe not tonight." Then he smiles. It carries a promise, too.

Before I can snarl and shove him off, he buries his face in my cleavage and nips one of my nipples with his teeth.

"Ow!" I slap him on the shoulder.

Chuckling, he strokes the stinging nipple with his tongue, looking up at me from under his lashes like he's daring me to stop him. I consider it until he pinches my other nipple, making me gasp.

"You like that," he whispers, intently watching my face. "What about this?"

He firmly pinches both nipples at the same time. A hot pulse of pleasure throbs between my legs. An involuntary moan breaks from my lips. It's followed by the dark, satisfied sound of his laugh.

"Less teeth, more tongue and fingers," he says. "Got it."

"Ryan—"

"Hush."

I glare at him. He's too focused on my breasts to appreciate my withering look. When he abruptly rises to his knees and tears off his shirt, I'm distracted, too.

His body is sculpture. Muscles ripple and flex with every movement. I think the temperature in the room has just shot up twenty degrees.

He lowers himself back into the cradle of my spread thighs. My hands automatically start to paw him, filthy addict that I am. He's so hard. Everywhere. Except his skin, which is inexplicably petal soft. It's like being embraced by a steel column covered in velvet.

He gets between my legs with some kind of Ninja move that's so fast, it's a blur. Then he shifts to slow-mo again. He nuzzles me right *there*, breathing me in with an audible sigh.

"These hardly even count as underwear." He tugs at my tiny thong. It's basically a two-inch piece of fabric held together by a few threads.

I breathe, "No panty lines."

He chuckles. "God forbid."

The next sound is my sharp inhalation as he slides his tongue under my panties and lazily licks my clit. "Oh!" I gasp, arching against the couch.

"Sweet," he mutters to himself.

A yank, the rip of tearing fabric, and my panties are disposed of, tossed over his shoulder to land in a small, shredded pile on the floor.

He slings my knees over his shoulders, grips my ass in both hands, and sucks my clit into the wet heat of his mouth. I sink my fingers into his hair and moan. Loudly. As I rock against his face. Trying to maintain consciousness.

The first raindrops hiss against the balcony tile.

"Yes," I whisper. "Oh God. That's good. That's so—*oh*—"

Without breaking the rhythm of his tongue, he slides a finger inside me. He reaches up with his other hand and thumbs over my hard nipple. Sounds are coming out of me that I don't recognize as my own. They don't even sound human.

When I stiffen and make a low whine in the back of my throat, he warns, "Don't you dare hold back on me!"

The words burst out of me in a desperate, breathless rush. "I'm too close. It's too fast. It's been too long, I'm already—oh God—"

He stops listening to me before I get three words out of my mouth. He simply goes back to his glorious torture, only now he's squeezing both my breasts in his hands, pinching and tweaking my nipples as he swirls his tongue between my legs. My hips rock in tandem with his tongue.

Sweat blooms over my chest. My heart goes arrhythmic. I groan, squeezing my eyes shut, the entire world narrowed to what's happening between my legs.

"Come for me, Angel. You know you need to." His voice is coaxing, wickedly soft.

I wish he'd stop calling me Angel.

Somewhere off in the night, a rooster starts crowing. They're all over the island, stupid, wild roosters who crow just as often at midnight as they do at dawn. It's to the sound of falling rain and a faint *cock-a-doodle-doo* that I come in a stranger's mouth, crying out his name.

Ryan groans into me as I writhe. Along with deep shock at finding myself here, the noise vibrates all the way through me. Then thought ceases, and everything is reduced to sensation.

The rough scrape of his jaw on the tender flesh of my thighs. His calloused fingers on my breast. The leather of the sofa, cool and smooth against my shoulders. The heady scent of flowers and sex in the air.

His mouth, owning me. Driving me. Forcing my surrender.

My fingers twist in his hair. I'm scratching his scalp, but I can't stop myself. I'm too far past restraint. I've jumped off an insanely tall cliff and am plummeting toward annihilation.

"Fuck yeah," Ryan whispers harshly. "Give it to me."

I do. I shudder and thrash and wring myself out against his clever tongue until I've got nothing left to give and I'm a mass of jelly limbs and random twitches, panting, sweating, laughing weakly with an arm flung over my eyes.

I get a tender kiss on the inside of each of my thighs and hear a low, satisfied chuckle. I look down to see Ryan with a pirate's jaunty grin, blue eyes shining.

"You can catch your breath on the way to the bed." He stands and picks me up.

I cling to his strong shoulders as he carries me to the large, four-poster bed. He sets me on my feet, steadies me, then peels off my dress like he's opening a present. He kisses my throat, strokes my skin, murmurs words I only hear as gentle sounds, soft as the evening air.

"Ryan," I whisper, trembling. My legs shake so hard, I think I might fall.

He takes my face in his hands. "I know. Me, too."

His kiss is like a mark of ownership. A firm and permanent seal.

*This is madness.*

He senses my rising panic. "Only a few hours, and then I'll let you run away." His voice turns dark. "For a while."

With his hands on my shoulders, he lowers me to the bed and lays me flat. He stands looking down at me, exposed and vulnerable beneath his gaze. His expression is one of perfect concentration and total control. He slowly rubs the heel of his palm along the bulge in his jeans.

When I lick my lips, his eyes flash.

"Tell me what you want," he demands.

"You."

His smile returns, only now it's edged in danger. He says softly, "Oh, you're gonna get me."

I shiver with equal parts anticipation and dread. I hear the unspoken *whether you like it or not*, and know without a shadow of doubt that he'll come looking for me after tonight is over.

I might have intended a casual fling, but Ryan intends something else entirely.

*He'll never find me. No one can. I'll vanish like I always do.*

Even as I reassure myself with those words, I'm doubting them. Something about this man makes me believe he'd follow me to the ends of the earth.

"I need to get you out of your head," says Ryan, watching me.

*Those damn eyes. They see everything.*

I sit up abruptly, scoot to the edge of the bed, and take the top button of his fly between my fingers. Looking up at him, I say, "How many times do I have to tell you to shut up?"

His laugh is husky, but turns to a groan when I rip open his fly and swallow his erection.

He's big and hard in my mouth, a pulsing heat against my tongue. I open my throat and take him all the way to the base, thrilling to the sound of his broken gasp. He settles his hands on either side of my head, and they're trembling.

Adrenaline surges through me.

I want him undone. I want him to feel what I just felt, that sudden, jarring loss of equilibrium, knowing someone else has taken over your body. Knowing someone else—a total stranger—is in command. I want to knock him off his smug pedestal and leave him whimpering at my feet.

I want to punch him in his pretty face.

Who is *he* to control *me*?

Then, without warning, I'm flat on my back with Ryan on top of me, his elbows braced on either side of my head.

"We're not doin' this if you're pissed off," he says, breathing hard.

Now I want to kill him. "I'm not pissed off!"

He growls, "Lie to me again, and I'll take you over my knee, woman."

I try to shove him off, but he weighs too much. Plus he's bracing himself with his arms and legs. Budging him is impossible. I grit my teeth, seething with frustration. He puts his lips next to my ear.

"Normally I'd tie you up right now and force you to tell me what the fuck is wrong, but since you don't like bein' restrained, we're just gonna have to have a conversation like adults."

I can recall with perfect clarity how many times in my life

I've wanted to commit murder. This is time number three. I want to strangle him. I want to squeeze his thick, tanned neck and choke the life right out of him, then maybe light him on fire and do a victory dance as he burns.

*I'm losing it.* I close my eyes and suck air into my lungs.

Ryan grips my head. His heartbeat thunders against my chest. His cock, wet from my mouth and rock-hard, presses between my legs. Into my ear, he says, "Be honest with me for once!"

A sob catches in my throat. Suddenly, I'm fighting tears, mortified by these ridiculous emotions, hating how powerless I feel.

"You make me feel weak," I blurt, then groan at my own stupidity.

A shade of tension leaves his body. His voice gentles. "You keep forgettin' you're the one in control, Angel. This is happenin' *because you want it to*. Just 'cause you're feelin' some kinda way about me, about this thing between us, doesn't change the fact that you're here, lyin' naked underneath me right now, by choice. Trust it. You're not the kind of woman who'd be here by accident, no matter how different this is from what you usually do."

My chest rises and falls in rapid bursts. "How do you know what kind of woman I am?"

Looking into my eyes, he says deliberately, "Because I see you. And I know that's what really scares you. No one ever gets to see the real you, but I do."

Knife to the heart, slicing it wide open.

God, the truth is awful. And this terrible intimacy is even worse. I think it's probably the worst thing in the world.

Ryan holds my head still when I try to turn it. At the end of his patience, he snaps, "Either you drop this hiding bullshit and be brave, or I'm kickin' your ass outta my room! What's it gonna be?"

His stare is blistering. I stare back, hating myself for liking him, cursing whatever gods might exist for putting him in this room. Anyone else and I'd have stuck to my plan. Anyone else and he'd be deep in a peaceful, sedative-induced sleep right now. Instead, fate decided to put me in the path of *this* man, the trained killer with a beautiful laugh and addictive kisses and eyes that see straight down to the bottom of my soul.

Finally, in a small voice I say, "I'll be brave."

It's not like I have a choice. If he kicks me out, I won't be able to climb the balcony to Prince Khalid's suite, and then I won't be able to steal the necklace, and the consequences of failure aren't something I allow myself to think about.

Better to suffer here in this bed than at the hands of the masters I serve.

Nostrils flared, Ryan inhales slowly. His gaze darts all over my face. "I mean it," he warns.

I swallow, muster my courage, then wrap my arms around his back. "I know." My voice is a pathetic, wavering thing. When the tear slides from the corner of my eye, I don't try to wipe it away. I just lie there and hate myself.

"Oh fuck, Angel," he breathes. He looks dazed, in happy disbelief, like someone just told him he won the lottery. Because of a *tear*.

I don't understand this person.

At.

All.

He kisses me so gently, I want to break every piece of furniture in the room. "Stop it," I beg. "Stop being so…*sweet.* I can't take it! Just fuck me like you would anyone else!"

"How do you know I'm not like this with anyone else?"

"The same way you know I'm a liar!"

He stares at me for a beat, blue eyes glittering. "Fair enough," he says with frightening calm. "But just so you know, me *not* bein' sweet is gonna leave marks."

I exhale in relief. "Thank God. *That* I know how to handle."

Not even a split second passes before Ryan shows me exactly what *not sweet* involves as his fingers, hard as stone, dig into my skin.

# 7

## RYAN

If she wants it hard, she's gonna get it hard, and God help her if she changes her mind.

Once I'm unleashed, there's no stopping me.

My kiss is savage. She returns it with a grateful noise, digging her nails into my back. She's luscious heat and satin beneath me, killer curves and a million contradictions and walls so thick, a man needs blast charges just to uncover a true smile.

*Who are you, Angel?*

I pull her head back and kiss her throat. She cries out when I bite her, scratches her nails down my back.

I'm glad she can't see my smile.

I flip her on her belly, then roughly drag her up onto her knees, hiking her beautiful bare ass in the air. Then I bite that, too, because I've wanted to do it since the second I saw her. Her face buried in the coverlet, she moans.

I slap her ass and bark, "Quiet!"

She gives me that kitten growl that tells me she wants to tear off my head.

I rip my wallet out of my back pocket, find a condom, and open the foil package with my teeth. I'm sheathed in seconds. I grab a fistful of her hair and steady her with my hand gripped around one of her hips.

Then without another word or any warning, I plunge my hard dick inside her.

This time when she cries out, it's guttural. Her back arches. She clenches her hands into the covers and bucks back against me.

"That's right, sweetheart," I say, my voice a rasp. "Fuck yourself on my cock."

She obeys without hesitation, thrusting her hips back to take me even deeper inside. My balls slap against her slick pussy. My hand tightens in her hair.

I haven't even removed my jeans. Or shoes. Or gun.

I'm in heaven.

I slap her ass again, laughing darkly when she curses. My handprint looks branded onto her skin. Next to the little indentations of my teeth, it looks like a mark of ownership.

Lust and possession surge through my body. I want to mark her all over. I want her to remember who had her, feel the ache of my passion tomorrow, see the bruises on her skin.

I reach around and pinch her swollen clit, stroking it between two fingers. She breathes my name, and I lose my mind. I bend over her body, wrap my arm around her waist, brace my other hand against the mattress, and drive into her over and over, grunting like an animal.

She fucking loves it. I know because she tells me.

"God yes Ryan so good I love it so good please oh God please—"

I growl, "Who told you you could speak, you bad girl? *Who?*"

She mews and buries her face deeper into the blankets.

When I can tell from her broken cries that she's right on the razor's edge of orgasm, I pull out and flip her over, manhandling her to get her on her back with her ankles over my shoulders. She hasn't even caught her breath before I'm inside her again.

She arches her back and grasps my biceps as I fuck her relentlessly, giving her exactly what she needs.

A sheen of sweat glistens on her chest. Her breasts bounce with every thrust. Her lips are parted, her eyes are closed, and she's so beautiful, it's like a dagger to my heart.

"Please," she begs in a ragged whisper. I know she's asking permission to come.

But I'm not in a generous mood. I've let the beast loose, and he says she can come when he's good and fucking ready.

I fall still, and she moans in frustration.

"One more sound outta you, and your ass'll be bright red and burning."

She bites her full bottom lip. Her eyes drift open. She stares at me from under lowered lids with a look like she wants to slit my throat.

I mutter, "I know. You hate me." I reach between us and slide my thumb over the wet, engorged nub of her clit. She gasps, which makes me smile in victory. "Only you *don't* hate me, Angel. You don't hate me at all."

She flexes her hips, trying to move against my cock. I lightly slap her thigh in warning. She sends me a look of nuclear rage, and I throw my head back and laugh.

Then I drop down on top of her, bending her in half. With her calves resting on my shoulders, I slide deep inside her heat, until I'm so deep, she's gasping.

Staring down at her, I order, "Take every inch of my cock, and don't you *dare* come until I say you can. Your orgasm is mine, and if you go off before I say you can, you'll regret it."

She loves every word coming out of my mouth, but still she has to grit her teeth and glower. She demanded it rough, but she fights against being made to submit. She wants it, but only on her terms.

Which I understand completely. She's a lioness. She needs a lion, but that doesn't mean her lion won't get clawed and bitten.

I pull out slightly, thrust into her, do it again. And again. And again, until she's pleading.

"You better not!" I roar, feeling her clench around my cock. She cries out in frustration, pounding her fists on my shoulders. I laugh.

She rakes her fingernails down my chest and shouts, "Laugh again and it'll be the last sound you make, you smug son of a bitch!"

The sting of my broken skin is nothing compared to the euphoria erupting in my chest. I can tell she doesn't like the shit-eating grin on my face because she slaps me.

Hard.

I laugh so loud, they can probably hear it downstairs in the lobby.

She tries to get out from beneath me, struggling and cursing, but it's all part of the game. As soon as I give her my full weight and take her face in my hands, she stills, panting, glaring at me with killer intent in her eyes.

"Wrap your legs around my back," I say, panting too, "and tell me how much you hate me while I make you come."

Her thighs become a vise around my waist. Her eyes burn. "I *do* hate you."

I flex my hips, and her lashes flutter. She whispers, "I do."

Her breasts are smashed against my chest. Our skin is slick with sweat. We're both breathing hard and our hearts are pounding in tandem and the electricity between us is gathering into a crackling, dangerous whirlwind, like the vortex of a tornado just before it touches the ground and destroys everything in its path.

I kiss her, biting her lips. I taste blood. Desperate for release, she sobs against my mouth. I know she can't hold back any longer.

"Yes, Angel," I whisper. "*Now.*"

Her back bows. Her neck arches. Her fingers claw into my ass.

Then, with a groan and a tremor that racks her entire body, she's over the edge, taking me with her as her pussy throbs rhythmically around my cock.

*Fuck. Fuck. Fuck.*

I'm aware that I'm grunting the word repeatedly, but my thoughts are incoherent. A white-hot ball of energy gathers at the base of my spine, pulsing, getting hotter and more unstable with every breath. The pleasure is almost unbearable. It's the most exquisite sort of pain.

Then she screams my name, and I lose it. I bite her on the shoulder and come so hard, the room dims.

I collapse on top of her, take a moment to get my bearings, then strip off my pants, shoes, and the gun strapped to my ankle, and start all over again.

Rain falls steadily outside in the humid night. Crickets sing. Frogs croak. Somewhere off in the distance, a dog barks. We listen to the symphony of nature in silence as sweat cools on our skin.

I murmur into her hair, "You okay?"

Angeline is lying on top of me, using my body as a pillow, her head tucked into my neck. She sighs in contentment, nods, and burrows closer.

For the past ten minutes, I've been combing my fingers through her hair, stroking my hands over her skin, memorizing every curve and plane of her body that's within reach. She's a delicious weight: warm, soft, and feminine. I'd like to keep her like this forever.

She says sleepily, "Who knew Mr. Happy would be such an amazing hate fuck?"

I pull a face and repeat in disgust, "Mr. *Happy*?"

"Yeah. Because you're such a shiny, perfect golden boy. Always smiling like you don't have a care in the world."

She makes me sound like a golden retriever. I don't know whether to be amused or insulted. "Excuse me, Angel, Mr. Happy is what some guys name their dick. And secondly, that wasn't a hate fuck. That was…"

Before I can come up with something that can accurately describe the sexual gymnastics we just engaged in, Angeline says, "Guys have names for their dicks?"

"Of course. You don't think we'd leave our most cherished body part anonymous, do you?"

She lifts her head and gazes at me. Her eyes are soft. "That must be an American thing," she says, kissing my chin. "You've all seen too many Arnold Schwarzenegger movies."

I stroke a lock of hair away from her cheek. "On behalf of Arnold Schwarzenegger, I'm insulted. Not *once* has he ever named his dick in a movie."

"So you've obviously seen them all."

"I fail to understand the correlation between the two."

She smiles. "That's because you're a man."

"Wait. You're telling me women don't have names for their unmentionables?"

She laughs, shaking us and the bed. "Unmentionables? Been reading one too many Victorian romances, have we?"

I purse my lips, assuming a prim librarian's expression. "I also enjoy needlepoint and decoupage, dearie."

"Sure you do," she says. "In between target practice and shopping for hotel room security devices."

"Thought we weren't gonna talk about work, Angel," I murmur. When she heaves a sigh that sounds almost regretful, I add, "Unless you're ready to tell me what you really do for a living."

"*Mon Dieu*," she mutters. "Could you *please* stop being so observant?"

I chuckle. "So don't be sweet, and don't be observant. You want a clueless asshole, that it?"

"They're generally a lot easier to handle," she grouses.

"But much more boring."

"And far less dangerous."

That gives me pause. When I speak, my voice comes out husky. "You're not in danger from me in any way."

She turns her face to my neck. "Silly man," she whispers. "You're the most dangerous thing I've run across in years. Maybe ever."

Pressure swells inside my chest. A sensation of warmth spreads through my limbs. I close my eyes and smell her hair because I can, because she's lying naked in my arms, probably more naked than she allows herself to be with anyone else.

I feel privileged. And I want more.

"So when I visit you in Paris—"

She laughs softly. "You're unbelievably stubborn."

"As I was saying, when I visit you in Paris, the first place I wanna take you is this bistro on Rue Vertbois that has decaying nineteenth-century décor, incredibly snobby waiters, and the most indecently huge portions that they don't allow you to share."

"L'Ami Louis," says Angeline, nodding. "I love that place. The *confit de canard* can make you cry."

I smile at the ceiling. For the same reasons I don't believe she's a writer, I don't believe she lives in Paris, but only someone who's spent a lot of time in the city could nail that description. And her Parisian accent, which only rarely slips.

Most notably when crying out my name when she comes.

When my dick stirs at that thought, she laughs. "Have you eaten a large quantity of oysters lately?"

"Hmm?" I'm distracted, smoothing my hands down her back. Her skin is smooth as glass.

"Never mind." She abruptly changes the subject. "I'm curious about the girl who was with you at the pool. Juanita."

I tilt my head on the pillow but can't see the expression on Angeline's face. "What about her?"

After a long silence, she replies. "She reminds me of someone I used to know."

When I wait but she remains quiet, I decide I have nothing to lose by telling her Juanita's story. And judging by the odd tone in Angeline's voice, I might have some valuable information to gain.

"She's Tabby's neighbor. The youngest of seven kids who all still live at home. Mother always working, no dad in the picture. Tabby sort of took her under her wing. Believe it or not, they have a lot in common."

"Because they're both prodigies."

My inner antennae twitch. "Yeah...but how could you know that? You only talked to Tabby for like an hour, and you didn't even meet Juanita."

"I didn't have to. Geniuses always exude a certain darkness. They don't fit, they know they don't fit, and being an outsider to the rest of the human race molds them in a way normal people can't understand. If you know what to look for, you can always see it."

Now I'm fascinated. "How?"

Angeline hesitates, thinking. "It's mainly in the eyes. Even when they're right in front of you, they're far away. But also it's a strange sense that they're..." She struggles to find a word. "*Other*. Almost like an alien. It's in everything they do. Once you're attuned to it, it's unmistakable." Her laugh is subdued. "Like knowing when someone's a killer."

Now my antennae are going crazy. "Oh really," I drawl, trying to sound nonchalant. "Known many killers, Angel?"

Because our chests are pressed together, I feel the way her heartbeat doubles in the space of two seconds.

*Bingo.*

In one smooth motion, I roll her over, throw my leg over her body, and capture her face in my hand. "I promised we wouldn't talk about work tonight, and I'm gonna keep my word. But tomorrow's a different story. Once the sun rises, all bets are off."

She swallows. In the low light, her eyes shine. "Yes," she whispers. "Once the sun rises."

I nod.

She adds, "But for now, you're going to tell me more about Juanita while I get something to drink. My mouth's a desert."

I kiss her softly on the lips. "Why're you so interested in Juanita?"

She rolls out from under me, sits up on the edge of the bed, and stretches her arms overhead. "I told you. She reminds me of someone I used to know."

I admire the way her long hair cascades down her back, a sleek brushstroke of mahogany against the golden canvas of her skin. "One more thing we're gonna talk about in the morning: who."

Angeline drops her arms and glances at me over her shoulder. Her eyes are unreadable. "Whatever you say, cowboy."

She rises from the bed and makes her way across the room toward the small refrigerator under a console near the television. I cross my arms under my head and indulge myself in the sheer pleasure of watching her nude body move. *Poetry.*

When I say, "She was kidnapped," Angeline whirls around and stares at me with a horrified look. She clutches her throat.

"Kidnapped! By who?"

"A psychopath. It's a long story."

Angeline is beginning to look a little green. "That scar on her back…"

I say flatly, "It's a long, *ugly* story."

She passes a hand over her face and exhales a hard breath. "Oh God, that poor baby."

There's so much more to her reaction than just average human empathy at hearing a terrible story about someone you don't know, but I won't be able to uncover it tonight. So I just add it to the list of things I'll get to tomorrow.

"Anyway, me and Connor and the crew found out where she was and went in and got her—"

"You *rescued* her?"

Angeline's eyes are wide. We stare at each other from across the room. I say softly, "It's what I do, Angel. It's the job. I find people."

For some bizarre reason, she looks like she might throw up.

Abruptly, she turns away and goes to the fridge. She yanks open the door, grabs a bottle of orange juice, slams the door, savagely unscrews the cap, and chugs half the bottle without taking a breath.

I lie still, giving her space for this newest freak-out, because I know instinctively that making any kind of sudden move will result in her running out the door. She stands with her back to me for several long moments until finally she draws a breath and turns back to me with a shaky smile.

She says, "That must be very gratifying work."

"Almost as good as being a travel writer."

Angeline closes her eyes.

"Sorry, couldn't resist. Come here."

She swirls the bottle thoughtfully. "Only if you promise to be nice."

I sit up and smile at her. "I'll be as nice as you want me to be. You know I'm good for that."

An attractive blush darkens her cheeks.

I hold out my hand. "Angel. Come here."

She approaches slowly, still swirling the bottle, holding my gaze with a wary look like she's not entirely convinced I'm not going to suddenly pounce. When she's close enough, I reach out and grasp her wrist. I pull her between my legs and nuzzle her breasts.

"You hungry?" I murmur. "I can order room service."

"In a bit." She taps me on the shoulder with the bottle. "You must be dehydrated."

"Yeah, I am, actually. Thanks." I take the bottle from her and swallow the rest of its contents. It's cold and deliciously tart. I set the empty on the bedside table, lie back on the bed, and pull her down on top of me, because it's my new favorite thing in the world. I wrap my arms around her and inhale the fresh, peppery scent of her skin.

Against my neck she says, "So you rescued Juanita…and now she's on vacation with you?"

"Her and Tabby are inseparable now. Oh—I didn't mention—we rescued Tabitha too. Same psycho had both of 'em."

When Angeline raises her head and stares at me, I shrug. "Like I said, long story. The upshot of it all is that the two of them somehow convinced Juanita's mother and psychiatrist that it would be good for Juanita to get away on vacation for a while, so here we are. One big, happy family."

My left ear starts to buzz like it does at high altitude when it needs to pop. I work my jaw, but no luck. *Why are my lips tingling?*

"I envy your happy family," says Angeline gently. She presses a tender kiss just below my earlobe. Her voice drops. "And I want you to know this was never the plan. I meant it when I said I don't do one-night stands. I never mix business and pleasure. Well…until you."

*Business?*

The bed does a lazy roll, like we're riding a wave on a boat.

Heart pounding, I jerk upright. Angeline leaps off me and backs away, keeping a watchful eye on my face. When I try to stand, the room slips sideways. I look at the empty orange juice bottle, her small handbag on the console above the fridge, and, with a bolt of horror, realize what happened.

"Angel! You didn't!"

"I'm sorry, Ryan. I'm so, so sorry."

She sounds like she actually means it.

I walk toward her, but in two steps, my balance fails me. I stumble and crash to a knee. The room spins wildly and begins to darken. Everything gets fuzzy around the edges. Indistinct. A sudden hot rush of anger is the only thing keeping my eyes open.

"What is it?" I demand, furious to hear my words slur.

"It's potent but not harmful, I promise," she says, wringing her hands. "You'll wake up with nothing but a headache. There are no lasting effects."

With the last of my willpower, I force myself to lift my head. I focus on her face. Her beautiful, lying face. "Oh there's gonna be *one* lasting effect," I growl, teeth gritted against the encroaching darkness. "And the next time I see you, woman, I'm gonna tell you *all* about it."

She has the good sense to look afraid.

Her face is the last thing I see before the room fades to black and I slump to the floor, unconscious.

# 8

## MARIANA

Even passed out, he's attractive.

I roll him onto his back and check his pulse. Normal. His breathing is deep and even. His mouth is slack. Those beautiful lips beckon me to kiss them, so I do.

Gently brushing a lock of gold hair from his forehead, I whisper, "*Lo siento, mi amor*. Sleep well."

It's a relief to drop the fake French accent.

I tuck a pillow under his head because I don't want him waking up with a crick in his neck to add to everything else he'll be mad about. Then I stand and look down at him.

He looks boyish *and* masculine. Sweet, but with all those muscles and tattoos and his manhood resting against his thigh, impressively large even when not erect. He looks…

Heartbreaking.

I press a hand over my chest, blink away the moisture in my eyes, and take a deep breath.

There's no time for regret. For wondering about might-have-beens. It's time to get to work.

From his drawers, I select a black T-shirt and a pair of his briefs and quickly dress. The gown I wore to dinner isn't made for climbing balconies, but it does have its purposes. I retrieve it from the floor and rip out the section of hem where I sewed the micro compass. I place it carefully in my mouth, tucked between my cheek and teeth.

I don't bother with the handcuff key or the razor blade sewn into different spots in the lining of the dress. Neither safeguard has become necessary. I do need the map with my bug-out route through the hills, however, so I find my heels and crack the left one sharply against the wall. The platform sole breaks off. The little folded map flutters out like piñata candy.

I tuck the map into the waistband at the small of my back. It's not snug enough. I'm wearing men's underwear, after all—they're not exactly made for curves. The only other place the map can securely travel during a climb in my present garb is my mouth or my crotch.

I head to the minibar, open a small packet of nuts, dump out the nuts onto the counter, and wrap the plastic packaging around the map. Then I stick it between my legs.

I'm nothing if not resourceful.

In the closet, I pull out two pairs of Ryan's dress shoes. I swiftly remove the laces and tie them into square knots. Wrapped around the drainpipe that runs the length of the building next to the balconies, they can then be tied into Prusik knots, the kind rock climbers use. They'll slide up a line, but downward pressure will cause them to lock.

Perfect for scaling walls.

I look at Ryan's laptop on the coffee table for a moment, but decide he'll have too much security on the device to make it worth an attempt at snooping. I'd never get past the login screen. Besides, my curiosity about him is useless.

No matter what he said about finding me, this is the end of our road.

I leave my handbag behind. Like all the clothing, cosmetics, and fake IDs in my hotel room, there's nothing in it of value to me anymore. I take one last look at Ryan, sleeping peacefully on the floor, and allow myself a final twinge of regret.

It's surprisingly painful.

*Adios, beautiful stranger. Maybe in another life.*

Then I step out onto the balcony into the warm evening rain, and look up.

# 9

## RYAN

A fist pounds on my hotel room door. Over and over, as relentless as the thudding inside my skull. The two are so perfectly in sync, in fact, that it's entirely possible the pounding fist is in my imagination.

Until I hear the muffled shout.

"Ryan! Brother! Open the goddamn door before I kick it down!"

It's Connor. He sounds pissed.

I open my eyes…and I'm looking at a smooth white ceiling. For some reason, I'm lying on my back on the floor. And Connor is pounding on the door, shouting like a maniac.

*What the fuck happened?*

When I lift my head, the room swims for a moment before settling. An unfamiliar bitter taste lingers on the back of my tongue. The faintest scent of pepper teases my nose before disappearing like a ghost.

Then I remember *exactly* what happened, and a searing bolt of anger jolts me to my feet. Heart hammering with adrenaline, I look wildly around.

It's morning. The rain has stopped. Everything is still and

quiet, including the dumbass roosters in the distant hills who can't tell time.

I'm alone, but alive, which honestly is more than I counted on.

"Brother!" Connor roars. "*I'm coming in!*"

Before he can smash through the door—because he will, he's dramatic like that, plus he loves to break shit—I shout, "I'm comin', you damn ape. Pipe the fuck down!"

My voice is hoarse. Along with the headache and the small bit of vertigo which has now cleared, it's the only aftereffect of whatever Angeline dosed me with.

Muttering, I stomp to the door and yank it open.

"What?" I holler.

Then I blink.

In the doorway stands Connor, bristling and veiny like Wolverine. Behind him, a small crowd has gathered, which includes Tabby, Darcy, Kai, Juanita—and Elvis, perched on her shoulder—several uniformed people who appear to be hotel staff, half a dozen police officers, and four burly Middle Eastern dudes wearing identical black three-piece suits and murderous expressions.

I peg them as security or bodyguards, judging by their size and general vibe of badassery.

Darcy looks down at my crotch. She snorts. "Well, *hello* there, big boy!"

This is when I realize I'm stark fucking naked.

I shout, "Juanita, cover your eyes!"

She rolls them instead. "Pfft. Why don't *you* cover your junk, perv?"

Darcy bosses, "Zip it, short stuff. A man needs to air himself out every once in a while."

Juanita says, "*Gross*!", which startles Elvis, who sits up on his hind legs on her shoulder and starts sniffing the air for danger.

Exasperated, I clap my hands over my dick. "As you can *see*, I wasn't expectin' company. Anybody wanna share why you're all standin' in front of my door at the crack of dawn?"

A young guy in a beige uniform peers around the bulk of Connor's shoulder. He speaks with a distinct Caribbean accent. "Good morning, sir. I'm Camilo Bembe, the general manager of the hotel. Uh, we're so sorry to disturb you…"

He clears his throat. He's trying desperately to pretend I'm not standing there with my dick in my hands. "But there's been an unfortunate incident. These officers need to ask you some ques—"

"WHERE'S THE GIRL?" booms one of the thugs.

The hotel manager jumps. Kai shrieks like a startled baby. Connor looks at the goon and growls low in the back of his throat.

I say, "Oh, you're lookin' for her, too? Popular little thing, isn't she? Can't help ya, though, boys. Wonder Woman roofied me before takin' off in her invisible jet, so I've got no fuckin' clue where she is. Maybe you should check her room."

Tabby coughs into her hand to stifle her laugh. The four thugs shift their weight from foot to foot. Connor looks at the ceiling and sighs.

"Get dressed, Mr. McLean. We need to ask you some questions."

That comes from one of the police officers to Connor's right. He's tall and slim as a reed, with unusual eyes the color of grass. His hand rests casually on the butt of the sidearm strapped to his waist. His tone is impassive, but the subtext is clear. *You're in big trouble, son.*

Yeah, well, wouldn't be the first time. I smirk at him. "You betcha. Anything to assist an officer of the law."

I turn and saunter toward the bathroom, leaving the door open and my bare ass on display.

Connor sighs again. Darcy says, "*Lawd.*" No one else makes

a peep, except for one of the swarthy bodyguards, who mutters something in Arabic under his breath.

I don't speak the language, but my life has been threatened enough times by dangerous men speaking foreign tongues that I get the gist.

But I don't mind. The sooner I discover how Angeline is connected to these men, the sooner I can start working on a way to find her.

By the time I'm dressed and emerge from the bathroom, the police officers are busy sniffing around my room. They've dismissed the crowd with the exception of Connor, who stands to one side of the bed with his legs spread and his bulky arms crossed over his chest. He's biting the inside of his cheek, trying not to smile.

I snap, "Okay, brother. Here's the part where you tell me what you think is so damn funny!"

His dark eyes dance with laughter. "You sure can pick 'em, my friend. This is even better than the time you hooked up with that Mafia don's wife."

"She said she was divorced!"

"Nobody divorces the mob, dummy. Remind me, *how* many goombahs did he send to kick your ass?"

He's having way too much fun with this. I make an impatient motion with my hand that basically translates to *get to the fucking point.*

"When you didn't come down for breakfast, I figured you were still…occupied…with your new friend. But an hour later when you didn't pick up your cell or the room phone, I knew something was wrong. The police were just about to have the hotel manager open your door when we got here."

"And the suits who'd like to separate my head from my body? Who're they?"

Connor says drily, "Personal security for one Ahmed Akbar Khan Khalid."

"Saudi?"

"Yep. Super rich. Oil money, of course. And a bona fide prince, to boot." He jerks his chin at the ceiling. "Honeymooning in the suite right above this very room."

We stare at each other for a beat as I process what he's told me. After a few seconds, it clicks. I feel like the biggest idiot on the planet.

"Aw, shit. What'd she take?"

From outside on the balcony, the head officer answers. "A Burmese pigeon's blood ruby necklace once owned by Queen Ingrid of Denmark. It's worth fifteen million dollars."

I look over at him. He's craning his neck to peer at something on the side of the building that's fluttering in the gentle morning breeze. He looks at me and points in the direction of the flutter. "You want to explain this?"

Connor and I join him outside. Hanging down from the railing of the balcony above mine is a makeshift rope composed of white bedsheets. We lean over and discover three more tied to the first, dangling down the side of the building, all the way to the ground.

My brain switches into Special Ops mode. "Four king-size sheets tied together with square knots. Readily available, easy to work with, anonymous…"

Connor and I glance at each other. He says, "And excellent weight support. Especially at a high thread count like these."

I look down again, assessing the distance to the lawn below. "Building stories are about ten feet tall. Each king-size sheet would provide about twelve feet of length."

Connor says, "And we're probably what, fifty feet up?"

Exactly what I'd calculated. I remind myself to unclench my jaw. "I gotta admit it. That's pretty smart." I look at the officer. "They're from Khalid's room. She wouldn't have burdened herself with the climb up from here to there carrying a stack of sheets."

He narrows his eyes at me. "How do you know she climbed up?"

I smack myself on the forehead. "You're right. She took the invisible jet."

Connor warns, "Ryan."

Ignoring him, I cross my arms over my chest and level the officer with a hard stare. "Okay. Here's every fuckin' thing you need to know in a nutshell. I met the woman who calls herself Angeline Lemaire yesterday at the pool bar at approximately fifteen hundred hours. No, I didn't know her before that. No, I'm not an accomplice. No, I didn't know anything about her plans. We went to dinner with my friends, including this big ape here, and then came back to my room.

"What happened after that is none of your damn business, except that she doped me with something she put in a bottle of orange juice." I jerk my head toward the bed. "The empty's on the nightstand. You can test for residue. My guess is Rohypnol, modified with somethin' to make it work faster. Took me down in thirty seconds. When I woke up, you were outside my door."

Though it hurts my ego something fierce to admit it, I add, "She obviously targeted me because I was stayin' in this particular room. If it were next week, you'd be talkin' to some other dude. End of story."

The officer is busy trying to think of something to say next when one of his compadres lifts a high-heeled red shoe from the floor. The platform sole is broken off. Examining it, he asks, "You two have a fight?"

Connor speaks before I can. "He doesn't fight with broads, only the husbands he didn't know they had. But that's a nice little hidey-hole carved in there. Perfect size for some cash."

"Or a flash drive," I say, grudgingly impressed. "Or a compass, an ID—"

"A map," he finishes, looking at me. His sharp gaze flicks to the bedsheets, then to the view of the verdant hills. To the head cop, he says, "Lemme guess. She didn't check out of the hotel. She hasn't been seen since she left dinner with Ryan. You don't have any video feed of her leaving the property."

The cop looks uncomfortable. "Correct. The hotel doesn't have security cameras pointing up at the outside of the building—"

"Hotels never do," I interrupt. "Security cameras are always trained down, toward doors and hallways. Any thief worth his salt would know that." Though I'm still mad as fuck, I can't help but smile. "*Her* salt."

I can tell by the cop's expression that he'd really like to throw my ass in jail, but he must've already decided I'm just some dumb lackey Angeline used to make her play.

A lightbulb goes on over my head. "Wait. You know who she is, don't you?"

He takes off his cap and scratches his head. Sounding weary, he says, "I can't comment on that."

Connor scoffs, "Oh come on! You wouldn't have even let me in this room if this was a real interrogation."

He scowls. "No one ever said anything about an interrogation!"

An odd combination of elation and anger electrifies my skin. "She's hit this hotel before?"

He looks back and forth between Connor and me, then obviously decides he might as well tell us, because he sighs heavily and starts spilling his guts.

"No. But I've got a friend in Interpol. Called him as soon as I was notified by Prince Khalid that his safe had been broken into while he was asleep. I knew it had to be a pro if he—she—could get past the armed security personnel posted outside the door and the biometric thumbprint scanner on the safe, and also be quiet enough not to awaken the prince or his bride for however long it took to finish the job."

He makes a face. "Though admittedly the prince is known to imbibe more than what could be considered a reasonable amount, and his wife said she fell asleep to a white noise app because of all his snoring." He turns to Connor. "Have you heard of Brain.fm? The princess claims it's very relaxing—"

I shout, "Cut to the fuckin' chase, man!"

He stares at me for a moment. "Let's just say this woman is on pretty much *everyone's* most wanted list."

I demand, "What's her name?"

He lifts a shoulder. "Who knows? She's got fifteen known aliases, probably plenty more that aren't known. Been doing big jobs for a long time. Jewels, mainly. The occasional piece of art. Never been caught."

I scoff, "How could a thief who looks like a supermodel never be caught? She stands out like a fuckin' neon sign!"

"If you saw the Interpol file, you might think differently."

"Disguises?" Connor sounds doubtful.

"Up the wazoo. Eyewitnesses describe her as anywhere from twenty to fifty years old. Five foot four to five foot ten. Blonde, redhead, short black hair, dreadlocks. Blue eyes, brown eyes, green eyes. Walks with a limp. Walks with no limp. Has a lisp. Has an Irish accent. French. Italian. Spanish. You name it. She's no one. She's everyone. She's impossible to pin down. Apparently she's known in criminal circles as The Golden Hand. But my Interpol friend says law enforcement calls her the Dragonfly."

Thinking of her gorgeous naked body trembling under my touch, I murmur, "Because of the tattoo."

The officer looks at me sharply. "Tattoo?"

"The dragonfly on her left hip."

His brows slowly rise.

I realize too late that this is new information to him. In spite of my gaffe, a flush of something like pride heats my neck.

If law enforcement doesn't know she has a tattoo, that means none of her marks have ever reported it. And if none of her marks have ever reported it, that means none of them ever saw her naked.

Goddamn. She was telling the truth about never having one-night stands!

I instantly forgive her for everything.

"No," says the officer. "It's because she leaves a drawing of a dragonfly somewhere at every job she pulls off. It's her calling card. The one in Prince Khalid's suite was scrawled on the bathroom mirror with his wife's lipstick."

"She wants everyone to know it was her," I say.

Connor adds ominously, "Or some*one*."

We lock eyes. I know him well, and right now I know he's thinking Angeline's calling card isn't meant as a taunt to the police. It's not an ego thing. It's a message.

But for who? And why?

Watching my face, the police officer chuckles. "Don't take it personally, Mr. McLean. She's duped some of the most sophisticated security personnel on the planet. She's a professional thief. The best in the business, by all accounts."

Connor claps his hand on my shoulder. He's chewing the inside of his cheek again. "Besides, I'm sure she thought you were real cute."

"Fuck off," I say cheerfully, because *I wasn't a one-night stand.*

The officer who was holding Angeline's shoe is now holding her red dress, retrieved from the floor. He's fingering it with his brows pulled together. "Got something here, chief."

"What is it?"

The officer removes a Swiss knife from his black utility belt, snaps open the blade with his thumb, and works it against a seam in the waist of the dress. The fabric gives way easily. He removes a small metal object, winking in the light. Looking surprised, he holds it up.

Connor and I say in unison, "Handcuff key."

The chief looks at me as if for confirmation. "She sewed a handcuff key into her dress?"

"In case she was apprehended and had to escape from cuffs." I shake my head, more impressed by the second. "It's fuckin' brilliant."

Another officer standing next to the television console opens the small beaded handbag Angeline left behind and dumps its contents onto the wood surface. Sifting through it with the tip of a pen, he catalogues his findings out loud.

"One rake pick. One tension wrench. One torch lighter. One folding tactical knife. One metal shim. Four plastic zip ties. One unmarked hotel keycard, possibly a master. And one lipstick."

He picks up the gold tube of lipstick and looks at the label on the bottom. "It's called Lady Danger."

A grin spreads over Connor's face. "I *like* this girl."

In spite of how completely fucked up this entire situation is, I grin back. "Me too, brother. Me too!"

The chief rolls his eyes. "You guys are idiots."

## 10

## MARIANA

Specializing in buying and selling rare coins, gold, jewels, diamonds, and valuables since 1979, Mallory & Sons Heritage Auctions has retail boutiques in most of the largest cities in the world. But the London boutique is the one I always visit upon completion of an assignment.

And not because it's company headquarters.

Ignoring the cold and the gray drizzle, I stand across the street for a few minutes before going in and just look.

The shop is charming glimpsed through its beveled-glass windows. It's brightly lit, stuffed with antiques, the walls crowded with original oils by artists of all levels of fame and importance, as well as the occasional exquisite forgery to be sold to a *nouveaux riche* collector more concerned with impressing his friends than demanding certified provenance.

Inside the shop, a man stands behind a massive oak counter carved with a relief from *Beowulf* of warriors on horseback battling a dragon. The man is examining a ring. He holds a jeweler's loupe to one eye, holds the ring up to the light. He's of average height and average weight with no distinctive features except an aquiline nose and an air of elegance.

His hair is more salt than pepper. His skin is lined around his eyes. His navy-blue suit is well tailored, but not couture. Judging strictly by appearance, he could be fifty…or seventy. Italian or Spanish. Scottish or Portuguese. Or pretty much anything else. He has no tattoos or scars, wears no jewelry or cologne, is perfectly forgettable.

He goes by Reynard, a name borrowed from the trickster fox from medieval fables.

He taught me everything I know.

That I love him is irrelevant to our business arrangement. If I said it aloud, he'd admonish me for it, so I keep it to myself.

I step off the curb, avoiding a muddy puddle, and hurry across the street. My heels click against wet cobblestone. The bell over the door jangles cheerfully when I come in. I'm hit with warmth and the sweet, smoky scent of the incense burning next to a votive candle in a cubby on the wall. Amy Winehouse plays softly in the background, crooning *you know that I'm no good.*

Reynard looks up. Catching sight of me, he smiles. "'By the pricking of my thumbs, something wicked this way comes.'"

I say drily, "It's good to see you too, Reynard."

He abandons the jeweler's loupe and ring to the counter and holds out his arms. "My darling."

I don't bother removing my rain-slicked overcoat. I simply go to him and let him enfold me in his arms.

"She's wet," he muses to himself, stroking my hair. "Silly child."

I pull back, grinning because I'm so happy to see him. "People don't catch cold from being wet."

"I wasn't talking about catching cold, my darling, I was talking about your hair." He smooths his hand over my head, clucking in disapproval. "It looks dreadful. Why aren't you wearing a hat? Or carrying an umbrella? One doesn't go about with no head covering in the rain when one has a tendency to frizz—"

"Be quiet, old man."

He blinks at me, insulted. "*Old?* Oh dear. You haven't eaten. You're light-headed. Shall I make us a cup of tea?"

"That sounds wonderful, thank you."

I kiss his cheek, smooth as a baby's behind. Then I have to suppress a rogue memory of the American's rough cheeks and how delicious they felt grazing the inside of my thighs.

That's what I've started calling him, my first and only lovely one-night stand. The American. It's more impersonal, therefore less painful. I'm hoping in time the dull ache will wear off his memory and I'll be able to sigh wistfully when I think of him, but for now it's like a jagged pill I've swallowed that's stuck just beneath my breastbone, slicing tiny cuts into my insides with every breath.

My body is sore in so many places from our lovemaking. My thighs. My lower back. My behind, faintly bruised by his hand.

My heart, bruised more than faintly.

Reynard intently studies my face. "Something's happened. Tell me."

This time, I have to force a grin. "I'm fine. Just tired from the flight. And the trek through the jungle to get to where I hid my bug-out bag. That resort was in the middle of nowhere! I was barefoot, if you can believe it. You should see the sorry state of my feet."

A faint smile lifts Reynard's lips. "Hmm. What's his name?"

"I have no idea what you're talking about."

"Of course you don't. What's that expression your face is attempting? It looks rather comical."

*I must be losing my edge.* "Stop harassing me about my face, or I won't give you what I came here for."

"You're in a delightful mood this evening, my darling. Let me go turn the sign."

Moving with panther-like noiseless grace, he walks to the front of the shop, locks the door, and flips over the small white sign in the window. Then he leads me through the shop to a large bookcase under a staircase at the back.

Neither of us mention that I don't have a choice about giving him what I came here to give him, but we act as if I do.

"Ladies first," drawls Reynard, with a flourish of his hand.

From the bookcase, I remove a slender volume bound in dark-green leather, its title stitched in gold along the spine. *Oliver Twist* by Charles Dickens. The story of an orphan who escapes the workhouse to join a den of thieves. Our little inside joke.

The bookcase swings slowly open to reveal a stone corridor. I replace the book, and we walk inside as the case swings closed behind us.

The tunnel is damp, smells of mold and mice droppings, and is badly in need of repair. After two turns, it opens into a large anteroom which is bare of decoration except for a trio of beeswax candles burning in a tall iron candelabra beside an arched oak door so thick it could probably survive a direct hit from a cannon.

"Any trouble with your mercenary?" Reynard inquires, removing an old-fashioned skeleton key from his breast pocket.

"Nothing I couldn't handle."

He flicks me an inscrutable look over his shoulder. Then he inserts the key into the lock. The door opens with a groan of rusted metal hinges to reveal a warehouse of staggering opulence.

There are so many priceless antiques, statuaries, paintings, sculptures, and artifacts from around the world stuffed into the space, it could make the Vatican turn green with envy. The first time I saw it, at ten years old, I stood gaping for a full five minutes, staring goggle-eyed like the rube I was.

Part of the complex of hidden tunnels beneath London used

during air raids in the Second World War, the vast, brick-walled space has been repurposed as a drop for purloined goods in transit. A quarter mile of heavy-duty steel shelving is stacked in tall, numbered rows down the center. Wood crates and boxes of all sizes overflow with booty, glinting under the lights. The larger items are kept along the walls—or on the walls, in the case of some of the oversized paintings and tapestries.

Regardless of their size, all items are barcoded and entered into an inventory software system Reynard developed himself. Some pieces come to cool for only a few weeks before being shipped out to their new owners. Some, like the 1727 Stradivarius violin stolen from the Manhattan penthouse of a famous conductor and still too hot to sell, have been here for decades.

As with everything seen through the lens of familiarity, however, I barely notice the glittering bounty now. As Reynard once famously said, *"If you've seen one gold-plated toilet, you've seen them all."*

I shrug out of my wet coat, shake the raindrops off, and drape it over the back of a velvet divan. Reynard turns on an electric kettle. The front part of the warehouse is set up as Reynard's office. Heavy brocade drapes in bloodred cover the walls. French crystal lamps spill light in fractured prisms onto a Louis XVI desk inlaid with gold. The bare stone floor is covered by a thick Turkish rug.

It has the air of an upscale French bordello.

Reynard turns to look at me. "You're not carrying anything."

"Aren't I?"

His gaze sweeps me up and down, gets snagged on my throat. He gasps. "Naughty!"

This time, my grin is sincere. "I couldn't resist. Took it out of Khalid's suite the same way." From around my neck, I slowly unwind the heavy cashmere scarf I'm using to hide the ruby necklace.

"Good God. Spectacular. Come into the light, my darling."

Reynard waves me closer. He removes a pair of spectacles from a drawer in his desk and slides them onto his nose.

"Since when do you wear glasses?"

"Since I'm old, as you so charmingly pointed out. Turn left a little. There." He examines the necklace without touching it. "Pity it'll have to be dismantled. The craftsmanship is exquisite."

I lift a hand and touch my finger to the center stone, a flawless twenty-carat ruby. It's heavy and cool against my skin. It *is* a pity the stones will have to be removed and sold separately, the gold setting melted down for scrap, but pieces like this inevitably are. It's simply easier to find buyers.

"Is that a *love bite* on your neck?" Reynard's eyes narrow at the mark the American's teeth left near my jugular.

*"Me not bein' sweet is gonna leave marks."*

I have to forcibly banish the memory of his face when he uttered those words. How his voice sounded, hot and rough with desire.

"I should be so lucky," I say breezily. "It's a bruise. Trek through the jungle, remember?"

"Hmm."

I can't tell if he believes me or not, but in another moment, it doesn't matter, because he says something that makes my entire body go cold.

"Capo wants to see you. Tonight."

"Tonight?" I repeat, my voice high. "He's in London?" My heart slams against my breastbone, sending my pulse flying.

Reynard meets my panicked gaze. His voice is steady when he answers. "He flew in when he discovered you'd be here."

I flush with anger. "You mean when you *told* him I'd be here."

Reynard removes his glasses and places them into his coat pocket. He says gently, "We all have to sing for our supper, my darling. We live and die at his leisure. You know this."

Yes, I do know. But I'm still childishly wounded by Reynard's betrayal. I look down, swallowing back tears.

When I stare at the ground a little too long, Reynard takes my chin between his thumb and forefinger, forcing me to look up.

"I need to keep him thinking I'm loyal, Mariana."

I jerk my chin from his hand. "He knows you're not loyal. Which is why we're in this situation in the first place."

I unhook the clasp on the necklace with a practiced flick of my fingers. It slithers down my chest. I capture it in my hands, thrusting it at Reynard because I'm suddenly filled with disgust for it.

At least he has the manners to look ashamed when he takes it from me. "I'm sorry, my darling—"

"Don't be. I knew what I was doing when I took the oath. And it was worth it, to keep you alive after everything you did for me. I'm just tired."

I find the nearest chair and sink into it, dragging my hands through my hair. He watches me silently, examining my face.

Again I'm reminded of the American. He and Reynard have that same hard speculation in their gazes, the way of making you feel utterly exposed in spite of all your careful disguises.

*Stop thinking about him, Mari. Don't waste time on foolish dreams.* Exhaling heavily, I pass a hand over my eyes.

Still holding the ruby necklace, Reynard says sharply, "What's going on? You're different tonight. What's happened?"

I lift my eyes and I lie again, because I have to, because the notion of honor among thieves exists in the same place as Tinker Bell.

Neverland, where children never age, and all it takes to keep you alive is faith, trust, and a little bit of pixie dust.

"Nothing," I say, keeping my face as blank as my voice. "Now why don't you tell me where I'm supposed to meet that son of a bitch so I can get it over with."

Reynard opens a drawer in the Louis XVI cabinet and removes a black velvet bag. Into it he carefully deposits the necklace. Then he draws the bag closed, puts it back into the cabinet, and lifts his gaze to mine.

"He's staying at the Palace. And please, Mariana. Be careful. He's in a strange mood."

"When isn't he?" I mutter.

"You'll need these." Reynard opens a different drawer. Another black velvet bag appears, this one much smaller than the first. From inside comes the soft *chink* of metal sliding against metal as he carries it over to me and places it in my outstretched hand.

I open the bag and peer inside, then look at Reynard with my brows pulled together. "I only need one to get past the doorman."

Reynard's pause could mean anything. It's short but weighty, and tells me he's carefully considering his words. "You never know what you're going to need when you're in the Palace, my darling. Better safe than sorry."

Those words echo in my ears long after I've had my tea and left.

~

From the outside, the Palace looks like a dump. It's an abandoned, decaying textile mill in a dodgy part of town, near the docks, a block or two away from a large homeless encampment. Tourists don't come around here. Neither do the police, who are paid handsomely to turn a blind eye.

The cabbie thinks I've given him the wrong address.

"Nuttin' here but trouble, miss," he says in a thick Cockney accent, peering through his window at the ten-story building outside.

It looks deserted. All the windows are blacked out. Old newspapers and the odd bit of trash decorate the sidewalk. A skinny orange tabby cat slinks around a corner, catches sight of the cab idling at the curb, and darts back out of sight.

"No, this is it. Thank you." I hand him a fifty-pound note through the opening in the plastic screen that divides us and get out of the cab.

He doesn't even offer me change before he drives off, tires squealing.

"Sissy," I mutter, flipping up the collar of my coat to ward off the chill of the evening.

It doesn't help.

I walk down a dark alley on the side of the building until I reach an unmarked door. The reek of the Dumpsters nearby is overwhelming. I rap my knuckles on the cold metal to the tune of "Shave and a Haircut," shivering as an icy wind whips around my bare ankles.

A small window in the center of the door slides open with a *clack*. An eyeball peers out at me. Then a deep male voice grunts, "Piss off."

I say, "New England clam chowder."

The eyeball gives me a searing once-over.

From my pocket I remove a silver coin and hold it up so the eyeball can see it. "Open sesame, amigo. It's freezing out here."

The eyeball disappears as the window slams shut. The quiet of the alley is broken by the scrape of the door opening and the doorman's greeting, friendlier now that he's heard the password and seen the coin.

"Evenin'."

He holds out his hand. It's the size of a dinner plate. Into his palm I set the piece of stamped silver. He nods and steps back, allowing me to pass.

I walk down a short corridor lit by a single bare bulb hanging from a wire on the ceiling. A freight elevator awaits at the end, its doors gaping open. I step inside and press a button marked "Limbo."

After a short ride, the doors open again to what appears to be the lobby of a posh hotel.

The Palace *is* a posh hotel. And bar, nightclub, neutral meeting space—even safe house if needed—all designed for a particular clientele.

A spectacularly beautiful redhead in a tailored ivory suit smiles at me from behind a marble counter to my left. Her fiery hair is gathered into a low chignon. Her skin is milk white. A gold placard on the counter reads "Concierge."

When I approach her counter, she smiles wider. "Dragonfly. How wonderful to see you again."

"Hello, Genevieve."

She notices I'm not carrying luggage. "I take it you're not staying with us long?"

"No. Do you have any messages for me?"

"One moment, please."

Her fingers move quickly over a keyboard as she glances at the computer screen tucked below the counter. "Yes. Mr. Moreno requests you join him on the seventh floor when you arrive."

Our gazes meet. Genevieve's pleasant smile doesn't waver. If she feels any pity at all for me at being summoned to the seventh floor by the head of the European crime syndicate, she doesn't reveal it.

"Thank you, Genevieve."

"You're welcome. Please let me know if I may be of any service during your stay."

Translation: If you require unregistered weapons, forged identity papers, armed escorts, or emergency disposal of dead bodies, I'm your girl.

We nod at each other in farewell. I quickly cross the lobby, noting several familiar faces. People are checking in and out, relaxing on sofas and reading newspapers, strolling around with drinks in their hands. Exactly like people do in a normal hotel lobby.

But this is no normal hotel, which I'm irrefutably reminded of as I enter the main elevators and look at the row of buttons on the panel on the wall. The floors aren't numbered. Inspired by Dante's *Inferno*, each of the nine floors in the Palace is named after one of the circles of hell.

I hit the button marked "Violence" and shiver as the elevator doors slide silently shut.

## 11

## MARIANA

The elevator dings. The doors slide open. I'm greeted by the sight of two men, naked from the waist up, beating each other bloody with bare fists in the middle of an open ring, with boundaries marked by a square of silver coins on the burgundy carpet.

Burgundy. Good for concealing bloodstains.

I steel myself against the revulsion that twists my stomach.

A barrel-chested man with no neck, a crooked nose, and a mouthful of disheveled teeth stands to the right of the doors. The only thing remotely attractive about him is his suit, a bespoke pinstripe Brioni with a midnight-blue tie and matching silk pocket square.

"Dragonfly." His voice is a rocky rumble, heavy with the mark of southern Italy.

"Enzo. You're looking well."

He chuckles. Somehow it sounds just as Sicilian as his accent. "Don't bullshit a bullshitter, *bambolina.* It's no good for your health."

His gaze drifts over my figure, lingering on the hint of

cleavage the collar of my coat doesn't manage to conceal. I curse myself for leaving my scarf at Reynard's.

Enzo murmurs something lewd in Italian, licking his lips.

Aggravated, I respond in Italian that his mother would smack him to hear him talking like that.

"Ya," he says, nodding. "But she's dead, so she don't hear nothing no more except the munching of worms. Capo's waiting on you."

*So much for the pleasant chitchat.*

Enzo turns, expecting me to follow because he knows I always do. I walk behind him as he leads me around the fighting men to a sitting area on the other side of the room.

The walls are painted black. The room is dim, smoky, and smells like sweat. Incongruent to everything, the gorgeous resonance of a pure, perfect soprano singing an aria from Puccini's *Madama Butterfly* plays on invisible speakers.

Trying to ignore the grunts of pain that punctuate the opera as blows are landed, I keep my gaze averted from the pair of bloody fighters and focus on the irregular mole on the back of Enzo's bald head.

But I've already seen enough.

Judging by the bruising on their bodies and how both men are panting and swaying on their feet, the fight has been going on for some time. Won't be long before one of them will collect his coins and the other is dragged out by his heels and disposed of.

Losers in one of Capo's fights don't leave the building breathing.

The sitting area is raised on a dais, flanked by a pair of floor lamps, wide enough to hold a long leather sofa and a few club chairs on either end. Six men in suits stand discreetly in the shadows at the rear, three on either side, hands clasped at their waists, faces impassive.

Capo's soldiers. Made men.

Assassins.

A glass coffee table in front of the sofa holds a magnum of champagne on ice and two empty crystal champagne flutes. The sofa itself holds two very young, nude girls—leashed with leather collars—and one large, dead-eyed man.

In one fist he holds the stub of a cigar. In the other he holds the girls' leashes.

He's thirty-five, maybe forty, wearing a tailored dark suit even more beautiful than Enzo's. His hair is thick and midnight black. His jaw is as hard as his eyes. He's handsome in an ugly sort of way, all the violence inside him barely contained, oozing out around the edges.

Vincent Moreno.

The most evil creature in the world, next to the Devil himself.

"Mari," he says softly. "You're here."

With a savage jerk of his arm, he drags both girls off the sofa. They land at his feet in a tangle of pale limbs and pained yelps, quickly silenced by another cruel jerk on their collars. They cower on the carpet, heads down, clinging to his legs.

My back teeth are gritted so hard, I think they might shatter.

"*Capo di tutti capi*," I say. Boss of all bosses. "I am."

Those dead eyes slice straight through me. For a long moment, he simply stares at me. Then, horribly, he starts to laugh.

"Enzo! Have you ever seen such a look!" He motions to me with his cigar. A fat clump of glowing ash falls onto one of the girls, burning her leg. She pulls her lips between her teeth and whimpers.

"Ya," drawls Enzo, popping a piece of gum into his mouth. He winks at me. "When some guy wants to kill me, he looks just like that."

Smiling, Capo tilts his head back and looks at me from under hooded lids. "You want to kill me, Mari?"

*Only every day, you worthless piece of shit.* "I'm not in the murder business."

His smile vanishes. "You're in whatever business I say you're in."

I swallow. A cold bead of sweat trickles down the back of my neck. Behind me, one of the fighters lands a vicious blow.

The crunch of bone makes the collared girls shudder.

"Yes, Capo. I meant no disrespect."

Gazing at me thoughtfully, he draws on his cigar. The tip burns red. He exhales a plume of smoke, then, without looking away from me, he raises the hand that holds the girls' leashes and says to Enzo, "Get rid of this garbage."

Enzo leads them off like they're a pair of dogs on choke chains. They crawl behind him on hands and knees toward a door on the far side of the room. I can't watch, because I can't help them, and I'm concentrating on swallowing the scream of impotent rage building in my throat.

I start counting all the places I've hidden weapons on my body.

*Left thigh. Lower back. Right forearm. Shoe.*

I'm not going to attempt anything because I'd be dead within seconds, but it calms me.

Capo motions for me to join him on the sofa. "Come. Take off your coat and have some champagne."

The six bodyguards watch me rebel for a moment against an order from their king. Try as I might to move, my body remains frozen.

Capo's hand is extended toward me. His eyes glitter with malice. Very quietly, he says my name.

I drag in a breath and find the will to get my shaking fingers to untie the belt on my coat. It falls open, Capo's eyes flare, and I freeze all over again.

Abruptly, he stands and comes to me. He cuffs my wrists in

his hands and gives me a short, hard shake. I smell his cologne, sandalwood and cloves, and almost groan in terror.

"You seem reluctant." His voice is low, his face close to mine. "Are you afraid of me, Mari?"

*I could die in this room, and no one would ever know. I'd never see Reynard again. I'd never see the sun again.*

*And the American... Will he think of me?*

I'm hyperventilating. It must be my fear that answers Capo, because I would never be so self-destructive to utter the words I say next.

"Yes. But I hate myself for it. You're not worth the wasted breath."

A muscle in his jaw flexes. He looks at my mouth. "I've killed men for less than that," he says, deadly soft. His gaze flashes back up to mine. His grip around my wrists is viciously tight.

I think of the American again, the way he touched my body with such reverence, how he was so sweet I couldn't bear it. It's comical that I should be thinking of him at this moment. Or maybe it's madness. Either way, it gives me a welcome boost of strength.

"I can't help it if you don't like to hear the truth."

Capo exhales slowly. His lids droop. He moistens his lips.

With a fresh dose of horror, I realize he's aroused by my defiance.

In a lover's tender murmur, he says, "Always so reckless, Mari. Always so proud. Do you know what I'd like to do with that pride of yours?"

My mouth goes dry. My stomach knots. I'm sure he can hear my knees knocking.

He leans closer. He inhales deeply against my neck, raising all the tiny hairs on my body. The tip of his nose nudges my earlobe as he breathes hotly into my ear, "I'd like to beat it out of you."

Then he releases me abruptly and snarls, "Now sit your ass down on the fucking sofa!"

He shoves me so hard, I stumble and fall to my knees. A hand grips my hair and yanks my head back. I look up into a handsome, unsmiling face.

Capo makes a clucking noise and chides, "Clumsy."

He drags me to my feet by my hair. I suck in a sharp breath from the pain but don't scream. I won't give the bastard the satisfaction. He pushes me onto the sofa, then stands glaring down at me while I wait, heart hammering, for him to pull out a gun and shoot me in the face.

But he only runs a hand over his hair and adjusts his tie, smooths a wrinkle in his beautiful jacket.

"You always manage to disrupt my equilibrium."

There's an edge like a knife in his voice. He sits next to me and pours champagne into both glasses. An acrid coil of smoke wafts up from the carpet beneath the coffee table where he abandoned his cigar.

I take the champagne he offers, ashamed to see how hard my hand shakes. Unsure if it will be the last taste of champagne I'll ever have, I swallow it in one gulp.

One of the fighters hits the other with a vicious undercut to the jaw. It sends him flying. As the soprano hits a high note, his body lands on the carpet with a dull thud. A tremor shakes the floor under my feet.

*Get up. Keep fighting. Please don't die in front of me. Please don't die and leave me here alone with him and his soldiers and nothing else to hold their attention.*

"I told you to take off your coat."

Capo has leaned back against the sofa, and is watching me from the corner of his eye. I do as he orders, my gaze averted. When I try to drape my coat over my legs, he warns softly, "Mariana."

I place the coat on the arm of the sofa and fold my hands in my lap. I'm sitting ramrod-straight, staring at nothing, when I feel his hand settle onto my thigh.

I flinch. He squeezes my leg. I grit my teeth and close my eyes. "So you know I finished the job."

He says casually, "Speak again without permission, and you won't walk for a week."

*"Who told you you could speak, you bad girl?"*

Why, *why* is the American in my head? Why can't I get him out? Why am I thinking of *him* as I'm sitting here with this savage of a man, my life in danger, my heart exploding in fear?

Even as I'm asking myself those questions, I know the answer.

Because the further away I get from that beautiful night, the more clearly I can see what I was given.

Capo asks sharply, "Why are you smiling?"

My eyes snap open. The fighter who was knocked out has rolled onto his side and is struggling to stand. It seems like a sign, so I decide to tell him the truth. "You remind me of the things I'm grateful for."

My honesty surprises him. Something like amusement flashes across his expression, but of course it can't be amusement because he doesn't have a sense of humor—because he doesn't have a soul.

He says, "How interesting. That almost sounded like a compliment. If you're not careful, I'll start to think you're sweet on me." After a beat, he adds, "Although those murderous eyes tell a different story."

We stare at each other. My fingers itch to claw into his eye sockets, to dig out his eyeballs and crush them under my feet, to feel vitreous liquid, warm and gelatinous, ooze between my bare toes.

*I wonder if evil is contagious.*

I ask politely, "May I please have permission to speak?"

His grin is unexpected. It's also terrifying.

"Do you know why I like you, Mariana?"

*He likes me? Dios mio*. His hand, heavy and warm, still rests on my thigh.

"No, Capo. Why?"

"Because you're a warrior. Even your submission is defiant. You'd rather die on your feet than live on your knees." He adds thoughtfully, "Like me."

*Like me? He thinks we have something in common?* Revulsion curls my tongue when I say, "Thank you."

My expression makes him laugh. When he lifts his hand from my leg, it feels like I've been sprung from prison.

"We could've made an incredible team, you and I. It's a pity you chose to take the oath to repay Reynard's debt instead of… the easier way." His gaze drifts down to my breasts. He sinks his teeth into his full lower lip.

I wish I hadn't guzzled all my champagne. I need something to wash the taste of vomit from my mouth.

He glances at my face. Whatever he sees there makes him prompt, "You may speak."

My plan was to try to get right down to business and find out why he called me here, but something has occurred to me that's much more important.

And far, far more dangerous.

I say haltingly, "I want…I want to ask for a favor."

For a long, tense moment, he stares at me. I wonder how long the fighters will be able to continue, because I sense I'm starting to run out of time.

Capo leans forward, sets his champagne glass on the coffee table, then rests his elbows on his knees and smiles. He's never looked more ruthless.

Holding my gaze, he says softly, "You know my favors aren't free."

I almost lose my courage then. But I'm gambling that the blood oath I've taken will give me some measure of protection against the worst part of his nature. Sicilians value blood oaths more than anything, except family and respect.

"Yes, Capo."

His eyes blaze with anticipation. He inclines his head, permission for me to speak granted.

"The girls who were with you when I came in…"

That muscle in his jaw flexes again. He looks hungry. Like a starving wild animal about to rip into a carcass with his teeth. "What about them, Mariana?"

My name on his lips is so sinister, I have to take several breaths before I work up the courage to speak again. "May I have them?"

He looks startled for a split second, then his face clears with understanding. His voice comes out as a hiss. "Save them, you mean. *Rescue* them. From me."

When I don't answer, Capo sneers. "They're two of hundreds. Thousands. All exactly alike. You can't save them all."

I stare at my hands. They're shaking. With fury or fright, I don't really know. "I couldn't live with myself if I didn't try."

He grabs my jaw and forces my head around so we're nose to nose, staring into each other's eyes. "This is about your sister, isn't it?"

My silence infuriates him. He snaps, "There are better ways to respect the dead than throwing yourself on their funeral pyre!"

I'm shocked. I thought he'd jump at the chance to degrade me the way I know he aches to.

"Is that a no?"

His nostrils flare. His hands clamp around my throat and start squeezing before I can react. He jerks me toward him. The movement is so violent, it lifts me clear off the sofa.

"You stupid fucking woman," he growls, veins popping out in his neck. "You stupid, proud, sentimental woman. You'd sacrifice yourself for a dead girl and two worthless whores who'll rob you and stab you in the heart the second they get the chance?"

He flips me onto my back on the sofa, a big, dark presence looming over me as I cough and struggle against his grip. My eyes water. I draw my knees up against my chest in useless defense.

He shouts into my face, "Do you know what I'd do to you? *Do you have any fucking idea?*"

I don't understand what's happening. I know he's furious with me, I know his hands are squeezing the life from my body, and I know that very soon I'll lose consciousness, because the room is starting to fade.

But I still don't get why I'm not already stripped naked and strapped to a St. Andrew's cross, watching Capo approach with nothing but a dark smile and a whip.

Enzo strolls back into the room, wiping his hands on a white handkerchief. Capo catches sight of him from the corner of his eye and abruptly releases me.

He stands and roars, "*Fuck!*" at the top of his lungs, then stalks to the ring outlined in silver, interrupting the two fighters.

He grabs one of the men by the throat and punches him so hard I can hear his nose shatter all the way across the room. The fighter crumples to the floor. Capo turns to the other man with an animal snarl and lunges at him, striking him with his fists over and over, mercilessly, even after the man falls motionless on his back on the carpet.

Enzo watches this outburst with vague interest, his lower lip puffed out. He's still wiping his hands on the handkerchief.

I sob when I realize what he's cleaning from his hands is blood.

The aria from *Madama Butterfly* ends. The only sounds now are ragged, heaving breaths, Capo's and mine.

Capo stands. He spits on one of the men on the floor. He wipes his mouth on the cuff of his sleeve, then drops his head back, closes his eyes, and inhales a deep breath.

I roll to my side on the sofa, get my feet under me, and

slowly sit up. My whole body is shaking. I cough and gag, dragging in excruciating breaths. My throat is so raw and bruised, I don't know if I'll be able to talk.

As if he's a bored waitress in a diner, Enzo asks, "You want I should order up some sandwiches, Capo?"

Sweating and disheveled, his gaze disoriented, Capo turns and squints at Enzo. He shakes his head like a dog coming out of water. He swallows, rakes his hands through his hair, and staggers away from the bodies in the ring.

I can't tell if either man is breathing.

"It looks like you're in luck, Mariana," says Capo, panting a little. "You won't have to owe me a favor after all."

He's looking at Enzo's bloody handkerchief.

I cover my face with my shaking hands. In a moment, another song starts up. Another aria. Another woman singing in her beautiful, soaring voice.

I'll never be able to listen to opera again.

Sounding more under control, Capo says, "Yes, Enzo. Order food. But not sandwiches. Steaks. Bloody rare."

"Sure thing, boss." Whistling, Enzo wanders to the elevator doors. He steps right over one of the unconscious fighters on the way.

Between my fingers, I see feet approach. A pair of big, expensive black wingtips polished to a mirror shine stop a foot or two away.

"I called you here because I wanted to discuss your next job. Only two left to go under your contract." Capo has regained all his control now and sounds like any boss addressing any employee in a staff meeting.

I can't look at him. My voice comes out as a painful croak. "One."

"It *was* one. Your dumb fucking Mother Teresa act just added another."

I stay silent, eyes lowered, impotent rage boiling in my veins.

A heavy sigh breaks from Capo's chest, stirring my hair. He lowers himself to the sofa beside me and pours himself more champagne.

He murmurs, "Ah, Mariana. This isn't how I wanted tonight to go. I wanted us to have a drink, visit, spend a little time together. But you always make me so goddamn..." His voice shakes over the next word. "*Angry.*"

I don't dare look at him. I don't dare speak. I think of tropical rainfall and roosters crowing at midnight and a man who called me Angel, and try not to cry.

After a moment, Capo whips the silk pocket square from his suit jacket and digs into the silver ice bucket, rooting around the magnum of champagne. He grabs a handful of ice, ties the ends of the pocket square together, and silently holds the dripping packet out to me.

I take it and press it against my burning throat.

Because this is my life.

Sounding tired, Capo says, "Listen to me. The job."

I nod. Ice water slides down my neck and trickles into my cleavage. It might as well be acid for how it burns.

"It's in Washington, DC. At the Smithsonian. I want the Hope Diamond."

I turn my head and stare at him with wide eyes.

"By the first of the month."

I drop the ice into my lap.

"And before you tell me it's impossible, remember what happens to Reynard if you fail." Capo takes a long swallow from his glass of champagne. Gazing at the unmoving bodies of the men on the carpet, he says bitterly, "You can do it. I have faith in you, Mari. Your loyalty to that old dog is even stronger than your need to be a hero to whores."

When he turns back to me, his eyes have changed. Gone is any hint of humanity. What I'm looking at now is the raw, brutal beast who would've strangled me to death if Enzo hadn't accidentally interrupted him.

The beast snarls, "Now get the fuck out of my sight before I lose my temper and tear you to shreds!"

He doesn't have to tell me twice.

I grab my coat and stumble away, vision blurred with tears of rage and desperation, vowing for the thousandth time that someday, somehow, I'll find a way to take him down. Until then, I've got to figure out how to steal a world-famous diamond from one of the most secure locations inside the capital of the United States.

Within ten days.

Or Reynard dies.

I grip the small velvet bag of silver coins in my pocket and hurry back down to Limbo to pay a visit to the concierge.

## 12

## RYAN

By the time the police finished poking around my room and collecting evidence, I'd missed my flight. I'd also discovered from my new friend the chief that a twin-engine Cessna was stolen from the local airport sometime during the night. Security cameras caught nothing but a glimpse of a woman—dressed in a black T-shirt and a pair of men's white briefs and carrying a small backpack—slicing through a chain-link fence with bolt cutters before sprinting away across the tarmac.

I got hard thinking about Angeline wearing my clothes as she flew off into the night. After breaking into an airport and stealing a plane. After breaking into a hotel suite and stealing a ruby necklace.

After breaking into my heart and stealing the whole goddamn thing.

I'd never spent time considering what my dream woman would be like, but apparently she's on Interpol's Most Wanted list.

My mother always said I didn't like things easy.

I spent another two days at the resort after Tabby and Connor continued on the rest of their honeymoon and Darcy, Kai, and Juanita headed back to New York. I was determined to assist the local police in their investigation, but when it became apparent they worked on island time, I took matters into my own hands.

I talked to everyone at the hotel who'd interacted with Angeline. I hacked into the resort computers and pored through the video footage. I broke into Angeline's room after the police were gone and hunted for any clue that might point me in the right direction. *Her* direction.

I came up with zilch. She was *Gone Girl.*

But only for now.

Tabby was amused by the whole thing. And ridiculously unhelpful. She liked Angeline nearly as much as I did.

"I'd help you find her, but I'm on her side," she'd said brightly, kissing me goodbye as she and Connor got into their taxi to head for the airport.

"Fuckin' Hello Kitty," I'd muttered, shaking my head.

"That too, but here's the thing, Ryan." Tabby looked me dead in the eyes. "She's living life on her own terms. She's nobody's fool. You know how I feel about women like that."

*Jesus. The fuckin' crazy chick mutual admiration society.* "She's an outlaw, Tab."

"She's a badass."

"She lied to me! She drugged me!"

Tabby's gaze softened. "She didn't want to."

"How the fuck do you know that?"

She shook her head. "What you understand about women wouldn't fill a thimble, you know that?"

Then she got into the cab and left with Connor, who was chuckling like a real asshole the entire time. I had to drop and do fifty pushups just so I didn't punch someone.

My plan at that point was to go back to New York and regroup, but then I got a hit on a search spider I'd set up on

Metrix's computer system that trawled all the online news outlets, and it changed everything.

*Cessna stolen from St. Croix found abandoned in a field in a rural part of Cornwall.*

Cornwall is in southwestern England. That's about as far as a Cessna could fly from the Virgin Islands on one tank. And one hell of a trip across the North Atlantic for a lone pilot. It would probably take nine hours nonstop, maybe ten, mostly in the dark, completely over water.

Talk about grueling.

But still…Cornwall. It has one city. It's one of the poorest parts of the UK. Not exactly a great place to fence a fifteen-million-dollar ruby necklace. I took a look at a map to see if it might jiggle anything in my mind. Sure enough, it did.

Cornwall is a four-hour drive from London, one of the richest cities in the world.

With some of the oldest and most powerful crime syndicates in the world.

When I did a search of police reports for stolen vehicles in the Cornwall area within the past seventy-two hours, I got one hit…and the stolen car was found with switched license plates less than a day later in a parking garage in Chelsea, a suburb of London.

For the first time in two days, I could breathe again.

I spent the flight to London thinking about something else my mother used to say: *It's all fun and games until someone gets hurt.*

I had a bad feeling the fun-and-games part was behind me.

# 13

## MARIANA

After I finish my business with Genevieve, I take a taxi to the Victoria Coach Station and retrieve my bug-out bag from the storage locker I rented before I visited Reynard. Then I use the burner phone in it to reserve a suite at the Ritz-Carlton for the night because there's nothing on earth that could compel me to stay at the Palace while Capo is there. And I can't stay with Reynard. He'd take one look at my black-and-blue throat and do something stupid like go and confront Capo and get himself killed.

Reynard might be a lot of shady things, but a man who tolerates violence against women isn't one of them.

I pay for the room in cash. When the front desk associate requests a credit card for room incidentals, I use a prepaid Visa gift card I bought at a grocery store. I've already changed from the dress, heels, and overcoat I wore to the Palace—all stuffed into the train station bathroom garbage bin—into a nondescript outfit any tourist might wear: comfy shoes, ill-fitting beige slacks, and an oversized knitted sweater the color of baby shit. My hair is hidden under a short, curly black wig. I stole the reading glasses from a rack at a dime store.

Glimpsed in a lobby mirror, I look like someone who owns too many house cats.

I mouth *meow* to myself and head to my second-floor room. I never stay higher in any hotel, in case I need to make a speedy exit out a window or there's a fire. Reynard taught me that fire trucks in most countries have ladders that only reach the third floor. Apparently, he found that out the hard way.

Once I'm inside the room, some of the tension leaves my body. I draw a bath, take a long, hot soak, and try not to think. Tomorrow is for thinking. Tomorrow is for planning. Tonight is for washing the stink of Capo's cologne out of my nose and trying to pretend I live a different sort of life.

Of course the only thing my brain wants to do is serve up some nice, juicy memories of the American.

Cursing to myself in four different languages, I rise from the tub, stalk naked into the bedroom, and call room service. I need food, and if I'm ever going to get to sleep, I need something strong to drink. Then I get dressed, lie down on the bed, stare at the ceiling, and count cracks to distract myself.

When the knock comes, I go to the door and glance through the peephole.

A guy in a black-and-white uniform stands behind a cart draped in white linen. He's looking down, fussing over a place setting, so I can't see his face.

My fingers curl around the folding blade in my pocket. "Yes?" I call through the door.

He looks up, smiling. "Room service, madam."

He's no one. Just a hotel employee.

Or is he?

"One moment, please. Just getting dressed." I go to the phone and dial room service. They pick up on the first ring.

"Good evening, in-room dining, this is Gwendolyn," says a friendly female voice. "How may I be of service?"

"Hi, I'm calling from room two-oh-five. The gentleman who

delivered my food…" I pretend to think, then mutter, "Shoot. What did he say his name was?"

"Christopher was sent up with your order, Ms. Lane."

Penny Lane is the name I used to check in. And Christopher is the name inscribed on the gold tag on the chest of the man standing outside my door.

"Oh, yes, that's it. I just wanted to tell you he was wonderful."

I hang up before the woman on the other end of the line can respond.

I go to the door, unlock the dead bolt, remove the security chain, and stand aside to let Christopher in. "Sorry about the wait."

"It's no problem at all. Shall I set the food out on the table for you, madam?"

"No, don't bother. You can just leave it the cart by the desk. I'll call down when I'm finished."

"Very good." He rolls the cart to where I'm pointing, then produces a receipt for me to sign. On his way out the door, he wishes me a good night.

An hour later, I've got a full stomach and a nice buzz. I recheck the bolt on the door, then turn off the lights and crawl into bed. I'm asleep within minutes.

I awaken sometime near dawn, my skin prickling with a sixth sense that something is terribly wrong.

Reaching for the knife I'd stashed under my pillow as soon as I checked in, I quickly glance around the shadowed room.

Everything looks normal. There are no strange sounds, no odd scents in the air. The security chain is still latched on the door.

My nervous system isn't convinced.

I ease the knife out. It catches a moonbeam spilling through a gap in the curtains and throws a silver flash along the wall.

"Careful with that. You could cut yourself."

The voice, deep and male, comes from the bed beside me.

I leap from the mattress like it's on fire. I'm caught midair by a pair of big arms that cinch around me and drag me backward on my heels. I fight, trying to stab my attacker in the thigh, but I can't get enough leverage because my arms are pinned. I jerk my head back in an attempt to break his nose, but he's too fast. He dodges my move with an expert countermove and a chuckle.

"Aw, you don't seem happy to see me, Angel. My feelin's are hurt."

I freeze. "*You!*"

"The one and only, darlin'." He puts his nose into my hair, inhales, and says in a husky voice, "Don't stab me. I look better without holes."

The relief that washes over me is almost as powerful and unexpected as the surge of joy. I drop the knife, spin around, throw my arms around Ryan's shoulders, and bury my face into his neck.

"Oh. Uh…okay. I see we're changin' gears." He sounds surprised, then suspicious. "Or are you about to offer me some orange juice?"

I shake my head and burrow closer. His arms wind around me again, this time with infinite gentleness.

Trembling with adrenaline, I blurt, "I'm sorry."

The chuckle again. "For what? Lyin' to me? Usin' me? Seducin' me?"

I answer truthfully. "Everything but the last part."

Ryan laughs. He takes my face in his hands. In the shadows, his smiling face is so handsome, my breath catches. He says softly, "Hi."

"Hi yourself. How did you find me?"

"Told you I would. I keep my word. You'll learn. By the way, do you always sleep fully dressed?"

The answer is yes, but I ignore the question and ask one of my own. "On a scale of one to ten, how mad are you?"

"Ninety-four. You got a lotta makin' up to do."

The innuendo in his voice sends a shiver of delight down my spine, but I don't want to get ahead of myself. He could be about to put me in handcuffs.

"Are you going to turn me in to the police?"

"Do I seem like I'm in a big rush to do that?"

I narrow my eyes and inspect his face, then admit, "Not really."

"There you go."

We stare at each other. He brushes a knuckle over the rise of my cheek. "So you're a thief."

"And you're a mercenary."

"Not my preferred term, but yes. Gotta say I like your voice even better without the fake French accent. Tell me your real name."

"Um…Elizabeth."

He sighs.

"Lauren?"

He says flatly, "Cut it out."

I make a calculated gamble, because I know he'll be able to tell if I'm lying. Besides, he can't get far without a last name. There must be millions of women with my first name.

"Mariana."

He examines my expression, then nods. "Pretty. And unusual. Suits you. Mariana what?"

"Let's not get carried away, cowboy. This is only our second date."

"Yeah, but look how good the first one went." He adds sourly, "Except the end. That sucked big-time."

The staring recommences. I can tell he really wants to kiss me. He also wants to take me over his knee and spank my ass.

And not in the good way.

I admit sheepishly, "You have every right to be angry."

He cocks an eyebrow, drawls a sarcastic, "You think?"

"Yes." I take a steadying breath. "But I'm just so goddamn happy to see you, I hope you can ignore how mad you are for a second while I do this."

I stand on tiptoe and kiss him.

He responds instantly, a low groan rumbling through his chest, a big, rough hand digging into my hair. The other hand grips my bottom, dragging me closer. He drinks deeply from my mouth, pressing me against him so I feel him grow hard.

He breaks away first, chuckling, and says in a throaty voice, "Guess Tabby was right."

"What?"

"Never mind. Listen. Here's how this is gonna go. I'm gonna get us both naked. Then I'm gonna make love to you. Sweet this time, not rough, 'cause you gave up the right to dictate terms when you pulled a spider monkey and crawled off the balcony and left me feelin' like a dipshit. Which is a pet peeve of mine, by the way. Then we're gonna talk—"

"Talk?" I repeat, a note of panic in my voice.

"Talk," he says firmly. "Like normal people do after sex."

I laugh a little breathlessly. "You think we're normal people?"

"Shut up. After the talk, you are *not* gonna dose me with drugs. You are *not* gonna disappear. What you *are* gonna do is tell me who did that to your throat so I can kill him."

All the air leaves my lungs. We're eye to eye, so he can see what his words have done to me, how terrified I suddenly am.

My voice breaking, I say, "I can't."

He growls, "You mean you won't."

I shake my head. "No. I mean I *can't*. And that's not a lie. It's just…" I blink away the sudden, awful memory of bloodied bodies lying motionless on burgundy carpet. "It's just that I work for monsters. One of the cardinal rules of monsters is you're not allowed to tell anyone they exist. And it's not only my life that ends if I disobey the rules."

He studies my face in silence. "So you're not a thief by choice."

"I've been a thief since I was six years old. It's what I do. It's who I am."

"It's how you survived, maybe, but it's not who you are."

I try to pull away, but Ryan doesn't allow it. He holds me in place, gently but firmly, and says, "I can help you."

My laugh is short and bitter. "Don't be a cliché. I'm not a damsel in distress, and you're no knight in shining armor."

"Not to toot my own horn, Angel, but my armor is so fuckin' shiny, it'd blind the sun. *I can help you.*"

This conversation is making me emotional, something I detest more than men who wear argyle socks. "I don't want to talk about this."

"Tough shit," he replies, and swings me up into his arms. Then he deposits me on the bed and lies on top of me.

If I didn't like it so much, I'd fish the other knife from the under the pillow and aerate him.

"Now look," he says, sounding reasonable. He braces his elbows on either side of my shoulders and props his chin on his hands. "You don't know about me, but I'm kinda the shit."

When I make a face, he smiles. I close my eyes and mutter, "Unbelievable."

"Ahem. As I was saying—I'm kinda the shit. I don't have my bio with me, but you'll just have to take my word that it's real impressive—"

"Oh. My. God."

"—and my major spec-i-al-i-ty—"

"That word doesn't have five syllables."

"—is rescuin' people from bad situations."

I think for a moment. "Like the Karpov situation?"

His eyes narrow. "You know him?"

"No. You mentioned him the night we had dinner with your friends at the resort restaurant."

Ryan looks pleased. "You were payin' attention."

Like a big baby, I hide my face under his forearm. "I paid attention to everything you said."

"Yeah?" he murmurs, his voice warm. "And why's that, Angel?"

I don't reply. What can I say? Because everything you said was interesting? Because I was infatuated with you from the moment I laid eyes on you? Because you're beautiful and sexy and so adorable, it melts my black heart?

No. Obviously I'm not saying any of that.

Ryan dips his head and nuzzles my ear. "Just admit it. I dazzle you," he whispers, then softly laughs.

"Shut up."

"Make me."

"Take off your clothes."

"Bossy!"

"We've already established that you like that, so do as you're told and get naked, cowboy. This room is only rented for one night."

There's a wicked gleam in his eyes that hints at secret plans. But he's not the only one with plans. He might be a good bloodhound, but I'm an even better escape artist. No matter what he's got planned for me, I'll be gone before he can play it out.

I don't want to go, but doing what I want is a luxury I don't have. I've got the world's largest blue diamond to steal within ten days. Time's a wastin'.

"I think *you* should take off my clothes," says Ryan, "since you have so much makin' up to do and all."

"If I do, will you tell me how you found me?"

"No. Duh." He pauses. "But I will if you leave with me tonight."

"Leave? What do you mean, *leave*?"

"You've got a nice big vocab, Angel, I think you know the meanin' of the word."

My heart thuds at a thunderous volume, like a fat person clomping down stairs. *Is he saying what I think he's saying?* "So...just to clarify..."

"You come back to New York with me and let me take care of your situation so we can get started on our happily ever after."

My mouth is open. I can't get it to close. I can't get any words to come out of it, either. I just stare up at him in disbelief while he smiles calmly down at me like he's just suggested we order in for pizza.

"You're cute when you're speechless, Angel. Can't wait to see what happens when I get down on a knee and—"

"Stop it! And stop calling me Angel! Get off me!"

"No, no, and no." He refuses to budge as I try to wrestle him off. The damn man is too big, too strong, and too stubborn to move an inch.

In that maddeningly reasonable way he has, he says, "You think this kinda shit happens every day? You think two people meet and have thermonuclear chemistry and make each other laugh and have mind-blowing sex, and then one of them steals a fifteen-million-dollar necklace and disappears and the other one finds the first one within a few days and breaks into her hotel room and almost gets stabbed but ends up on top of her in bed?"

When I don't respond because I'm too mind-fucked to answer, Ryan says, "The answer to all that is no. Now get on board, Angel, because this train has already left the station."

After a long time, I manage to say, "Who told you how much the necklace was worth?"

He sighs like I'm the biggest idiot who's ever lived. "You have a bad habit of focusing on all the wrong things, you know that?"

I blow out a breath and close my eyes because my clomping heart is making me dizzy. I say in a strangled voice, "That's an amazing offer, cowboy, but I can't leave with you. It would be a death sentence for someone I love."

He's quiet for a moment, stroking a thumb over my earlobe, then he presses the softest of kisses to my jaw. "Mariana, I can help you. That isn't bullshit. It isn't ego. It's the truth. I've got a team of badass motherfuckers trained by the United States military in heroics and general mayhem who can be here within hours to back me up. We'll get your people, and then we'll get the fuck outta Dodge."

"There's nowhere I can run! They'll find me!"

"*Who* will?"

I open my eyes. Ryan stares down at me with dangerous intensity burning in his gaze. It breaks my heart how serious he is about helping me.

He doesn't realize I'm a lost cause, or that I've already got one foot out the window.

"The monsters."

"Not if I get them first."

I want to scream in frustration. "You don't understand!"

"So educate me."

"I can't!"

"You keep sayin' that word. Like you forgot you have somethin' called free will."

I say bitterly, "Free will is for people who haven't sworn blood oaths to—"

The words die in my mouth. Horror at my blunder rises up in their place. When I look up at Ryan, a wolf is looking back down at me.

"Blood oath?" he repeats, deadly soft. "We talkin' Cosa Nostra? The Sicilian mob?"

My entire body breaks out in goose bumps. I say firmly, "No."

His laugh is short and dark. "Oh, okay. Sure. That was totally believable."

I turn my face to his arm and close my eyes again, cursing myself for my stupidity and him for seeing through me like a pane of clear glass, which no one—with the possible exception of Reynard—ever does.

Ryan says, "So this is good. We're makin' progress! Now all you gotta do is tell me who else we're takin' with us and—"

"Please don't."

"Don't what?"

I swallow a sob. "Make it sound like a hypothetical. Like it could actually happen. I stopped believing in fairy tales a long time ago."

Ryan takes my face in his hands. He says softly, "Maybe they didn't stop believin' in you."

When he kisses me, it's like a promise. Like he's making a blood oath of his own.

*This man is going to be the death of me.*

I wrap my arms around his neck and kiss him back with everything I have, my heart shattering into a million jagged pieces.

Because his kiss is a promise, but mine is a goodbye.

# 14

## RYAN

Just when I'm about to rip off all her clothes, Mariana breaks the kiss and looks away. Sounding embarrassed, she says, "Um. I have to…before we…I have to go to the bathroom."

"I really don't care if you shaved your legs or not, sweetheart."

"I have to pee!"

"Well, why didn't you just say so?" I sit up, help her sit up, and grin at her, because she's wearing a look like she can't decide whether or not to smack me or start kissing me again.

Then I catch sight of her neck, mottled with bruises above the collar of the hideous turd-colored sweater she's wearing, and my grin dies a quick death.

Whoever the bastard is that did that to her, he's gonna have to answer to me.

And then he's gonna wish he'd never been born.

"It looks worse than it is," she mutters, covering her throat with her hand. Before I can say anything, she goes into to the bathroom and closes the door. The water turns on. I picture her standing at the mirror looking at her bruised neck with those big, beautiful eyes, and I want to break all the furniture in the room with my bare hands.

I blow out a hard breath and stand, turning on the bedside lamp. I can't stay in one place, so I start to pace. I remove my leather jacket, toss it onto a chair, and listen to the sound of the toilet flushing.

*There's nowhere I can run. They'll find me. It would be a death sentence for someone I love.*

Whatever shit she's mixed up in, it's bad. And if it's really Cosa Nostra, it's pretty much the worst it could be. The real Italian Mafia makes *The Sopranos* look like *Sesame Street.*

Thinking about it makes me antsy. I go to the sliding-glass door of the balcony and step out into the cool, misty night. The fresh air is bracing. Even at this hour, the sounds of taxis honking and people talking drift up from the street below. Like New York, London is a city that never sleeps.

I don't know how long I stand there looking out at the city lights, but at some point it occurs to me that Mariana is taking a really long time to pee.

I whirl around and stare at the closed bathroom door. I'm across the room in a few seconds, knocking on it.

"Angel? You okay in there?"

No response.

*Fuck.*

I try the door handle. Locked. "Mariana?"

Nothing.

"Okay. You wanna do this the hard way? We're doin' it the hard way." I step back, wind up, and give the door a brutal kick.

It splinters off its hinges and flies open, crashing to the tiled floor with an echoing *boom.* I stride into the bathroom, my head whipping from side to side, already knowing what I'll find.

Or, more correctly, what I *won't* find.

"This fuckin' broad," I mutter, staring at the open window above the bathtub. The bathtub is the old-fashioned claw kind, made of cast iron, heavy as a cement coffin. Around one of the feet is tied the corner of a bedsheet.

The rest of the bedsheet hangs out the window.

I rush to the tub, jump in, and lean over the windowsill. Sheets dangle all the way to the manicured boxwood shrubs planted along the side of the building two stories below. An elderly couple with a Corgi on a leash are staring up at me from the sidewalk. The dog is staring at me, too.

The man's voice drifts up on a current of cool air. "Lost something, have you, mate?"

His wife titters. I resist the urge to flip them off.

Mariana is nowhere to be seen.

I don't bother asking the couple if they saw the direction she ran. I simply withdraw into the bathroom, untie the knot from the foot of the tub, toss the sheet out the window, and pull the window shut. Then I go into the other room and turn on the TV.

She said she had the room for the night, after all. Pity to waste it. Besides, I need to give her a head start.

What's that old saying about giving someone just enough rope to hang himself?

I call room service and order a cheeseburger and a beer. Then I pull my cell phone from the pocket inside my jacket and navigate to the tracking app synced with the tiny GPS I stuck on the back of Mariana's ugly sweater.

The screen glows with a red dot, moving steadily south of the Ritz.

Smiling, I settle into the big armchair in front of the TV and wait for my food.

~

Standing across the street from Mallory & Sons Heritage Auctions in the morning fog, I think it could be a different century for how old-fashioned the place looks. Even the street feels like something out of a period movie, with its gas lamps and cobblestones. Only the taxi trundling by ruins the illusion. I almost expected a horse and carriage to turn the corner instead.

A cheerful bell rings when I push through the front door. The place smells like incense and old books. Jazz plays softly in the background. A man looks up from a big oak counter carved with a weird battle scene involving dragons and meets my gaze with a level one of his own.

We size each other up.

He's somewhere north of fifty, neither young or old, neither handsome or ugly, dressed in an average dark-blue suit. Joe Average.

I get the sense his average appearance is carefully crafted.

I also get the sense he's been expecting me.

Strolling in his direction, I take in everything about the room, including the security cameras masquerading as speakers on the walls. When I get to the counter, I lean my elbow on it and give him a corn-fed, backcountry dumbass smile meant to convey I'm not a threat, and might even be a little slow on the uptake.

He stares at me. His left eyebrow slowly lifts into a condescending arch. In a tone so dry it's practically dust, he says, "Is that what they're teaching in the American military now? How subtle. I've seen bulldozers with more finesse."

I instantly decide I like him. "Haven't been in the military for a long time, pal," I reply. "I'm just a smiler."

His tone grows even more disapproving. "The smiling American. How cliché."

I say softly, "I'm anything but a cliché, friend. Where is she?"

His lips purse. He exhales a small, annoyed breath. If he rolls his eyes, I might have to punch him in the face.

"She?" he repeats, a little cattily, I think.

"Mariana."

He blinks, taken aback, but quickly recovers, smoothing a hand over his tie as his face shifts into a neutral expression.

"You're surprised she told me her real name." I'm feeling all kinds of macho and self-satisfied. I resist the urge to puff out my chest and calmly gaze at him instead.

He folds his hands on the counter and drills me with a look. "If you knew her the way I know her, you'd be surprised, too." His gaze drifts over my leather bomber jacket to my jeans, then flicks up to my hair, which I combed by dragging my fingers through it. His mouth takes on the shriveled appearance of a prune. "You'd be *very* surprised indeed."

I dig that he's not trying to pretend he doesn't know who I'm talking about. And I don't take it personally that he obviously thinks Mariana's too good for me. We're pretty much on the same page there.

Even if she is an international jewel thief wanted by *all* the police.

I straighten, fold my arms across my chest, and smile wider.

He closes his eyes and shakes his head.

"Listen, buddy—"

"It's Reynard," he interrupts. "Please refrain from calling me any more nicknames. A grinning American addressing me as friend, buddy, and pal is quite literally my definition of hell."

"No need to get pissy. And what d'you have against Americans, anyway? We saved your asses in World War II. If it wasn't for us, you'd all be speaking German."

"Let's not get into a debate about history, Mr. McLean. I never enter into a battle of wits with an unarmed opponent."

Bypassing the zinger—which I have to admit is a good one—I say smugly, "So she told you about me."

From his coat pocket, Reynard withdraws a pair of glasses. Snooty as shit, he puts them on and looks down his nose at me. "Don't flatter yourself. I looked you up in a database."

By now my grin must be blinding. "But you had to know my name in order to look me up."

After a pause, he says, "I'm jealous of all the people who haven't met you."

"Tell me where she is."

His irritation is palpable. "Mr. McLean—"

"I can help her," I insist, bracing my arms on the counter and getting into his face. "Whatever trouble she's in, I can get her out of."

He stares at me for a long time, his gaze sharp and assessing. "You're an interesting man, Mr. McLean, I'll give you that. But you seem to be operating under the mistaken impression that your help is wanted."

"You talkin' about you, or her?"

A muscle in his jaw flexes. "I think it's time for you to leave."

I drop the nice-guy act and growl, "And I think it's time for you to realize that dumb motherfuckers who stand in the way of something I want have extremely shortened lifespans. Tell me where she is and where she lives, or I'll break every bone in your body."

His patience finally snaps. Eyes blazing with fury, he whips off his glasses and lays into me.

"This might surprise you, you gargantuan idiot, but you're not the first man on earth to threaten my life, nor would you be the first to cause me harm for protecting her! And if you had even *one* functioning brain cell, you'd realize that a woman in her position would *never* tell *anyone* where she lived—especially someone like me who could be pressured by someone like you into giving up that information! For the love of all that's holy, I have no idea what she sees in you! You're proof that evolution can go in reverse!"

Red-faced, he huffs. He jerks the glasses back onto his face.

Then he peers at me through them and shouts, "Why the bloody hell are you smiling again?"

I cross my arms over my chest and drawl, "So she told you she likes me."

He grits his teeth so hard, I think they might shatter. "Get out."

I cock my head, pretending to think, then say, "Nah. I think I'll just wait for my buddies from Interpol to show up and take a little gander 'round the place. You looked me up in a database? Well, I looked you up too, brother. Real nice establishment you got here. Real legit. Squeaky clean, at least on paper."

I peer over his shoulder toward the back of the shop. "I'm sure you don't have anything to hide, right? No random ruby necklaces hangin' around? Big ones, maybe a hundred carats?"

I already knew it wasn't Reynard Mallory who bruised Mariana's neck, even before I set foot in his shop. I pegged him as her fence the minute I entered his address into Metrix's search program and took a look at his business. If anyone can move a hot, one-hundred-carat ruby necklace, it's Mallory & Sons Heritage Auctions. It has branches all over the globe and a sterling reputation unvarnished by its secret, long-standing ties to every underworld organization that exists.

He says stiffly, "Your bluffs are as unfortunate as your fashion sense, Mr. McLean. I have a high-ranking friend on the police force who would have alerted me if Interpol were about to pay me a visit."

Then, with no small satisfaction, he says, "But I do have a GPS tracking device you might be interested in. It's small and extremely light, excellent for hiding in clothing. Unfortunately it's nonfunctional, due to being smashed by the heel of a shoe—whose owner was spewing some rather colorful language at the time, I might add—so it won't do you much good."

*So that's why I lost the signal. Somehow Mariana found the tracker and destroyed it.*

*Which means she knew I'd come here…which means she's gone.*

*Again.*

*Shouldn't have ordered that cheeseburger.*

As a jazz number that sounds like five different guys are playing five different songs comes on the speakers, Reynard and I glare at each other. After a while, I say, "Okay. Two things. Number one, I'm gonna give you a cell phone number. It's unregistered and untraceable. Only one other person in the world has it—"

"Your therapist?" he asks sweetly.

"Funny. I'm gonna give you my number, and you're gonna give it to Mariana."

His expression sours. Before he can tell me to go jump off the nearest bridge, I add, "In case of an emergency, she can call me twenty-four seven on that number. I mean it. Day or night. From anywhere in the world, she can call me, and I'll come."

I grab a pen from a cup next to the cash register and scribble my number on a yellow Post-it note, then stick it to the center of Reynard's tie. He peels it off with two fingers, his pinky held out and his lip curled. I'm surprised he doesn't pinch his nose.

He mutters "Stupendous" and puts the Post-it between the pages of a book he lifts from under the counter. Then he tosses the book back into place with derision, dusting off his hands.

*Cheeky son of a bitch.*

"Number *two*, I want you to tell me who did that to her neck so I can have a talk with him. And by talk, I mean beat him to a pulp."

Reynard freezes. "You're playing a very dangerous game, Mr. McLean," he says with a strange stillness in his entire aspect, even his voice.

I send him a hard stare. "I'm not playing any game, Reynard. I've never been more serious in my life. Someone hurt my girl. That shit doesn't stand. He's lucky if I leave him breathing."

He blinks rapidly, as if clearing his vision. "Your…*girl*?"

I make a dismissive gesture, then park my hands on my hips. "She's not a hundred percent on board with the program yet, but I'll get her there. I'm irresistible, as you can tell."

His laugh is faint and disbelieving. He reaches for the porcelain teacup sitting to his left on the counter and gulps from it, his Adam's apple bobbing. Then he reaches under the counter again, this time to produce a slender silver flask. He uncaps it, pours a small measure of what looks like whiskey into the tea, then decides to drink directly from the flask instead.

When I say, "She loves you, you know," he violently coughs, spraying a mist of golden liquid over the counter. When his coughing fit is over, he stares at me with watering eyes and an open mouth.

Man, I dig shocking the shit out of people.

"At least I'm *assuming* you're the person Mariana was talkin' about when she turned down my offer to take her back to the States with me because it would be a death sentence for someone she loved. She ran straight here like she was runnin' home. Figured this had to be her safe place."

He makes a strangled sound and clutches his throat. He wheezes, "*Take her with you?*"

"And you, if she wants. Both of you would have my protection."

He looks me up and down with wide eyes, like I'm off my fucking rocker.

"Christ," I say, insulted. "The two of you are really shit for my ego, you know that?"

"She took advantage of you. She lied to you. Why on *earth* would you offer to take her anywhere but prison?" Reynard asks, like he really can't fathom it.

I shrug. "Because I care about her."

He gapes at me. "Are you on drugs?"

"She moves me, Reynard. You have any idea what it takes for a man like me to be moved? By anything? Ever?"

His face goes through several different expressions before settling on something I can't quite comprehend. There's a darkness there, an old memory maybe, something rattling around in a grave.

He murmurs, "Yes. Yes, actually, I do."

I sense an opening and press my advantage. Leaning closer to him, I say, "Let me hel—"

The bell over the door in front of the shop jangles.

Reynard looks over my shoulder. Instantly, his eyes shutter. Something about his posture changes, softens. Even his face somehow becomes more indistinct. Suddenly, I'm looking at Average Joe again, the man you couldn't pick out of a crowd, who could easily vanish into it instead.

In a voice meant to carry, he says, "You just have to continue east for two more blocks, sir. The entrance to the tube is on Chancery Lane. You can't miss the signs."

His eyes convey a warning as real as his words are fake.

*Go. Now.*

I glance over my shoulder. Two beefy olive-skinned men in suits with suspicious bulges in odd places flank the door. They look at me with that flat, killer gaze I've seen a thousand times before.

"Thanks, man," I say cheerfully, turning back to Reynard. "This city's just so huge, ya know?" I laugh an unselfconscious, touristy laugh. "Way bigger'n my hometown. I keep gettin' lost! Have yourself a nice day!"

I turn and saunter toward the men, smiling my dumbass backcountry smile again. On them, it works, because they both give me a quick once-over, then dismiss me and turn their attention to Reynard. I walk out the front door, whistling, then stand on the sidewalk and pretend to look for a street sign while I memorize the plates on the stretch limo parked at the curb across the street.

The back window is rolled halfway down. I catch a glimpse of a face in the shadows of the interior. It's a man, black-haired and unsmiling, with hard, shining eyes swimming in darkness, like coins glinting in the bottom of a wishing well.

Every nerve in my body slams into Defcon One. If I were a fire alarm, I'd have sirens sounding and emergency lights blazing.

*"I work for monsters,"* Mariana had said.

I damn sure know a monster when I see one.

I turn and casually stroll down the sidewalk, keeping my posture easy, not looking back even though there's an animal inside me, clawing at my skin, roaring at me to go back and introduce the black-haired man to the barrel of my gun.

When I'm safely around the corner and out of sight, I yank my cell phone from my pocket and dial Connor's number. When his voicemail picks up, I say, "Sorry to bother you on your honeymoon, brother, but I'm gonna need to borrow your wife."

This situation calls for a bigger brain than my own, and if anyone knows how to root a monster from its nest, it's Tabby.

I hang up and put a pair of earbuds in my ears. From my phone I activate the bug I stuck under Reynard's counter when I came in. I start to listen as I duck into a pub across the street.

## 15

## MARIANA

"All clear! You can come out now!"

Reynard's voice is muffled through the heavy stone lid of the sarcophagus I'm lying in. I press a button next to my left hand and the lid slides open on pneumatic rollers installed specifically for its current use: hiding people.

I climb out, dust myself off, and look at Reynard. He stands with his arms folded over his chest, staring at me with such disapproval, I wince.

"Don't say it. I already know."

He says acidly, "Know what, my darling? That you led your *inamorato* right to me? That you broke every rule we have? That he could single-handedly ruin us both?"

Groaning, I walk past him on my way to the back of the shop and the hidden exits I can access through the warehouse. "I said don't say it!"

Reynard follows right on my heels. "Not to mention you got another job added to your oath because of a foolish impulse—"

"Trying to help those girls wasn't foolish!" I whirl around, heat crawling up my neck, and glare at him. "What was I supposed to do, sit there and drink champagne while their throats were slit in a room down the hall? Let them suffer like Nina did? Is that what you would've had me do? Not even *try* to save their lives?"

My shouted words die in lingering echoes in the rafters.

More gently, Reynard says, "Capo would've savaged you, Mariana, and still would've done as he pleased with them. As it is, we're fortunate he even let you walk out of that room. I told you to be careful. Instead, you took a sharp stick and poked a sleeping bear."

"Well, he has his necklace now," I say bitterly. "So he got what he wanted."

"That's not what he wants, and you know it."

I swallow the bile rising in the back of my throat.

"I don't know why he didn't take advantage of your offer. Perhaps he still has some small shred of humanity left. But I dare say that kind of luck is once in a lifetime. Poke the bear again, and I have no doubt you'll be eaten alive."

I told Reynard everything when I arrived, including what happened with Ryan in the Caribbean, what Capo did to me at the Palace, and how Ryan found me at the Ritz. It was only by chance that I pulled off my sweater and a strand of my hair caught on the small metal tracking device under the collar. I destroyed it immediately, but not before swearing a blue streak mostly directed at myself.

Mostly.

"Thank you for the advice. Now, if you don't mind, I have a plane to Washington, DC, to catch and the world's largest blue diamond to steal, or the bear is *really* going to have something to be angry about."

I turn and continue down the aisle. Again, Reynard follows so closely behind, I'm surprised he doesn't trip me.

"We need to talk about your American."

"He isn't my American."

"Oh-ho! Really? Perhaps someone should inform *him* of that fact. The man is completely infatuated with you!"

"He's probably taken a lot of hard hits to the head. He's a soldier."

"Good God!" he scoffs. "If what you know about men was made into a book, it would be filled with blank pages! He *was* a soldier. Now he's a hired gun with a hard-on for a woman whose life is beholden to one of the most dangerous criminals who's ever lived. It's a Shakespearean tragedy in the making!"

"If you're trying to make me feel better, you're completely failing."

"I'm trying to make you have a conversation. Mariana, stop."

Reynard clasps my shoulder, pulls me up short, and turns me to face him. He says, "Do you know what a hero needs more than anything else?"

"Great hair? A compelling backstory? A cool name and a cape?"

"A *villain.* And do you know what happens when a hero *finds* his villain?"

"They live happily ever after in the pages of a comic book?"

Radiating annoyance, Reynard purses his lips and exhales.

I ditch the jokes and answer seriously. "War."

"Exactly," Reynard replies softly, nodding. "And if you don't shake your American, he's going to start a war with the Devil and drag us all into hell."

"You're forgetting that I already shook him."

"Did you? Because I get the feeling the man is a little more resourceful than you're giving him credit for."

Aggravated—because he's right—I pull *Oliver Twist* from the bookshelf. It yawns open, revealing the dank tunnel beyond.

Reynard sighs, realizing I'm not going to respond. When he speaks again, he sounds resigned. "He'll be watching the shop.

We have to assume he'll have video surveillance on us within hours, if he doesn't already."

"I know."

"Which means you can't come back—"

"I *know*!"

At my sharp tone, he stiffens. I blow out a hard breath and scrub my hands over my face.

"I'm sorry. I know this is my fault. I know I messed up. He's just so…he's so…" I search for the right word, but can only come up with one. "Beautiful. In every way. I've never met anyone like him. He makes me feel like I'm worth something." My voice breaks. "He makes me feel like I could be someone better than I am."

With infinite gentleness, Reynard strokes a hand over my hair. "We're creatures of the underworld, my darling. We have no business in the dealings of heroes."

My throat constricts. I whisper, "Just once, I'd like to be a hero, too."

Reynard watches in astonishment as a tear crests my lower lid and slides down my cheek. Then he surprises me by engulfing me in a hard, heartfelt hug.

"It will all be over soon," he whispers, an odd vibration in his voice. "You'll honor the oath and then you'll be free. Then you can live whatever kind of life you like, anywhere in the world."

I squeeze my eyes shut, loving the sound of those words, but knowing in a dark part of my soul that they're untrue.

Capo will find a way to keep me, blood oath or no. All these years and all these jobs to pay off a debt have been more than promises kept. They've been a safety net.

Without that safety net, it's going to be a fast and hard fall straight into the arms of a monster.

I pull away, wipe my cheeks, and force a smile. "Here." I hand Reynard the copy of *Oliver Twist*. "Keep this safe for me. You know it's my favorite."

He takes it, cradles it against his chest, and looks at me with a goodbye in his gaze. His next words almost break my heart.

"See you on the other side, my darling."

I run into the tunnel before he can see the fresh tears welling in my eyes.

~

At two o'clock in the morning a week later, I'm breaking into the Smithsonian Institution.

I've left my hot-wired Mini Cooper not far from the Federal Triangle Metro station and am headed swiftly on foot toward an industrial heating unit adjacent to the butterfly habitat garden on the museum grounds. I've already switched the Mini's plates, but if it's somehow identified in my short absence, the Metro will provide another quick escape route.

On the side of the large aluminum heating structure, I crouch down behind a thicket of shrubs, sling my backpack off my shoulders, remove a pair of safety goggles and thick nitrile gloves, and don them both. Then I uncap a glass beaker filled with a viscous greenish liquid and tip it against the aluminum, working quickly to draw a four-foot square.

In a few moments, the liquid reacts with the metal and starts to bubble. Soon it has eaten through enough for me to pry the square loose with a flathead screwdriver. Leaving it and the empty beaker on the grass, I put the screwdriver and goggles back into my pack, sling it over my shoulders, and crawl inside the heating duct on hands and knees, carefully avoiding all the corroded edges.

It's silent and black as a crypt, except for the hazy yellow beam from the pen-size Maglite clenched between my teeth.

From my entry point, I navigate slowly through the heating ducts into the southeast wing on the second floor of the Natural

History Museum. At this time of night, the security staff is at its thinnest, but I'm careful to make as little noise as possible. Contrary to how it looks in the movies, breaking into buildings through HVAC vents can be extraordinarily loud if one isn't careful.

And extraordinarily dangerous if one isn't light. Aluminum ducting isn't made to hold the weight of a grown man. A two-hundred-pound male would crash right through the ceiling.

And judging by the dent my left knee just made, I should probably cut back on the carbs.

After what feels like forever, I reach the Gems and Minerals Hall, where the Hope is displayed. I pop the grating off an access panel and peer down into the museum. It's dark, quiet, eerily still. The only sound is the wild thrumming of my heart.

Since the floor is a dozen feet below me, I've brought a rope knotted with footholds. I tie it off around a metal connector fitting, then slither down, leaving the Maglite on the lip of the duct for the trip back.

I land on the floor in a soundless crouch on one hand and one knee. Then I'm up in a whip-crack movement, headed toward my next target, the museum's computer system, only a short jog away from where I've entered. The lock on the door is a biometric fingerprint scanner, but it's a simple pattern-matching sensor unit, easily fooled.

Inside the room is a large computer terminal that runs the museum's custom software. It's secured by a username and password, but I already have those, too. I log into the system and navigate to the security portal. Then I alter the museum's hours of operation, setting opening time to one minute ago.

Before I hit *save changes*, I scrawl my signature dragonfly icon on the screen with magic marker and take a deep breath.

The interior of the museum is about to light up like a football stadium. Once that happens, I only have sixty seconds at most to get the diamond and get back into the ducts before guards swarm the entire wing and I'm trapped.

I exhale, say a silent prayer, and press the button.

The room floods with light.

As fast as I can, I run out of the computer office and through a door that leads into the Geology Hall. Almost instantly, I spot the Hope Diamond's display case. Because I've set the museum to open, the case has erected itself from the floor as it does automatically during public viewing hours.

And because every light in the museum has turned on and all the perimeter doors have unlocked, all the guards in the vicinity of the west wing are now aware that something is wrong.

Forty seconds.

The illuminated pedestal of marble and security glass that holds the Hope stands alone in the middle of the room. The glass is too thick to break with ordinary means like a hammer, and it would take far too long to cut through with a UV laser or dental bur, so I'm manipulating sound frequencies instead. I take a battery-operated ultrasound shock wave generator from the backpack, press the focus tubes against the glass, turn the dial to the highest decibel setting, and switch it on.

Alarms blare overhead. The noise is deafening. I can't even hear the sound of the safety glass as it splinters into a spiderweb of cracks.

Thirty seconds.

Because the glass is laminated, it stays in a single sheet instead of exploding. I have to punch out a hole with a rubber mallet to get to the diamond, which—because the excessive vibration has triggered an internal sensor—is rapidly descending into the base. I snatch it from its velvet perch just before the vault closes over it.

The Hope is as big as my fist, dark as a sapphire, glittering like it's alive. I stuff it into my backpack and sprint back to my rope, still dangling from the ceiling. Using the footholds, I climb up to the ducts, pull the rope in, then crawl like mad, listening to the sirens and men's frantic shouts. Boots pound against the floor below as guards flood Geology Hall.

I make it out with seconds to spare. Now I don't have to be quiet, I only have to be swift.

When I finally see the square opening I entered through, the night sky sparkling with stars beyond, elation floods me like wildfire.

My skin is electric. Every sense is sharpened. Every nerve is a firecracker.

I'm invincible. Euphoric.

Alive.

Grinning like mad, I tumble out of the duct and sprint through the butterfly garden. The Mini is still parked right where I left it. I gun it and fly down a side street toward my safe house, cold wind whipping through my hair from the open window, a hot pulse of victory burning through my veins.

*I did it! I did it! I actually pulled it off!*

I take a corner at top speed, but am immediately forced to come to a screeching, tire-smoking halt, because the street in front of me is blocked by a line of police cars.

My heart stops. My stomach drops. My mind wipes blank, except for a name, played on repeat.

*Reynard.*

My capture equals his death warrant.

In front of the line of black-and-whites stands a large man with his legs braced apart, his arms crossed over his chest. I can't see who it is because all the police vehicles have their headlamps on and emergency lights running, but then he steps forward, and his face clears from the shadows.

All I can focus on is his grin.

His perfect, shit-eating, American grin.

Rage erupts inside me like a supernova exploding into space. "*SON OF A—*"

"Peach farmer, actually." Ryan leans down to look at me, his blue eyes shining with mirth. "But you probably already knew that, didn't you, Angel?"

He reaches through the open window and wraps his hand firmly around my wrist.

# 16

## RYAN

Whoever coined the phrase "If looks could kill" would have to create something substantially worse than death if he saw the expression on Mariana's face right now.

Her look isn't simply murderous. There's a war behind her eyes. Planets are being destroyed. Entire universes are getting incinerated by the sheer heat, power, and enormity of her fury.

It's so cute, I want to kiss her.

I open the door and pull her from the car, listening to her sputter, "You lying, scheming, untrustworthy *prick*!"

I chuckle. "Uh, hello, kettle? Yeah, it's the pot calling. We'd like our hypocrisy back. At least I didn't drug your OJ."

Her back is so stiff, her spine might be in danger of snapping. The whites of her eyes glow all around the pupils. She's pulling hard against my grip, but she's not going anywhere.

Not without me, anyway.

I lean in close to her ear. "I like this outfit, by the way. Very heroin chic. Nice touches with the filthy hoodie and the dirt smudged on your face. You must fit in real nice with all the drug addicts and indigents at that fleabag motel you've been holed up in for the past week while you planned the job, hmm?"

She makes a noise I heard a man make once right before he shot me. It's a real hair-raiser of a hiss, vicious as all get-out, like some unholy combination of a badger and a rattler and Nosferatu on the hunt.

Coming from her, it's as hot as a naked roll in a habanero patch.

If I didn't have the wool to pull over everyone's eyes right now, I'd drag her off into the bushes and have my way with her, filthy clothes and dirt stains be damned.

Her voice a raw scrape of betrayal, she says, "You just killed him, you know! I hope you're proud of yourself! I hope you can sleep easy knowing you've got Reynard's blood all over your hands, you heartless—"

"Oh ye of little faith." I tweak her nose. "Be quiet now, woman, your man's got work to do."

Her expression is priceless. *Priceless.* I wish I had a camera. This is one for the books.

Grinning, I turn back to the squad cars and yell, "Zuckerman! C'mon over here and meet my colleague! I told you she could do it!"

Mariana goes slack against my grip. She makes a small retching sound, like a cat trying to expel a hairball.

I have to bite my lip to stop from laughing out loud.

A pudgy, sweating, middle-aged bald man in a gray suit pushes past the policemen milling around their squad cars and heads toward us with a sheepish smile. He sends Mariana a little wave.

She mutters, "What. The. Ever. Loving. Fuck."

Smiling at the approaching Zuckerman, I reply under my breath. "Just savin' your ass, honey. You can thank me later. I've got some real good ideas how."

"Ms. Lane!"

In his enthusiasm, Zuckerman practically falls on top of Mariana. He grabs her hand and pumps it up and down like he's trying to inflate her. "I'm so pleased to meet you!" He laughs nervously, his cheeks a damp, cherubic pink. "I know I probably shouldn't be thrilled that you pulled it off, but I've been telling the board for *years* that we needed to update our security protocols. And now I have proof, thanks to you! We'll definitely get that funding I applied for now!"

In response, Mariana faintly wheezes.

I suggest, "Why don't we go inside and have some coffee, and Ms. Lane can debrief you and your head of security about what holes you need to plug in your system, yeah?"

"Oh yes, definitely, I want to hear *all* about it!" Zuckerman says with glee. "Oh goodness. I hope I get a promotion out of this. You're a *genius*, Ms. Lane. When Mr. McLean approached us this week with his offer to do a penetration test, I must admit I had my doubts that this kind of thing actually worked, but I'm so happy to say I was wrong!"

He claps, hopping a little.

Mariana looks like she's been Tasered.

Zuckerman waves us toward a squad car. "Let's have one of the boys drop us off at the main entrance. I hate to go anywhere on foot, don't you?" He turns and starts to amble away, but stops when I call, "Mr. Zuckerman."

He turns back to me. "Yes, Mr. McLean?"

"Aren't you forgetting something?"

He blinks like a baby bird. Then he throws his hands in the air. "Oh my stars! Ha ha! Silly me! How could I forget?" He hurries back to us, says behind his hand, "Don't tell the board I forgot to ask for the diamond back. They'll have me skinned!"

Smiling, he holds out his hands to Mariana.

When she doesn't move, I take the backpack from her—wresting it off her shoulders when she resists—and hand it to Zuckerman.

"Heavy!" he exclaims, wide-eyed.

"Tools," Mariana says, the way someone might say "Shoot me."

"We're right behind you, Mr. Zuckerman. Lead the way!" I clamp my arm around Mariana's shoulders, ignoring the blistering string of curses she lets loose under her breath.

Thirty minutes later, we're in Zuckerman's office with the head of the security team and the Secretary of the Smithsonian Institution, both of whom have been called in from home, where they'd been fast asleep.

They're pissed as hell. Apparently, they weren't in on the pen test idea.

Zuckerman, meanwhile, is glowing like his wife just gave birth to his first child.

As for me? I'm having what could be described as the time of my life.

Mariana still wants to slice off my balls and shove them down my throat, but her rage has settled from thermonuclear to merely atomic. She's only glanced at me once since she sat in a chair across from Zuckerman's desk. I handed her a coffee, and she sent me a look that could liquefy steel.

When I winked at her in response, the air around her shimmered.

Pretty sure she didn't dig the wink.

"How the hell did you get past the biometric fingerprint scanner on the computer room door?" barks the head of the security team, a man unfortunately named Butts. He's a big guy with a big gut and a big ego who's having a hard time accepting the truth: a woman snuck onto his turf and snatched the world's most famous diamond.

If he wasn't such an arrogant dick, I'd almost feel sorry for him.

Mariana calmly takes a sip of her coffee. Even though she's disguised as a junkie in mangy jeans and that filthy hoodie, she can't hide the elegance of her every move. She brushes a strand of hair from her face, and it's like art.

I have to concentrate on a hideous still life of rotting fruit on the wall to distract my rising boner.

She says, "The scanner is a pattern-matching sensor, the simplest of all the biometric units on the market. The algorithm compares the basic fingerprint patterns of arch, whorl, and loop between a stored template and the image pressed to the glass. Unlike the ultrasonic or capacitance models, it doesn't require a live, three-dimensional finger to unlock, so the only thing I needed to fool it was a photocopy of a registered user's print."

"And how did you get that?" Butts asks, sounding dubious.

Mariana replies, "I took a tour of the museum several days ago and followed one of the security guards to the men's restroom near the employee lounge. He left a perfect thumbprint on the metal push plate on the main door. I got it off the door with a lump of Silly Putty, then took a high-resolution digital picture. I printed the image on a piece of photo paper, and voilà."

When everyone gapes at her, she rolls her eyes. "Don't look so shocked, boys. That's Thievery 101. There are as many ways to pull a print from a smooth surface as there are ways to fool scanners. I could've used silicon gel to make a mold, etched a print into the copper of a photo-sensitive printed circuit board, you name it. The only kind of biometric that would have really given me a problem is an active capacitance sensor, which uses a charging cycle to apply voltage to live skin. For that, I'd need an actual finger."

Because I'm curious myself, I say, "Tell them what you'd do in that case, Ms. Lane."

She looks at me and replies seriously, "Take a hostage."

I frown at her. "That's not funny."

In response, she merely smiles.

Butts snaps, "So we had your face on camera days ago. That's just stupid! If anyone had reviewed our security footage and saw you follow the guard into a restricted area—"

"No one ever reviews the footage unless an alarm is tripped. Correct?"

He stares at her, a flush crawling up his neck.

She answers her own question. "Correct. Even if for some improbable reason the tapes were reviewed, your surveillance system was installed decades ago. It's not exactly high fidelity. And my head was covered then as it is now, and I was also wearing thick glasses. You'd have a hell of a time identifying me from your shitty outdated cameras."

Her lips lift into a smile that would look at home on a serial killer. "Besides," she says softly, staring at Butts, her eyes poisonous. "I'm sure you'd be looking for a man anyway, right?"

From behind his desk, Zuckerman laughs in glee. Butts starts to pace like a caged animal, hands on his hips, every so often shooting Mariana a death glare.

I wipe a hand over my mouth to hide my smile. "So to recap, you used a homemade mixture of common table salt and H2S04, the liquid found in car batteries, to corrode an opening large enough for you to fit through in the side of the heating duct unit."

Starting to look exhausted, Mariana nods. "It works great on aluminum, but has little effect on other metals, and none on glass. I'd probably have used a laser cutter if the unit was steel, but they're a lot more cumbersome, and the light might have drawn attention to me."

I nod, fascinated and, frankly, fucking impressed. "Would you explain why you chose the soundwave generator to break the safety glass on the diamond's display case?"

She blows a lock of hair off her forehead and takes another

swallow of coffee before answering. "Think of it as the high-tech version of an opera singer using her voice to break a wineglass. All glass has a natural resonance, a frequency at which it will vibrate. The water white safety glass installed by Diebold to secure the diamond is no different. The glazing and laminates make it tricky, but if blasted with a complex sonic shockwave, the amplitude is sufficient to propagate cracks. And cracks were all I needed."

Looking utterly defeated, the secretary, a thin man with a shock of white hair and bleary blue eyes, speaks up. "But how did you get the computer login information? How did you know how to traverse the vents? Where to get in, what turns to make to get you to your target, all of that?"

Mariana shrugs. "The Internet."

He makes a high-pitched deflating sound like a punctured tire, his bloodshot eyes wide.

She explains, "Almost everything in the world is available on the web. You just have to know where to look. For the login information, it was a darknet market where someone—my guess is a disgruntled employee—had linked to your internal server's security software. As the passwords changed weekly here, they were also updated online. It cost a pretty penny but was obviously well worth it. In the case of the vents, it was architectural drawings from the archives of the DC building inspector's office."

Zuckerman, the secretary, and Butts look at each other. There seems to be an unspoken agreement that someone's ass is getting kicked, but no consensus on whose.

I take advantage of the pause in the conversation. "It's late. We're all tired. Why don't we reconvene in a few days after Ms. Lane has had a chance to compile a detailed written report with her findings and our suggestions for how Metrix can further assist the Institution with its security needs? Mr. Zuckerman, you know how to contact me."

Before waiting for anyone to speak, I lift Mariana to her feet with a hand under her arm and head for the door.

"One more question before you leave, Ms. Lane."

Mariana and I stop and turn back. Zuckerman is standing behind his desk, patting his moist forehead with a folded handkerchief. He asks, "What's with the drawing of the dragonfly?"

*Fuck.* My hand reflexively tightens around her arm. It's a protective response, but she calmly shakes me off and even manages a small, mirthless laugh.

"Oh, it's just an inside joke. When we conduct these high-level pen tests, we always pretend we're some famous thief. Like a role-playing thing." She jerks her thumb at me. "This one always pretends he's Butch Cassidy. Wanted to be a cowboy when he was a kid."

Zuckerman beams. "How fun! What does Mr. McLean leave behind, a toy pistol?"

"A plastic burro." When all three men frown, Mariana deadpans, "Because he's an ass."

"Isn't she a hoot, guys?" My grin is stretched so wide, I can't feel my lips. "Well, we're off. See you in a few days!"

I turn and drag her out the door.

At least I get a dark chuckle from her on the way out.

Mariana doesn't speak again until we're in the truck I rented when I arrived in DC. As soon as she slams the door shut behind her, she turns to me and snaps, "Give me one good reason why I shouldn't bury my knife in your thorax."

I start the car, rev the engine, and put it in reverse. "Which knife? The stiletto in your back pocket, the Tanto in your waistband, or the utility blade in your boot?"

I tear out of the parking spot in the museum's lot to the sound of squealing tires and growling female.

"How did you know I was going to hit the museum?" she demands.

"I bugged Reynard's place the minute I walked in last week."

She gasps, and I grin. "You mentioned DC and the world's largest blue diamond. Two plus two equals four, etcetera. Yeah, you had a *real* interestin' conversation after I left and you popped out of wherever you'd been hiding. If memory serves, you called me gorgeous. No, wait. It was better than that."

I pretend to think, as if I haven't been thinking about it for seven days straight. "Handsome? No. Magnificent? No—oh yeah! *Beautiful*."

I glance at her. She stares back at me in silent fury, nostrils flared, hands clenched to fists.

I say softly, "You called me beautiful, Angel. I been called a lot of things by a lot of women, but that's a first." My grin shows up again, twice as big as before. "So naturally I had to follow you across the Atlantic so I could make you say it to my face. Ingenious the way you exited Reynard's place through the Chinese laundry down the block, by the way. I'm guessing it's all connected by tunnels?"

She bites the inside of her cheek. Her fingers flex. She's itching to wrap them around the hilt of one of her knives and slice me up like deli meat.

"Reynard—"

"Is perfectly safe."

"How do you know?"

"How do you think I know?"

Another growl. She's starting to sound like a grizzly.

"Maybe for *now* he's safe. But when I don't show up with that diamond, the person who ordered me to get it is *going to kill Reynard*! And he's going to take his time doing it, because causing pain is his passion!"

"I know it is. Been readin' up on the guy. And imagine how

angry Vincent Moreno would've been when you gave him a fake diamond."

She shakes her head, blinking fast. "*Whaaa…*"

It's so comical, I almost laugh.

But I don't, because I know she's one laugh away from making me and a colander have a lot in common.

"The Hope Diamond on display at the Smithsonian is a fake, Angel. Has been since the seventies, when it was stolen by an unidentified group of thieves who posed as tourists, then hid in a utility closet after the museum closed and rammed through the vault wall with a forklift pinched from the loading dock. They were never caught. There's a lot of politics involved and something about a hinky insurance policy, but the upshot of the story is that the powers that be at the time decided it would be a financial and PR disaster for the Smithsonian if word got out that a smash-and-grab crew filched the Hope, so instead they put a replica in its place, and that's what's been on display for the last forty years.

"It's right up there with KFC's recipe as one of the world's best-kept secrets. Only a handful of the bigwigs at the Institute knew about the theft, and all but two of them are dead now. Even Zuckerman and the secretary don't know."

I take a corner too fast, but Mariana doesn't even notice. She just keeps on staring at me with big eyes and a wide open mouth. Finally, she asks, "How do *you* know?"

"Because, like I've told you before, I'm the shit, baby."

We zoom through the dark streets, trees and streetlights flying past, with no noise for miles but the sound of the engine and the radio on low. After a pause, she speaks again. "How do you know about Capo?"

My sigh is extravagant. "How many times do I have to tell you I'm *really* good at my job before you'll believe me?"

She slumps down in the seat, drops her face into her hands, and exhales a long, slow breath. It's several minutes before she speaks again, and when she does, her voice is so low, I almost can't hear it.

"So...basically...you just saved my life."

"*And* Reynard's," I point out, trying not to sound smug and completely failing.

"But..." She lowers her hands and gazes blankly out the windshield. "I can't go back empty-handed. If I return to Capo with nothing—"

"You're never going back to him, Mariana," I cut in, my voice hard. She stares at me, looking confused. "You're gonna let your man handle this, you hear me? Now, do you need to pick up anything at your fleabag safe house before we head to New York?"

She makes a soft, incoherent noise of shock.

I take it as a no and stomp my foot on the gas, headed toward the interstate.

Headed toward home.

17

# MARIANA

I don't know how long I slept, but when I awaken, morning sun streams through the windshield as Ryan opens the passenger door.

"C'mon, Angel," he murmurs, hoisting me into his arms. "We're home."

I mutter a protest at being handled like luggage, but I'm so exhausted I give up without a fight. I sag against the broad expanse of his chest as he kicks the car door shut behind him.

He chuckles. "You're heavier than you look."

I mumble, "And you're dumber than you look. Another crack about my weight and you're a dead man."

"God, I love it when you threaten me with bodily injury."

My legs dangle over his arm as he walks across a gated parking lot to a squat, brick building with no windows on the first floor. In front of a metal door with no handle, he stops.

"Supercalifragilisticexpialidocious," he says to the door.

Bewildered, I lift my head and squint at him.

He shrugs. "So I love *Mary Poppins*. Sue me."

The door slides open soundlessly, revealing a lighted steel box about five feet wide and eight feet tall. When Ryan walks inside, the door slides shut behind us. With a subtle clang, the box begins to descend.

I say to Ryan's profile, "Do you live near the center of the earth?"

"Yep," he answers instantly. "That's why I'm so hot."

He slants me a grin. I close my eyes against its brilliance and tuck my head into his neck.

"Where are we?"

"I told you. Home."

"No, *where*?"

"The Bronx. Ish."

"Either it is, or it isn't."

"Normally, I'd agree with you, but in this case, there's a little wiggle room considering we're not talkin' horizontal coordinates."

The elevator stops, the doors open, and Ryan walks out into pitch blackness. He calls out, "Raindrops on roses."

Overhead lights blink on in orderly rows, revealing a bachelor pad that has probably starred in every male's fantasy of a bachelor pad since the term was invented.

High ceilings. Exposed brick walls. Polished cement floors. Lots of steel beams and glass surfaces, and a smattering of leather furniture. A television the size of a school bus hangs on the wall, along with black-and-white abstract art suggestive of nude women. Not a single throw pillow or bright color in sight.

"Raindrops on roses?"

"And whiskers on kittens," he says, nodding.

I look at him. "Bright copper kettles and warm woolen mittens?"

He beams. "Angel! You know *The Sound of Music*!"

I gaze around his underground sanctuary that sizzles with machismo and is operated with voice commands taken from Julie Andrews movies, and ponder my predicament.

Only one reasonable explanation comes to mind.

"I'm dead, aren't I? Just give it to me straight. I was shot sometime yesterday, and now I'm dead. And this is…purgatory?"

He scoffs, "This is *heaven*, baby!"

"Heaven? I am dubious."

"That's a one-hundred-ten-inch ultra-high-definition TV! And that"—he swings me around so I'm pointed in the direction of a large kitchen, gleaming with stainless steel appliances—"is a professional-grade chef's kitchen complete with a grill, a griddle, a double-walled pizza oven, *and* an infrared salamander broiler—"

"Maybe purgatory was being too generous."

Ryan purses his lips and considers me. "I know what you need," he pronounces, then strides through the living room, past the gargantuan television and arty nudes, past the built-in wine cellar and wet bar, around a wall composed entirely of live succulents in different shades of green, brown, and gray, and into his bedroom.

He stops in front of a bed approximately the size of a train platform. The duvet and sheets are black, as are the pillows. A trio of red candles reside on a black bedside table. A fuzzy black rug sprawls over the floor.

I ask, "So how many vampiresses do you usually sleep with in this thing?"

"Vampiress?"

"A vampire of the female persuasion."

"Why isn't that just vampire? Do you say poetess too? Seems a little sexist, Angel."

"You're avoiding the question about your abnormally large bed, which I find suspicious."

"The bed, or the avoidance?"

"Both. I also find your choice of black and red as a palette for your boudoir suspicious. Especially when you're trying to convince a person this is heaven, which I'd like to think is decorated in more cheerful tones."

"Boudoir?" he repeats, sounding insulted. "I'm a badass, sweetheart, not a French escort. This is called a bedroom. And it's awesome."

Ignoring his obvious delusion, I point with my foot across the room. "What in God's name is that?"

"You've never seen a grand piano before?"

I exhale with what I hope is sufficient disgust. "I've never seen one in a *bedroom* before. It's ridiculous. I'm picturing you in a velvet smoking jacket, serenading your harem of vampiresses with a little post-bloodsucking Rachmaninoff."

Ryan kisses the top of my head. "You're delirious. It's probably the proximity to all this grade A testosterone I'm manufacturin'."

"Undoubtedly," I say, trying hard not to find him charming, but failing.

"Let's get you to bed."

Without waiting for an answer, he strides over to the black behemoth and gently deposits me on it. He kneels at my feet, unlaces my boots, and pulls them off, then peels off my socks and tosses those aside while I watch in something like shock. Only achier.

He glances up and catches me watching him. "What?"

"What are you doing?"

He looks at my feet, then back up at my face. Like you would speak to someone very drunk, he says, "I'm takin' off your shoes, darlin'."

"No." I close my eyes, inhale, then make a little motion with my index finger indicating the two of us. "What are you *doing*?"

When he squeezes my ankles, I open my eyes. Looking straight into them, he says, "Takin' care of you. And before you ask why," he says when I open my mouth, "the answer is because that's what I'm gonna do from here on out. Take care of you. You're the priority now. You're mine."

I mull over this ludicrous pronouncement.

Is he a professional stalker? Does he have a screw—or ten—loose? This can't possibly be how he lives his whole life, just making one rash decision after another, with no more fore-thought than you'd give what pair of socks you were going to wear.

"I don't understand."

"I know," he says warmly, pulling my hoodie over my head. "But you will."

"How can you just decide like that?" I ask, sounding petulant as he discards my hoodie. I stare at my bare feet. They appear startlingly vulnerable, naked and pale, a visual metaphor for my heart. I insist, "We don't even know each other."

When I see that dimple appear in his cheek, I mutter, "Biblically doesn't count."

The dimple turns into a pit you could fall into and disappear. "So says you. Lie down."

I'm gently pushed onto my back. Swimming in confusion, I stare at the ceiling but find no answers there, because ceilings generally aren't good for that sort of thing.

Ryan unbuttons my jeans and drags them down my legs in a no-nonsense, businesslike way, as if I'm an uncooperative patient and he's my long-suffering nurse.

"People make things way more complicated than they need to be," he says, flinging my jeans over his shoulder. I notice he isn't nearly as fastidious with my clothing as he is with his own. "If you'd just listen to your gut, nine times out of ten you'll make the right decision without havin' to do any hand wringin' or hair pullin'. Your instincts will tell you what you should do."

"Except for that pesky tenth time." I yawn as he pulls the covers up to my chin. My eyelids are so heavy. "Then you're fucked."

He leans over and kisses me on the forehead. Then he makes a face and wipes his lips. "Stay there," he commands, as if I have a choice in anything.

He leaves. I let my eyes drift shut and listen to the sound of running water. Then his footsteps return, along with him, bearing a wet washcloth.

He begins to clean my face.

"This is too much," I protest, but only half-heartedly, because the warm, wet cloth feels delicious on my dirt-caked skin. "Ryan. I don't think I can handle this...whatever this is. Us. You're giving me a mental breakdown."

"Nah, you're doin' that all on your own, darlin'. Just go with it. I promise it'll all work out. Jesus, what is this, like, industrial-strength dirt?" He scrubs harder.

I mumble, "Had to make sure...you know...disguise."

"Yeah, well, you get a gold star for effort. When you wake up, I'm gonna have to throw you in the shower to get the rest of this shit off."

"Throw?" I say, drifting off to sleep. "Sounds a little aggressive, cowboy."

He sighs, stirring my hair. "Always focusin' on the wrong things," he mutters to himself.

I fall asleep to the sound of his breathing and his hands gently caressing my face.

~

I dream of burning buildings and firetrucks with ladders too short to rescue people hanging from windows on upper floors. When I wake, I bolt upright, sweating, heart thundering, with no idea where I am.

Then I see the polished bulk of the ridiculous grand piano, the all-black everything else, and realize there's only one place on earth besides Dracula's castle that I could possibly be.

I rub the sleep from my eyes, throw off the covers, and pad into the adjoining bathroom. My bladder isn't so much full as it is ready to burst. I use the toilet, then wash my hands and face and brush my teeth because my breath is poisonous. When I realize I've used Ryan's toothbrush without a second thought, I have a *lot* of second thoughts, and stand there staring at it in my hand.

From the doorway comes his amused voice. "I can see the smoke pourin' from your ears, Angel. Don't pop a blood vessel over there."

I glance at him. He's shirtless and barefoot, wearing only a pair of faded jeans, leaning against the doorframe with his arms folded over his chest and a wry smile on his lips.

As always, he's beautiful. A big, muscular, tattooed, golden beauty of a man who claims I'm his.

My heart feels like it might explode.

I say quietly, "I've never used anyone else's toothbrush before."

"I've never let anyone else sleep in my bed before."

That gives me a start. He sees my surprise and drawls, "Nope, not even the vampiresses. I kick 'em out right after I play Rachmaninoff. Come here."

Moving at the speed of refrigerated molasses, I return his toothbrush to its small glass tumbler and walk toward him. He holds a hand out, wiggling his fingers.

"Any slower and I'll be an old man by the time you get here."

"Give me a sec. I'm trying to control my freak-out."

"Over how spectacular I look without a shirt?"

I step into his arms and hide my face in his chest. "Over how spectacular you are in general."

He wraps his arms around me and pulls me in tight. I'm engulfed in warmth and the scent of a male in his prime, clean skin and warm musk and a delicious, indefinable something that's so damn sexy I make a little noise deep in my throat.

Ryan nuzzles my ear. "You've got it bad for me, don't you, Angel?" he teases, a chuckle rumbling through his chest.

That sound coming from my chest is a whimper.

In one smooth motion, he bends and picks me up in his arms. He heads toward the glassed-in shower on the opposite side of the room.

"Is this going to be a thing?" I ask, my arms wound around his broad shoulders. "You carrying me around like a sack of potatoes?"

"It makes me feel macho bein' able to lift all this weight—ow!"

"Serves you right," I grumble, releasing his earlobe from my front teeth. Then I feel guilty and kiss the spot I've just bitten, making him chuckle again.

"So she has a conscience after all," he muses. "Who knew?"

"Shut up."

"Put somethin' in my mouth and make me."

I roll my eyes at his suggestive wink. "It's like you're twelve."

"You're not the first person to tell me that."

He's not insulted, just matter-of-fact. We arrive at the shower door. He sets me on my feet and, with no further ado, pulls my T-shirt over my head.

"Matching bra and panties," he says, hungrily eying my underwear. "Lacy. Nice. Take 'em off."

"You're an incredibly pushy man, you know that?" I'm grousing but obeying at the same time, reaching around to unsnap my bra. When the straps fall down my arms and my breasts spring free, Ryan bites his lower lip.

"Yes," he says, his voice husky. "Now get those fuckin' panties off and let me look at you."

I let my bra dangle from my fingertips for a moment because

I love the way the delay makes his eyes burn. Then I let the bra drop to the floor, and slip my thumbs under the top of my panties, just over my hips.

"These panties?" I say, teasing. I do a little shimmy. Ryan narrows his eyes.

"Tyrant," I say, and edge the panties down an inch.

His gaze flashes up to mine. It's a look that could ignite a forest fire.

I slide the panties down another inch. "You're not the boss of me, you know that, right?"

He growls, "As soon as you get those goddamn panties off, I'm gonna prove you wrong, darlin'."

How I'm beginning to adore that sleepy, slow Southern drawl. I never guessed a dropped *g* at the end of a word could be so sexy.

I push the panties past my hips. They slither down my legs and pool around my ankles. Ryan takes one long, silent look at me—head to toe, his gaze blistering—then drops to his knees, grabs my ass, pulls me into his face, and bites me right between my legs.

It's not a hard bite. It's just like…*mine. This is mine, and I'm gonna bite it because I can, and I want to.*

My entire body shudders. I've never been this aroused—this quickly—in my life.

Then he slips his tongue between my folds, and my arousal sprouts wings and launches into outer space. I dig my fingers into his hair and rock against his hot, wet mouth. My nipples tighten and tingle with every swipe of his tongue.

"That feels so good," I whisper.

He opens his eyes and looks up at me. It's almost painfully intimate, watching him suckle me on his knees as I struggle to remain standing. The sound of my ragged gasps echoes off the bathroom walls. When his teeth scrape over my clit, I moan.

He reaches down between his legs, yanks open his fly, grabs

his erection in his fist and starts to stroke it as he eats me, looking up at me the entire time with hooded, heated eyes.

I love it that he likes to taste me. That the first thing he wants to do is put his mouth between my legs. It's carnal, a little animal, and makes me feel sexy and dirty and gloriously desired.

I flex my hips in time to the strokes of his tongue and am rewarded by a low, guttural groan of approval deep from within his chest.

I arch back. My shoulders hit the glass shower wall with a hollow noise. Bracing my weight against the wall, I cant my hips forward and spread my thighs open wider. Ryan takes advantage of the new angle and plunges his tongue deep inside me.

My moan is loud and broken. My nipples are so hard, they ache. I'm panting, no longer simply flexing my hips but riding his face like a rodeo bull as he pumps his cock in his fist.

I gasp as a wave of heat blasts through me. Deep inside my pelvis, there's a throb and a hard, abrupt clench. I whisper, "Oh fuck. Ryan. *Ryan.*"

He knows I'm there. He slides two fingers inside me, reaches up with his other hand and pinches my nipple, and gently bites down on my engorged clit.

I come, screaming his name with my head thrown back, my eyes closed, and my whole body jerking. Wave after wave of pleasure pulses through me. It's violent and soul-searing hot.

He's on his feet before it's over, slinging one of my legs over his bent arm so I'm wide open for him. He plunges inside me with a groan. Then he starts to fuck me, his strokes short and fast, thrusting into me as my body clenches around him, holding us up against the shower door.

I scream and come and cling to his shoulders, lost to all of it. To him. Us.

This earthquake of emotion that's splitting me open and shattering all my walls.

He laughs a dark, satisfied laugh. "What were you sayin'

about me not bein' the boss of you?" he says gruffly into my ear. When I sob brokenly, he whispers, "Yeah, baby. Who's your daddy now?"

He's so hot and so hard and so fucking *male*, I'm absolutely wild for him. *But oh shit, this is a complete disaster. What the hell am I doing?*

I must make another noise, because Ryan stills. Breathing heavily, he says, "Easy. You're safe. I've got you."

Still trembling with aftershocks, I groan and bury my face in his neck.

"Hush, Angel," he whispers. "C'mon now. Shh."

"I can't—I can't—"

"You can. You will. *We* will. I promise."

I start to cry, and can't stop. I'm making ugly, raw noises, like an animal in pain. Hot tears stream down my face and drip onto his chest. I'm horrified at myself, at this awful show of weakness, but he takes it all in stride, as if dealing with emotional females is par for the course.

"It's okay. Get it out. Get it out, baby, you'll feel better."

His arms are a cage, or a refuge, I don't know which. I only know that suddenly I'm scared shitless. All I want to do is run and hide from the enormity of this thing unfurling between us—this dangerous, addictive, overpowering thing.

He's still inside me.

After a while, when my sobs turn into muffled hiccups, he exhales a long breath and kisses my hair. "Well. I knew I was amazing in bed, but tears are unprecedented."

I sniffle and blow out a hard breath. "It's just that I like you," I grudgingly admit. "Like…a lot."

His laugh starts deep in his belly, a silent clenching and unclenching of his abs that leads to a chuckle burbling up into his chest and breaking free. He throws his head back and laughs, shaking us both. It goes on forever.

I wipe my nose on the back of my hand. "You're going to be insufferable now, aren't you?"

"*Yes*," he says, full of enthusiasm. "Oh my God, I'm gonna be such a giant, chest-beatin' pain in the ass, you have no idea!"

I glance up at him. His smile could cause blindness. "I have a pretty good idea," I mutter.

He takes my face in his hands and gives me a deep, heartfelt kiss. I wonder if he's getting covered in snot, but the kiss is too nice to spend much time worrying about that.

"Whew! You're a handful, darlin'," he says when he finally breaks the kiss. "Lucky for you, I dig difficult women. Now, if you don't mind, I'd like to fuck you in the shower. Try not to fall apart again until after I come. Blue balls make me ornery."

He opens the shower door, lifts me up with both hands under my bottom, and walks in.

Still wearing his jeans.

Still inside me.

# 18

# RYAN

"Take off your pants, you idiot!" Mariana says, laughing softly.

Her laugh somewhat eases the big knot under my breastbone formed by her tears, but I'm still worried. Beneath that tough exterior, she's as fragile as glass.

All I want to do is make her feel safe. Make her smile. Banish forever those scared little whimpers she makes in her sleep.

I've never felt more protective of anything. Or more sure of what I want.

The only problem with what I want is that it comes with so much baggage, it could sink a Navy destroyer.

But I've got a plan to fix that.

"If it means puttin' you down, the answer's no." I turn on the water, holding her up with one arm, and adjust the knobs until it's nice and warm.

She looks appreciatively at the muscles flexing in my biceps. "Now you're just showing off."

They're pretty impressive, if I do say so myself.

I set her against the tile wall, brace my legs apart, and go in for another kiss. Her arms and legs are wrapped around me, and she's holding on tight. The moment my tongue touches hers, she moans softly into my mouth.

It makes my heart take off like a rocket, that sweet little sound. I love it the way I love football and barbecues and fireworks on the Fourth of July. The way I love Thanksgiving and Buzz Lightyear and guns with high-capacity magazines.

I love it like it's a religion.

In a way, I suppose it is.

"Goddamn, Angel. You're so fuckin' sweet." My voice is as rough as my breathing. She looks up at me with those big brown eyes, and suddenly, it's hard to breathe at all.

"*You* are," she whispers. "You're the sweetest man I've ever met, and if you're not careful, I'll—"

She breaks off and looks away, sharply inhaling.

I've felt like this precisely once before, as a senior in high school. I scored the winning touchdown on a game a bunch of college recruiters had come to see me play. My team carried me off the field on their shoulders, chanting my name. My parents were in the stands, glowing with fucking pride. Everyone was jumping up and down and screaming. An entire stadium of fans was losing their minds.

I was a king. I was a god. It was the best moment of my life.

Until now.

"You'll what, baby?" I whisper. "Say it."

She swallows hard, blinking.

I drop my head and nuzzle her neck, pressing my lips against the pulse throbbing near her ear. "Be brave."

"You already know."

"I want you to say it. Out loud."

Digging into my shoulders, her fingers tremble. She gazes up at me from beneath long, curving black lashes. "I'll…fall in love with you."

You'd think the sound of your heart bursting would be like a wet, messy, booming thing, but really, it's the gentlest little *plink.*

I groan and kiss her, hard. She kisses me back with wild abandon, her heart pounding against my chest, her whole body shaking. When she flexes her hips, I instantly lose all control.

I thrust deep into her, so deep she gasps into my mouth.

Then I close my eyes, bury my face in her neck, and revel in the feel of her body and the sounds of her cries as I drive into her over and over again. I'm as helpless to slow down or hold back as I am to stop the tsunami of emotion breaking over me. I'm flying, or falling, or being flung through space at a million miles per hour.

My voice breaks over her name.

Her pussy clenches hard around my cock.

My orgasm tears out of me like a ripcord tearing open a parachute.

I grunt like an animal, my fingers dug into her ass, every muscle in my body flexed and straining, a little voice in the back of my head commenting casually, *Well, this should be an interesting development—*

"I'm coming, Angel! Fuck!"

She's coming, too, throbbing hot around my pulsing dick, both of us hoarsely crying out and shuddering.

It's too late to pull out. I try anyway, but just end up staggering. Hot water cascades between us, spraying our faces and bodies and the walls. Mariana is arched back in my arms, her mouth open and her eyes closed, her skin slick with sweat and water. My biceps and thighs are burning, and I'm still coming, my pelvis jerking compulsively, my cock buried deep and spilling.

Suddenly, Mariana realizes what's happening. Her eyes fly open. Into my face she shouts, "Tell me you had a vasectomy!"

Hand to God, I don't know why, but I erupt in laughter. "Do I seem like the kind of man who'd let a scalpel anywhere near his balls?"

Her horrified face tells me that isn't the right answer.

I give her my most winning smile. "This seems like a good time to discuss how many kids you think we should have."

During the thundering silence that follows, I hope there aren't any sharp objects within easy reach.

"Are we gonna talk about this?"

"No."

"Angel—"

"Ryan, don't push me. Do. *Not*."

Mariana paces back the way she just came. We're in the living room. I'm on the couch, and she's wearing holes in the rug. Suffice it to say, I'm feeling a lot less anxiety about what may or may not have taken root in the shower, so to speak.

I mean, I'm not an idiot. It's not an ideal situation. If it even *is* a situation. But it's also not the end of the world.

I love kids. Being a dad is something I've always wanted.

If Mariana lets me live long enough to become one, which is up in the air at this point.

Finally, she stops pacing and crucifies me with a look. "I need to call Reynard."

Unease clenches my gut. "What you need to do is eat something. I'll make us—"

"No," she says sharply, cutting me off. "You don't get to decide what I do or don't do."

I stand and draw in a breath. Keeping my voice low and controlled, I say, "I know you're upset—"

"You know nothing, Ryan Tiberius McLean," she says bitingly, her eyes as hard as diamonds. "You know exactly *nothing* about me, not even my last name."

She waits for me to challenge it, but of course I can't. She's right.

I don't know her goddamn last name.

Heat creeps up my neck.

"Don't get me wrong. I'm not putting this on you. I accept full responsibility for what happened in the shower. But we need to be very clear that you're not calling the shots here. You stopped me from stealing a fake diamond and giving it to a man who's killed many people for far less, and for that I'm grateful. But my gratitude is where my obligation to you ends."

My face stings like I've been slapped. I take several slow breaths to cool my rising temperature. "Okay, let's dial this back a notch. You've been through a lot. You're tired and stressed—"

"Don't you *dare* patronize me," she snaps, eyes blazing. "I've been through more than you'll ever know, more than most people could live through, and I survived. Clawing and biting and eating worms when I had to, eating fucking *dirt* when that's all there was, I survived. Long before you, Ryan, I survived."

Her face is red. Her hands are shaking. I've never seen her this angry.

"You don't know what it means to have nothing, because you were born in a country where you could speak out against the government without being killed. You were born to parents who knew how to read and write, who had opportunities to make life better for their children. You weren't born a girl in a culture that valued girls as much as horses or cows, good only for buying or selling or putting to work. You weren't orphaned at six when your parents and almost everyone else you knew was murdered in a midnight raid. You didn't live for years like an animal in the hills, filthy and starving, hiding from guerrillas who'd sell you to the highest bidder, only coming out at night to steal what you could from the villages. You didn't have to watch your sister—"

She breaks off abruptly, swallowing a sob.

I'm frozen in shock at her words. "Angel," I breathe.

She swallows hard several times, swipes at her eyes, then straightens her shoulders, lifts her chin, and pierces me with her gaze.

With exquisite dignity, she says, “My name is Mariana. I’m a professional thief wanted by authorities in twelve countries for crimes committed in the service of honoring an oath that saved the life of the only man I’ve ever loved. That man is Reynard. If it wasn’t for him, I’d have died a horrible death as a little girl, the worst kind of death a little girl could ever suffer. And now I want to call him. God help you, gringo, if you try to stand in my way.”

My mouth hangs open. I’m stunned, heartsick, and deeply, deeply impressed. If I thought she was a goddess before, now I might as well kneel at her feet and start babbling prayers.

“Yes,” I say, finding my voice. “Of course. I’ll bring the phone.”

We stare at each other across the room, silence yawning wide between us. I want to say more but know any words I could speak would be useless.

I bring her one of the spare cells I keep in the safe in the wall of my bedroom. “It’s a crypto phone. Untraceable. Totally secure. You can keep it.” I turn and head back toward my bedroom, assuming she’ll want privacy.

Shows how much I know.

“Ryan,” she calls.

I stop and look over my shoulder. I washed her jeans and hoodie while she was asleep, and she’s wearing them now, her damp hair loose around her shoulders, her feet bare. Even with no makeup, dressed down, exhaustion seeping through all her movements, she’s the loveliest thing I’ve ever seen.

She drags a hand through her hair and sighs. “Is your offer of food still on the table?”

I nod, not daring to speak.

She looks at the phone in her hand like she’s looking for

answers. She exhales in a gust and lifts her gaze to mine. "That would be nice. Thank you. And thank you for the phone. I didn't mean to be such a bitch…it's just that…"

"You don't owe me an explanation," I say softly.

After a moment where I can tell she's struggling to find the right words, she says, "I've always been alone. I've always worked alone. I don't know anything about taking care of other people, or being part of a team. I've never even had a pet. Trust isn't a luxury I've ever been able to afford. So this…you…"

She falters, making a helpless gesture with her hands. I don't want to push her to say more, but I also don't want her to stop talking.

This is exactly the kind of shit we need to work out.

Her eyes shining, she says, "You're like a dream that's so good, I don't want to wake up, but I know eventually I'll have to. And the longer I stay dreaming, the worse it'll hurt when I'm finally awake."

*Fuck.* If my heart didn't already burst in the shower, it would shatter into a million tiny pieces now. I have to stand there and breathe for a few seconds before I can speak. When I do, my voice is rough with emotion.

"Life isn't always unfair, Mariana. Lots of bad shit happens, but good things happen, too, and you need to be able to recognize the good when it comes along. You need to be able to accept it and deal with it, same as you deal with the bad. Love is as real as hate. Trust is as real as hunger. You know how to survive. But that's not the same as living."

She stares at me, swallowing, the color high in her cheeks.

I say more softly, "And if what happened in the shower turns out to have consequences, we'll deal with it. Together. Now make your phone call, woman. I'm gonna make us some chow."

I kiss her forehead as I walk past her into the kitchen.

The sound of her faint laugh follows me as I go.

# 19

## MARIANA

"Reynard," purrs a cultured British voice on the other end of the line.

Flooded with the same relief I always feel when I hear his voice, I close my eyes and rest my forehead in my hand. I'm sitting at Ryan's glass kitchen table, my nose filled with the delicious scent of frying bacon, my heart like a grenade with the pin pulled inside my chest.

How do people live like this? How can anyone survive this feeling, this agony of tenderness and hope? It's madness, I know it is, and yet…

"Hello, Reynard," I say quietly. "It's Dragonfly."

A brief pause follows before he asks, "Are you all right?"

"Yes and no. Mostly yes, nothing to worry about."

Another pause. "It certainly sounds like something to worry about."

I chew my lip, thinking. "The job was…difficult."

This time, his pause is deafening. "Have you completed it?"

I clear my throat. "Yes. And no."

He says drily, "How esoteric. Care to elaborate?"

"I'm just calling to find out if you're safe. Are you safe? Are you well?"

"Of course. Whatever are you going on about, my darling?"

When I don't respond, his voice turns dark. "Oh, bollocks. The American."

I let my heavy sigh serve as my answer.

Reynard turns businesslike, his tone clipped. "If I'm not mistaken—and I never am—your deadline is in forty-eight hours. Do you need an extension?"

"I want you to promise me something, Reynard."

I can almost hear him pull himself up short. "Good God. That sounds bad. Let me sit down. All right, go ahead, I'm sitting. No, wait, let me get my flask." Through the phone comes the sounds of a gulp and some lip smacking. "There. Sorted. Tell me."

I open my eyes and look at Ryan, frying bacon in a pan at his ridiculously enormous stove, and listen to what my heart is emphatically telling me.

"If Ryan McLean contacts you for any reason, I want you to promise to do exactly as he says. No questions asked."

At the stove, Ryan freezes.

A bristling silence, then Reynard says flatly, "He's taken you hostage. That bloody grinning idiot is holding you hostage, isn't he?" His voice rises. "He has a gun to your head right now, doesn't he? Put him on the phone! That colossal wanker! I'll give that smiling arsebadger something to stew on—"

"Reynard—"

"Does he have any idea who he's meddling with?" Reynard shouts. "That smarmy, second-rate John Wayne impersonator! That swaggering, insufferable, cock-swinging, pathetic excuse for a man—"

Wincing, I hold the phone away from my ear. Reynard is still going. I wait until I hear a pause, then I put the phone against my ear again and loudly interrupt the tirade.

"No one has taken me hostage, Reynard. No one is forcing me to say anything. *I'm* asking."

Ryan stands perfectly still at the stove. It doesn't look like he's even breathing.

Cool and controlled, Reynard says, "*Why* are you asking?"

Wavering one final time, I bite my lip so hard, I almost draw blood. Then I jump off the cliff that's in front of me, hoping against hope that somehow I'll fly instead of smashing face-first into the ground.

"Because I think we can trust him. And I think we're going to need his help."

I've stunned two men, thousands of miles apart, into shocked silence. After a while, Reynard makes a sound like he's choking on his tongue.

"Oh, for fuck's sake." I exhale in a gust. "I don't like it, either, believe me! But it is what it is. We're going to trust the American. This is the new normal. I just decided right now."

If Ryan can do it, then I can, too. *Gut, you better be on track with this, or I'll cut you out of my body myself.*

Reynard hollers, "Are you *mad*? You only have one job left! One! After all these years, freedom is within reach, and you—"

"The diamond is a fake, Reynard. What do you think Capo would do to me—to *us*—if I gave him a fake? Do you think he'd believe me when I said I had no idea? Do you think he'd be forgiving?"

Reynard's voice drops an octave. "Who told you it was fake?"

My gaze flashes up to Ryan's back. He hasn't moved an inch. From the pan of bacon, smoke rises in billowing gray plumes. It's started to burn.

For a moment, I fall through a bottomless chasm of pure panic, but I wrestle it into submission long enough to answer. "That's not the point."

"Au contraire, my darling, it's *exactly* the point. Take a

moment and consider who you're dealing with. This stranger you've decided to trust." He says *trust* sarcastically, like he's putting air quotes around it because the concept is so ridiculous. "Take a moment to consider what his motives might be. What his endgame is." Reynard's voice turns hard. "Wipe the stardust and rainbows from your eyes and *think*."

Anger crawls up my neck in a hot, prickling rush.

I really detest being patronized, and that's twice in ten minutes.

"My eyes *are* wide open, Reynard. Sometimes I wish they weren't, because life would be easier, but they are. Now here's something for *you* to think about: what if Capo *knew* the diamond was fake? What if he set me up to fail? You want to talk about motives and endgames? Let's talk about Capo's. Let's talk about what he really wants, because we both know it isn't more jewels!"

A buzzer sounds. It's a smoke alarm. Ryan finally breaks his statue impersonation and jabs his index finger into a button on the hood above the stove. A fan starts to suck the smoke from the burning bacon into a vent, lifting it in eerie, ghostly whorls.

It reminds me of the way the smoke rose over the avocado fields the night my parents were murdered.

I can't sit any longer. I jolt from the chair and start to pace around the table, chewing my thumbnail as I go.

Reynard says flatly, "You have forty-eight hours to get that diamond and get back to London. Capo's expecting you. If you don't arrive, he'll kill me. That's not so alarming, I've been expecting it for years, but what should alarm you is that *he will hunt you down*, using all his considerable reach and power to find you. And when he finds you, my darling…" His voice darkens. "He'll take his time with you. He'll make you beg for death long before it arrives."

My hand lifts to my throat. I think of the girls with collars, the red stains on Enzo's handkerchief, and all the blood drains from my face.

"You're suddenly so interested in trust?" asks Reynard, chillingly soft. "Trust *that.* Trust in the dependability of evil, because unlike lust and infatuation, it will never fade. It will never let you down. Unlike handsome American Marines, evil always keeps its promises."

I inhale a soft, shuddering breath, my entire body going icy cold.

Ryan finally turns from the stove. He takes one look at my face, and thunderclouds gather over his head. He strides over to me, holding out his hand, his eyes burning.

"Gimme the phone."

"What?" I say, startled.

"Woman. Give. Me. The. Phone."

I decide now isn't the time to be my usual sassy self. I silently place the phone in his hand.

He lifts it to his ear and growls into it, "Listen up, you snobby motherfucker! I don't care how much Mariana loves you, if you ever say anything to her again that makes her look like she does right now, I'll break both your legs!"

My lips part, but the man has rendered me incapable of speech.

On the other end of the phone, Reynard says something unintelligible. All I hear is a bark.

To which Ryan barks back, "*Yes!*"

He listens for a moment, shifting his weight from foot to foot, then thunders, "You better fuckin' believe it!"

I drop my face into my hands and groan.

*A pissing contest. Divine.*

After a moment, when I don't hear any more barking, I peek through my fingers. Frowning furiously, Ryan listens to whatever Reynard is saying. He nods, says a curt, "Mmhmm," huffs out a breath, looks at the ceiling with his nostrils flared, then nods again. Then he proceeds to answer what must be a series of rapid-fire questions with a series of rapid-fire answers, punctuated by jaw-clenching pauses.

"None. Yeah. Yep. I do. I will. I *know*." Then, more irritated, "Despite what you think, dickhead, I didn't fall off the back of a fuckin' turnip truck!"

Then, just to bake my brain completely, he breaks into a grin. "Okay, man. Will do. Good talk, brother." He ends the call and looks at me.

After a while, I manage to say, "What the hell was that all about?"

Ryan shrugs. "He doesn't like me much, but we're workin' it out."

I stare at him in blank disbelief, all the cogs of my brain frozen.

He says, "Okay, look. I know it's hard to believe, but I'm not perfect. Don't make that face, it's true. I'm fuckin' stubborn, and I've got a hair-trigger temper. I curse too much, I don't exactly have finishing school manners, and I can be overbearing. And overconfident. And a bunch of other unflatterin' words that start with 'over.' I'm also opinionated, sarcastic, easily frustrated, more than a little conceited—"

"This is quite the list," I say.

"I could go on for days. My point is that I'm aware of my shortcomings. Because I know I'm not perfect, I don't expect other people to be perfect, either. The only thing I demand from anyone—whether they like me or not—is that they're real. Whatever and whoever they are, they own it. They don't make fuckin' excuses. I hate excuses."

When it becomes evident he's done speaking, I venture a hesitant, "Okay?"

"Reynard is worried about you. More worried about you than he is about himself, which I dig. Means he loves you, which is good, 'cause I know you love him. So no matter how much he doesn't like me, I'm gonna respect him because he's bein' real with me. Understand?"

I squint at him, hoping it might make things clearer. "Um…"

Ryan reaches out and gathers me in his arms. He lifts my chin with a knuckle so I'm forced to meet his level, serious gaze. "Chalk it up to another one of those things about me you'll eventually understand. The more important topic here is that you told him you decided to trust me."

He waits for me to answer, his eyes glowing bright blue with emotion, like a pair of sapphires held up to the sun.

I flatten my hands over his chest, loving how hard it is, how wide and warm, how his heart thumps strong and steady beneath his sternum like it's confident it will never fail. I run through a dozen different explanations in my mind before distilling my decision down to its essence.

I say softly, "You're worth the risk."

For this, I'm rewarded by the sight of a big, badass Marine getting all choked up.

"Angel."

His voice is raw. His eyes glimmer. He wears the euphoric expression of someone who's just been granted his dying wish.

This is how I know my gut is on the right track, even if my brain is trying to stomp on the emergency brakes. I smile at him and stand on tiptoe to kiss him gently on the lips.

"I keep telling you my name is Mariana."

"Yeah," he says hoarsely. "But you're my angel, so that's what you're gonna get called."

Now I'm the one getting choked up. "I'm no angel, Ryan. I'm trouble with a capital *T*. You have to know that. However this all turns out with the diamond…I'm no good."

"You're not trouble, you're *in* trouble. Two different things."

"I'm a fugitive from the law."

Unimpressed with my evidence, he lifts a shoulder. "The law's overrated."

My brows arch. For a smart man, he's utterly failing to grasp the general concept of our predicament. "Is prison overrated? Because if I'm caught—"

"I'm gonna take care of that."

Examining his face gives me no clue as to what he could possibly mean, so I prod an explanation. "'That' being…"

"Your record. The rap sheet of one nameless, international thief known as the Dragonfly. That's all gonna go away."

Because my brain is incapable of directing any of my bodily functions in the aftermath of that outrageous statement, my mouth falls open and expels a small, astonished breath on its own. It takes every ounce of focus and determination I have to form a coherent sentence, and even then, it's only three sputtered words.

"Th-that's *not* p-possible!"

In his supremely casual, confident, infuriatingly-vague-yet-dripping-with-overt-sexual-innuendo-Ryan-like way, he drawls, "You just worry about how you're gonna show your gratitude when your man's done fixin' all your shit that's broke, okay?"

He kisses the tip of my nose and makes a move to turn away, but I grip his biceps and give him a hard shake, which fails to move him even a single inch. This time it's his brows that arch.

"Stop it! Just stop with the random, over-the-top, incomprehensible pronouncements! *How* are you going to fix it?"

He produces a dazzling smile that, if it showed up on anyone else's face but his, would inspire me to commit homicide.

"That's what heroes do, baby. We save the motherfuckin' day."

When it becomes apparent that *that's* his idea of a reasonable explanation, I say between gritted teeth, "I will kill you where you stand."

"Damn, you're gorgeous when you're angry."

I close my eyes and inhale a deep breath while mentally adding another few choice words to his list of faults.

"Ryan. Please. This is my future we're talking about. My *life*. No more jokes. *Tell me*."

He strokes the pad of his thumb over my cheekbone, following its path with his gaze. "I made a deal with the FBI to get the charges against you dropped. I'm gonna give 'em somethin' they want a lot more than a jewel thief."

My heart slams against my breastbone, sending my pulse flying, my blood roaring through my veins. *The FBI? A deal?* He can't be serious. He can't possibly be speaking the truth.

Past the roaring in my ears, I manage to ask, "What are you going to give them?"

The wolf slips back into Ryan's eyes and is there in the growl in his voice when he answers.

"A monster."

# 20

## RYAN

Mariana stares at me, breathless, speechless, her eyes wide and her face bone pale. For a while, I'm not sure if she's happy or angry, but then she releases my arms, stumbles backward, and drops heavily into a chair.

Gazing up at me like I just arrived from outer space, she breathes, "Capo?"

"Yeah. Vincent Moreno, aka Capo, head of the European crime syndicate, head of a transnational human and drug trafficking organization, head of a big fuckin' violent snake that specializes in suffering and exploitation. Your boss."

"My jailor," she corrects vehemently. "My *master*. The man who holds my leash!"

I force myself not to react to the image those words invoke of Mariana on her knees, the man from the limousine with the dead eyes gripping the chain to the choke collar around her neck. But rage has a way of making itself known in spite of all efforts to contain it. In this case, it's the flush of heat climbing my neck that gives me away.

She glances at my throat and sniffs in disapproval. "If all it takes are those few words to get you mad, you'll never be able to take him down. He's a siphon for negative emotions. He'll feed off anything—anger, fear, shame, doubt—grow stronger from it, and turn it around and use it against you."

The heat on my neck flames hotter. "There you go underestimating me again."

Mariana looks into my eyes. Her shock has vanished. Now she's simply practical, all business, her tone as flat as her expression.

"Put your ego aside, cowboy. That wasn't an attack on your manhood. It was the truth, gained from years of experience earned the hard way. If you're even a little bit serious about getting close to him, you're going to have to do it surgically, methodically, without an ounce of feeling to mar your perspective. And even then, you probably won't be able to pull it off."

Does this woman have no idea that she can crush me with her words? I snap, "Gee, thanks for the vote of confidence."

She shakes her head, annoyed with me. "This isn't a street thug we're talking about. Vincent Moreno is a psychopath with hyperactive paranoia and a genius-level IQ. He's filthy rich, vastly powerful, and extremely connected. Everyone who's anyone in the crime world owes him favors. He's a god among bastard kings."

Her voice grows softer. "And he owns me."

I growl, "Not for long!"

She shakes her head again. "You don't understand what I'm saying."

"Then make it fuckin' clearer!"

After a frigid beat, she says, "Number one: use that tone with me again and you'll be missing a cherished body part. I won't make it painless. Number two: I'm Capo's favored pet. I can go places you can't. Whatever your plan to get to him is, it has to include me."

This entire conversation has veered off into unexpected and extremely unwelcome territory. I stare at Mariana, my blood boiling like a cauldron of poisonous witches' brew in my veins. Quietly, with deliberate enunciation, I say, "That is out of the fuckin' question."

She gathers herself, inhaling and sitting up straighter in the chair, then leans back and folds her arms over her chest. "Fine. Let's hear your plan."

It sounds like a challenge, like she's already decided whatever I'm gonna say will fail big time, so of course I get more pissed off, even though she just told me to can it.

"My *plan*," I shout, "is to let him know *I've* got the Hope Diamond, and if he wants it, he's gonna have to *meet* with me, and when he does, the FBI's gonna swoop in and *bust* his ass, and then he's off for a nice long soak in a sensory deprivation chamber before bein' *interrogated* by a bunch of agency spooks who get off on roughin' guys up as much as *he* gets off on sellin' little girls into sexual *slavery*!"

My fevered rant is met with a cavernous, icy silence, timed by the hollow ticking of the clock on the wall. Then, in a voice an executioner might use to call up his next victim to the gallows, Mariana says, "Repeat the part about the Hope Diamond again? The part where you said *you* have it?"

We stare at each other with open hostility, like pistoleros in a Mexican standoff. I wonder if the vein pulsing in my temple is in imminent danger of bursting, it's throbbing so hard.

"Yeah," I say gruffly. "I've got it. The real one." Acidly sarcastic because I'm bent by her reaction—I was expecting gratitude and got attitude—I add, "Surprise."

Her jaw works like she's chewing on something that's really, really tough to swallow. Saddle leather, maybe. And I've never seen a pair of brown eyes glow so fucking bright, like they're lit from within by hellfire.

With perfect control, her voice Arctic cold, she says, "And how, may I ask, did that come about?"

If I were a smarter man, I'd probably be getting real nervous right about now, but I'm obviously not that bright a bulb, because all I'm getting is more and more pissed. "It *came about*," I repeat mockingly, "when I asked the guy I know who owns it if I could borrow it to snare a snake."

She does this thing that brings to mind a cartoon tea kettle right before it explodes. All the shaking and rattling, bolts popping off like popcorn, steam escaping, sounds like train whistles and splitting metal screeching in the air…yeah, that's what my girl starts to do, only it's a helluva lot more intense.

"I planned that job for a *week*," she says, rising from her chair, her voice shaking, her eyes flaming incinerator hot. "I lived in a shitty, cockroach-infested motel room for seven days, working twenty hours a day on research and logistics, listening to junkies tripping and hookers howling through fake orgasms and homeless guys fighting over cigarette butts they found in the street. I sweated every detail, had nightmares about what would happen if I failed, risked my neck breaking into that museum not once, but *twice*."

Her voice rises to a shout that could disrupt flight paths with its thundering vibrations. "And the whole time *you* had the diamond?"

She takes a step toward me.

I've stared the grim reaper down a hundred times in as many different ways, yet the look in her eyes still makes me take a step back.

"In my defense," I say placatingly, hands held up, "we weren't on speaking terms at the time. You'd ditched me again, remember? Sheets out the window? Vanishing act? Any of this ringing a bell?"

"Oh, I hear ringing bells all right, cowboy, and they're tolling for you."

I get that's some kind of reference to death from a Hemingway novel, but can't remember specifically which one. Not that it matters, because she's advancing like an M1 assault tank, and I'm about to get ripped a new asshole. Among other things.

"Honey, now stay calm—"

"Too late. That ship has sailed. Now we're taking a nice, long cruise on the SS *Cut A Bitch*. Guess who's the bitch? I'll give you a hint: it's not me."

My laugh sounds nervous. "Jesus. And I thought *I* was temperamental."

"Oh, smart. Insults and sarcasm are a *great* choice right now. Just keep digging that hole, cowboy." Mariana nods slowly, her eyes pinwheeling in full serial killer mode. "Because I'm about to shove you over the edge and bury you in it."

She's still advancing, I'm still retreating, and I'm starting to sweat.

I had no idea that five and a half feet of female could be so terrifying.

*Maybe she's about to get her period?*

In fear for their life, my testicles scream at me in no uncertain terms that I shouldn't make that observation aloud. Instead, I start to toss out rationalizations like a nervous zookeeper might toss raw meat into the alligator moat, hoping to pacify all the snapping, ravenous teeth.

"It's not like I could waltz into the fleabag motel and interrupt your planning! Knock, knock, who's there, it's your kinda-sorta boyfriend who you keep runnin' out on! Hey, look, shiny object, you don't have to hit the museum after all!"

"That's *exactly* what you could've done!" she retorts hotly, steam billowing from her ears.

"You ran out on me!"

"You crossed an ocean to find me!"

"You needed time to miss me!"

She rears back with an expression of shock and horror, like I just shoved a big, rotting rat corpse under her nose. "*What?*"

At least she's stopped advancing.

In my best macho-dude-who-is-NOT-intimidated-by-his-woman impersonation, I fold my arms over my chest, brace my legs apart, and peer at her down my nose.

"You heard me," I say, then exhale in annoyance, wishing I didn't sound like somebody's elderly, prissy aunt.

Birdlike, Mariana cocks her head. "You wanted me to miss you?"

I narrow my eyes at her suspiciously rational tone. "Well…yeah."

"Why?"

Now the heat crawling up my neck is embarrassment. Trying to maintain a shred of masculine dignity, I say stiffly, "I wasn't sure if you would."

When she just stands there staring at me in confounded silence, I figure the cat's already out of the bag, might as well go for broke. "So, did you?"

"I don't know," she says, sounding thoughtful. "Is that what you call it when you think about someone every second of every day, dream about him every night, know without a doubt you'll never experience anything quite as wonderful as the way he made you feel? When you ache that it's over, yet still feel privileged to have experienced it anyway?"

I have to swallow before I answer, because someone has shoved a rock down my throat. "Yes."

Her smile is so beautiful it could end wars. "Then I definitely didn't miss you."

That rumbling sound echoing through the kitchen is the growl emanating from my chest. It only serves to piss me off even more that hearing it makes her smile grow wider.

Full of sass and tartness, she says, "And if you want me to decide I like you again and start telling you the truth, you better count me in on any plan you have regarding Capo and tell me everything from here on out. *Including*," she adds when I open my mouth to talk, "any other things I've been instructed to steal that you already have in your possession."

My eyes narrow to slits. "You better sweeten that demand with a kiss, woman."

She lifts her chin and looks at me the way one might look at a piece of debris in the gutter that fell off a passing garbage truck. "You'll get your kiss when I get my promise."

My brows shoot up my forehead. "You think you can blackmail me?"

"Yes, Ryan," she replies with supreme confidence, a queen addressing her lowly subject. "That's exactly what I think. Now, do you want your kiss or not?"

"I've negotiated with terrorists before, you know."

"You're calling me a terrorist?"

"I'm calling your bluff."

"I'm *not* bluffing."

"Oh, yeah?" I rub my chin and give her a long and lingering once-over, calculating the odds of being stabbed depending on what I say next. There's a butcher's block of knives on the counter to her left that I'm pretty sure she's been eyeballing during this conversation.

"So you don't care if you ever kiss me again? You can totally live without my mouth on yours?" A hint of a smile lifts the corners of my lips. "Or any other parts of your body?"

Her cheeks faintly darken with color. Her chin lifts another inch in the air. "That's right."

I chuckle. "You used to be a better liar, darlin'. But okay. You're on."

She blinks, a little frown forming between her eyebrows. "I'm *on*?"

I shrug, turn back to the stove, and start to scrape out the burned bacon from the frying pan into the sink. Whistling cheerfully, I reach under the counter for the dish soap, then proceed to wash the frying pan, taking my time to scrub off all the little black bits, one ear trained behind me for a different kind of whistle, the sound the edge of a knife makes as it slices through the air toward the tender space between my shoulder blades.

That sound doesn't come. By the time I'm finished with the pan, Mariana has settled into a chair at the table, legs crossed, fingers tapping, searing my face off with her eyes.

I smile at her.

She smiles back with the sharpness of a viper's fangs. "Enjoying yourself?"

"Just cleanin' up the mess, baby. It's kinda my thing, cleanin' up messes."

If a man could be struck dead from a look, I'd already be six feet under.

"Funny," she says lightly. "And here I thought your thing was causing blindness with your teeth. How much work have you had on those chompers? That shade of white must've cost a fortune. They're as pearly as a unicorn's backside."

I make spokesmodel hands at my smile. "These old things? Oh no. These are bona fide, baby. I never even had braces."

She makes a face like she's sucking on a lemon wedge. "What about that nose? And that jaw you're always parading around like it should be chopping a cord of wood? I've seen axes with softer edges. There's a history of cosmetic surgery there, right?"

I mouth *You wish* and stroll over to the fridge, where I open the door and stand peering in. "You feel like breakfast or lunch?" I ask over my shoulder. "It's kinda brunch time, which is why I went with bacon—though really, bacon's apropos for any meal on account of it bein' so delicious—but I've got fixin's for sandwiches, omelets, pasta, crepes—"

"Crepes?" she repeats loudly.

I turn and look at her, glaring at me like a warlord from the kitchen table. Blinking innocently, I say, "I knew I was gonna have a guest from Paris, so I stocked up." My lips twitch, but I try very hard not to smile. I'm only marginally successful. "Got escargot, too. You want some of those? Not really my thing, but I figure with you bein' French and all"—I add emphasis on the word *French*—"you'd enjoy 'em."

She flattens her hands over the tabletop and exhales. I imagine plumes of white frost emanating from her nostrils, like the smoke from dry ice, and suck in my cheeks to keep from bursting into laughter.

"No, thank you," she replies, in a voice like brandished swords.

"Okay. I'll surprise you then, how 'bout that?"

"For a change," she mutters under her breath.

*Now who's the sarcastic one?*

I set about making brunch and ignoring the waves of hostility pulsing at me from all angles. I'm whipping eggs and milk with a fork when I hear, "So where are you keeping the diamond, anyway?"

"Ha! Wouldn't you like to know?" I keep on whipping, then am struck by an idea. I turn to her with a smile, which she curls her lip at. "I'll make you a bargain."

*Tap, tap, tap* goes her index finger on my kitchen table. "This should be interesting."

"Tell me your last name and where you're from, and I'll tell you where I'm keeping the diamond." When she hesitates a moment too long, I remind her, "You decided to trust me, remember?"

She shoots back, "That was before I decided I wanted to kick you in the balls."

I lift a shoulder like I could care less either way, and turn back to the eggs. "Suit yourself."

She starts to mutter in Spanish. I think I hear curses involving my mother and a few imminent threats on my life, but I'm not proficient in the language, so maybe I'm imagining it.

"My last name is Lora. L-O-R-A." She spells it out like I'm

too dense to guess, her tone loud and condescending. I swallow a chortle.

"And where do you live when you're not traveling the world in search of booty, Ms. Lora?" I glance at her over my shoulder. "The jewel kind, not the other kind. I wasn't implying you travel the world in search of men."

"How gallant," she deadpans. "Thank you for clarifying."

I send her a wink. "No problemo."

She appears to be doing deep-breathing exercises for several moments, complete with closed eyes and pursed lips on slow exhalations. Then she opens her eyes. "My home is in Morocco. But that's not where I'm from."

I instantly lose interest in the eggs.

*Morocco.*

I slip through a basement door in my memory to a place I visited once and never forgot. A place teeming with life, color, noise, and scents, so many exotic scents assaulting the nose, it was dizzying.

Orange blossom and cardamom, mint tea and jasmine oil, roasting meat and sweat. Dusty markets called souks filled with tourists and snake charmers, food stalls and laughing children, henna artists and musicians, a labyrinth of alleyways leading in like tributaries from the mazelike medieval city beyond. Lush gardens shimmering amid golden desert sands. Quiet *riad* courtyards adorned with mosaic-tiled fountains. Lapis lazuli glittering on ancient tomb walls.

Opulence and poverty and beauty, such beauty everywhere, you could drown in it and be grateful for such a glorious death.

I look at her with fresh eyes, this exotic creature regarding me with disdain at my kitchen table, and feel the sharp, painful throb of my heart.

"What?" she asks, nonplussed.

"I can picture you there, among the date palms and veiled women. I can picture you stealing into a locked room at dawn with the morning call to prayer echoing over the empty medina, the sun on red-tiled rooftops already hot."

By her expression, I can tell we're both surprised at the thickness of my voice.

After a moment of stillness, she murmurs in Arabic. It's the opening recital of the *Adhan*, the call to worship that rings out from minarets atop mosques five times a day in Islamic countries.

I listen the way an alcoholic drinks wine. Her singing is like the song of angels. It inspires the exact same kind of dumbstruck reverence in my heart.

Over the roar of my thrumming pulse, I ask, "Do you practice Islam?"

She shakes her head. "But the prayers are beautiful." Looking at her hands, she adds more quietly, "And so are the people. Morocco is the most beautiful place in the world."

I'm struck with realization. "You miss it."

Her shoulders round the way they do when you're bent with exhaustion or remorse, your body unable to hold itself upright any longer. In a voice so low it's almost a whisper, she says, "Like someone chained to the wall of a cave for a hundred years misses sunlight."

I take a breath that feels like inhaling fresh-fallen snow.

This.

*This* is why I answered Reynard the way I did when he asked me why I didn't turn her in to the police. This feeling of awe, for lack of a better word. This powerful, mysterious force that makes my chest ache with yearning, though I don't even know its proper name. This magic of hers that drew my eye and held it from the second I caught my first glimpse.

For me, Mariana holds an allure I've never encountered, something elemental, a pull as strong as gravity and just as impossible to resist. She makes me wish I had a talent for sonnets or sketching so I could capture the essence of it on paper, put it down for others to marvel over the way I do, the way people marvel over the magnificence of the Grand Canyon or the Taj Mahal.

She makes my pulse quicken, my blood run hot, and every cell in my body and soul come alive.

She moves me.

And I'd move mountains for her.

Our petty game of tit for tat abandoned with the next beat of my heart, I stride over to the table, bend down, and take her startled face in my hands. I give her a kiss, firm and potent, letting all the joy singing in my veins leach through my lips. When it's over, I pull away and stare into her lovely brown eyes, the rich hue of fine, barrel-aged bourbon.

My voice all gravel and sandpaper, I say, "All right. I'll show you the diamond and I'll tell you the whole plan. Then you're gonna tell me everything *I* want to know. Your life story, where you grew up, everything you love and hate and are proud of and regret. Your favorite music, your favorite food, the name of the first boy you ever kissed. And I'm gonna tell you mine."

Mariana laughs breathlessly, her eyes alight. "You kissed a boy?"

"Smartass," I growl, falling, falling, falling, head over heels and around again.

## 21

## MARIANA

I once heard insanity described as doing the same thing over and over and expecting different results. That was Albert Einstein, a much more intelligent person than myself. I'm thinking of him now as Ryan drives me to wherever he's keeping the diamond. I'm in the passenger seat, mulling all my life choices that have led me to this moment as the cityscape of Manhattan flashes by outside the windows, a silent movie of color and light.

It's silent inside the car, too. For once, we're not fighting or fucking. We're just sitting side by side, holding hands.

Such a simple thing, yet so painfully tender. My whole life, I've felt lioness-strong, toughened by the cruelty of fate and circumstance, but meeting Ryan has taught me that my heart isn't the fortress I thought it was.

Instead, it's is a newborn baby bird, blind and vulnerable to predators and the elements, trembling with hunger and terror in its nest.

I want to kick my own ass for being so weak. This whole thing has disaster written all over it.

"Pretty grim over there," Ryan observes, squeezing my hand.

I keep my gaze turned to the window when I answer, because I know how good he is at reading what's in my eyes. "Just ruminating on the vagaries of life and how arbitrary it all is."

His chuckle is warm. "I understood about half the words in that sentence, but my advice is not to worry. It'll all work out in the end."

Now I do look at him, because my curiosity is overwhelming. The sunlight treats him differently than it does other people, caressing him in a hazy, lover's glow, gleaming the tips of his hair and burnishing his skin to gold. Before I met him, I never even considered a man could be pretty, but he's beyond merely pretty. He's mind-meltingly beautiful.

Yes, that's it. He's melted my mind. No wonder I'm having trouble thinking.

"You're an optimist," I say flatly.

"You say that like you're accusing me of murder."

"Have you always been like this?"

He glances at me sideways, the flash of dimples in his cheek annoyingly adorable. "Like what? Awesome? Amazing? Unbearably cool?"

"Guess you weren't kidding when you said you were conceited," I mutter.

"The only difference between me and you, Angel," he says, squeezing my hand again, "is that you're a plotter and I'm a panster. You sweat every detail, and I live by the seat of my pants. We both get where we want to go in the end, I just don't waste time fussin' over what-ifs."

I suffer a brief but violent pang of jealousy that he doesn't have the worry gene, but then am insulted that he'd refer to all my careful planning—for instance, on a job like stealing the Hope—as "fussin'."

"I don't *fuss*. I deliberate. I consider all the options. It's called being professional."

"It's called bein' anal."

"It's called being an adult!"

He sighs like every man has ever sighed when dealing with a woman who doesn't agree with him. That "here we go" sigh. That "maybe it's PMS" sigh.

I'd like to hear the sigh he'd use if I stabbed him in the neck.

He says, "You're awful dramatic for someone who's so anal."

"I bet your brain feels as good as new, seeing as how you never use it," I grit out.

His shoulders shake silently. While I'm over here steaming, the bastard is trying not to laugh! When I try to extricate my hand from his, he just holds on tighter.

"Nope," he says with infuriating cheer, "you don't get your hand back just 'cause you've got your panties in a twist."

Instead of trying to force it or argue, I just smile sweetly. "Okay. But when *you* get *your* hand back, it might be missing the rest of your arm."

"We're here anyway, so there's no need for violence, darlin'."

Pulling up to a solid steel gate, Ryan winks at me, then rolls down his window. He punches a code into a black box, then he grins up at a camera pointed down from the top of the brick wall that flanks the gate, and flips it the bird.

"Were you in a fraternity?" I wonder aloud, watching him in all his cocky, Captain America football-hero glory as he makes lewd gestures at a piece of electronic surveillance equipment.

"In?" he scoffs. "No. I was a *founding father* of the Kappa Alpha Delta fraternity, *the* coolest frat on campus."

"It's all starting to make sense now." I shake my head as the gate swings open.

We pull into a large lot similar to the one at Ryan's home and park near a building similar to his, too, only much bigger. It looks like a converted industrial warehouse. All the windows are blacked out and there's only one entrance, a huge hammered steel door that's at least ten feet tall and about as wide. A fleet of hulking black Hummers lurks on one side of the lot, windscreens and chrome rims gleaming. They look like a group of metal sharks ready to feed.

The whole effect is über-masculine and weirdly threatening.

"Is this your other bachelor pad?"

"This is Metrix Security's headquarters."

"Oh. Yes, I guess it makes good sense to keep the diamond at the headquarters of a security company. This place must be as impenetrable as Fort Knox. Or your tooth enamel."

His only answer is a smile as he exits the car. I undo my seat belt, but before I can open the door, Ryan is holding it open for me, his hand extended to help me out.

"Thank you."

As we walk hand in hand toward the colossal door, he says, "The camera at the gate has facial recognition software—so nobody who isn't supposed to get in doesn't, even if they have the entry code—but there's also a guy watching the camera who mans the submachine guns set into the walls on either side of the gate."

"Machine guns?" I repeat, astonished. "Who're you expecting, the Terminator?"

Ryan says darkly, "Never know who's gonna come knockin'. Better armed to the teeth than caught off guard."

Our eyes meet. I think of acrid clouds of smoke over avocado fields, the rank, rusty smell of blood on dirt, and shudder. "I couldn't agree more."

His gaze sharpens, but he doesn't comment further because the steel door is silently sliding open. It reveals a beast of a man, dressed all in black, a gun strapped to his waist.

"Hey, brother," says Ryan, breaking into a grin.

In a rumbling baritone, the man replies, "Hey yourself." His eyes, dark and flinty as obsidian, flick toward me. "Lady Danger.

Nice to see you again, sweetheart. Stolen anything since I last saw you?"

"Yes. Bought any clothes that aren't black since I last saw you?"

Ryan laughs, and so does Connor. They look at each other, something silently passing between them.

"Nope," says Connor, glancing back at me, his eyes warm. "Don't hold your breath for it, either. C'mon in, kids, everyone else is already here."

My brows shoot up. *Everyone else?*

Seeing my look, Ryan sheepishly explains, "They kind of insisted."

"They? Who's *they*?"

"You didn't think the crew would let this opportunity pass by to say hello, did you?" Connor throws over his shoulder as he walks away into the gloom of the warehouse.

I stare at his retreating back with rising panic, then I stare at Ryan. "Who are we talking about? The FBI?"

"Worse. Come on, the sooner we go in, the sooner it'll be over with."

When I balk, he adds, "I have *one* word for you, Angel." He lowers his head and looks at me from under his brows.

Regretting I ever mentioned it, I exhale heavily. "Trust."

"Bingo. Now loosen that Vulcan death grip you've got on my hand. You're cuttin' off the circulation in the right side of my body."

He turns and drags me inside. As soon as we're over the threshold, the steel door slides shut behind us. We're swallowed in shadows. It's cool and dim inside, the cement floor polished to a subtle sheen. As we walk farther, my eyes adjust. I glimpse black computer towers extending the length of one wall in blinking, softly humming rows. Dozens of cubicles on the east wall house hard-jawed men wearing headphones, staring at computer screens. Another wall has a huge collection of weaponry displayed behind glass cases.

"Wow," I murmur.

"Impressive, isn't it?"

"Yes. There's enough free-floating testosterone in this place to get a convent of nuns ovulating in sync."

Ryan wrinkles his nose. "Don't be sacrilegious. Nuns don't ovulate."

When he doesn't smile, I say, "Please tell me that was a joke."

"What do you mean?"

"God, you're serious."

"Why would they ovulate if they don't ever have sex?" His voice rises. "Hey, Connor. Back me up, here, brother. Nuns don't ovulate, right?"

A few steps in front of us, Connor stops short. He turns and looks first at Ryan, then at me. He points to his own face. "You see how I don't look surprised by that question?"

"I'm guessing these little gems of his aren't that unusual."

Connor says, "It's not that he's dumb, don't get it wrong. The man's got an IQ of 156, which, by any standards, is way above genius level. Einstein himself clocked in at about 160."

"Funny you should mention Einstein, I was just thinking about him on the way over."

Ryan says, "Uh, guys? You realize I'm standin' right here, right?"

We ignore him. Connor says, "It's just that he has no idea—literally, *none*—about the inner workings of the female body."

Ryan extravagantly rolls his eyes. "Excuse me for not bein' a gynecologist."

"Don't they teach sex education in schools in the United States?" I ask Connor, genuinely curious.

"Oh yeah. But this one gets weirdly squeamish at any

mention of menstruation, so his mother had to write him a note to get him out of the days in class where the teacher covered it."

My brows lifted as high as they can go, I look at Ryan.

He's glaring at Connor. He says accusingly, "Bro."

Smiling, Connor replies, "It's one of my favorite stories."

"You're not supposed to *tell* anyone!"

"She's not anyone." He glances at our clasped hands. "She's your girl."

Ryan is in a kerfuffle for a moment after that, unsure of how to respond. "Fine, but just don't tell her I'm afraid of spiders!"

I ask laughingly, "You're afraid of spiders?"

Connor says, "Screams like a little girl when he sees one."

Ryan says, "*Bro!*"

"You're the one who brought it up, idiot."

Bypassing all the spider talk, I ask Ryan, "Have you seen a psychiatrist about your fear of bleeding women? That seems extremely Freudian."

"Some deep-seated shit, for sure," Connor agrees, nodding.

On an aggravated exhalation, Ryan says, "When I lived at home before college, my sisters used to fuck with me by hiding their used pads and tampons in my stuff. I never knew when I was gonna stick my foot in a sock or put my hand in a coat pocket and have it come away covered in period blood."

Connor and I make identical faces of disgust.

"What the hell?" Connor says.

"Oh, yeah, they thought it was hilarious. Meanwhile, I'm traumatized for the rest of my life. Every time I walk by the feminine products aisle in a grocery store, I feel like I'm gonna have a heart attack."

I picture him as a teenager, freaking out over a maxi pad he found in his sock drawer and shrieking every time he sees a spider, and I start to laugh.

Connor looks at me, and he's laughing, too. "Can you believe this shit?"

"Unfortunately, yes, I can."

"Glad to know my psychological wounds are so entertaining," says Ryan drily, but I can tell he's not really angry. I love it that he can take a joke at his own expense.

On impulse, I kiss his cheek.

His blinding grin comes on in full, megawatt voltage. "By the way, I know *all* I need to know about how the female body works." He looks at Connor and waggles his eyebrows.

Connor's sigh is the aggrieved but fond one of a mother whose favorite child is misbehaving again. Shaking his head, he turns and walks away. We follow like a pair of ducklings.

When we arrive at Connor's office, there's a welcome party waiting.

Darcy reclines in a big leather chair, her feet propped up on an even bigger black oak desk, her eyes closed as Kai, standing behind her, massages her shoulders.

Tabby, pacing a three-foot section of floor in the corner, has her nose pressed against her cell phone screen. Her thumbs fly over it as she types.

Juanita is lying on the black leather sofa against the far wall in a Catholic schoolgirl's uniform of plaid, pleated skirt, white shirt, and knee socks. She's watching something on a tablet propped on her stomach and feeding Cheetos to the fat black-and-white rat lounging contentedly on her chest.

When we walk in, everyone stops what they're doing and looks up.

And for a moment, just a few stuttering beats of my heart, I allow myself to remember what it feels like to have a family.

Because it's obvious they're all happy to see me.

Darcy lets out a whoop and jerks upright, knocking over the desk phone and almost falling out of the chair in the process. Kai jumps up and down, maniacally clapping. Tabby's grin is almost as huge as Ryan's. Juanita is grinning, too, and even the damn *rat* looks happy, whiskers twitching like mad.

"Oh," I say in a small voice, my heart thumping with surprise, my eyes wide.

Ryan slings his arm around my shoulder and gives me a reassuring squeeze, as if he knows I'm in need of a little emotional fortification before I face the firing squad.

"Miss Thang!" Says Darcy, finding her footing with the help of Kai. "You made it!"

She charges.

"This will only hurt a little," says Ryan regretfully, before jumping out of the way.

Darcy throws her arms around me, engulfing me in her bosom.

She smells sweet and fruity, like coconuts. It's pleasant, but I'm being suffocated, and so I make a bleating sound of distress.

She releases me to hold me at arm's length. "A travel writer. Ha! We all knew that was baloney, girl. No writer in history has ever had ta-tas like that!" She leers at my chest.

"That's what *I'm* sayin'," drawls Ryan, leaning against a bookcase.

Darcy turns scolding, shaking her finger in my face. "Now don't worry about us telling anyone you got sticky fingers, girl. We're real used to keeping each other's big, hairy secrets in this crew, you hear?"

"Um…"

She leans in and says in a stage whisper, "You know, me and you gotta stick together because the redhead is nuts. Tattoos of green fairies, and building computers that think and shit. And don't get me started on all that Hello Kitty nonsense. It's like she thinks that cartoon cat is alive."

Tabby looks at the ceiling. "Darcy. I'm literally four feet away."

Darcy mutters under her breath, "Lurk much, nutty?"

Exasperated, Tabby throws her hands in the air. "Still! Four! Feet!"

Darcy ignores her. "Now I know you and the boys got some business, so me and my baby"—she blows a kiss to Kai, who giggles and waves with his fingertips—"and short stuff over there with the rodent just stopped by to say hi real quick on our way to lunch. So. Hi."

I can tell I'm supposed to say something now, so I pretend this is a completely normal situation and say pleasantly, "Hello. It's very nice to see you again, Darcy."

She nods in solemn satisfaction, like we just made a blood pact. Then over her shoulder, she bosses, "Kai, say hello to Miss Thang!"

Kai makes a formal little bow. When he straightens, he says in his charming German accent, "I would like to cook you a meal when this is all over, Miss Thang. Do you enjoy strudel? I make an *excellent* traditional strudel."

Wondering what he means by "ven zis is all over," I reply, "That sounds wonderful. Thank you, Kai. And you can just call me Mariana."

I notice Connor and Ryan are both trying hard to keep straight faces, and not having much luck.

Juanita rises from the couch and skips over, tossing the rat onto her left shoulder in a smooth, practiced move. All gangly limbs and soft clouds of dark, curly hair, she inserts herself between Darcy and me, dusts orange Cheetos powder from her hands, then stares up into my face.

As if picking up where we left off in an earlier conversation she says, "Me and Elvis have a bet about where you're from. He says Brazil, but you don't have a Portuguese accent—"

"I don't have *any* accent," I interrupt, a knot forming in the pit of my stomach.

Everyone else seems to have suddenly fallen silent.

Juanita slowly shakes her head, not in disagreement, but as if I'm not listening. She repeats firmly, "He says Brazil, but I say Colombia. So which is it?"

Her eyes are large and velvet brown, black-lashed and penetrating. They're also devoid of childlike innocence, or any of the bashful self-consciousness adolescents usually display in a roomful of adults.

I'm looking at a fifteen-year-old girl, but the person looking back at me hasn't been fifteen in an eternity.

Ghostly pale and unsmiling, my sister's face swims into my vision. I inhale a hitching breath.

"You remind me so much of someone I once knew," I whisper in Spanish, reverting to my native tongue without a thought, dragged back by the weight of ancient memory and the kind of wounds that scab over, but never fully heal.

Juanita replies instantly in Spanish, "I knew it. Elvis, you owe me five bucks."

"Okay, no secrets now. Everybody talks in English from here on out."

It's Tabby, her tone light and joking, but she's looking at me with a gaze that's anything but light. I realize that she understood everything Juanita and I have said to each other at the same time I understand that she won't mention another word to me about it, or divulge to anyone else what we've said.

This is turning out to be one hell of an interesting day.

## 22

## RYAN

While Tabby and Mariana stare at each other, mentally transmitting some kind of weird, girl-code shit, Connor and I share a look of our own.

His look says *She okay? You okay?*

My look says *I'm good, but my woman's hangin' on by a thread.*

He nods. His piercing gaze flicks over to Mariana. "All right, kids," he booms, addressing the room. "Visiting time at the zoo is over. Say your goodbyes."

Darcy says, "C'mon, Kai, let's roll. It's Badass Big Guy Meeting Time. Short stuff," she says to Juanita, "you got a restaurant picked out for lunch? And don't say anything with the words *kale bar* in it, or I'll be forced to kick your tiny Catholic behind."

Juanita replies, "I'm an atheist, Darcy. I only go to a Catholic school because I'm fifteen and have no legal rights, and that's where my mother wants me to go. And I was thinking that new Thai-French fusion place on sixth. Elvis loves Thai food."

Aghast, Darcy cries, "*Atheist!* Hush, you silly child, God will hear!"

Juanita turns to look at Tabby. "Is it worth it?" she asks.

"Nope."

Juanita shrugs and flips her hair over her shoulder. She looks at Mariana and sticks out her hand. They shake solemnly, an ocean of unspoken words between them.

I can't wait to find out what their little exchange in Spanish was all about.

Darcy, Kai, and Juanita take their leave. Connor lowers his bulk to the big captain's chair behind his desk, Tabby perches on a corner of the desk and folds her hands over a knee, and Mariana and I sit in the two leather guest chairs opposite them. For a moment, we all simply look at one another.

Then Mariana says quietly, "I hope I didn't ruin your honeymoon."

"Are you kidding?" laughs Tabby. "You were a highlight!"

Connor swivels his head slowly to look at her, his dark brows climbing his forehead.

Tabby smiles tenderly at him. "Not *the* highlight, honey."

"Don't need to hear any details about the other highlights!" I interrupt before Connor forces Tabby to make a list of all his talents in the sack. I know I've got an ego on me, but Connor's got an egosaurus. If he gets a burr under his saddle, we'll be here all day trying to calm that bucking bronco down. "Connor, you wanna start?"

For a moment, he drums his fingers on the desktop, thinking. Then he looks up at Mariana. "Yeah. Let's start with Vincent Moreno."

She stiffens. I reach over and touch her arm. She clutches my hand, threading her fingers through mine and squeezing. The whole time, Connor watches us with unblinking intensity. I can see the wheels turning behind his eyes.

Mariana asks, "What do you want to know?"

"When Ryan told us your situation, we made some inquiries," Connor says, referring to himself and Tabby.

"Inquiries?" Mariana repeats cautiously.

It's Tabby who answers this time. "As I told you before, I work for the government. Specifically the NSA. Freelance, but at the highest clearance. We've also got contacts in the FBI and the CIA, and the international security and law enforcement communities. All this adds up to a very powerful network of information."

Mariana sits perfectly still, listening, a look of intense concentration on her face. A faint tremor runs through her hand.

Her voice lower, Tabby continues. "This man you work for… He's very dangerous."

"No," says Mariana without a second's pause. "Ebola is dangerous. Sharks are dangerous. Live electrical wires are dangerous. Vincent Moreno is pure evil."

Connor says curtly, "Yet you're on his payroll."

Mariana's eyes slice through him like a hot knife through butter. A vein throbs on the side of her neck. "When the devil tells you to jump, the only question you ask is how high."

I resist the hot, crackling urge to come to Mariana's defense only because I already know Connor and Tabby are on our side, and I know this is a conversation that has to be had. But *fuck*, seeing Mariana upset touches nerves I didn't even know I had.

Maybe my feelings for her are making me grow new ones.

"I understand that," says Tabby. "I know something about psychopaths myself."

"Then you know that they can't be reasoned with, or easily fooled."

"Yes."

"So when Ryan tells me *he's* going to return the Hope Diamond and set Capo up with a sting, you'll understand my opinion that not only is that a particularly stupid plan, it's also destined to fail."

To my horror, Tabby replies, "Yes. I happen to agree with you completely."

I shout, "Tabby! What the fuck?"

Connor says wearily, "Save your outrage for the end, brother. It gets worse."

Before I can protest further, Tabby continues. "There's no way a man like Vincent Moreno is going to accept a meet with a stranger, especially when all he has to do to find out who you are, Ryan, is dig a little. Then he discovers your identity, easily guesses what you're up to, and puts out a hit. You're dead before dawn. So is Mariana."

"He wouldn't kill me right away," says Mariana, looking at her hands. "There are things he wants from me much more than my death."

That sucks the air right out of the room. We all stare at her in silence, until Tabby finally breaks it.

"Submission?"

Mariana shakes her head, closing her eyes. "More than that. More like surrender. I've been defying him for years. But mostly he just wants my pain."

She opens her eyes and looks at each of us in turn, me last. "He wants to wring every drop of anguish from me the way you'd wring water from a towel. He's come close a few times, but always manages to hold himself back. And if I'm being honest, I think the reason he can resist has less to do with self-control or honoring the blood oath I took than it does with heightening his anticipation. All these years, all these jobs, this noose he holds over Reynard's head… I've finally realized it's not really about repayment of a debt."

"What's it about?" I ask, in a raw voice, like I've been screaming.

She swallows then says faintly, "Foreplay."

"That *motherfucker*!" I growl, hackles bristling, but before I can continue what threatens to be an epic rant, Connor thunders, "Can it, soldier!"

I whip my head around and glare at him.

"You going ballistic isn't gonna help anything!" he snaps, meeting my blistering glare with a steely one of his own. "Now fucking can it. Your woman needs you steady, not bleedin' rage outta your eyes."

He's right. He's right and I know it, but that doesn't make it any easier to swallow.

I jerk out of my chair and start to pace the floor, dragging my hands through my hair and muttering. I want to *kill* Moreno, I want to tear him *limb from limb*, but if I can't control myself, I've got zero chance of doing either.

So I pace and breathe and force myself not to think of the word *foreplay* and how it's now ruined for me forever.

Eyeing me with surprise at my forceful reaction, Tabby says to Mariana, "I'm sure Ryan's already told you he's spoken with the FBI about getting all the charges dropped against you in exchange for Moreno."

Mariana glances at me, hesitates, then nods.

"And he's told us that you have approximately forty-eight hours to get the diamond to Moreno before the clock runs out on your friend Reynard."

Mariana nods again.

"Well then, I think we need to give you the diamond and get you on a plane."

I stop dead in my tracks and stare at Tabby in complete disbelief, my rage erupting all over again. "We're not sending her back to him! Under no circumstances is she even gonna be in his general *vicinity* again!"

"The rest of the plan we talked about stays the same, Ryan," Connor interjects, his voice tight. "The FBI will have whatever meeting place we designate surrounded. Snipers on rooftops, agents ready to swarm in, you know the drill. All she'll have to do is wear the wire like you were going to, get him to admit a few damning things on tape—"

"Absolutely not," I say flatly, blood pulsing in my ears.

"Fuck no with a capital *F*. Would you send Tabby in if the situation was reversed?"

Tabby asks archly, "You think it would be up to him?"

Sounding thoughtful, Mariana answers. "Capo's never searched me before any of our meetings. He trusts me. He'd never know if I was wearing a wire."

*He trusts me*. That makes my stomach roll like my breakfast might make a reappearance.

"What would I have to get him to say?"

"No, Angel," I say, gripping the back of her chair. When she looks up at me, I shake my head to underscore my words. "*No*. Never. Gonna. Happen."

The look in her eyes tells me I've already lost this fight.

Unflinchingly holding my gaze, she says, "Reynard bought me from Capo when I was ten years old. Did you know that? Did you find that out in your talks with the FBI?"

The only sound I hear is the pounding of my pulse. The whole room narrows to a small tunnel of black, focused on Mariana's face. I sink into the chair next to hers.

"What?"

"With money he'd been skimming from Capo's operation for years," she continues as if I haven't said anything. "Very small amounts, nothing that would raise suspicions. My sister Nina and I were in a group of girls being trafficked to Europe from South America in a shipping container. There was no food, only jugs of water, and no receptacles for waste. Twenty-seven of us went into that shipping container. Twelve of us survived the trip to London. We were all children. The oldest, my sister Nina, was fourteen."

From the corner of my eye, I glimpse Tabby recoil and cover her mouth with her hand, but I can't look away from Mariana. I can't move. I can't even breathe.

"Normally, girls taken from the villages in my country are smuggled to Tenancingo, Mexico, which is a hub for human trafficking and forced prostitution, but we were sold abroad because we were pretty. Pretty girls get higher prices. And Capo pays the highest prices of them all. Especially for virgins." She waits a beat, looks at her hands, then whispers, "He gets a new container every month."

Connor breathes, "Jesus Christ."

Mariana takes another moment, then shakes her head as if pulling herself from a bad dream. She speaks more briskly, her voice clear and level, but there's an undercurrent of rage.

"To make a long story short, Reynard went to the docks thinking he was meeting a shipment of stolen paintings, but got the surprise of his life when the workers opened the doors. Somehow the manifests got mixed up, and there we were, a dozen starving, terrified little girls in collars and chains, huddled among corpses.

"Reynard only had enough cash on him to bribe the workers for one of us. They were Capo's men, of course. The story became that only eleven girls had survived."

I remember putting a hand around her neck in passion and her stiffly saying *"I don't like to be restrained,"* and I have to swallow the bile rising acidly hot in the back of my throat.

"Later I found out that my sister and the others were brutally raped by their transporters before they ever got to Capo. But my sister escaped. She got her hands on one of the men's guns and blew her brains out. She was lucky, in a way. I understand not one of the other girls made it to sixteen."

I'm aware that my mouth is open. I'm aware that the silence in the room is one of the most awful sounds I've ever heard, filled with the horror of three adults who've seen plenty of terrible things in their lives. But I can't move. I'm frozen. All I can do is stare at Mariana.

She sighs heavily, passing a hand over her face. It's obvious the toll this tale is taking on her. I wonder if she's ever spoken about it to anyone before.

"It was another ten years before Capo found out what Reynard had done. I don't know how. All I know is that one day he came to the shop and said I had a choice to work off Reynard's debt in one of two ways."

Her mouth pinches in distaste at some memory. More quietly, she says, "So instead of becoming Capo's whore, I became his puppet. His obedient minion, sent to fetch whatever bauble struck his fancy. I was already an accomplished thief by then. By seven years old I could sneak into any locked room, pinch a wallet or a watch from a man without him knowing it was gone. Reynard only refined my skills. So it made sense for Capo to recruit me, though he would've preferred I choose the other path. And all these years later, here we are."

Mariana looks at Tabby and Connor, both of whom are obviously in the same shock I am. She says, "I've wanted to kill him for as long as I can remember. So if there's anything I can do to help take him down, I'll do it."

Tabby and Connor look at me.

"Angel," I say roughly, hunting for her eyes. When I get them and she looks at me, I say, "Let me kill him for you."

Connor says quickly, "If we don't give the FBI Moreno, she doesn't get a clean slate."

I'm not really listening. It's hard enough to concentrate on sitting still when every nerve is screaming for me to go cut off Moreno's head and present it to Mariana on a silver platter.

I want to destroy him for what he's done to her. I want to obliterate him. I want to rip him apart with my bare hands and feast on his bones. I've never felt such all-consuming fury.

Looking deeply into my eyes, Mariana smiles.

"That might be the most romantic thing I've ever heard, cowboy. Thank you. And please, please don't take this as an insult, or a lack of faith in your abilities, but the possibility of you getting close enough to kill him is very small."

When I start to protest, she presses a finger against my lips.

I love it when a woman does that. It silences me instantly.

"He travels everywhere with six assassins. He's never in a public setting where he could be trapped, surrounded, or caught in a sniper's crosshairs. No one outside of the assassins—all Sicilians, unimpeachably loyal—knows where he lives."

She looks at Tabby for confirmation. When Tabby nods regretfully, Mariana turns her attention back to me.

"He's avoided many different attempts on his life, simply because he's always expecting the next one. He lives prepared to die. When they invented the term criminal mastermind, they were talking about him. The smartest, most straightforward way to catch him is with bait he already knows and trusts."

She drops her finger from my lips and adds with quiet vehemence, "And in my mind, it wouldn't count as avenging my sister's death if I had nothing to do with Capo's demise. I can't be a spectator, letting everyone else do the work. To use your words from earlier, how would you feel if the situation was reversed?"

I want to answer that the situation is totally different because she's mine and it's my job to protect her in any way and every way, but the words are curdling like spoiled milk in my mouth.

Because the truth is that if someone did to one of my sisters what Vincent Moreno did to Mariana's, to all those nameless girls who were someone's sisters and daughters and best friends, there'd be no force in heaven or hell that could stop me from getting my revenge.

I swallow hard and think for a long moment, wrestling with my conscience, my ego, and every male instinct in my body.

It might be the hardest battle I've ever fought.

Finally, after an eternity of silent debate, the scales tip to one side and I take a deep breath.

"All right."

I have to force the words past my teeth with an enormous effort of will.

"But if I even get a *whiff* that things are going sideways, I'm pulling you out and going in myself, guns blazing." I look at Connor, letting him see the kamikaze warrior in my eyes. "And this plan better be air-fuckin'-*tight* or I'm not signin' off on it. You hear me?"

He says quietly, "I hear you, brother."

I stand, pace around the room a few times, breathing in another few deep breaths as I try to get myself under better control. Everyone watches me, silently waiting.

Eventually I trust myself to talk without blowing up.

"First things first. We need to decide on a place for the meet. It can't be public, not only because Moreno wouldn't agree to it, but also because we want to mitigate as much collateral damage as we can if things go south and the guns come out. But it also has to have enough cover for the FBI spooks to hide, and multiple ingress and egress points for them to come in and for us to get out. Somewhere neutral enough that it won't arouse his suspicions, yet ideally close enough to an airport that he can be moved quickly before his men can regroup and form a counterassault to get him back."

Mariana's lips curve into a small, unnerving smile.

"How about an inferno?"

# 23

## MARIANA

For the next hour, we talk logistics. Or Connor, Tabby, and I do, while Ryan paces the floor like a caged tiger and tries not to break anything.

His protectiveness shouldn't surprise me. He's a soldier, after all. Generally they have no problem putting their lives on the line to protect what they hold dear. He's trained to think of others first, to focus on the mission first, to focus on goals and outcomes rather than dwelling on feelings and the *why*.

But his reaction to my story does surprise me. Both his immediate and heartfelt offer to kill Capo for me, and his willingness to swallow his protective urges—and his pride—to allow me to take part in a plan he so obviously doesn't want me to have anything to do with.

In other words, he's respecting my wishes. Against his better judgment and what must be a considerable onslaught of testosterone pounding against the inside of his skull and demanding that he lock me in a closet to keep me safe, but he's going along with what I want. And by the looks of it, it's killing him to do so.

If I wasn't already so infatuated with him, that alone would do the trick.

I've never met an alpha male who could be described as liberated.

"So just to recap," I say into a lull in the conversation, "I'll arrange to meet Capo at the Palace. I'll come in wearing a wire and an earpiece, which will receive and transmit from an FBI van set up close by. I'll show Capo the diamond, making sure to mention how he ordered me to take it, like he did with the other jobs. I'll ask him what my next job will be, make small talk about his business, lead him into discussing our history together or whatever specifics I can to get him to disclose about his criminal activities. If he's got girls with him, as he usually does, that will be easy. How will I know when you've got enough?"

"You'll hear the agent in charge give the signal to go over your earpiece," says Connor. "And then all the lights will go out. You need to hit the ground and stay there until we've got Moreno in handcuffs."

"She'll be a sitting duck!" Ryan interjects hotly. "When the lights go out, he'll know something's hinky—and who's gonna be right there for him to blame it on?"

"I doubt if he'd suspect me, but if he does, I can defend myself. Last time I met with Capo, I walked in wearing half a dozen knives. The main problem is his men. They're never more than a few feet away from him, and they're heavily armed."

"Can you get him alone somehow?" asks Tabby.

Ryan stops pacing, stiffens, and curls his hands to fists.

Glimpsing his murderous expression and nuclear body language, Tabby says, "Whoa. You just went full transformer-mutant mode, dude. Chill for a second. We're only parsing the possibilities."

Livid, he answers with a tight jaw. "Parse *other* possibilities."

"Sweetie," I say softly.

Ryan cuts his freezing gaze to me.

Ignoring the fact that there are two other people in the room, I say, "You're the most amazing man I've ever met."

He blinks, and his iceberg eyes go all melty.

I say, "Thank you for being so protective. I know this is very hard for you."

His hands slowly unclench. He takes a big breath.

"And I know you'd rather have this go any other way than the way it's going, and that it's killing you to think I'll be in danger."

He swallows, folds his arms over his chest, and glares at the floor. He says gruffly, "Killing is too soft a word."

"I know. Look at me."

He lifts his eyes, but not his head, so he's standing there glowering at me from under lowered brows.

God, he's adorable.

"When this is over, we're going to have that dinner at L'Ami Louis in Paris and gorge ourselves on champagne and oysters and *confit canard* while we hold hands and watch the sun go down over the Seine. Then we'll discuss how much of the year we want to live in Morocco versus Manhattan. Then we'll go back to our hotel and make love. For days. Weeks, maybe. We'll see how it goes, depending on how many oysters you eat. Deal?"

He toes the floor with his boot and pretends to think about it. He also pretends to scowl to cover the smile that threatens to consume his face. Eventually, he says grudgingly, "Fine. But only because you called me sweetie."

The astonishment on Connor's face is epic. Tabby, meanwhile, has little hearts for eyes.

"You guys are too cute!" she exclaims.

"I am not *cute*," grumbles Ryan. "Don't push it."

He takes my face in his hand and gives me an angry kiss, then goes back to pacing.

I'm considering it a success.

Tabby snaps back into planning mode as if there was no interruption. "Are you sure we have to show Moreno the diamond? What if he hands it off to someone before Mariana gets the information we need? I know Karpov won't be happy if he doesn't get that rock back."

I slowly swivel in my chair and look at Ryan. "So that's where you got it."

Ryan nods. "Yeah. Noticed it on display in his mansion when we brought his daughter back to St. Petersburg from her kidnappers. His father was the one who originally coordinated the theft from the Smithsonian back in the seventies. Now it's like a family heirloom. I told him it might lift the curse if he lent it out for a good deed."

"Curse?" Connor says, intrigued. "What curse?"

Tabby answers as if she wrote the leading book on the history of the stone.

"The one put on it by the priests who discovered it was missing from their Hindu temple in India in the seventeenth century. Jean Baptiste-Tauvernier, its first recorded owner and the man who stole it from the temple, came down with a raging fever soon after. His body was later devoured by wolves. King Louis XIV bought the stone in 1673 from Tauvernier, then died —painfully—of gangrene. Louis XVI inherited it, and he Marie Antoinette lost their heads during the French revolution. It was stolen from Versailles during the revolution and lost for a while, but surfaced many years later when a Dutch jeweler, Wilhelm Fals, recut it and sold it off in two parts. Fals's son murdered him…and then killed himself.

"There was a Greek merchant who later owned the diamond and then killed himself, his wife, and their child by driving off a cliff. The heiress who owned the *Washington Post* had the diamond for a while, and everyone in her family died in tragic circumstances—including her—broke and owing huge debts.

That heiress's kids sold the diamond to Harry Winston, who donated it to the Smithsonian by *mailing* it—and the mailman who delivered it had his leg crushed in an accident right after. *And* his house burned down. And finally, Sergei Karpov, the Russian oligarch who arranged for the stone to be stolen from the Smithsonian, was poisoned by a business rival. His wife died in a mental hospital. His son and daughter-in-law suffered four stillbirths before finally giving birth to a healthy girl…who wound up getting kidnapped by a brutal gang of thugs."

"And saved by me," says Ryan, tidily summing up the tale.

Connor corrects him drily. "*Us*."

"Oh. Yeah. That's what I meant. Us." He shrugs.

Connor shakes his head and sighs.

"Capo won't hand off the diamond to anyone," I say. "He *will* be curious about why I want to meet at the Palace to give it to him instead of him picking it up from Reynard's like he usually does and meeting him there afterward, so I'll have to come up with something plausible."

I look at Tabby and Connor for ideas. Tabby answers first.

"Because you're worried Reynard's place is bugged. Yes, this is good," she says, warming to the idea as the rest of us stare at her like she's been drinking. "It will appeal to his paranoia, make *you* look trustworthy, and deflect suspicion, all at once. You can say you saw a man who looked strange hanging around the utility box down the street, heard an odd click on the phone when you last spoke, whatever. It's a classic hide-in-plain-sight diversion technique. Look at this suspicious thing over here so you don't notice this even more suspicious thing happening right under your nose."

I say, "If I tell him that before the meet, he'll just send his guys over and sweep the shop for bugs."

"So tell him you can't discuss over the phone why you need to change the meet spot. Make it sound like you think your call is being monitored. Then use some kind of code only he would know to suggest the Palace."

"That won't work," Ryan interrupts. "He'll suggest a meeting place of his own, somewhere he can control, somewhere probably on *his* turf."

My brain turning, I say slowly, "Unless I give him a more compelling reason to meet me at the Palace. A reason he won't be able to resist."

Ryan and I lock eyes. When he reads what I'm thinking, he says loudly, "No."

"I'd be able to get him away from his men that way, too."

Another no, even louder, punctuated by an index finger pointing at my face and a thundered, "DON'T EVEN THINK ABOUT IT!"

Connor says, "I feel like I'm missing something."

Tabby responds, "Mariana wants to use herself as bait."

"She's already doing that."

"No, honey." She looks at him meaningfully. "*Bait* bait. The kind a sadist with a yen for virgins can't resist."

"Ah. Gotcha." Drumming his fingers on the desk, he glances at Ryan, at me, then back at Ryan. To me, he says, "I can't sign off on that unless your man does."

"He *doesn't*!" hollers Ryan, rattling the framed picture of the American flag on the wall.

Connor leans back in his chair and laces his hands together over his flat stomach. "Any other ideas?" he asks me mildly. "'Cause that one's not gonna fly."

I hold Ryan's supercharged gaze for a moment. Finally, I say, "I'll think of something. Let's talk about the rest of the plan. What happens after the FBI has Capo in custody? Won't they want to keep the diamond and return it to the Smithsonian? How are you going to explain that?"

Ryan says, "The FBI doesn't give two shits about the diamond. They want Moreno."

Tabby asks, "Why do you have to bring the real thing to the meet? Wouldn't a fake suffice if he's not even going to keep it?"

I shake my head. "He can spot a fake a mile away. Gemology is one of his passions. He'll have a jeweler's loupe to magnify it, but there are a dozen easy ways to test a phony diamond without bringing it to a lab. He'll know as soon as I set it in his hands."

"We need to put her in body armor," says Ryan abruptly. "She's gonna be in a room with six armed assassins, then the FBI's gonna blow down the doors—"

"Like a bulletproof vest wouldn't be obvious," says Connor, dismissing the idea with a shake of his head.

"I don't need body armor. I'll have my seamstress make me a dress."

When everyone looks at me blankly, I smile. "She's not a regular seamstress."

Tabby asks, "Nanotechnology?"

I take a moment to marvel at how she seems to know something about everything, then say, "Yes, exactly."

Ryan asks, "Like the Kevlar suits the troops used in Iraq?"

I nod. "Only the fabric is much thinner, and far more stylish. It will look like just a regular dress, not impenetrable body armor."

"Cool."

I can't help but smile at Ryan's and Connor's identical expressions of awe. "Just one of the perks of being an international criminal, guys."

Something happens to Ryan's face. His expression changes, but I can't tell what he's thinking until he says, "You gonna miss that? Your old life? Your old friends?"

"I don't have any friends, or what you could call an actual life." I answer more sharply than I intend because I'm still rattled by all the terrible memories that talking about Nina and Capo have evoked.

But Ryan softens all my sharp edges when he says, "You have friends, Angel. They're right here in this room."

My throat tightens. The hot prick of tears threatens at the back of my eyes.

Connor drawls, "And as for a life, it sounds like you and lover boy here got all sorts of plans for that already. Paris, Morocco, oysters…" His grin is huge. "He's not ever gonna want to come back to work."

"That's right," says Ryan, staring hard at me. "Gonna need some paid sick leave, 'cause I'll be too chapped and dehydrated to work for a few months."

Tabby wrinkles her nose. "Yuck. Just got a gnarly visual of your chapped junk. Thanks for that."

"We done for now?" says Ryan to Connor, but he's still looking at me.

"Yeah, go on. I'll call the agency and get it together. Mariana, what's the address of this joint you call the Palace?"

I give it to him.

"They're gonna need to meet with all of us before the op. Paperwork, briefing, the whole enchilada. Seeing as how we don't have much time until you need to be in London, it'll be soon. Why don't you both go home and get some rest." Connor chuckles as Ryan and I continue to stare at each other. "Or whatever."

Tabby gives me a hug before we leave. Ryan and Connor hug, too, thumping each other on the back so hard, I'm sure there will be bruises.

As we walk out the door, I say, "Wait! You haven't shown me the diamond!"

Ryan only smiles. "I never said it was here, darlin'."

I spend the ride back to Ryan's in even deeper thought than I spent on the ride over. Thinking of what's ahead of us, of all the possible things that could go wrong, my brain is scrambled eggs. I keep a calm demeanor, though, and keep my hand in Ryan's loose and light so he doesn't guess what I'm going through and change his mind about allowing me to take part in what's by far the most dangerous job I've ever attempted.

If I fail, Reynard dies. If I fail, *I* die. If Capo discovers Ryan's part in the plan, Ryan dies. So do Connor, Tabby, anyone associated with Metrix…basically everyone I've been in contact with, including people I haven't been in contact with yet, but will, like the FBI agents I'll meet before we go. Hell, the boys from the Smithsonian might even be in danger.

Basically, the plan should be called If Anything Goes Wrong, Everyone Dies.

Ryan says firmly, "I promise it's gonna work out."

I should've known he'd guess what I'm feeling. The man's intuition is almost female. "This telepathy of yours is spooky. Have you ever considered a job in the field of psychic readings? You'd make a fortune."

"Nah," he says, sending me a wink from the driver's seat. "I can't see the future. Only what's right in front of my face." He lifts my hand to his mouth and kisses it.

"That's because your teeth have an unearthly glow. You could find your way through a haunted forest just by smiling."

"Your jealousy of my dental perfection is flatterin', darlin', but considering *you* have beautiful teeth, it's also a little weird."

My teeth were crooked as fishhooks until I was fifteen and Reynard paid for my braces, but I keep that to myself. I'm suffering a serious bout of superstition that saying his name aloud will cause something bad to happen. Instead, I say, "Not as weird as the way you drive. You are aware that we're not currently engaged in a high-speed pursuit with the police, right?"

"Excuse me, woman, but I'm an *excellent* driver. Example."

He swerves hard to avoid a squirrel that has darted into the road, then cuts back into his lane just as quickly, saving the squirrel but leaving a swath of squealing tires in his wake from other drivers slamming on their brakes to avoid colliding with us.

"Hmm," I say, my heart thumping. "Seeing as how your example was accompanied by a chorus of horns and what is probably a nasty case of whiplash on my part, I reject it out of hand." A black BMW speeds by us in the next lane. "Oh, and that guy wants you to know you're number one. Boy, does he have a long middle finger."

"What does he know? He's driving a Beemer!" Ryan scoffs. "Douche."

I sense this is some vestigial prejudice from his fraternity days and decide silence is the most intelligent reply.

"Oh no. Don't tell me you're a fan of German cars."

He's looking at me in dread, like I might be about to sprout horns. Despite my better judgment, I decide to engage in this ridiculous line of conversation.

At least it will keep my mind off how difficult it's going to be to meet Capo with a blank, innocent face.

"I'm guessing by your tone and expression of horror that that would be a terrifying development in our relationship?"

"Nothing is *terrifying* to me," he says with utter disdain. "I'm a Marine."

"You *were* a Marine," I point out with what I consider solid logic.

He makes a face like I've just said his mother is ugly and he has a small dick. "Once a Marine, always a Marine, woman! *Semper fi!*"

I sigh. "Great. I've awakened the Macho Kraken."

"You know you get that face you have right now from Reynard, right?"

When I look at him with one eyebrow cocked, he says,

"Yeah. *That* face. That 'How've you managed to live to this age with your gnat-size IQ?' face. That 'How did you get here, did someone leave your cage open?' face. That 'You must have a terribly empty feeling inside your skull' face!"

I can't help myself. I clutch my stomach and dissolve into laughter.

"Good," he says, sounding satisfied. "Laughter is better than worry lines. Trust me, darlin', *it's all gonna work out.*"

This is when I realize the entire back-and-forth was a ploy—a very effective ploy—to make me feel better and put my mind at ease.

He doesn't give a shit about German cars one way or another. He just gives a shit about me.

My laughter abruptly ends, and I'm fighting tears.

I don't deserve this. I don't deserve *him.*

I'm a thief. A professional criminal. An outlaw and a miscreant, down to the marrow of my bones. I take things from people, things that don't belong to me, cherished things that hold meaning to their owners. I lie and cheat and steal, I have since I was a small child, and I don't deserve anything even close to the goodness of this man, the hugeness of his heart, the promise of a better tomorrow that shines in every one of his beautiful smiles.

*"We're creatures of the underworld, my darling. We have no business in the dealings of heroes."*

Reynard's words echo in my head like a bitter winter wind. I suck in a breath and stare out the passenger window, my vision blurred by all the water in my eyes.

"Ah, darlin'," Ryan sighs, squeezing my hand. "It's not what you're forced to do to survive that shows your character. It's what you do when no one's looking. Perfect example? You puttin' that pillow under my head after you roofied me. That was fuckin' sweet, Angel."

I start to laugh again. How could I not?

"Better," he says, pulling me closer. "C'mere and snuggle up. You need some body contact."

*No, cowboy. I just need you.*

When I sigh into his neck as I fit myself against his body, Ryan squeezes me tight.

I hope he's strong enough to hold on for the both of us, because I think we're in for one hell of a roller coaster ride.

# 24

## MARIANA

"God," I groan. "You're carrying me again! I'm not an invalid!"

Ryan, holding me in his arms as we descend in the elevator, kisses my temple. "I'm a man, you're a woman," he explains, apropos of nothing.

"I don't understand your logic."

"That's 'cause your primary hormone is estrogen."

"Are you *trying* to get yourself killed?"

"No need for you to walk when you've got a man around who wants to carry you."

The elevator doors open, and we enter the house. Ryan calls out the cue for the lights and they flicker on. Then he turns and heads toward the bedroom.

"Keep this up and my legs will atrophy," I say. "Wait. Are you just using me as a workout for your biceps?"

He doesn't answer, but his smile is highly suspicious.

"Fine. Moving on. Where's the diamond?"

"You're obsessed with that fuckin' thing, you know that?" he grumbles, but spins around and heads back to the kitchen. In front of the refrigerator, he sets me on my feet.

He takes out a carton of milk and puts it on the table, then gives me a meaningful look.

"Do you think I'm deficient in calcium?"

His eye roll is extravagant. He picks up the carton and shakes it back and forth.

When it rattles, I gasp, covering my mouth with my hand. "No! You didn't! In *there*?"

"Why not? It's not gonna spoil. And who's gonna think to look in the fridge for a big ol' blue diamond? Anybody tries to hit this place—they'd totally fail, by the way, not even a spider's gettin' in here—they'd be lookin' for a safe. Which I do have, but I only keep crypto phones in it. You wanna see it?"

He rattles the carton again. Speechless, I nod.

He turns to the cabinet, retrieves a drinking glass, and sets it on the table, then pours milk into the glass until a big chunk of something falls out with a *plop*, spraying milk on the tabletop.

He fishes the diamond from the glass with his fingers and holds it up. Even dripping milk, it burns with an eerie gray-blue brilliance.

He offers it to me. I take it without a word and simply stare at it glittering in the palm of my hand. I think of an heiress who died broke and a king who lost his head, and am filled with trepidation.

After a moment, I find my voice. "Do you also have the crown jewels in the vegetable drawer?"

"Freezer," he answers without hesitation. "Wrapped up in white butcher's paper marked *pork roast*."

It's disturbing that I actually believe him.

He holds out his hand. I give him the diamond back, watching in silence as he casually drops it back into the milk carton, then pours the glass of milk in over it. He folds the top of the carton closed, sticks it back into the fridge, rinses his hands and the glass in the sink, then turns around and looks at me.

"What?" he asks when he sees my face.

"That stone is worth more than two hundred million dollars. And you're keeping it in a nonfat milk carton in your refrigerator."

"It's just a pretty rock, darlin'. It's only worth what people believe it's worth. For me, it's just a means to an end."

"What end?"

He walks slowly toward me, then takes my face in his hands. "The end of you havin' to work for a monster. The end of you tyin' sheets together and disappearin' after a night with me. The end of anything that doesn't make you happy or keep that beautiful smile on your face."

He kisses me softly, cradling my head. It's deep and slow and achingly sweet, the kind of kiss that could make you fall in love.

I pull away with a little gasp.

"Don't run away," he says, his voice soft and earnest. "Promise me you won't ever run away from me again."

My heart thrums like the beat of a hummingbird's wings inside the cage of my chest. "You know they say promises are made to be broken. Let's not tempt fate."

He finds my mouth again, takes it like he owns it, like all of me belongs to him and always will. I curl my hands into his shirt, taking fistfuls of it as he eats me with kisses.

"I don't want you to do this," he says roughly, breaking away only long enough to speak those words, then kissing me again, hungrier this time, his hands around my head tighter. "This shit with Moreno. It's that last thing in the world I want."

"I know," I whisper.

He bites my lower lip, sucks it into his mouth. "You also know why I agreed to it, right?"

I nod, clinging to him. His arm slides around my waist. His hand fists in my hair. Into my ear he says, "Why?"

I know what he wants me to say, but I can't. I can't say those words out loud. So I only make a small noise in my throat and shake my head.

He whispers, "Chicken."

Without warning, he swings me up into his arms and turns for the bedroom.

This time, I don't make any smartass comments about his biceps. I hold on to him as he strides past the wall of succulents and stare at his handsome profile. A rising pulse of heat starts to simmer through my body because I know what he's going to do as soon as we get to the bedroom.

And he does. He lays me down on the bed, shucks off his boots, wordlessly strips off all my clothes, gets on his knees, and puts his mouth on me.

I arch and cry out his name, already desperate.

"Shh," he hushes me gently. "We're gonna go slow this time. Slow like I've wanted to every time, but we always ended up goin' hard and fast."

He dips his head and presses the softest of kisses to my clit. I jerk and suck in a breath.

"Hush, Angel," he whispers. "Just feel this."

His breath is warm on my exposed flesh. It feels decadent and so sexy, knowing I'm totally exposed to him and he can see *everything*, but he's just languidly running his rough palms over my belly and breasts, hovering between my legs like we have all the time in the world, stroking my skin like there's no tomorrow.

He nuzzles his nose gently in the space between my thigh and sex, inhaling deeply. It sends a rash of tingles up my spine. My heartbeat goes jagged. I get small bites all along the insides of my thighs, tender bites, like he's testing my flesh, tasting it. Every so often, a soft swipe of his tongue chases away a sting where his nip was a little too strong.

He kisses me between my legs again, reaching up to squeeze my aching breasts, and I moan, unable to keep it in.

"God, I love that sound," he breathes, and slides his tongue deep inside me at the same time he pinches my hard nipples, rolling his thumbs over the rigid peaks.

Heat erupts along all my nerve endings. I close my eyes and rock my hips, wanting to get closer, needing his mouth all over me, inside me, everywhere at once. I feel like I'm starving, like I'll break apart if he doesn't get inside me soon, and I tell him in a breathless whisper that I need to feel him, *now*.

"Oh, she thinks *she's* in charge." He chuckles. "How sweet."

He continues to flick his thumb over my nipple as he draws the other hand down my body, spreading it open under my ass and using it to lift me closer to his face. Then he suckles me slowly, his tongue wet and hot, his lips making suction while the rough pad of his thumb strokes my outer lips.

"Please," I whisper, writhing against this mouth, the pressure building. "God. Please."

"Tell me how it feels," he says harshly. The tremor in his voice tells me he's getting closer to losing his control—and knowing it's all because of me, because of how I'm reacting to him and what he's doing to me—makes it so much hotter.

I whisper, "So good. So amazing. It feels…it feels like I'm yours."

His groan sends a vibration through my core that feels so incredible I jerk. His tongue laps faster against my clit. His thumb slides inside me, but it's not enough.

"Please," I beg again, a pulse of pleasure throbbing between my legs.

"Don't come yet, baby. Just feel this. Just breathe."

His whispered command makes me shudder. His voice is so soft yet so hard, so confident, so fucking sexy I can't help but rock faster against his mouth, cupping my breasts so I can pinch my nipples while his hands dig into my hips, trying to hold me in place.

"Look at you all swollen for me," he says softly, then slides his tongue up and down my cleft, flat, lapping, until he gets back up top and he does a swirling thing that makes me groan and shudder. "Fuck," he whispers. "I love how you respond to me, Angel."

He can't wait anymore. He rises up, drags his shirt over his head, rips open the fly of his jeans, then takes his erection in his fist. "Need your mouth, sweetheart," he rasps.

I sit up, scoot closer to him, wrap my hand around the thick base of his cock, and slide the head between my lips.

His soft moan is my reward.

I stroke his shaft as I get the head of his cock wet all over, then take it deeper into my mouth, sucking, feeling him tight and hot against my tongue. He hisses in a breath, digging his hands into my hair, and flexes his hips, looking down at me as I suck him deeper into my mouth.

He gasps when I take him all the way to the base.

When I circle my other hand around his balls, he shudders. I start a rhythm, achingly slow, a drag and pull with my mouth that allows me to feel every ridge and vein, to savor his heat and taste, to listen as his moans grow louder and more broken.

"Not yet," he pants. "I want to come in your mouth, but not…oh *fuck*."

I'm circling my tongue around and around his engorged head. He's watching me, eyes half-shut, mouth open, hair falling into his eyes as his chest heaves with every breath. His hands on either side of my head are shaking.

Then suddenly I'm on my back again. He hovers over me, big and powerful, a mountain of a man, his half-lidded eyes filled with lust and possession. "Spread your legs," he orders softly, "and fuck that sweet pussy on my cock."

I obey him, reaching down for his erection, finding it and sliding it back and forth between my legs until it's slick. He holds himself still above me, arms braced and every muscle flexed as I guide the head of his cock inside me, canting my hips to get the angle right.

"*Slow,*" he warns as I immediately start to buck against it. I drop my head against the mattress, drag a ragged breath into my lungs, and very slowly flex my hips so he eases inside me, inch by beautiful, hard inch, until he's fully sheathed.

"You've still got your jeans on," I say breathlessly.

He answers in a voice like gravel. "I'll take 'em off in a minute. Need you like this first. Now rock against that cock, baby, and kiss me."

I pull his head down and kiss him deeply, my thighs trembling on either side of his hips, my heartbeat like thunder. Then, very slowly, I start to move my hips in a circular motion. It feels so good I clutch the hard globes of his ass and grind against him, rubbing my sensitive clit against his pelvis while keeping the entire throbbing length of him inside.

"Oh God, this is my new favorite thing," I pant. "You're so hard. God, you're rock-hard for me."

"Let it build. Don't rush it. Just feel me. Feel how good we are together."

He lowers his head and sucks on my nipple. I arch into his mouth, gasping, wanting to laugh and cry and scream all at the same time, every emotion pummeling me so I have to fight for breath.

"My beautiful Angel," Ryan murmurs against my skin, moving his mouth to my other breast and sucking it, his soft hair tickling my skin. His voice drops to a whisper. "You have my heart. You know you have my heart."

I swallow a sob.

He lowers his chest to mine so his whole body is pressed against me. Then he inhales against my neck, makes a deep sound of pleasure, and flexes his hips. "C'mon, baby," he gently prompts when I fall still. "That's your cock. Fuck it."

I close my eyes and run my hands up his muscular arms, loving the strength I feel in them. Then I exhale the breath I've been holding and roll my hips.

Ryan growls in pleasure, so I do it again. And again. And again.

He's hot and heavy and hard against me. His whole body is hard and masculine, and I love it so much, I can't help but paw him like a greedy little animal. I turn my head to his arm and sink my teeth into the muscle as I listen to him pant and softly groan. I'm so wet, I hear the sounds it makes as I grind against him, but I don't care. I'm past rational thought. I'm nearly delirious.

He takes over and starts to pump into me, deep and slow, his mouth on my neck. My nipples drag against his chest with every move, sending shock waves of pleasure throughout my body as a coil of pressure winds tight deep inside me, tighter and tighter with every stroke of his cock.

"I'm close," I breathe, shaking with the need for release.

"Hold on, baby. Draw it out. It'll be so much more intense if you can hold on."

He keeps pumping, flexing his hips in that agonizingly slow, steady rhythm, his breath hot at my ear. When I cry out, almost tipping over the edge, he falls still and peppers sweet, gentle kisses all over my neck and shoulder.

I pull his hair, wanting to scream, wanting to come but also wanting to hold on, gulping big breaths and shaking uncontrollably beneath him.

"Oh, fuck you're right *there*," he whispers when I clench around him. He raises his head and stares into my eyes. There's a moment, a long, bottomless moment, where we simply gaze at each other, our hearts in our eyes, everything laid bare between us.

Then he exhales and thrusts into me, and I'm over the edge.

My body bows as my orgasm slams into me, stiffening my muscles and stealing the breath from my lips. I cry out, mindless, thrashing, going crazy underneath him as he drives into me again and again, grunting through his pleasure, watching me come through slitted eyes.

*Ryan Ryan Ryan.*

I'm screaming his name, or sobbing it, I don't know and I don't care. I'm past caring about anything but him, but this, this whirlwind of thunder and lightning, of howling gales and scalding rain. This could be heaven or it could be hell, and when I realize it doesn't matter as long as he's with me, it finally shatters what's left of the wall around my heart.

It all crumbles away. All my doubt. All my fear. All my stupid excuses.

I *do* belong to this man, no matter how much I might try to deny it, no matter how much my rational mind might scoff. No matter how crazy it is. How impossible.

I'm his.

Then he's laughing. Loudly, with his head thrown back, a wild, crazy laugh like he just broke out of prison.

"Yes, you *are*," he says, still laughing, which is when I realize I've said it aloud.

He rolls flat onto his back, taking me with him in a smooth motion, made simple by the strength of his arms. My hair cascades around my shoulders and breasts as I stare down at him with heavy lids in a fog of sheer pleasure, feeling him so deep and hard inside me. I'm still throbbing around him, and my body is still pulsing inside, so I follow the beat of the pulse and rock against his cock, throwing my head back and closing my eyes.

His hands grip my hips. He thrusts up into me, his breath harsh and guttural.

He whispers, "Look at you, oh fuck, you're so fucking beautiful, Jesus, *Jesus*—" He cuts off with a groan, his body bowing up into mine. "Fuck! I'm gonna come! Fuck, Angel, your mouth, gimme your *mouth*—"

He breaks off with another groan, this one desperate.

I manage to clamber down and get him into my mouth just as

he starts to come, spilling hotly onto my tongue. He's shouting, his head pitched back onto the pillow, all the muscles in his abdomen and arms standing out.

I swallow. He gives me more. He's twisting in the blankets, pulling my hair, out of control, grunting like an animal as he pumps against my mouth. I love every second of it, his taste, his total abandon, everything.

He comes like he does everything else, 1,000 percent committed. Crying out until he's hoarse, praising me, making me feel beautiful, like fairy tales could be true and happily ever afters might be an actual possibility. When it's over and he's spent, lying motionless and panting, his chest slick with sweat, I sit back on my heels and just look at him. I drink him in with my eyes, memorizing every golden line of his body.

Because in some dark part of my heart, no matter how much I want to believe in them, I know that fairy tales aren't true.

He cracks an eye open and peers at me. "Oh no. I see smoke. You're thinking."

"No, I'm admiring the picture I've made."

"What picture is that?"

"The picture of a big, strong man wrung out and helpless against me."

"Well," he says, his voice husky, "not *totally* helpless." His cock, still erect, twitches against his belly. When I laugh, he holds out his arms. "Get up here."

I crawl up and fit myself against him, snuggling under his arm and throwing my leg over his. He kisses my forehead, one arm tightening around me in a possessive embrace. The other hand trails up my arm, raising gooseflesh in its wake. I rest my head against his chest, listen to the steady thump of his heart, and close my eyes.

"Tell me a story, Mariana," he whispers, lips moving against my forehead.

"A story? What kind of story?"

"A story about a little girl who lived in the hills and ate dirt to survive," he says with infinite gentleness. "The story of you."

I turn my face to his neck. He squeezes me tighter when he feels the tremor run through me. Then, when I've gathered the courage and decided where to start, I take a deep breath and begin.

## 25

## MARIANA

"Once upon a time, there was a shy little girl named Mariana. She was born in Colombia, in a small village called Chengue, in the Sucre province, a northern coastal mountain range near the Caribbean Sea. Most people there were cattle farmers, but Mariana's parents farmed avocadoes. No matter what they farmed, however, the people of that region were poor. Peasants. The little girl didn't understand that until many years later. She thought the wild hills she roamed with her scruffy yellow dog were paradise."

I pause to draw a breath, wondering if Ryan knew it would be easier to tell this as if it happened to someone else—just a girl in a story, not me.

I decide he probably did.

"Colombia was—and is—a country of great beauty, but also great violence. It's been embroiled in civil war for more than fifty years. People think coffee and drugs are the main fuel of its economy, and they are, but there are also kidnappings for profit, assassins for hire, and death squads that roam the countryside, paid by the government to quell any rebellion.

"Misery is big business there. Death is an accepted part of life. But all was well in tiny Chengue. Mariana and her older sister, Nina, helped her parents on the farm, and they went to school in the village and led a normal, happy life."

Beneath my cheek, Ryan's heart beats faster. He instinctively knows what's coming before it even leaves my lips.

"Until one night, the paramilitary came before dawn and started pulling people from their homes."

I close my eyes and listen to the beat of Ryan's heart, the ache of devastation burning through me even after all these years.

"The soldiers took everyone to the center of the village. There was so much screaming, so much confusion, so many shiny black pools of blood. A few, including Mariana and her sister, escaped to the hills. They couldn't escape the screams, though. They lasted all through the night, horrible screams and gunfire and shouting that echoed up into the hills like the voices of angry ghosts.

"When it was over, the paramilitary set fire to everything. Mariana and her sister huddled together high up in the branches of a tree they'd climbed, and watched the only home they'd ever known burn to the ground."

"I know this story," Ryan says in a low, raw voice. "I've heard of Chengue. It was alleged that the Colombian government assisted the FARC guerillas with the killings."

"Alleged, but never proven. Not that it matters either way. When dawn rose over the village, both Mariana's parents and nearly everyone else she'd ever known were dead. The avocado fields were smoking and black. The cattle had been slaughtered. Her beloved yellow dog lay still in the dirt, missing half his head.

"Mariana was six at this time. Her sister, Nina, was ten. For the next four years, they hid in the hills with a few other children, living like scavengers, little nocturnal animals stealing what they could from nearby villages to survive. They hid from the guerillas who swept through every so often, starving and filthy and forgotten by the rest of the world."

"Jesus," says Ryan, his voice choked.

I smile sadly. "No. He never showed his face in Chengue. He forgot about them, too."

Ryan rolls us to our sides, pulls me up against him so my back is nestled against his chest, and draws his knees up behind mine. He pulls me tight to his body, his arm an iron band around my waist, and buries his face in my hair.

"One day," I continue, my voice sounding very faraway to my own ears, "the guerillas finally caught the children. They were so weak by then. Just skin and bones, their eyes huge and sunken in their lice-ridden heads. The few boys in the group were quickly killed. Their necks were so brittle, so easily snapped. But the girls…well. Unfortunately, the girls were pretty. That's what they said, anyway, the men who dragged them kicking and screaming from their hiding places. They said words like *pretty* and *money* and *pure*, and although the girls didn't know what they meant, they knew enough to be terrified.

"And so they were sold to a trafficker named Beatriz, a woman with gold teeth and no soul, who took off their clothes and inspected them to see if they'd ever been had by a man."

Behind me, Ryan's breathing is uneven. His body is shaking in reaction to my words, when strangely I feel more and more calm as I continue to speak, as if I'm releasing poison from my veins.

"The girls were taken to the port. They were loaded with other girls from other villages into a shipping container. There were no lights. There was no food. Each girl was chained to the wall, a collar around her throat, steel cuffs around her ankles and wrists, one gallon of drinking water in a plastic bottle by her side. They sat in the darkness for days that were like decades, listening to each other's pitiful cries and retching from seasickness, until one by one they fell silent and there were only a few more whimpering voices left.

"By the time the rocking stopped and the doors creaked open, none of them were making any sounds at all. Mute and wretched, they lifted their eyes to the light."

I have to stop. My throat has closed in on itself as it did when that container door creaked open and I caught my first glimpse of Reynard's horrified face.

I was nothing by then. I wasn't even human. I was an animal. The only instinct I had left was primal rage.

As if it's a movie projected directly onto my mind's eye, I see Reynard press a handkerchief to his nose. He staggers back several feet, overcome by the stench of human waste and rotting corpses.

"I was the last one taken out of the container. I couldn't walk, so they dragged me out by one arm. They dropped me at Reynard's feet. I lay in the dirt while they corralled the other girls into a bus that was waiting to take us to Capo's. I thought I would die. I didn't care. Even the sound of my sister crying my name didn't move me. Then Reynard knelt down and brushed the hair off my face. When I looked up at him, I saw tears on his cheeks."

I realize I've reverted to first person when I feel tears on my cheeks, too. I don't bother to wipe them away. It's almost the end of the story.

"The last time I saw my sister was through a dirty window of a yellow bus. She had blood running from her nose. Her hands were pressed to the glass, and I could tell she was screaming, but for some reason, I couldn't hear her. I couldn't hear anything. Then the bus drove away, and Reynard picked me up in his arms.

"As he carried me to his car, a dragonfly landed on his shoulder. It had iridescent blue wings. I'll never forget the color of those wings. The dragonfly looked at me and said, 'Survive.' I know I must've been hallucinating, but that's what it said. 'Survive.' And somehow in my mind, the dragonfly was my sister, and she was telling me to live, to live for all of us, all the girls in that dark cage who would never grow up to be wives and mothers and lovers. All the girls who'd had their childhoods stolen, who were abused so brutally, who were sold off by adults with no more care than you'd sell a used car.

"So I did what the dragonfly told me to. I survived. Reynard nursed me back to health. He was kind to me. He raised me and gave me an education and continued to skim money from Capo's operation so that every once in a while he could save a little girl from a nightmare.

"And every time I steal something at Capo's request, I honor the memory of my sister and those dead girls by leaving the totem of the dragonfly, a beautiful creature that has a very short life. A creature that visited me when I was close to death and gave me a reason to live. Without that dragonfly on Reynard's shoulder, I know I wouldn't have made it past that night."

After I stop speaking, there's total silence. Ryan's heartbeat thuds against my shoulder blades. His breathing is shallow, and there's a small tremor in the arm he's bound around me. Finally, he presses the softest of kisses to the nape of my neck.

I turn over and throw my arms around his shoulders, burying my face in his chest.

He cradles me close, his feet tangling with mine, a low sigh slipping from his lips. "Angel," he whispers gruffly, "you're a miracle. I'm so grateful you lived. And for as long as you do, I want to be beside you."

I burst into tears.

He lets me cry without shushing me, just holding me tight against his body, letting me take strength from him, giving me a soft place to fall. When it's over and I'm sniffling and snot-faced, he goes to the bathroom and comes back with a wet washcloth and gently wipes my cheeks and nose. Then he strips off his jeans and underwear, crawls under the covers, and spoons me again, one arm under my head and the other tight around my waist, his breath warm and soft on my shoulders.

I fall in love with him the way the dying give up their last breath: irrevocably, with both hope and terror for what lies on the other side.

We sleep.

I don't know for how long, but we both come awake at the same time, our hands and mouths finding each other, our bodies and hearts perfectly in tune. Ryan makes love to me with a tenderness that's painful because it's so raw. I've been stripped of the hard, protective skin I've worn for so long. I'm nothing but exposed nerves and a beating heart and a ravenous, insatiable hunger. Hunger for him, for this beautiful man who saw me from the beginning, who so easily saw what I really was and accepted me without judgment or fear, only good humor and open arms.

He gives me hope for mankind.

"What time is it?" I ask hours later, when we're both sated and sweaty, a tangle of arms and legs under the rumpled sheets.

"Dunno," he replies sleepily. He turns his head on the pillow and gazes at me, smiling. "Why, you ready to go again?"

My laugh is low and happy. "Sure, if you have a wheelchair handy. I don't think I'll be able to walk right for a week."

Ryan looks like this is the best compliment he's ever received. Beaming, he lifts himself up to an elbow and kisses my shoulder. "You don't need to walk, remember? You've got your own personal wheelchair right here." He flexes his arm, making his biceps muscles bulge, and me laugh.

"You're crazy."

"Crazy for you." He smiles into my eyes, and I'm so floating and light, I must be hooked up to a helium tank.

"I need a shower," he says, throwing back the covers. "You in?"

"Get the water warm for me. Be right there."

"Don't take too long, Angel. I'm a hot-water hog."

He winks, rises from the bed, and treats me to the sight of his gorgeous backside as he swaggers naked into the bathroom. I stretch under the covers, feeling the soreness in all my muscles, trying not to let darker thoughts of what's going to happen tomorrow intrude on my happy little oasis.

But as soon as I try to push my worries away, they come back in full force and the moment is ruined.

As the water goes on in the bathroom, I sit up in bed and scrub my hands over my face. The need to check in with Reynard has been scratching at my brain for hours, and now it's finally turned into an all-out assault I can no longer avoid if I want to stay sane.

I don't know exactly what I can tell him, but at the very least I need to let him know I have the diamond, and I'll be back soon.

Ryan is whistling in the shower when I rise from bed. I dig the phone he gave me out of the pocket of my jeans, discarded on the floor hours ago, and dial Reynard's number.

It rings. And rings.

And rings.

He's never not answered my call before.

My fear is an invisible fist that reaches out and grabs my heart. It's impossible to breathe. My pulse beats fast and fluttery. I wait, holding the phone tight to my ear, fighting a sense of doom so strong it makes my hands tremble.

Finally, the ringing stops as the call clicks through.

"Reynard?" I say into the silence, my voice high with panic.

There's a strange sound I can't identify. A wet sound, almost like a rheumy cough, but weaker. Then, as horror blooms over me like a pestilent flower, Reynard's voice finally comes over the line.

"Dragonfly," he says, his voice raspy and low, a death rattle. "My darling. Don't come ba—"

He cuts off abruptly. I'm about to frantically shout his name, but the words die on my lips when I hear what comes over the line next.

"Hello, Mariana. We've been waiting for your call."

Cold with horror, I sink to my knees on the floor. Clutching the phone in both of my shaking hands, I whisper, "Please. Please don't hurt him."

Capo's chuckle is soft and dark. "Oops. Too late."

My groan is a terrified animal's. "No. Please. I-I have the diamond, I'll be there soon—"

"With your boyfriend the mercenary? I think not. I understand he has quite close ties with American government agencies that go by three initials. Now listen carefully. A plane is waiting for you at JFK Airport. Go to the Sheltair private jet terminal and tell the gate agent your name. Your real name, please, none of your covert identity nonsense—"

"Capo, *please*," I beg, "Reynard had *nothing* to do with this—"

"Don't insult my intelligence!" he thunders, his patience snapping like a twig. "I've been recording everything that goes on in that fucking trinket shop for *years*!"

I think of our plan to tell Capo that I thought Reynard's shop was bugged, and sob.

It *was* bugged. When Ryan went in and demanded Reynard tell him where I was, after he left and I emerged from my hiding place inside the sarcophagus…the whole time, Capo was listening.

*"If you don't shake your American, he's going to start a war with the Devil and drag us all into hell."*

I recall Reynard's warning to me that day, and sob again.

"Tears won't help you." Capo's voice is softer now, his control regained as quickly as it was lost. "You know what I want. Come to me, or Reynard dies. Try to run, and your boyfriend dies, too. I know where he lives, Mariana. I know everything there is to know about him."

"You'll kill them both no matter if I come to you or not," I say bitterly. "You'll kill us all."

Capo's voice drops an octave and gains an intimate, seductive edge. "I could have killed you a lifetime ago, Mari. But you have something I want. And I'm tired of waiting for it. Come to me now, and you have my word I'll let them live."

"The word of a *murderer*," I hiss, shaking so hard I almost can't keep a grip on the phone.

He turns nonchalant. "Well, it's up to you. Don't come, and they die. Not easily. Not quickly. You will, too, because I don't tolerate disobedience. Come, and all of you live to see another day. The way I look at it, your only real option is to see if I'll keep my word. The odds are fifty-fifty. Flip a coin, make a choice. Heads, everyone dies. Tails…"

His voice drops again. "Everyone lives, and you and I get to spend a little quality time alone together before I decide what to do with you. Maybe you can convince me to be lenient."

I don't speak. There aren't any words in any language for this moment.

Except "Fuck you."

Capo laughs. After a split-second pause, I hear a scream in the background, high and wavering, full of anguish.

"He won't last much longer, Mari. Better hurry. Come alone and don't be followed, or all the blood will be on *your* hands."

A *click*, final as the last nail in a coffin, and he's gone.

I thought I knew what hell was before, but now I realize that, like the circles in Dante's *Inferno*, you have to go through many different layers before you finally reach the center where the Devil waits, licking his lips.

I take a moment to say a silent farewell to my beautiful dream, and to Ryan, the beautiful dreamer who made me believe in fairy-tale endings.

Then I rise, wipe the tears from my cheeks, and quickly dress.

# 26

## RYAN

I stand in the shower with my hands flat on the wall in front of me and my head bent under the spray, letting the hot water pummel and soothe my muscles. I'm calm, my mind focused and clear, my heart like an eagle with spread wings riding an updraft over the crest of a mountain.

I always thought falling in love would be like falling apart somehow. Like losing your mind. Well, there's that too, I admit with a wry chuckle. But it's more like…finding something you didn't even know you'd lost.

I feel like me, only better. Bigger. Turbocharged. With Mariana by my side, I could take on the world and win.

I really hope there's an opportunity for me to take a shot at Moreno during the op, because a life behind bars isn't enough punishment for that scumbag.

A bullet isn't, either, but I'm sure the government would frown on me going full *Hurt Locker* on him like I want to. Like the son of a bitch deserves.

I shake the water from my eyes and thoughts of Vincent Moreno from my head and straighten. "Angel!" I call out, my voice echoing against the tile. "Water's gettin' cold!"

I picture her snuggled in my bed, warm and soft under my covers, her hair messy and her dark eyes lit with fire like they always are when she looks at me, whether pissed off or turned on. My dick gets heavy just from the thought of it.

I smile down at the big guy. "Still got some juice left in you, huh?" *Better fix that.* "Angel!" I call again, louder this time.

I grab the bar of soap and start to lather my chest, but something stops me. I don't know what. Intuition, maybe. I cock an ear toward the door and listen.

Nothing. No answering call.

I crank the knob, turning off the spray of water. "Mariana?"

Not a sound.

*No. It's not that. It's only your mind playing tricks on you. You're becoming an old woman, worrying over everything. She's in the kitchen, grabbing something to eat.*

Then I remember what's in the kitchen.

"No." This time I say it out loud, and firmly, because I'm being an idiot. After what we just shared, after everything she told me, there's no way in hell she ran out on me again. There's no fucking way…

I'm out of the shower and into the bedroom before I can even finish the thought.

She's not there.

"Mariana!"

I stride naked into the living room.

She's not there.

I run into the kitchen.

She's not there.

I run, wet and frantic, shouting her name through every room in the house.

It's only when I see the note taped to the elevator doors that I stop running. Unfortunately, I stop breathing then, too. I read what she's written and inhale what feels like my last breath.

. . .

*Ryan,*

*I'm not saying goodbye, because goodbye means going away, and going away means forgetting. And I'm never going to forget a single moment with you.*

*Forever,*

*M.*

My enraged bellow of "FUCK!" echoes throughout the whole house.

When I yank open the fridge and find the milk container empty, the roar that tears from my chest isn't even human.

## 27

## MARIANA

I don't have any money, so when the cab I flagged down on the street pulls up to the curb at the private jet terminal at JFK, I throw open the door and run out before the driver can stop me. His angry shouts quickly fade as I run into the terminal, and I head straight for the nearest customer service counter.

"Mariana Lora," I say breathlessly the moment I get there. "My name is Mariana Lora. I was told—"

"Yes, Ms. Lora." The woman behind the counter, an attractive, middle-aged brunette in a navy-blue suit, smiles at me with all her teeth showing. Then she gestures like a spokesmodel to a set of sliding double glass doors to her left. "Right through those doors. The jet is waiting on the tarmac."

Of course I don't need a ticket, or identification. I don't have to go through security, either. Such is Capo's power.

I run through the glass doors into the cool evening, my hair blowing wild around my face. There are a dozen jets of different sizes spaced up and down the tarmac, but the one closest to the doors is large and has a man in a black suit waiting at the bottom of fold-out stairs. He lifts his hand in greeting. I wonder how long he's been waiting there like that for me.

I wonder who else is on that plane.

As it turns out, two other men in suits. I enter the plane and find gleaming luxury: large, buff-colored leather seats and a few small tables, and a pair of big, unsmiling guys seated at the back who stand when I come in, adjusting their suit jackets like they're hoping for a chance to use the weapons under them. The man on the tarmac follows me inside, folds the stairs up, and locks them into place. Then he raps twice on the closed cockpit door and asks if I'm carrying a cell phone.

I debate whether or not to give it to him, but judging by his expression and the gun glimpsed in the holster at his waist, it would be a bad decision to lie.

I hand it over wordlessly. He removes the SIM card, smashes it under the heel of his shoe, and tosses the phone aside.

He motions for me to extend my arms. I obey silently and he frisks me for weapons, head to foot. When he doesn't find any, he asks if I'd like a drink.

I decline. He pours me one anyway—vodka, straight—and points to the closest chair.

"Why don't you sit there for the flight?" he says, his voice as quiet as his eyes are hard.

It's not a request. I sit. Then he gives me the drink and a smile so chilling, I shrink back into the chair.

He switches to Italian. "The vodka will help."

I answer in English. "With what? I'm not afraid of flying."

"Not the flight," he says, still in Italian, still smiling. "With what comes after."

He leaves the bottle on the table in front of me and goes to sit at the back of the plane with his two friends as the engines roar to life.

## 28

## RYAN

"Take it easy, brother, calm down, I can't understand you—"

"She took the diamond!" I holler as I take a corner at top speed, tires squealing. "She's gone, Mariana's *gone*!"

The Bluetooth in the truck emits a crackle, then silence. Then Connor says, "Well, that fucking sucks."

"I'm on my way to Metrix right now! We need to scramble the team and get everyone locked and loaded—"

"The team?"

"—and ready to go within thirty minutes!"

"Sorry, I'm not following. You know where she went?"

"Thirty minutes!" I shout at the top of my lungs and disconnect the call.

I fly so fast through the streets of lower Manhattan, it's a miracle I don't kill anyone, including myself. By the time I arrive at Metrix, I've achieved a tenuous grip on my fury and am able to slow at the gate and punch in the security code instead of gunning it and trying to crash straight through like my adrenaline would like. I park, jump out of the truck, and hump it across the parking lot without even closing the driver's door.

Connor has already beat me here.

The big steel door slides open, and he's standing with his arms folded over his chest, wearing his usual black boots, cargo pants, T-shirt, and Glock, along with a credible poker face—although I can tell he's on high alert.

"What's the 411, brother?"

I hold up my cell phone. "Let's get the satellite up. I've got a bead on her."

He turns and strides beside me as I head to the war room. Even at this hour, all the computer stations are manned. We don't even get a single curious glance as we blow past the crew. They're used to seeing us in combat mode.

"You wanna tell me what happened?"

"You know what happened," I growl. "She took the diamond and left."

"Uh-huh. And what precipitated that?"

I stop dead in my tracks, swing around, and stare at him. "*Precipitated?* Are you fuckin' kidding me?"

Connor spreads his hands wide in a placating gesture, so I know what's about to come out of his mouth is gonna be something I won't like.

"All I'm asking is, did you two have a fight?"

I grind out, "Jesus. Fucking. Christ."

"'Cause when you guys were here earlier, I was getting the vibe that she was basically…in love with you."

"Of course she's in love with me, dickhead!" I roar, my face exploding with heat.

Connor blinks. He drags a hand over his dark hair, shorn short like he always wears it. "Yeah, you lost me again, brother."

I lift a hand and start to count the obvious facts on my fingers.

"One: everything was peachy keen one minute, afterglow like a motherfucker painting my bedroom walls pink, the next minute, she's gone. With the diamond. Two: she left a cryptic fuckin' note with some weird Peter Pan quote her and Tabby were yakkin' about the night they met. Three: She made a call on the cell phone I gave her right after I went into the shower and right before I discovered her gone. A call that lasted exactly forty-six seconds before bein' disconnected from the other end. Guess who she called?"

Connor says immediately, "Reynard."

"Bingo. Only the number she dialed was rerouted all over the fuckin' place and bounced off practically every fuckin' telecom satellite we got up in space before bein' encrypted and obfuscated all to hell, then pingin' back to a Chinese restaurant a block away from my house."

Connor's eyes turn poison black. Crazy-person black. The black of a man who's getting ready to go to war. "Vincent Moreno. And that ping-back was his way of telling you he knows where you live."

"And Mariana's headed to him with the diamond in exchange for Reynard's life."

After a beat, he says, "She's lucky you trust her. After her history of running out on you, most other guys would've figured this was the same thing."

I turn and head toward the war room again. "Yeah, well, don't give me a medal yet, 'cause I told her the phone was untraceable, which it isn't."

Connor says, "Good thinking. Unless Moreno or one of his men take it away from her at some point, which we have to assume they will."

"We'll still be able to locate her."

"Oh? How's that?"

"I might've put a tracker on her sweatshirt," I grudgingly admit.

When he doesn't say anything, I add, "And one on her belt. And another one in each of her boots."

He chuckles, shaking his head. "Ain't love grand?"

"Don't judge me!"

"I'm not, brother. I've got GPS on every piece of Hello Kitty shit in Tabby's closet."

I push through the glass doors of the war room, muttering, "You must need extra bandwidth."

The command center in Metrix—referred to by everyone as the war room—is exactly what its name suggests. All our ops are planned and monitored in the large rectangular space. It's the central hub for every mission, the beating heart of the company, the one place I know that will be able to pinpoint Mariana's location to within a five-foot radius.

An array of electronic equipment bristles from every wall and flat surface. Computers, video screens, satellite monitoring systems, you name it. In the center of the room is a long black table surrounded by leather captain's chairs. One end of the room has a raised dais with computer terminals. I think it was modeled after the combat ops center at the Cheyenne Mountain nuclear bunker complex in Colorado Springs, but Connor won't admit it.

He'd never fess up to getting ideas from the Air Force.

I jog over to the nearest computer terminal, pull up the tracking program linked to my phone, and navigate to the map. And there's Mariana, designated as a cluster of red dots, her location irrefutable.

Six thousand feet above the Atlantic Ocean and climbing.

Connor says, "Shit. She's in a bird. Gonna need to scramble the FBI."

"They'll take too long!" I growl in frustration. "Fuckin' paper pushers!"

When I look over at him and he sees my expression, he says, "Oh no. Are you thinking what I think you're thinking?"

"Ask Tabby to hack into air traffic control and see which

flight has those coordinates." I point at the screen. "Find out where it's going. And see if she can fiddle with the onboard flight management system to get it to slow down a little, or at least tamper with the fuel gauge readout or something else so the pilot has to make an unscheduled landing."

His brows lift. "Would you like her to make it rain, too, brother?"

After a moment, I ask, "Can she do that?"

He just shakes his head, sighs, and removes his cell phone from his pocket.

## 29

## MARIANA

The flight is hours long. I don't know exactly how many because I don't have a watch and there aren't any clocks on the plane, but when we begin to descend, the sun is rising over the distant horizon in a brilliant orange glow, and I can finally see land.

I unbuckle my lap belt and rise. Instantly, all three men behind me rise, too, watching me like hungry vultures.

I don't bother pointing at the lavatory. They can fucking figure it out on their own.

Slamming the door behind me, I turn on the faucet and splash cold water on my face. I'm exhausted. I need a shower, clean clothes, and to brush my teeth. I use the toilet, flush, then comb my fingers through my hair. I'm hot, so I drag the hoodie over my head and enjoy the relief of cool air on my bare skin.

A tinny metal *plink* catches my attention. I look down.

In the sink, caught next to the drain stopper, is a round metal object the size of a dime. I instantly recognize it, because I've seen this thing before. I pick it up and stare at it until my hand shakes with the hot rush of adrenaline flooding my veins.

GPS.

I have to stuff my fist in my mouth to stifle my groan.

What do I do? If Ryan follows me, Capo will kill him. And me. And Reynard.

*Which he'll probably do anyway,* my brain unhelpfully reminds me.

I stand holding the tiny tracker until there's a knock on the door and a sharp question in Italian.

"Give me a minute!" I snap. Then I'm overcome with terror at the thought of what will happen if Capo or his men discover this device.

I look frantically around the small lavatory for a hiding place, but the knock is coming on the door again, louder this time, and I decide there's really only one thing to do.

I swallow the tracker in one gulp.

I yank the hoodie back over my head, take a breath, smooth my hands down my stomach to calm myself, then open the door and stare up into the glowering face of one of the black-suited triplets. His hand rests menacingly on the butt of his sidearm.

"Had to go number two." I push past him to go back to my seat.

The assassin takes a long, narrow-eyed look around the bathroom, then closes the door and moves silently past me toward the back of the plane. I stare out the window and watch a rugged coastline rise up to greet us. In a few minutes, we've landed at a small airport and are taxiing off the runway and toward a gate.

A cell phone rings behind me. It's answered with a curt "Ya." There's a short silence, then a deferential "*Si, Capo. Certo.*"

Then one of the assassins is lifting me to my feet with a hand wrapped around my upper arm.

"Ouch! You're hurting me!" I try to yank away, but his grip is steel. He gives me a quick, hard shake that makes my teeth clatter.

He tells me in Italian how he'd love to hurt me in other ways, to which I furiously respond, "Capo will kill you if I come to him with even a bruise!"

It's a long shot, but it hits the mark. The assassin's nostrils flare and his lips thin, but his grip loosens so it's no longer cutting off circulation.

"Be nice," I add bitingly, "or I'll tell him some pretty lies about what you did to me in the bathroom."

He smiles, a dark, lazy smile that makes my skin crawl. In succinct English, he says, "Who do you think gets his leftovers, bitch?" He drags me closer as I try to pull away. Into my ear, he says hotly, "The three of us share them. You're a little old, but you'll do."

He grabs my other arm and pushes me in front of him down the aisle. I stumble but quickly regain my balance, throw him a poisonous look over my shoulder, then stand with my arms folded protectively over my chest in the galley near the cockpit door.

All three men in black come to stand in a row in front of me and stare at me with identical small, knowing smiles.

It's so creepy, I have to look away, even though it makes me feel like a coward.

"First dibs," one of them says to the others.

Their smiles grow wider when they see my expression. Then I grow so angry, I want to spit.

"Well, I hope you like AIDS," I say with as much dignity as I can muster, "because I've been HIV-positive for eight years, and it's recently taken a turn for the worse." I motion to my mouth. "I get these sores. Painful, pus-filled things, and skin rashes like you wouldn't believe, and right now I've got a *really* nasty yeast infection—"

"We're allowed to subdue you if you fight," interrupts the one I think is their leader. "What do you think, Sal? Is she fighting?"

My blood runs cold, but Sal merely shakes his head. "She's just scared."

"Ya," says the leader, softly. "Scared." He adjusts a thickening bulge in his crotch, and I want to throw up.

Mercifully, I'm saved from any further conversation with the sicko squad when the cockpit door opens. The pilot emerges, tall and slim with hair the color of cast iron, and a nose that's been broken more than once. He looks sharply at the four of us. His gaze lingers the longest on me.

"Change of plan." He turns his attention back to the assassins. "You're to take a Cessna from here. It's already fueled up and waiting down the tarmac. No need to go in the terminal, just head straight over to gate forty-two. It's a two-minute walk south."

*Two minutes.* A lot can happen in two minutes. In two minutes, a person can die of a heart attack, achieve an orgasm, post a Facebook status update, fall in love.

In two minutes, a person could find a way to escape from her captors.

But no. I have to see this through, because Reynard's life is in the balance and maybe, *maybe* there's a way for me to escape or make a new plan after I know Reynard is alive and safe. Until then, I'm stuck.

We exit the plane. The morning is cool and bright, the salt air bracing against my heated cheeks. There are a few airport workers within sight, a luggage handler unloading bags onto a conveyor belt, a guy with neon signaling sticks and headphones steering a twin-engine jet into a nearby gate, a woman driving by in a pushback tug. The urge to scream to all of them for help is almost overwhelming.

I choke it back with thoughts of how Reynard sounded on the phone, that bloodcurdling shriek he made when Capo did whatever horrible thing he did to cause it.

Waiting for us at the Cessna is another man in a black suit.

They seem to be in endless supply. He motions for us to come quickly, but as soon as we're at the steps that lead up into the plane, he stops us and produces a long, black plastic wand from behind his back.

A metal detector.

With brisk efficiency, he swipes it over my head and neck, my chest and arms, my stomach and back, then stops abruptly at my waist when the wand emits a frazzled squawk.

He yanks up my hoodie and stares at my belt.

Then he glares at my three companions. "You fucking idiots."

"What?" says the leader, offended. "We searched her!"

"Not good enough." New guy rips off my belt and throws it on the tarmac.

I stare at it in disbelief. *Another GPS?*

I decide that if I ever see him again, Ryan and I are going to have a nice, long talk about this "trust" thing he keeps harping on about.

The man proceeds to slowly wand down both my legs, then around my feet, where the wand squawks again. Muttering curses, he straightens and glares at me. "Take the boots off."

I do as I'm told and shuck them off. He kicks them aside, then begins another careful full body wanding until he's satisfied I'm clean.

Thank God the wand doesn't penetrate flesh, because I don't want to imagine what horrible thing would happen to me if my bare midriff gave off an alert.

I'm roughly loaded onto the plane. There are only enough seats for me, the three assassins, the pilot—who's already seated—and the new guy. After a short wait on the runway and clearance from the tower, we take off once more, banking hard into the glare of the morning sky.

*God, if you're up there, now would be a good time to prove it.*

The small plane lands on a tiny island, deserted except for the concrete strip of runway and the black helicopter waiting at one end. No one has spoken for the duration of the flight, so I have no idea where we are or where we're going, but if the next leg of the journey involves a helicopter, it must be close.

The pilot coasts to a stop at the end of the runway but keeps the engine running, the props spinning.

"Out," commands the lead assassin, opening the small door.

He barely moves aside to let me pass, so I'm forced to press against him. He grins down at me, leering, and I quickly jerk away and hop down to the cracked runway.

It's obvious he's not worried about me escaping at this point, which makes sense. Unless I had a mind to drown myself, I've got nowhere to go. There's nothing on this island except sand, scrub brush, and seabirds wheeling overhead, their lonely cries like the wails of lost children.

The assassins follow me out of the plane, one by one. They lead me over to the helicopter as the Cessna turns around. The plane takes off again as I'm climbing into the chopper. I watch it go, getting smaller and smaller until it's just a glinting speck against the sky.

Blue as a dragonfly's wings, that sky. Blue as my lover's eyes.

The chopper starts up with a mechanical roar and a burst of wind, the blades rotating until they're a silver blur above us. When we lift off, I'm praying again, only this time with all my might.

For a long time, there's nothing below us but water. Endless water, in every direction. But then I glimpse a spot of white in the distance against the unceasing navy blanket, and it all makes sense.

As we fly closer, the size of the yacht grows and grows until we're hovering over it, and I get a better sense of how massive it truly is. I've seen city blocks that are shorter. The helipad we're headed toward is on the lowest of the vessel's six decks, to the rear of an oval swimming pool which is situated at the extreme forward tip. There's another helipad on the aft deck, an enormous bridge deck topped with bulbous satellites, and a tender on the starboard side that's about the size of an average ski boat, only it looks miniscule in comparison to the sheer enormity of its berth.

The megayacht's name is spelled out in italic lettering on one section of white siding:

*Sea Fox*.

"She has a two-seater submarine, too," says the lead assassin, startling me. When I stare at him, he smiles. "In case Capo wants to take you for a deep-sea dive after dinner."

His smile turns evil. Heart pounding, I look away.

We land on the helipad with a gentle bump.

A manservant in a white uniform opens the door from the outside. Ignoring everyone else, he gestures at me to disembark. I do, with the assassins following at my heels. We're led off the deck and through an outer lounging area of tables, cushioned sofas, and a large, built-in fire pit. Then we enter the yacht through electrically operated sliding-glass doors.

The first thing I hear is opera music. Muted and beautiful, it plays over hidden speakers and instantly makes my stomach curdle. I force back memories of the last time I heard opera and try to remain calm.

I fail. Every part of my body that has sweat glands is working overtime.

The interior of the yacht is decorated in muted earth tones of sand, brown and gray, with ultramodern furnishings and a lot of polished wood. Colorful, contemporary art adorns the walls. We head toward a glass staircase in the center of a lobby-like area, and I follow the manservant as he mutely motions me on.

*Why doesn't he speak?*

"Loose lips sink ships," says one of the men behind me with a low, sinister chuckle. I realize he's read my mind at the same time I realize the probable meaning of those words. The manservant is missing his tongue.

*Breathe, Mari. Just breathe. One foot in front of the other.*

We walk for what feels like a lifetime, navigating through a warren of rooms—each more spectacular and luxurious than the last—until we arrive at a pair of mahogany doors flanked by marble statues of roaring lions, fangs bared, crouched to pounce. The manservant raps twice on the doors, waits until he hears a murmur from within, then pushes open the doors and stands aside.

The suite is vast, maybe five thousand square feet from glass wall to glass wall, with a private outside deck at the opposite end. It's tall, too, three stories capped with the brilliance of a modern, sculpture-like chandelier suspended from clear cables so it appears to float in midair.

The floor is white marble, the view is of sparkling ocean, and the man looking out the windows across from me with his hands in his trouser pockets and his back turned in my direction is Vincent Moreno.

My heart stutters. For one long, breathless moment, I'm transported back in time to that fateful night, the last time I saw my sister alive, when I was so near death and a dragonfly saved me.

*Reynard saved me. I owe him my life. That's why I'm here.*

The thought gives me strength as Capo turns around and meets my eyes.

Our gazes lock.

I'm certain one of us isn't leaving this room alive.

He's wearing a crisp white linen suit, which sets off his dark tan. The collar of his shirt is open, revealing a strong neck. A small gold medallion nestles in the hollow of his throat. He's calm and spotless, and I hate him so fiercely, it's like I've swallowed fire.

His lips curve upward. "Mari. You made it."

His gaze flicks over me, taking in my tangled hair, rumpled clothing, and bare feet. "Though worse for wear, it would appear." His gaze slices to the three assassins, who've taken up positions against the wall to my left and stand with hands clasped behind their backs, faces impassive.

He wanders across the room, in no particular hurry, stopping midway to inspect a bowl of green grapes set out on a glass coffee table. He selects a few, then continues toward me, popping a grape into his mouth.

My hands shake so hard with the urge to curl around his throat that I have to flex them open to get them to stop.

When Capo's within arm's reach, he pauses. He lifts his chin at the manservant, who bows and silently backs from the room, closing the doors behind him. Then he stands looking at me for a while, obviously relishing the moment.

"Were you treated well by my men?"

"What difference does it make?"

A fleeting frown crosses his face. I can't decide if it's irritation or something else.

"I asked you a question, Mariana. Answer it."

It serves no point to bicker or refuse, so I do as he instructs and glance at the row of assassins behind me. I point at the one closest. "That one called me a bitch and hurt my arm." I point at the one on the other end. "And that one said he wanted first dibs on me."

In the middle of bringing a grape to his mouth, Capo pauses. He looks at the men. "Santino. Fabrizio. Is this true?"

Neither man hesitates to answer. In unison, they say, "*Si*, Capo."

In the next instant, Capo pulls a silver handgun from under his jacket and fires off two rounds, one in each of the assassin's foreheads. Blood and brain matter splatter the wall in a lurid, chunky pattern of red.

I jump and scream as the assassins crumple to the ground.

"What about Salvatore?" Capo calmly asks, casually waving the gun at the assassin who's still standing. "Did he behave?"

Salvatore hasn't moved, not even to look at the bodies of his compatriots on the floor. Blood—not his own—drips down his cheek.

"H-he didn't do anything," I whisper, my stomach violently churning.

"Good." Capo slides the pistol back into its holster inside his jacket and pops the grape into his mouth.

I manage to make it to a wastebasket near the potted palm to my right before I vomit.

In between heaves, I catch a glimpse of a small, round object at the bottom of the trash can, glinting metallically among the putrid yellow bile.

# 30

## MARIANA

"All right now," says Capo in a soothing voice, gently patting my shoulder. "Take it easy. Just breathe."

I rock back to my heels, wipe the back of my hand across my mouth. "Don't touch me!" I say hoarsely.

His sigh sounds disappointed. "Oh, Mari. You always were a bleeding heart. So easy to hurt. So quick to love." His voice changes, hardens somehow. "That was your downfall, you know."

*My downfall? What's he talking about?* I stagger to my feet, shrugging off his hand in disgust and contempt, and turn to look at him, keeping my gaze off the floor and the widening pools of red around the lifeless bodies. "I've brought the diamond. Where's Reynard?"

Capo gazes at me for a long time, a strange, probing expression in his eyes that's especially unnerving because it's a look I don't recognize. Without glancing away from me, he instructs Salvatore to leave us alone.

"*Si*, Capo." Salvatore ignores the bodies on the floor and exits through the mahogany doors as if nothing is amiss.

*Maybe it isn't. Maybe this is situation normal and bodies aboard the* Sea Fox *drop like flies.*

Something about the name of the yacht bothers me, but I've got bigger problems to think about. When Capo just stands there staring at me, I ask again. "Where *is* he?" A touch of hysteria raises my voice.

Capo wordlessly holds out his hand and makes a "give me" gesture. I pull the Hope from the pocket of my hoodie where I've been carrying it and set it into his open palm.

He looks down at it. "What's on it?" he asks with a curled lip.

"Dried milk."

He cocks one dark brow at me and waits for more of an explanation. When it doesn't come, he shrugs, removes a jeweler's loupe from under his coat, then holds the diamond up to the light and peers at it through the magnifier. Satisfied, he makes a low sound in his throat.

He pulls a silk handkerchief from another pocket, wraps the diamond in it, and returns it to his pocket. "Have you ever wondered, Mariana," he asks thoughtfully, "what stayed my hand all these years?"

His eyes are dark brown, like mine, only his reflect no glimmer of light or mercy.

"Stayed your hand?" I repeat in confusion, resisting a primal urge to back up.

Haltingly, as if he can't help himself, he reaches out and touches my hair. I notice his hand is slightly trembling. Now there *is* a light in his eyes, but it's got nothing to do with mercy.

"From what I've always wanted," he whispers. "From what I've always *really* wanted from you." His fingers tighten around a strand and pull.

My swallow is a loud gulp. The taste of vomit is sharp in my mouth, stinging the back of my throat. There's a rancid stench in my nose I can't get rid of. I jerk my head to free my hair, but he doesn't let go, and so several strands are torn from the root. He stands there gazing at them in a weird kind of fascination while I curse and press a hand to my stinging scalp.

"*Where is Reynard?*" I say loudly, hanging on to my control by the slimmest of threads.

"Where I've always been, my darling," says a familiar voice to my right. "Wherever you needed me."

I whip my head around. There he stands in his typical blue suit, smiling his typical warm smile, healthy and whole, not a mark on him.

"Reynard!" I sob in relief and fly into his outstretched arms, slamming into him so hard, he staggers back a few steps.

Chuckling, he holds me tight against his chest, rocking me and reassuring me he's all right, everything is all right, everything is going to be so much better from now on.

Only his words are wrong, all wrong, so wrong that my sweet relief quickly turns to bitter, choking ashes in my mouth.

Because the words he speaks are in Italian.

A language Reynard doesn't know.

I pull away abruptly and stare at his face. His smiling, *uninjured* face.

*The* Sea Fox.

*Reynard, who borrowed his name from the trickster fox from medieval fables.*

*Reynard...the fox.*

In blossoming horror, I whisper, "No."

Reynard cradles my face in his hands. "What was the most valuable lesson I taught you, my darling?" he asks gently. "The *one* lesson you never could have eluded your enemies without?"

The answer burbles up from inside me on a wave of dizziness that almost makes me fall. "Disguise."

Reynard nods slowly, holding my gaze, the meaning in his eyes unmistakable, and all that I am or ever thought I was is gone with an intake of breath.

I push him away, screaming, "NO!"

"I told you she'd overreact," says Capo, moving around me to stand beside Reynard. Standing next to each other like that, looking at me with identical expressions of calm inevitability, the resemblance is clear.

If I hadn't just regurgitated the contents of my stomach, I'd do it now.

"Impossible. Impossible." I keep repeating it in a ragged whisper as I back away, my mind going a million miles per hour in a desperate quest to make sense of this insanity.

Reynard takes a step toward me. "Mariana—"

"You saved me from him!" I scream, pointing at Capo.

"Yes," he replies calmly. "I did. Were it not for me, you'd have been chewed up and spit out years ago, like all the others. Like your sister would've been, had she not taken her own life."

The tears are coming now. I can't stop them, or the ugly way my voice breaks, betrayal and disbelief warping my words as they're coursing like poison through my body. "This isn't happening. This can't be happening. *You raised me like your own daughter!*"

Reynard nods, and his eyes are kind. "I always wanted a daughter. My wife died giving birth to our only child."

He lifts his hand and rests it on Capo's shoulder.

The sound I make is one of pure anguish, ripping from my throat the way my heart is being ripped right out of my chest. I stagger backward, my hands pressed to my ears, shaking my head and sobbing.

Aroused by my distress, Capo licks his lips. He takes a step forward, but Reynard stops him with an arm held out over Capo's chest.

*"Have you ever wondered what stayed my hand all these years?"*

Here, then, is the answer.

Reynard, who isn't Reynard, but Vincent Moreno's father,

the real *capo di tutti capi*, boss of all bosses, head of the snake, power behind the throne, secret leader of an international empire of human and drug trafficking, master of disguise and man I have loved my entire life.

The man responsible for my sister's death and oceans of human suffering.

Tears stream down my cheeks, blurring my vision and dripping from my jaw. My chest heaves with my hitching breaths. I'm hot and cold, sick with rage and heartbreak, everything inside me screaming *NO!* straight down to the marrow of my bones.

I bump against the glass coffee table with the bowl of grapes. I pick up the bowl—it's crystal, heavy—and hurl it at Reynard with a guttural roar of pain.

He and Capo jump aside, easily avoiding the bowl and the flying grapes. With a crash, it shatters into a million glinting splinters on the marble floor. Reynard sighs as if I'm testing his patience. "I want you to listen to me now, Mariana—"

"Why? Why would you do this? Why would you save me and raise me and *pretend to love me*?"

He blinks at my screamed accusation, genuinely surprised. "I *do* love you, my darling. I've always loved you, from the moment you were dropped at my feet. You looked up at me with those huge brown eyes like I was a god, like I was your savior, and I was moved. I'd never felt a thing for any of the other girls in my stable, but you touched me."

When I groan at the way he refers to his victims as stock—like horses, only less valuable—his expression hardens.

"Your problem, my darling—aside from a ridiculous sentimental streak I was never able to train out of you despite my determined efforts—is that you think only in terms of black and white. Good and bad. People aren't black or white, and neither is life. Everything is a sliding scale of gray, some paler, some darker, but nothing pitch black or pure white. Those extremes don't exist, except in your mind. Take me, for example. Haven't I cared for you? Haven't I shown you love, given you skills, a job, a *life*?"

"Lies," I whisper, breaking apart, piece by jagged piece. "All of it was lies."

"No," he says firmly, shaking his head. "It was real. And when you get over this little shock, you'll realize it."

"Little shock?" I repeat, a crazy laugh bubbling out of me. "*Little fucking shock?*"

He makes a dismissive motion with his hand, like he's tiring of the conversation and my lack of cooperation in moving it along. "You took an oath years ago, and now by bringing us the Hope, your marker is honored. Don't pull that face at the mention of honor, Mariana. It's second only to family in importance to me. I grant that the blood oath you took was under clouded circumstances—"

"I thought I was saving your life!"

He smiles. "But in reality, you were saving *your* life. You were proving your loyalty to me and your worth to the organization. You were earning your spot at the table."

I have an inkling where he's going with this and I can't help but stare at him, speechless, powerless to grasp the real scope of his plan. But he lays it all out for me neatly so my battered brain doesn't have to do any work at all.

"Outsiders aren't allowed to do business with the family, except in very rare circumstances where their loyalty and value can be proven beyond a shadow of a doubt. Once you'd grown to adulthood and I'd seen countless times how clever you were, how quickly you learned and mastered all the tasks I set before you, I decided it was time to see if you could be trusted. Not trusted the way thieves or criminals trust each other, trusted the way *family* is trusted."

Trust. Fucking *trust*. I think if I ever hear that word again, I'll lose my mind.

His tone slightly more somber, he continues. "But there are rules that govern these things. Even I must abide by them. So an oath was made and your name was entered into the logbook. Now there's only *one* final thing you must do to close the log and satisfy the marker, and properly join the family. Only blood can pay for blood."

When I just stare at him, he says, "You need to kill your American."

My mouth falls open. Every drop of color drains from my face.

Capo chuckles. "God, look at her. She didn't see *that* coming."

"Prove your loyalty to me," murmurs Reynard, his gaze hypnotic, "and inherit an empire."

I whisper, "You're insane."

He flips his hand. "Hardly. I'm a businessman. You know me, Mariana. *This is me*."

I snap, "Yes, I do know you! And you're nothing but a pimp and a liar and a despicable piece of shit!"

He strides toward me. Before I can lift my arm to defend myself, he slaps me hard across the face.

It's so sudden and violent, I lose my footing and fall on my ass, the breath knocked out of my lungs in a gust. Shocked, I touch my fingers to my nose. They come away bloody.

Looming over me with a red face and wild eyes, Reynard thunders, "*Show some respect for your father!*"

Behind him, Capo is excited by seeing me stricken and bleeding on the floor. He reaches between his legs and fondles himself, stroking his growing erection through his trousers.

Something inside my mind snaps.

I feel it go, like a tether unwinding and pulling free, a spool abruptly spinning out of thread. In an instant, I'm blank and emotionless, a robot with no heart or soul, no past or future, no hope or love or fear. I look up into Reynard's face, feeling as calm as morning.

"I'll show you the same respect you showed my sister, *Dad*."

I curl my hand around the gun shoved into the waistband of my jeans, in the small of my back, hidden under my sweatshirt. I pinched it from the assassin on the plane when he forced me to press against him and point it now at the chest of the man who taught me how to expertly steal things right off people's bodies without them ever knowing.

Capo screams, "*No!*" and lunges at me.

Without a breath of hesitation, I pull the trigger.

# 31

## RYAN

I'm an hour behind her. Only a single hour, but sixty minutes has never felt so goddamn long.

I'm at the rinky-dink airport in Abruzzo, Italy, where Mariana touched down briefly before taking off again, heading east. I hitched a ride out of New York with an old military buddy I once took a belly of lead for in a firefight against insurgents in Iraq, who now flies a transatlantic run for FedEx. But this is as far as his route goes, and I need another plane.

Fast.

"She's on a yacht in the Adriatic Sea, just off the island of Vis, in Croatia," Connor tells me over the sat phone. "We've got it up on the satellite now. I'm sending you the coordinates."

"A yacht? Fuck."

"Yep," says Connor, sounding grim. "You're gonna have to jump in. And watch your six, brother, because some of these big-ass megayachts like the one we're looking at are equipped with surface-to-air missiles."

"Jesus! Why the hell would you need a missile defense system on a nonmilitary boat?"

"Because, as a for instance, you're the paranoid head of an

international criminal empire and lots of people would like to see you dead."

"Good point."

"Even if there aren't missiles, there will definitely be a bunch of hired guns. Wait there for the rest of the team, I don't want you going in alone. They'll be to you in less than—"

"No."

Connor growls. "Goddammit, Ryan—"

"Twelve guys in combat gear parachuting out of a plane's gonna get a lot more attention than one. I'm going in alone. Have the team rally on Vis and wait for my call."

He's silent for a moment. I know he's pissed I insisted on taking off on my own before the rest of the team was assembled, because that's not how we do things, but this is one time I wouldn't—couldn't—wait.

My woman's in danger. If God himself told me to wait, I'd tell him to suck my dick.

"Copy that," Connor finally says. "But when you get back, we're gonna have a chat about teamwork, Rambo."

"If you're done lecturing me, Grandma, can you send me the number of the nearest skydiving outfit? I'm gonna need to rent a rig."

Connor mutters, "This shit is so much easier in the movies."

"You're tellin' me."

"Tabby's pulling up the info. The number's on the way."

"Thanks, brother."

"No problem. And Ryan?"

"Yeah?"

There's a pause before he speaks. "Keep frosty, brother. This guy Moreno's a real piece of work."

"I will, brother. See you soon."

I disconnect the call, thumb over to my texts, and click the link to the phone number of Skydive Italia that just popped up on my screen.

32

## MARIANA

A deafening bang, a blinding flash of light, and a violent recoil jolting up my arm are the three things that happen simultaneously when I shoot Vincent Moreno at point-blank range in the chest.

He staggers back, arms flung wide, eyes bulging. He lands on his back with a *whump* that shakes the floor. Blood flowers from the hole in the center of his chest, quickly seeping crimson through his pristine white shirt.

Reynard is frozen, staring blankly at his son. I don't know if his shock is due to finding himself standing when only seconds before my gun was pointed at him, or if he's still trying to understand what happened.

In case it's the latter, I provide him with an explanation. "He lunged. It was instinct."

Reynard shifts his gaze to me. His eyes are so wide, they show white all around the irises. His face is the color of the marble floor.

I stand slowly and face him. My body feels like it's a thousand years old. As if the words are coming from someone else, I say in a hollow voice, "Only blood can pay for blood?" I gesture to Vincent, still alive but gasping for air, his hands fluttering uselessly at his sides. "Consider us even."

Alerted by the sound of a gunshot, four assassins slam through the closed doors. They see Vincent on the floor and me standing there with a gun, and all of them pull up short, draw their weapons, and point them at me.

"Stop!" shouts Reynard in Italian, holding out a hand. "Don't shoot! This is my daughter! You will *not* hurt her!"

They freeze. They glance at each other, then at me, then at Vincent, who's making awful gurgling noises, desperately trying to suck air into lungs that are most likely collapsed.

I can tell by the expression on Vincent's face—past the pain and panic—that he's unhappy with this development.

The men slowly lower their weapons. Reynard turns his attention back to me.

"You were the son I should have had," he says, his voice shaking with emotion. "You were always the strong one. The dedicated one. The one without the sickness in the head." He gestures to Vincent, who wheezes in outrage.

Blood seeps from one corner of his mouth, and has gathered in a slick, shining pool under his body. His eyes are like a rabid dog's, rolling viciously in his head. Even fighting death, he's full of rage.

Reynard says, "You were always the one I intended to pass everything to, Mariana. *You* are my true heir."

I blink, the assassins gasp, and Vincent roars like a wounded lion.

Then everything takes on the quality of a dream. It all seems to happen in slow motion. I see Vincent reach into his jacket. I see him withdraw his silver pistol. I see him point it at his father. I smell the acrid stench of gunpowder in the air, still lingering from the shot that took him down. I see another burst of brilliant light, hear another bang, and a *crack* like thunder.

Reynard's head explodes like a pumpkin. He spins a fast half circle, then crumples facedown to the floor.

An eerie stillness follows. I'm untouchable, inside a cocoon of unreality that's softening all the hard edges of things, keeping my pulse even and my mind clear, removed from it all, like I'm a spectator watching a movie, serene and safe behind a gauzy screen.

Vincent takes one last, ragged breath, shudders, then closes his eyes. The gun drops from his hand and clatters against the floor. After that, he doesn't move, his chest stops rising, and I gather from all the evidence that he's dead.

I feel nothing.

I feel nothing when I look at the mangled pulp that was Reynard, either. I'm aware I must be deeply in shock, that my body is responding to severe trauma by instinctively defending itself with psychological detachment, and that later I'll probably develop PTSD, but right now, I don't care.

When I look at the armed men standing frozen and gaping at the doors, I still don't care. My utter lack of fear or feeling must show in my face, because they stare back at me in obvious trepidation.

Then one of them whispers, "*Capo di tutti capi*," and slowly takes a knee.

He isn't looking at Vincent or Reynard, lying there motionless.

He's looking at me.

One by one, the other assassins sink to their knees.

Then they bow their heads, paying their respects to the new leader of the empire.

# 33

## RYAN

"Which one is it?" I shout over the roar of the engines as I stare though the Cessna's window at the ocean, fourteen thousand feet below me.

And the *three* fucking megayachts floating within a mile of each other off the coast of Vis.

This was as far as the GPS got us before the final working tracker blinked offline. One mile of ocean, not five feet.

Serves me right for only attaching four trackers to Mariana's clothing.

When I get my woman back, she's not going anywhere without a dozen.

"We can't dial down tight enough on the satellite images to get the hull identifiers to see who owns them, but there's a huge heat signature coming from the one farthest west," Connor says in my ear. Our connection is shitty, and his voice is cutting in and out, but I can still hear him when he says, "There's gotta be hundreds of people on that craft."

Which would make sense if your business is trafficking bodies.

Imagining a ship full of scared little girls in addition to Mariana, I seethe with anger. I can't wait to bury a bullet in this sick motherfucker's skull.

"Copy that. Out."

I hang up the sat phone before Connor can say anything else. At this point, there's nothing else that can be said. Except maybe good luck.

Or sayonara.

I zip the phone into a pocket in my jacket, shove a pair of tactical goggles on my face, and give the thumbs-up to the skinny guy with the dreads from Skydive Italia. He was more than happy to take me up solo when I gave him five thousand cash, plus another few thousand for the chute and rig he won't get back, but he isn't too happy now, after watching me pull a shit ton of guns and ammo from my ruck and strap 'em all over my body.

He'll get over it.

He yanks open the door and steps aside. Freezing wind slaps my face. The roar of the engines becomes deafening. At this altitude, I don't need supplemental oxygen, but breathing's still gonna be a bitch until I'm under canopy. I sit on the overhanging platform and scooch all the way to the edge, then arch my body and kick my feet back as I jump.

This shit is way more fun when you're running out the back of a C-130 with your buddies.

Within seconds, I'm falling at terminal velocity. The force and roar of the wind is enormous, but the fall itself is peaceful. I lie on my belly in the void of the sky, the earth a huge blue crescent below, curving at the horizon, the sun a brilliant white gleam above. The sound of freefall is like an everlasting, crashing wave.

And all I can think is *Mariana. Mariana. Mariana.*

She's a pulse in my blood. Knowing that I'm this close to her, that I'm almost *there*, is a kind of madness. I force myself to focus and count the seconds until my altimeter tells me it's time to pull my chute.

Once I do, the noise level drops. The roar of the wind abates and there's only a whistle through the lines of the canopy. Breathing is easier, and everything is peaceful.

And now I'm a sitting duck.

If there are antiaircraft missiles on Moreno's yacht, this is when I'll find out.

As I rush closer to the yacht, I see how massive it is, longer than a football field and wider, too. No one is in view on any of the decks, which is a stroke of good luck.

With the handles on the chute, I steer toward the aft deck. It rises up fast underneath me. As soon as my feet touch down, I'm out of the harness, dropping it over the side of the ship so the chute sails away, drifting down toward the surface of the water. Crouching low, I run to the back of a massive teak bar and take cover behind it. I've instantly got my Glock in hand and my ear trained for warning shouts.

They never come.

The first niggle of worry crosses my mind, but I shove it aside.

Keeping low, with my Glock at the ready, I run inside the first deck. The doors are wide open. The interior is just as luxurious as the exterior, but there's no one here, either.

*Where is everyone? Where are the armed guards?*

I sprint through a living area—bypassing a huge dining room and media room—and head toward the spiral-glass staircase toward the back. I'm on security cameras somewhere by now, but nobody's coming out to meet me. This ship is as quiet as a graveyard.

*Find the master suite.*

I don't allow myself to think about why I assume Moreno will have taken Mariana to his bedroom, I only know that's where I'm headed next.

The top deck is obviously the helm, encased in glass and deserted, so I've got four other decks to clear. I silently ascend the staircase, every sense trained for noise or movement, but I move unhindered through the ship.

Until I reach the fourth level. Then my heart drops like a rock to my feet.

The entire deck is a huge nightclub, running the length of the ship, fore to aft. There's an enormous white dance floor, two bars, sofas lining all the mirrored walls, stripper poles dotting the perimeter, disco balls glittering from the ceiling, a DJ booth on a riser in one corner, and a dozen or more suspended metal cages I have to assume hold dancers.

And there are bodies *everywhere.*

Naked, half-dressed, in bikinis and miniskirts and thongs, young, well-endowed women lie together in sleeping piles, tanned limbs entangled like snakes. There are men as well, but far fewer. Young men in loud, tropical print shirts and board shorts, baby-faced but muscular, college-aged.

In between all the dozing frat boys and the army of passed-out Playmates are empty bottles—literally hundreds of them—champagne and tequila and wine strewn all over the place, obviously dropped wherever they were emptied. Beneath the bodies and bottles, the floor sparkles with confetti.

This isn't a human trafficking operation.

It's a fucking *bachelor party.*

The point is driven home like a stake through my heart when a guy, not even thirty, wearing nothing but tan cargo shorts and holding an orange drink with an umbrella in it, wanders into the room. He sees me standing there in camouflage, gun drawn, bristling with weapons, and stops in his tracks.

"Uh, hey, man," he says, eyeing me. "You part of the show?"

I bellow, "FUCK!"

He jumps. A few of the girls stir, yawning and mumbling, but go right back to sleep.

This is a fucking nightmare. I'm having a nightmare, and a heart attack, and a fucking mental breakdown, all at once.

I stride over to the guy, point my gun at his nose, and snarl, "Who owns this boat?"

He peeps out a name, not Moreno's.

"*Take me to him!*"

He spins around so fast, the umbrella flies out of his drink. Then he runs to the door he came through with little skittering steps, like a mouse. I follow on his heels, a volcano erupting from the top of my head.

He takes me to a large bedroom decorated all in white, where the hairiest man I've ever seen is lounging in a big leather chair, smoking a cigar, and playing *Grand Theft Auto* on a huge TV. His chest hair is like a bear's pelt. On the bed are two naked girls, gently snoring. A fat Burmese cat wearing a diamond collar lounges between them, licking its tail.

When we come in, the hairy guy glances at me, at my Glock, then presses a button on a remote that pauses his game.

He asks, "That a .40 cal or a nine millimeter?"

I say, "Are you fucking kidding me?"

The kid in the cargo shorts blurts nervously, "Armin, this dude was just *standing* there in the middle of the disco—"

"Shut up, Kenny. The reason I ask is 'cause I got a few nines, but I'm thinking about adding the .40 cal to the collection." Armin calmly smokes his cigar.

"I'll give you this one if you let me borrow your tender to get to the yacht next door," I tell him.

Armin's brows lift. He's Middle Eastern, Turkish maybe, built like a wall and completely unfazed by my presence. I'm not sure if he's nuts or if I should offer him a job. Maybe all that hair doubles as body armor.

He assesses my state of agitation and my outfit of deadly weapons. "Why, you got somebody to kill over there?"

Kenny draws in a horrified breath and shrinks away from me.

"Nope, I got somebody to save, and I don't have time to dick around with conversation."

"The ship next door belongs to the Oracle software guy, Larry Ellison. Came in last night with his family. We cruise the same waters lotta the time, recognized his yacht."

"Thanks for the intel. You just saved me from crashin' another bachelor party. You gonna let me borrow your tender or what?"

"Oh, this wasn't a bachelor thing," Kenny meekly chimes in. "Armin gets paid to party by all these different brands. Like, to post pictures on Instagram with all the girls while he's wearing expensive watches and drinking top-shelf tequila and stuff. He's totally famous, I can't believe you don't recognize him—"

"Shut up, Kenny!" Armin and I say in unison.

Kenny shuts up. Armin scratches his bushy beard. "I got a sub on board if you'd rather take that. You look like a guy who likes to take people by surprise."

I'm liking this guy more and more with every word coming out of his mouth. "Yes. That's fuckin' brilliant. Thank you."

Armin smiles. "Cool. But I'm driving."

# 34

## MARIANA

In my cocoon of shock, it doesn't seem at all strange to order the kneeling assassins to rise. They do, holstering their weapons and clasping their hands in front of their waists as I've seen them do countless times before, but never for me. Then they stand there, waiting for my command.

"Salvatore," I say quietly, addressing the only one I know by name.

His gaze cuts to me. "*Si*, Capo?"

*Capo*. I swallow the sick laugh tickling my throat. If I start laughing, I might never stop. "How many other people are on this boat?"

"Fourteen crew, the captain, and us." He makes a gesture to encompass his companions, me, and the bodies on the floor.

"Will the tender hold that many?"

"Yes."

"I see." I stand there trying to think for a moment, forcing my thoughts around the cotton candy of my mind.

Salvatore clears his throat, and I focus on him again. He obviously wants to speak.

"Yes?"

With surprising dignity, holding himself tall, he says, "I disrespected you earlier, Capo, on the flight. I didn't know who you were. We weren't told…" He thinks better of whatever he was going to say and falls silent for a moment. Then he continues in Italian. "It would be my honor to end my life in payment for this disrespect."

An aria plays in the background, a pair of soaring sopranos singing about betrayal and heartbreak, their love for the same man. I never would have guessed opera would be the soundtrack in hell.

"That won't be necessary. We've had enough bloodshed this morning. Thank you, Salvatore." After a beat, I add, "Your loyalty is appreciated."

I feel his pride at that statement, that I've said it in front of the other men, his chest swelling with it, and the urge to laugh returns tenfold.

I'm losing my sanity. Perhaps I've already lost it.

Perhaps I never had it at all.

"I want you to take everyone except the captain and get on the tender," I instruct, walking slowly to Vincent's body. In my gauzy dream, I bend down, fish the Hope Diamond from his jacket pocket, and curl my fingers around the stone as I gaze down at his lifeless face.

There's blood and spittle in the corners of his lips. He didn't shave this morning. His chest is still warm.

I straighten and direct my gaze to Salvatore again. "Everyone who's alive, I mean. Get on the tender and go to the nearest island. Do it now. Take nothing with you. Before you go, tell the captain to come to me here."

His brow creases, but he doesn't contradict me or ask for clarification. He simply murmurs, "*Si*, Capo."

He turns and leaves the room, the other men right behind him. I'm left alone with four dead bodies and the muggy chaos of my thoughts.

I walk to the outside deck and raise my face to the morning sun. It's warm and sunny, the smell of the ocean strong. A light breeze plays with my hair. I don't know how long I stand like that, in a trance, but when I hear an engine roar to life, I look down. There on the surface of the white-capped water below is a boat with four men in black suits, and fourteen others in navy-and-white uniforms.

Salvatore is at the helm. He guns the throttle and makes a heading for the island in the far distance, not turning to look over his shoulder even once.

Absolute power corrupts absolutely, said Lord Acton. Now, for the first time, I have a true idea of what he means.

I head inside to wait for the captain.

## 35

## RYAN

Armin and I are trotting out of his bedroom when we hear the explosion.

It's huge and somewhere not far away, judging by the concussion that rattles all the windows a second later.

We look at each other at the same instant. He says, "That doesn't sound good."

My heart stops. *Mariana.*

I shove past Armin and run through the yacht the way I came in until I reach an outside deck and see what caused all the noise.

On the eastern horizon, a big orange fireball illuminates the sky.

It's not the sun.

"Get us over there!" I scream at Armin when he appears on deck. He pulls a cell phone from his pocket, touches a number, lifts the phone to his ear.

"Let's go check out that explosion, Captain. Somebody's gonna need help. Full steam ahead." He listens for a moment. "All right, as close as you can." He clicks off, then stands looking at the fire in the distance with his arms folded across his chest. "She can do thirty knots when she's up to speed. We'll be there in under ten minutes."

Ten minutes is too long. I pull my own phone out and call Connor. He answers on the first ring. "What's your status, brother?"

My voice comes out hoarse with stress. "I'm on the wrong fuckin' yacht! The one Mariana's on just blew up! You got satellite feed?"

"Blew up?" Connor mutters a curse. "We're not live streaming. I won't have an updated shot for about ten minutes."

Ten minutes, again. I throw my head back and roar my frustration. Beside me, Armin doesn't even blink. The man is unflappable.

"It's gonna be okay, Ryan," says Connor firmly. "Listen to me—"

"I'll never forgive myself if anything happens to her," I say, struggling to breathe, adrenaline lashing through me, my stomach in ropes. "If she's hurt, or worse—"

"Stop!" shouts Connor. "Focus!"

I close my eyes, drag air into my lungs, drawing on all my training for high-stress situations. But no mission has ever been this personal before.

No mission I've ever been on has included the possibility that the woman I love dies in a fiery explosion.

"Can you get closer to the other yacht?" Connor asks in my ear.

"We're on the way."

"We?"

"Long story. Call the FBI. Call Interpol. Call everyone. Get that fuckin' boat surrounded and get a medical emergency response team out there as fast as you can." I hang up before he can answer and spew a blistering string of curses, panic pulsing through me like another heartbeat.

Watching black smoke rise in the distant horizon, Armin says, "I take it someone you care about is on that ship?"

My heart pounds so hard, I'm surprised he can't hear it. Through gritted teeth I say, "Yes."

He nods, his expression thoughtful. "We can get over there faster if we take the speed boat. She'll do up to eighty knots on calm waters."

When he looks at me, I say, "*Let's go.*"

~

As we slice through the water toward the burning yacht in Armin's yellow cigarette speed boat with the busty pin-up girls painted on the sides, I try not to think of worst-case scenarios or all the horrible possibilities. I try not to think of anything at all. But the closer we get to the ship, the more obvious it is that the *only* possibilities I'm dealing with are bad.

Worse than bad.

Not only is the yacht on fire, it's sinking.

Listing on her starboard side, flames roaring through all the decks and spitting high up into the sky, the craft is almost completely demolished. The satellites on the helm have been blown off. All the glass on every deck is shattered. Smoke and chemical fumes billow from the length of the hull in acrid clouds that sting my eyes.

There's an enormous debris field around the remains of the yacht, chunks of fiberglass and furniture and metal, partially submerged, bobbing in the waves, blackened and twisted into ugly shapes. There's diesel fuel, too, a slick film floating on the water, reflecting oily rainbows in the light.

I don't see any bodies, but it's obvious by the level of destruction and the blistering heat of the fire that if anyone was on board, they couldn't have survived.

Armin cruises in slow circles around the hulking carcass of

the ship, keeping a safe distance from the roaring flames as he steers carefully through the field of debris. I lean over the side and hunt desperately for any sign of life, for anyone waving from the water, for the smallest hint that would give me hope.

There's nothing.

The yacht is a burning, blackened husk of death, the ocean all around eerily silent.

It isn't until I hear the helicopters and look up into the sky that I realize I've fallen to my knees.

And that awful animal scream that seems to be coming from everywhere is coming from me.

The next few hours are a blur. People. Activity. Noise. Questions.

So many fucking questions.

The Croatian coast guard arrives on scene first, followed by their navy, search and rescue teams, Interpol, and finally, the FBI. There are also plenty of lookie-loos in boats cruising around, along with news and paparazzi choppers whizzing overhead.

Field officers from the FBI and Interpol team up to debrief me while the search and rescue teams get to work. I remember nothing of what was asked or answered. I do remember having to be physically restrained as I was removed by police from the scene, and Armin telling them to chill out because I was cool.

But I wasn't cool. I'd never been less cool. I was a rage and self-blame machine, desperate for any other reality than the one I was living.

In the port at Vis, I'm released by the FBI and told I'm free to go on my way, that they'll contact me if necessary. I think they were just sick of dealing with me by then. I heard more than a few mutterings of "lunatic," "head case," and, "meltdown." I meet up with the rest of the team from Metrix, who, as a unit, take one look at me and call Connor for support.

I can't talk to him, though. All my words have dried up. I stand in a parking lot in the waning hours of the day, holding a phone to my ear, listening to my best friend speak, anguish roiling inside my belly like a nest of snakes.

For a moment, when he tells me there are satellite pictures of a tender leaving the yacht just before the explosion, hope floods back in a sweet, heady rush that leaves me trembling. But then he says video footage from security cameras at the port captured good quality images of everyone who got off that vessel, and Mariana wasn't among them.

Neither was Moreno.

The implications of that…of what she might have gone through, of why he'd send the entire crew away to be alone with her…

I go numb then. Blank. Everything is put on pause, except the nasty little voice inside my head telling me if I'd only landed on the right yacht, everything would be different.

If I hadn't failed, Mariana would still be alive.

Afternoon fades into evening, and still I stand on the docks, gazing west, watching smoke rise in the distance, hoping for someone to come and tell me there's been a miracle, that it was all a mistake. That she wasn't on that yacht, that she was found safe and sound with Larry Ellison and his family, or floating unharmed on a piece of flotsam, or had escaped Moreno and was waiting for me on the other end of the docks the entire time.

That moment never comes.

With every hour that passes, I die a thousand little deaths until there's nothing of me left but my shadow.

Like a ghost, I haunt the port of Vis for weeks, mute and grieving, soaking up every nugget of information that comes in from the various authorities about the explosion—what's been found, how the cleanup process is going, what they're trying to do to contain the huge diesel spill from the engines. I stay there long after the news crews have left, long after the rest of the guys from Metrix have returned Stateside, long after logic tells me there's no more reason to stay, until finally, the reality can no longer be denied.

Mariana's gone.

Again.

Only this time, she's gone for good.

# 36

## RYAN

*Two months later*

"Tell me you're eating, at least. Last time I saw you on Skype, you looked like a chemo patient."

"Christ, Connor, you sound like my grandma. And that's not a compliment, by the way. The woman was a giant pain in the ass."

His answer over the line comes across gruff. "Brother, tell me you're eating so I don't have to ask my wife to hack into the traffic cams in Paris to get me photographic fucking evidence!"

My lips lift to the closest thing approximating a smile I'm now capable of. I practiced it in the mirror of my hotel bathroom just this morning, aware that people have started to cross the street in apprehension when they see me walking toward them.

I'm sure it's the crazy look in my eyes, but it could be the wild hair and scraggly beard, too.

"I'm eating. As we speak, which should make you happy."

"I don't believe you."

I sigh, shaking my head. He's *worse* than my grandmother.

"Here, listen." I lean over the table and shove another big

hunk of country bread smeared with duck confit into my mouth, chewing into the cell phone as loudly as humanly possible.

Cows are quieter eaters. Champion pie eaters are quieter. I sound like a blue-ribbon hog at the trough.

Several people at nearby tables turn to send me outraged stares, like I've offended their ancestors with my abominable chewing, but I ignore them.

"All right," says Connor grudgingly. "I'm not totally convinced that's food in your mouth and not a live octopus and a barracuda having a fight, but it sounds disgusting enough that I'm gonna let it go for the moment. Moving on."

I swallow, take a big swig of my champagne, sit back in my chair, and close my eyes. Food doesn't have much taste anymore —not even the ridiculously expensive meal I'm now eating—but sunshine warming my skin is one thing I can still enjoy.

Every time I close my eyes and lift my face to the sun, she's there, smiling that angel's smile, and even though it hurts like fuck, I do it every chance I get.

"Moving on," I agree.

Connor hesitates for a moment. "Got a call from Karpov today."

That doesn't even cause a blip on my radar. "I wondered when that would happen."

"Yeah, he's, uh…a little agitated."

"Just tell him, bro. Tell him his big blue diamond is at the bottom of the fuckin' Adriatic."

"No," he responds sharply. "If I tell him that, you'll be missing your head within twenty-four hours. I know you don't use it too often, but still. It's your head. You need one."

I don't agree. Heads are for people with working brains. All I've got inside my skull is a big, moldy lump of mozzarella. "I'll call him. I'll give him the coordinates where the yacht sank. He can go deep-sea diving."

"That isn't funny."

"It wasn't a joke."

The phone emits a growl that would do a grizzly proud. "You have a death wish now, is that it?"

When I take a beat too long to reply, Connor curses. "Do I need to be worried about this? I mean more than I already am? Do you need me to come out there? Because I'm on a plane as soon as you give me the word—"

"Like I told you when I took a leave of absence, I just need some time to get my head straight," I say quietly.

I'm pretty sure Connor's about as convinced as I am that getting my head straight isn't going to happen, but for now, we're pretending it is. We're pretending I'm not completely mind-fucked and useless, that I might one day be able to go back to work.

I can't see myself ever doing anything but sitting here at a table on the quaint outside patio of L'Ami Louis under the dappled shade of the trees, eating the meal Mariana and I should have been eating together. I've been in Paris for a month and I'm here every night, wasting my savings, wasting what's left of my sanity, wasting my time.

I don't have anything better to do.

Even if I did, I wouldn't want to be anywhere else. Part of me keeps hoping she'll show up one night, sit down beside me, and we'll pick up right where we left off, as if the past two months never happened.

As if I'm not a ruin of a man. The zombies on *The Walking Dead* have more life in them than I do. I've seen mummies in better shape.

*If only I'd landed on the right yacht.*

"If only" is my best friend now. We spend a lot of quality time together, beating each other up.

Connor sighs. I picture him sitting behind his big black desk, running a hand over his big square head. "Okay. Take all the time you need. But don't take forever, brother. I need you back here at some point. For comic relief, if nothing else."

I try out my fake smile again. It doesn't feel right on my face, so I drop it.

"Did you see the final police report on what caused the explosion?" I ask, pouring myself more booze.

"Yeah," says Connor. "Fuel leak in the bilge ignited by the engines."

"And the secondary explosion that caused most of the damage was the missiles blowing up from the heat of the fire."

"Fucking antiaircraft missiles on a yacht," Connor mutters.

"Apparently it's not that uncommon on those megayachts. Armin's has 'em, too."

"Your buddy, the Instagram star? Why the fuck would *he* have them?"

"Because he's got too much money and a fetish for things that blow other things up. And things that go fast. And boobs."

Connor chuckles. "Yeah, I checked out his site. That dude is living every teenage boy's wet dream. His father's some kind of media billionaire?"

"Telecom and cable. They've got all of Europe wired."

Armin and I have kept in touch. He keeps pestering me to sail up to Monaco with him, says there's a lot to distract me there, but I'm not in the mood for the kind of distractions playboy gazillionaires like.

Connor and I chat for a few more minutes. Neither of us mentions the part of the report about the human remains recovered from the wreckage of the yacht. More specifically, the *bits* of human remains. They were so badly charred and in such small pieces that the only thing the forensic anthropologists were able to identify was a section of splintered femur bone from a Caucasian male in his sixties.

That had to be Reynard, considering his age and that he vanished without a trace after the phone call with Mariana. He must've been on the yacht, too, Moreno's surefire lure to get her there.

Of Mariana and Moreno, there was no trace. One of my recurring nightmares now is of sea creatures munching on barbequed body parts.

But there's a lot of ocean out there. I'm bracing myself for the day when I read in the paper that pieces of a female skeleton washed up on some remote Italian beach.

At least I'd have something then. I don't even have a picture of her. I've got nothing left but memories and a hole in my chest big enough to drive a tank through.

"Another bottle, sir?"

The waitress stands tableside, holding up my second empty bottle of champagne.

I actually hate the stuff, but it's what Mariana said we'd have when we came here, so I'm having it.

When I nod, the waitress leaves without another word or a bat of her eyelashes. She knows I'm just getting started. All the waitstaff know me now, and know to put me in a taxi and tell the driver the name of my hotel when I can no longer walk at the end of the night.

I tip good, so nobody complains.

"All right, brother, I gotta go," I tell Connor, squinting into the setting sun. It's a gorgeous day, warm and clear, a hint of crispness in the air. The leaves on the trees are starting to turn bronze and gold. In the distance, the Eiffel Tower glints like a jewel.

"Go and get drunk again?" Connor asks.

"Yes, Grandma, go and get drunk again."

"I'm worried about your liver."

"You're worried about everything. Stop it. I'm a big boy."

There's a fraught pause. "You're my best friend. You're my brother. And I love you, man. Don't forget that, okay?"

I love you. Three words Mariana and I never said to each

other. Three words I'll never be able to hear again without being swamped with pain and regret.

"Yep," I say, my throat closing. "Call you later."

I hang up without saying goodbye, because I know how my voice would crack. He's already worried enough as it is.

The waitress returns. She sets a big glass of milk on the table in front of me and turns to leave.

"Wait." I gesture to the glass. "I didn't order this."

She shrugs. "I was told to bring it."

She walks away without a backward glance, leaving me in a fizzy champagne haze. I glance around at all the tables nearby, wondering which asshole thinks I've had too much to drink and should be switching to milk, but no one's paying any attention to me.

Then a gentle breeze stirs the leaves of the trees shading the patio, and a ray of light hits the glass in a way that illuminates it from behind.

I've never seen milk sparkle before. Rainbow prisms dance over the white tablecloth before disappearing as the wind shifts the leaves again.

*What the fuck?*

I pull the glass nearer and stick my finger in it. I can't get all the way to the bottom, so I take my spoon and dip it in. It hits something hard.

There's something in the bottom of the glass.

Something that *sparkles*.

I jolt out of my chair so abruptly, it topples over backward with a crash. Ignoring the gasps and disapproving mutters arising around me, I stare at that glass of milk like it's a bomb. Like it's going to explode any second, the same way my heart is going to explode inside my chest.

With a shaking hand, I reach out and tip over the glass.

Milk sloshes out, spreading over the white linen, pooling around my dinner plate, dripping off the edge of the table until the glass is empty except for the large chunk of blue ice left behind.

It's the Hope Diamond.

"Mariana!" I holler at the top of my lungs, spinning a wild circle, staggering, arms failing as I look for her, for any glimpse. "*Angel!*"

Everyone in the restaurant has stopped to stare at me. All conversation has ceased. The only sound is the traffic on the street beyond the patio and the wind gently rustling through the trees.

I grab the diamond and run into the restaurant, knocking aside everyone in my path. There are shouts, curses, the crash of plates against the floor. When I find my waitress taking an order from an elderly couple at a table near the front window, I fall on her like a pilgrim at the end of a thousand-mile journey through the desert when he catches his first glimpse of the holy city.

"Where is he? The person who ordered the milk! Who is he, and which way did he GO?" I grip her arm so hard, she lets out a little scream of panic.

"I don't know! I didn't see who ordered it! My manager told me—"

She jerks her head toward the squat, black-haired man with a beak of a nose steaming toward us from the kitchen. He obviously is *not* happy with me right now.

"Monsieur!" he shouts, wagging his finger as all the restaurant patrons look on, agog. "Monsieur, we have had enough of you! Get out! I can no longer tolerate this kind of—"

I grab him by his lapels and drag him against me so we're nose to nose. Then I thunder into his face, "WHO ORDERED THAT FUCKING GLASS OF MILK?"

He blinks, once, exhaling a terrified breath, then blurts, "A woman, a woman in a black veil. She came in and ordered it, she said to send it to your table, she said you would know what it meant, she tipped me one hundred euro—"

I shake him so hard his eyes roll around in his head like marbles. Pounding through my veins is a drumbeat of *a woman, a woman, a woman*.

"WHERE DID SHE GO?"

The manager points to the front door. "Sh-she disappeared! I don't know anything else! She didn't say anything else!"

I shove him aside and sprint out the door. On the sidewalk, I turn in every direction, frantically hunting for any glimpse of black. Everything is spinning and I can't see straight. My heart is a firecracker, my pulse is wildfire, and electricity blisters my skin.

Then, around the corner of a building half a block away, I see something dark billow and snap like a sail in a breeze before disappearing from sight.

The hem of a long black veil.

I run faster than I've ever run in my life. I'm a bolt of lightning crackling over the sidewalk. I'm a supersonic sound wave.

I'm Lazarus, risen from the dead.

When I round the corner, panting and out of my mind, I see a figure draped in black far ahead on the crowded avenue. The figure walks briskly, looking straight ahead, her gait purposeful as she weaves through the throng of strolling pedestrians. She ducks into an alleyway just as I break into a run.

When I reach the alley, I find it deserted except for a pair of reeking Dumpsters and scattered trash. Windows in the tall brick buildings on either side stare down like blank eyes. A lone pigeon pecks at the ground, wings beating in a panic when I run past it with a bellow of frustration.

But in my rush, I've missed something. There's a door halfway up the alley, a door cracked open so light from inside spills out onto the cobblestones in an inviting yellow slice.

My heart in my throat, I slowly backtrack and push open the door.

I step into an art gallery. It's bright and airy, filled with stylish couples mingling and chatting, drinking chardonnay. I move like a dream walker through the gallery, gazing in cold shock at all the colorful framed oils hanging on the bright-white walls.

In every painting, the subject is a dragonfly.

"Mr. McLean? Excuse me, sir, are you Ryan McLean?"

I turn toward the voice. It's a woman I've never seen before, an elegant redhead in a tailored ivory suit. She's very beautiful, with milk-pale skin and secretive eyes, her fiery hair coiled in a low chignon. She smiles at me, waiting for a reply.

"Yes," I say gruffly, finding my voice. "I'm Ryan McLean. Who are you?"

"Genevieve," she replies, as if the name should mean something to me.

I swallow, fighting to maintain my composure when everything inside me is howling wolves and hurricanes. "Where is she? Where's Mariana?"

Genevieve's smile deepens. "I'm sorry, I don't know anyone by that name. But I was instructed to give you this."

She holds out a folded piece of stationery. I take it, my hand shaking like a leaf.

"Good luck to you both, Mr. McLean," says Genevieve warmly. "She was always a favorite of management."

Without another word, the redhead turns and melts into the crowd.

I stand with the note in my hand until I become aware I'm garnering a lot of curious glances. Then I unfold the paper and read the words written in precise, slanting black ink.

*I can picture you there, among the date palms and veiled women.*

*I can picture you stealing into a locked room at dawn*

*with the morning call to prayer echoing over the empty medina, the sun on red-tiled rooftops already hot.*

I recognize the words instantly, because they're my own. And now I know exactly where I'm going.

I drop my head back, close my eyes, and inhale my first real breath in months.

# 37

## MARIANA

*Morocco*

Once upon a time in another life, I was a little girl.

I had a little girl's dreams of fairy tales and handsome princes. I had parents and a sister and a scruffy yellow dog named Dog. I went to school in a ramshackle schoolhouse with a dirt floor and woven banana leaves for a roof, and picked avocadoes on my parents' farm. I didn't know I was poor, or powerless, or cursed.

Once upon a time, I was happy.

Then…I grew up.

I grew up and learned that happiness is like heaven, a thing everyone yearns for but few ever find. I learned about death and betrayal and sex and longing, about hunger and sadness and fear.

I learned that dreams are only for dreamers.

I learned to survive.

Then one day many, many years later, I learned about love.

I discovered love was nothing like a fairy-tale. It was more like a bad poem written in indecipherable meter by a drunken poet who couldn't keep a job, so he lived with his mother his whole life while writing the most outrageous roadblocks and outcomes, based on nothing but the whims of his own inebriated brain. It had an awkward beginning, a wildly improbable middle, and an awful, painful end. And nothing rhymed.

Love was the *worst*.

Inconveniently, it was also the *best*.

I didn't trust it from the get-go.

What I didn't realize is that love isn't like Tinker Bell. Love exists whether you believe in it or not.

And whether you believe in love or not, *it* believes in *you*.

~

He finds me on the third day. Three long days, three unending nights, and then I look up from my mint tea and he's there.

Standing across the medina, his gaze fixed on me, a bare glint of yearning bright in his eyes, he's there.

He looks terrible.

Like he's been sleeping on park benches and dining on scraps from trash cans to survive. Like all he's ever known is heartbreak and violence. That I'm the cause of the pain he's wearing like a second skin makes all the broken parts inside me grind together and bleed.

I rise from my table, shaking and breathless, my nerves channeling fire. Between us, the square is a riot of color and noise, food stalls, trilling laughter, dancers and dusty barefoot children. Freshly dyed silks flutter indigo and saffron in the breeze. I turn and make my way through the winding alleyways, draped in carpets and thick with people, until I reach an azure door.

I push through the door into a quiet courtyard, Ryan's presence behind me so vivid, it's almost like touch.

Past a splashing fountain, up a winding staircase to a quiet room at the top with a view of distant mountains and walls painted the same blue as the door. By the window, I turn and wait, holding my breath.

He eases into view in the open doorway, moving carefully, silently, as if approaching a wild animal trapped against a wall. When he sees me, his eyes flare. He inhales through parted lips and stands staring at me for a long, silent moment, drinking me in, his hands trembling at his sides.

In a low, hoarse voice, he says, "How?"

"There was a submarine on the yacht. A little two-seater. That got me as far as Tunisia. From there, I took the train to Casablanca, then a bus here."

His brow creases in confusion.

"I had the captain take me. He knew how to operate the sub…and how dangerous a gas leak on a yacht loaded with munitions would be. He knew what to do to make it look accidental."

He processes that, then slowly takes a step forward over the threshold. His gaze darts around the room, questioning, cataloging the furniture, the timbered ceiling, the colorful pillows on the bed. Then it snaps back to me again, as if magnetized.

When he doesn't speak, I say, "The crew on the yacht were prisoners. Forced to work for free, their silence guaranteed because their tongues were cut out. When I explained to him what I wanted to do, the captain was more than willing to help me. He wanted to disappear, too. Become someone else. Live a different life. We parted ways in Tunisia."

Ryan takes another few halting steps toward me, then stops, the tremor in his hands getting worse. He's focused on me with an extraordinary intensity, his eyes burning with questions and need. He swallows, his Adam's apple bobbing. There's a pulse of heat like a heartbeat between us.

With a break in his voice, he says, "Why?" and I know what he's really asking.

Why did you make me believe you were dead?

"I went a little mad," I whisper, closing my eyes. "When I found out Reynard was Vincent's father—"

Ryan's sharp intake of breath makes me open my eyes. I nod at his expression of disbelief.

"Yes. And I loved him. My whole life, I loved him, and he'd been lying to me about everything. It was all a test."

I have to stop and breathe around the vise winching closed in my chest. When the pain eases and I can speak again, I say, "He was grooming me to take over as his heir. He said it in front of his men, so I knew that if they didn't think I was dead, I would be hounded. Hunted. Cosa Nostra doesn't let people go. So I died. Only I didn't. And now I'm here…"

I trail off into silence, suddenly miserable with the strain of this moment, with everything so raw and aching between us, with so much left to be said.

"Well," he murmurs after a moment, "the FBI thinks you're dead, too. I mean, the Dragonfly. Case closed. You're free now. You can go anywhere, do anything you want."

He swallows hard, so clearly struggling, I'm forced to bite the inside of my cheek until I taste blood so I don't run to him and fling my arms around his shoulders.

With his heart in his eyes and a rasp of hope in his voice, Ryan asks very softly, "What *do* you want?"

I break then. All my careful control, all my pretense of calm, it all falls away with a shudder. "The same thing I've wanted since I saw the most beautiful smile I've ever seen dazzling the crowd at a pool in St. Croix. *You*, cowboy. I want you."

We move at the same moment, arms reaching out for each other, and meet in the center of the room in a hard, breathless embrace. His arms tighten around me, and he's shaking just as hard as I am. My name on his lips is a prayer, his voice ardent and sweet and so full of love, it splits me wide open. I kiss him, and it feels like homecoming, his unshaven jaw rough in my hands, a thrum of pleasure and happiness like wildfire burning through me.

"Why did you wait so long?" he says hoarsely. "Angel, why did you wait so long to let me know you were alive?"

When I look up at him, his cheeks are wet.

I kiss his face, his soft lips, his closed eyelids. "You needed time to miss me. Did you?"

As I hoped he would, he laughs, a sound that makes my heart leap with joy. He hugs me so tight, I think my ribs might be crushed, but I don't care.

"I'm not capable of witty repartee right now, so I'll just say yes."

I wrap my arms around his waist and nuzzle my face into his neck, breathing him in, feeling like I've been living under a thundercloud for a thousand years and the sky has just opened up and bathed me in rays of golden sunlight. "That isn't the real reason," I whisper.

He's serious again in a heartbeat, his smile gone and his brows drawn together.

I say haltingly, "I…I did go a little crazy, after I found out about Reynard. I didn't believe in anything for a while, not hope or trust or love. I didn't even recognize my own face in the mirror. I thought I might be ruined, or that maybe I was cursed because of the diamond, but then…"

Ryan takes my face in his hands, searching my eyes. "But then what?"

"But then I got proof that I wasn't."

He slowly shakes his head. "I don't understand."

I draw away from him and go to the bathroom. I return holding a little white stick that shakes in my outstretched hand.

Ryan takes it, looks at it, at the little window on the front, and sinks to his knees on the floor. I crouch down beside him, wind my arms around his shoulders, and close my eyes.

Against my neck, he whispers, "There's a blue line on this pregnancy test."

"Yes," I say, my eyes filling with water. "There's a *very* blue line."

Blue as a dragonfly's wings, that line.

Blue as my lover's eyes.

# EPILOGUE

"We're going to be late," says Mariana, sifting her fingers through my hair.

"So we'll be late. I'm busy, woman. And be quiet! With all your yammerin', I can't hear the bean."

Her laugh makes my head bounce. We're in bed, naked, and I've got my ear pressed against the gentle swell of her belly. It's my new favorite activity, second only to having my lips pressed here. I do a lot of talking to this growing belly, and singing at it, too, so much so that I think Mariana is more tired of having a grown man clinging twenty-four seven to her stomach than of the nausea she's dealing with about as much of the time.

"Maybe the bean is sleeping. Did you ever think of that? Maybe you're giving the poor child insomnia with your constant harassment."

I lift my head and look at my woman, sleepy-eyed against the pillow, her hair mussed and her skin glowing, and try to send her an appropriately outraged glare. I end up smiling instead. My pretend outrage is no match for her beauty.

"*Harassment?* No. This is called communication."

"It's a little one-sided to be accurately described as communication, honey. It's more like an extended monologue. *Very* extended."

The wry twist to her lips makes me chuckle. "Okay," I say, moving up the bed. "I'll give the bean a break. For now."

I kiss Mariana softly, prop my head on one hand, and flatten the other over her bump. It's not too big yet—she's only four months along—but it's irresistible to me. Along with all the other parts of her gorgeous body.

I had no idea pregnant women could be so damn sexy. I never looked at them that way before. It's probably that she's pregnant with *my* child that's bringing out the beast in me, but I swear my knocked-up woman is the most erotic thing I've seen in my life. If it were up to me and my perma boner, we'd spend every minute of the day naked in bed.

Unfortunately, it's not up to me, which Mariana proves by pronouncing, "Go start the shower. We need to get ready!" and giving me a little shove in the chest.

"Bossy," I grumble.

She smiles sweetly at me, batting her lashes like a debutante. "Which you love, so stop your fake complaining."

I nuzzle her neck, running my palm up her rib cage until I find the soft fullness of a breast. "I do love it," I murmur, swiping my thumb over her nipple. "I love it all."

"Stop trying to distract me. It's not going to work."

"It's already working," I say, chuckling darkly as she shivers and arches into my hand. I lower my head and suck her hard nipple into my mouth.

"Dinner," she reminds me, but her voice is breathy and she's twining her legs between mine. I use a hint of teeth on her nipple, chuckling again when her fingernails dig into my chest.

"We're already late." I lift my head and capture her mouth in a long, sweet kiss.

Mariana breaks away reluctantly. "Kai's making his special schnitzel! He's so excited about it, I don't want to be rude!"

"Schnitzel for Thanksgiving dinner." I shake my head. "It's un-American."

Mariana rolls her eyes. "There's going to be turkey, too. *And* apple pie, because I told him you'd throw yourself on the floor and have a tantrum if you didn't have a 'proper' Thanksgiving meal."

"Really?" I brighten at this news, but then grow suspicious. "What about stuffing? Cranberry sauce? Green-bean casserole? Those poufy white dinner rolls? I bet he doesn't do the rolls. He seems like one of those weird, multigrain, no-yeast, gluten-free, non-GMO bread stick kind of guys."

Closing her eyes, Mariana sighs. "And I'm having a child with this man," she mutters.

"Yes, you are, you lucky girl!" I say, grinning like mad. Then I kiss her all over her face until she's helplessly laughing.

She pushes me away, still laughing, and rises from the bed. She shakes her hair out, tossing it over her shoulders so it cascades in a dark wave down her back. I look on, feeling like I might burst with the happiness pounding inside me.

"I know you're staring at my ass, cowboy," she says as she walks, hips swaying, into the bathroom. "I can feel it tingling."

"Oh, I'll give you a tingle." I throw off the covers and leap out of bed, running after her.

~

By the time Darcy opens her front door, we're an hour late to Thanksgiving dinner, but I'm feeling so self-satisfied with how loudly I made my woman scream in the shower, not even an asteroid plummeting toward earth could put a dent in my cheer.

"We thought you mighta got lost!" says Darcy crossly, standing in the doorway with her hands on her hips. When she glimpses my shit-eating grin, however, she starts to smile.

"Oh. I see how it is." She shakes her head, pulling Mariana

into a hug, and gives her a motherly pat her on the back. "It's a wonder you can still walk at all, girlfriend."

The color is high in Mariana's cheeks when they break apart. She sends me a sour glance, but I can tell she's trying not to smile. "When I can't, he carries me."

"Lawd," says Darcy, fanning herself. She eyes my crotch, and I have to laugh.

"Happy Thanksgiving, Darcy." I give her a hug, then hold out the bottle of wine I picked out for the occasion. "I hope this goes okay with schnitzel."

"Aw, that's so sweet! C'mon in, everybody's waiting on you."

She waves us inside and closes the door behind us. It's the first time we've been to Darcy and Kai's place, a bright, airy loft in a funky neighborhood in SoHo, and their taste is reflected in every eclectic, colorful piece of furniture and artwork. I admire an interesting bronze sculpture on a pedestal in the entryway, which Darcy informs me was crafted by Kai himself.

"It represents man's struggle to survive in a chaotic, meaningless universe."

"Huh," I say, inspecting it. "Looks like a big comma to me."

Darcy snorts. "Don't tell my baby that," she says, voice lowered. "He thinks he's the next Michelangelo. You should see his paintings."

"That bad?" Mariana asks.

"They look like somebody gave a hyperactive five-year-old child a box of crayons and told him to draw the contents of his stomach."

I look at Mariana. "Forget about the rolls, now I'm worried about the turkey."

"There they are!"

Kai's happy greeting—*zere zey are!*—comes from across the loft. He's in the kitchen, wearing an orange apron and one of those tall chef's hats. Also orange, because it's Kai.

"Come in! Come in!" He waves at us with a spatula. "You're just in time for the schnitzel!"

"Goody," I say under my breath.

Darcy laughs. "Don't worry, Ryan, he's not much of an artist, but he actually *can* cook!"

I help Mariana remove her coat and drape it over a nearby chair, then scold, "Wait for me!" as she turns and starts to follow Darcy toward the kitchen. I take her elbow, wind my arm around her waist, and usher her inside, all the while listening to her grouse about overprotective cavemen.

"Get used to it, Angel, 'cause it's only gonna get worse once the bean gets here."

"Hmm. I almost feel sorry for this kid. He has no idea how many GPS trackers he'll have attached to his body the minute he pops out."

"*Her* body," I say with utmost confidence. "Don't gimme that look, woman. The bean is a girl!"

"Oh, really? And how do you know that?"

"Same way I know everything else." I wink at her and tap my temple.

"Is he bragging about his big brain again?" asks Connor from the purple sofa in the living room.

He's sitting with his arm slung around Tabby's shoulders. Juanita's sitting cross-legged on the floor at their feet with a bunch of open schoolbooks strewn around, chewing a pencil and absentmindedly scratching the belly of Elvis the rat, who's sleeping on his back between the pages of a textbook. On the wall across from them, a flat-screen TV is turned to a news channel.

"I don't need to brag. My big brain speaks for itself."

Connor and I grin at each other. He and Tabby stand up, and we all share hugs.

"Careful, brother!" I bark when Connor squeezes Mariana, his biceps bulging.

He pulls away with a sigh and looks into Mariana's eyes. "He's gonna be like this for the next five months, isn't he?"

"Oh no," says Mariana with a straight face. "He's going to be like this *forever*."

"Heya, short stuff." I nod at Juanita, who's looked up from her books. "Whatcha' doin'?"

She pushes a lock of curly brown hair away from her face. "Just finishing up some extra credit for a class."

"Oh yeah? What's the class?"

"Topological spaces and the fundamental group."

I blink. *Is that like…gardening?*

When she sees my blank look, she explains. "It's the advanced geometry and topology stream of the one-hundred-level math curriculum at the new school I'm transferring to in the spring."

I try to look like I have a clue about what she just said. "Cool. So no more Catholic school?"

"I got accepted into Harvard," she says with a shrug, like it's no big deal.

"At *fifteen*?"

Tabby laughs at the expression on my face. "How's your big brain feeling now, jarhead?"

"Shriveled," I admit.

"And how are *you* feeling, Mariana?" Tabby gestures to the bump under Mariana's pretty red dress.

Mariana looks down at her belly, smiles, and rests her hand on top of the bean. "Good," she murmurs. "Other than the morning sickness, which should really be called all-day sickness, I feel great." She glances at me, and her smile grows deeper. "It helps that I'm not allowed to lift a finger to do even the smallest bit of housework. I went out for a few hours yesterday afternoon to do some shopping, but mainly I spend my days napping and eating."

"There's a few other things you spend time doing, too." I grin down at her and pinch her ass.

"TMI, bitches," Juanita says, and goes back to her books.

"Got a call from Karpov this morning," drawls Connor, looking at me.

"Karpov!" I say, surprised. "I know it wasn't about the Hope, 'cause he got that back weeks ago."

"It was about another job he needs us for."

My brow creases. "Another job? What's wrong this time? Don't tell me his daughter was kidnapped again!"

Connor chuckles. "Nope. Now his son's gone missing from his rich-kid prep school in London."

A little chill runs down my spine. *Maybe there's something to the curse on that diamond after all.* Mariana must sense what I'm thinking, because she squeezes my fingers and sends me a reassuring smile.

Darcy says, "Everybody to the table! Dinner's on!"

We walk into the dining room, everyone oohing and aahing over the extravagant place settings and crystal, and take our seats while Darcy and Kai proceed to bring out enough food to feed an army. I'm happy when I see the turkey, golden brown and traditional, and even happier when I see fluffy white dinner rolls appear, wrapped up snug in a linen napkin in a basket.

"Oh, baby, turn off the TV, would you?" says Darcy to Kai.

His hands are full, so I offer to get it. I rise and amble into the living room, pick up the remote from the coffee table, and am about to hit the power button when something the perky blonde newscaster is saying stops me cold.

"—haven't yet apprehended the perpetrators who broke into the store yesterday afternoon after it had closed early for the Thanksgiving holiday, but the theft is being called 'incredibly well planned and executed' by the police, who wouldn't answer many of our specific questions, citing the ongoing investigation. One thing of interest they did share with the press, however, was the unusual method the thieves used to gain entrance to the flagship Harry Winston store on Fifth Avenue. Apparently, they came in through the air-conditioning vents."

I turn slowly, the remote control in a death grip in my hand, and look at Mariana. "Angel?"

Radiant, she glances up at me with an expectant smile. "Yes?"

I gaze at the diamond studs glittering in her earlobes. "Are those new earrings?"

She says innocently, "These? Oh, they're just a little something I picked up in my travels."

"Your *travels*," I repeat flatly. I fold my arms across my chest. "You got somethin' you wanna confess?" I growl.

Her smile glows as brilliant as the sun. "Only that I love you, sweetie!"

When I growl again, she bursts into laughter. She pushes her chair back from the table and comes to me, her eyes shining, that brilliant smile lighting up her whole face. She puts her arms around my shoulders and rises up on her toes to give me a kiss.

"You're too easy to wind up, honey. I wouldn't risk the bean or my future with you for a pair of earrings." Then she whispers into my ear, "By the way, the answer to the other question you haven't asked yet is yes."

"Other question?" I say gruffly, holding her tight and inhaling her scent, pepper and clover and something sweet that's all her. "What other question?"

She presses another kiss to my lips. Then she lifts her left hand next to her face and wiggles her fingers.

The big diamond on her ring finger sparkles with rainbow prisms that catch the light.

Shocked, I shove my hand into the pocket where I'd put the ring box before we left the house, and find the little velvet box gone.

"I can spot jewelry hidden in clothing at fifty paces, cowboy," says my love, smiling that heartbreaker smile.

My heart going a million miles per hour, I say gruffly, "The answer is yes?"

"The thought of you having any other woman in your abnormally large bed makes me want to break every bone in your body, so I figure that's a pretty good indicator that I should keep you around."

I take her face in my hands. "*The answer is yes?*"

"Yes," she replies, staring deep into my eyes. "I love you with every cell of my heart and soul, and I'll be so proud to be your wife."

I throw my arms around her and squeeze her tight, my laugh part groan, my hands shaking. Then I kiss her with everything I have until we're both breathless.

From behind us comes a teasing shout. "Get a room!"

I flip Connor the bird over Mariana's shoulder, not even bothering to open my eyes.

# ACKNOWLEDGMENTS

Thank you to my editor, Linda Ingmanson, for catching all my gaffes, and to my cover designer, Leticia Hasser for her time and talent.

As always, my deepest gratitude to Jay, without whom nothing I do is possible. Being married to my best friend is so much more fun than any fairy tale could promise.

Finally, big thanks to all my readers and the members of my Facebook group, Geissinger's Gang, for making this job so fun and rewarding. I so appreciate you!


During research for Mariana's character, I read many heartbreaking tales from victims of human trafficking. UNICEF estimates more than twenty million people are trafficked around the world, the majority of them women and children who are forced into prostitution. These victims suffer unimaginable violence, exploitation, and abuse. To learn more, please visit the US Department of State's Office to Monitor and Combat Trafficking in Persons at www.state.gov.

# ABOUT THE AUTHOR

J.T. Geissinger is a #1 international and Amazon Charts bestselling author of emotionally charged romance and women's fiction. Ranging from funny, feisty romcoms to intense, edgy suspense, her books have sold over ten million copies and been translated into more than twenty languages.

She is a three-time finalist in both contemporary and paranormal romance for the RITA® Award, the highest distinction in romance fiction from the Romance Writers of America®. She is also the recipient of the Prism Award for Best First Book, the Golden Quill Award for Best Paranormal/Urban Fantasy, and the HOLT Medallion for Best Erotic Romance.

Find her online at www.jtgeissinger.com

## ALSO BY J.T. GEISSINGER

***Standalone Novels***

Pen Pal

Perfect Strangers

Rules of Engagement

Midnight Valentine

***Queens & Monsters Series***

Ruthless Creatures

Carnal Urges

Savage Hearts

Brutal Vows

***Beautifully Cruel Duet***

Beautifully Cruel

Cruel Paradise

***Dangerous Beauty Series***

Dangerous Beauty

Dangerous Desires

Dangerous Games

***Slow Burn Series***

Burn For You

Melt For You

Ache For You

***Bad Habit Series***

Sweet As Sin

Make Me Sin

Sin With Me

Hot As Sin

***Night Prowler Series***

Shadow's Edge

Edge of Oblivion

Rapture's Edge

Edge of Darkness

Darkness Bound

Into Darkness

Made in the USA
Monee, IL
18 January 2024

51949845R00194